Julian Home

Frederic Farrar

Julian Home

The present edition is a reproduction of previous publication of this classic work. Minor typographical errors may have been corrected without note, however, for an authentic reading experience the spelling, punctuation, and capitalization have been retained from the original text.

ISBN: 978-1-64799-342-9

CONTENTS

CHAPTER ONE

SPEECH-DAY AT HARTON

"A little bench of heedless bishops there,
And here a chancellor in embryo."

Shenstone

It was Speech-day at Harton. From an early hour handsome equipages had been dashing down the street, and depositing their occupants at the masters' houses. The perpetual rolling of wheels distracted the attention every moment, and curiosity was keenly on the alert to catch a glimpse of the various magnates whose arrival was expected. At the Queen's Head stood a large array of carriages, and the streets were thronged with gay groups of pedestrians, and full of bustle and liveliness.

The visitors—chiefly parents and relatives of the Harton boys—occupied the morning in seeing the school and village, and it was a pretty sight to observe mothers and sisters as they wandered with delighted interest through the scenes so proudly pointed out to them by their young escort. Some of them were strolling over the cricket-field, or through the pleasant path down to the bathing-place. Many lingered in the beautiful chapel, on whose painted windows the sunlight streamed, making them flame like jewellery, and flinging their fair shadows of blue, and scarlet, and crimson, on the delicate carving of the pillars on either side. But, on the whole, the boys were most proud of showing their friends the old school-room, on whose rude panels many a name may be deciphered, carved there by the boyish hand of poets, orators, and statesmen, who in the zenith of their fame still looked back with fond remembrance on the home of their earlier days, and some of whom were then testifying by their presence the undying interest which they took in their old school.

The pleasant morning wore away, and the time for the Speeches drew on. The room was thronged with a distinguished company, and presented a brilliant and animated appearance. In the centre was a table loaded with prize-books, and all round it sat the secular and episcopal dignitaries for whom seats had been reserved, while the chair was occupied by a young Prince of the royal house. On the other side was a slightly elevated platform, on which were seated the monitors who were to take part in the day's

1

proceedings, and behind it, under the gallery set apart for old Hartonians, crowded a number of gentlemen and boys who could find no room elsewhere.

"Now, papa," said a young lady sitting opposite the monitors, "I've been asking Walter here which is the cleverest of those boys."

"Ahem! young men you mean," interrupted her elder sister.

"No, no," said Walter positively, "call them boys; to call them young men is all bosh; we shall have 'young gentlemen' next, which is awful twaddle."

"Well, which of those boys on the platform is the cleverest—the greatest swell he calls it? Now you profess to be a physiognomist, papa, so just see if you can guess."

"I'm to look out for some future Byron or Peel among them; eh, Walter?"

"Yes."

The old gentleman put on his spectacles, and deliberately looked round the row of monitors, who were awaiting the Headmaster's signal to begin the speeches.

"Well, haven't you done yet, papa? What an age you are. Walter says you ought to tell at a glance."

"Patience, my dear, patience. I'll tell you in a minute."

"There," he said, after a moment's pause, "that boy seated last but one on the bench nearest us has more genius than any of them, I should say." He pointed to one of the youngest-looking of the monitors, who would also have been the most striking in personal appearance had not the almost hectic rose-colour of his cheeks, and the quiet shining of his blue eyes, under the soft hair that hung over his forehead, given a look of greater delicacy than was desirable in a boyish face.

"Wrong, wrong, wrong," chuckled Walter and his sister. "Try again."

"I'm very rarely wrong, you little rogue, in spite of you; but I'll look again. No, there can be no doubt about it. Several of those faces show talent, but one only has a look of genius, and that is the face of the boy I pointed out before. What is his name?"

"Oh, that's Home. He's clever enough in his way, but the fellow you ought to have picked out is the monitor I fag for—Bruce, the head of the school."

"Well, show me your hero."

"There he sits, right in the middle of them, opposite us. There, that's he just going to speak now."

He pointed to a tall, handsome fellow, with a look of infinite self-confidence, who at that moment made a low bow to the assembly, and then began to recite with much force a splendid burst

2

of oratory from one of Burke's great speeches; which he did with the air of one who had no doubt that Burke himself might have studied with benefit the scorn which he flung into his invective and the Olympian grace with which he waved his arm. A burst of applause followed the conclusion of his recitation, during which Bruce took his seat with a look of unconcealed delight and triumph.

"There, papa—what do you think of that? Wasn't I right now?" said the young Hartonian, whose name was Walter Thornley.

But the old gentleman's only answer was a quiet smile, and he had not joined in the general clapping. "Is Home to take any part in the speeches?" he inquired.

"Oh, yes! He's got some part or other in one of the Shakespeare scenes; but he won't do it half as well as Bruce."

"I observe he's got several of the prizes."

"Yes, that's true. He's a fellow that grinds, you know, and so he can't help getting some. But Bruce, now, never opens a book, and yet he's swept off no end of a lot, as you'll see."

"Humph! Walter, I don't much believe in your boys that 'never open a book,' and, as far as I can observe, the phrase must be taken with very considerable latitude; I still believe that the boy who 'grinds,' as you call it, is the abler boy of the two."

"Yes, Walter," said his brother, an old Hartonian, "whenever a fellow, who has got a prize, tells you he won it without opening a book, set him down as a shallow puppy, and don't believe him."

By this time four of the monitors were standing up to recite a scene from the Merchant of Venice, and Home among them; his part was a very slight one, and although there was nothing remarkable in his way of acting, yet he had evidently studied with intelligence his author's meaning, and his modest self-possession attracted favourable regards. But, a few minutes after, he had to recite alone a passage of Tennyson's Morte d'Arthur, and then he appeared to greater advantage. Standing in a perfectly natural attitude, he began in low clear tones, enunciating every line with a distinctness that instantly won attention, and at last warming with his theme he modulated his voice with the requirements of the verse, and used gestures so graceful, yet so unaffected, that when with musical emphasis he spoke the last lines,—

> "Long stood Sir Bedivere
> Resolving many memories, till the hull
> Looked one black dot against the verge of dawn,
> And on the mere the wailing died away,—"

he seemed entirely absorbed in the subject, and for half a minute

3

stood as if unconscious, until the deep murmur of applause startled his meditations, and he sat down as naturally as he had risen.

"Well done, old Home," said Walter; while Mr Thornley nodded rapidly two or three times, and murmured after him,—

"And on the mere the wailing died away."

"Really, I think Julian did that admirably, did he not?" said a young and lovely girl to her mother, as Home sat down.

"By jingo," whispered Walter, "I believe these people just by us are Home's people."

"People!" said his sister; "what do you mean by his people?"

"Oh, you know, Mary; you girls are always shamming you don't understand plain English. I mean his people."

Mary smiled, and looked at the strangers. "Yes, no doubt of it," she said, "that young lady has just the same features as Mr. Home, only softened a little; more refined they could not be. And they've been hearing all your rude remarks, Walter, no doubt."

The boy was right, for when the speeches were over, they saw Home offer his arm to the two ladies and lead them out into the courtyard, where everybody was waiting, under the large awning, to hear the lions of the day cheered as they came down the school steps. Bruce was leading the cheers; he seemed to know everybody and everybody to know him, and as group after group passed him, he was bowing and smiling repeatedly while he listened to the congratulations which were lavished upon him from all sides. Among the last his own family came out, and when he gave his arm to his mother and descended the school steps, one of the other monitors suddenly cried—

"Three cheers for the Head of the school."

The boys cordially echoed the cheers, and taking off his hat, Bruce stood still with a flush of exultation on his handsome face, in an attitude peculiar to him whenever he was undergoing an ovation.

"Pose plastique; King Bruce snuffing up the incense of flattery!" muttered a school Thersites, standing by.

"Green-minded scoundrel," was the reply; "that's because he beat you to fits in the Latin verse."

"How very popular he seems to be, Julian," said Miss Home to her brother, as they stood rather apart from the fashionable crowd.

"Very popular, and, on the whole, he deserves his popularity; how capitally he recited to-day," and Julian looked at him and sighed.

"And now, mother, will you come to lunch?" he said; "you're invited to my tutor's, you know."

They went and took a hasty lunch, heartily enjoying the simple and general good-humour which was the order of the day; and finding that there was still an hour before the train started which was to convey them home, Julian took them up to the old churchyard, and while they enjoyed the only breath of air which made the tall elms murmur in the burning day, he showed them the beautiful scene spread out at their feet, and the distant towers of Elton and Saint George. Field after field, filled with yellowing harvests or grazing herds, stretched away to the horizon, and nothing on earth could be fairer than that soft sleep of the golden sunshine on the green and flowery meadowland, while overhead only a few silvery cloudlets variegated with their fleecy lustre the expanse of blue, rippling down to the horizon like curves of white foam at the edges of a summer sea.

"No wonder a poet loved this view," said Mrs Home. "By the bye, Julian, which is the tomb he used to lie upon?"

"There, just behind us; that one with the fragments broken off by stupid picturesque tourists, with the name of Peachey on it."

"And so Byron really used, as a boy, to rest under these elms, and look at this lovely view!" said his sister.

"Yes, Violet. I wonder how much he'd have given, in after-life, to be a boy again," said Julian thoughtfully; "and have a fresh start— a rejuvenescence, beginning after a summer hour spent on Peachey's tomb;" and Julian sighed again.

"My dear Julian," said Violet, gaily rallying him, "what a boy you are! What business have you to sigh here of all places, and now of all times? That's the second time in the course of an hour that I've heard you. Imagine a Harton monitor sighing twice on Speech-day! You must be tired of us."

"Did I sigh? Abominably rude of me. I really didn't mean it," said Julian; and shaking off the influences which had slightly depressed him for the moment, he began to laugh and joke with the utmost mirth until it became time to meet the train. He accompanied his mother and sister to the station, bade them an affectionate farewell, and then walked slowly back, for the beauty of the summer evening made him loiter on the way.

"Poor Julian!" said Violet to her mother when the train started; "he lets the sense of responsibility weigh on him too much, I'm afraid."

But Julian was thinking that the next time he came to the station would probably be at the end of term, when his schoolboy days would be over. He leaned against a gate, and looked long at the green quiet hill, with its tall spire and embosoming trees, till he fell into a reverie.

A slap on the back awoke him, and turning round, he saw the genial, good-humoured face of one of his fellow-monitors, Hugh Lillyston.

"Well, Julian, dreaming as usual—castle-building, and all that sort of thing, eh?"

"No; I was thinking how soon one will have to bid good-bye to dear old Harton. How well the chapel looks from here, doesn't it?—and the church towering above it."

"The chapel being like a fair daughter seated at her mother's feet, as your poetical tutor remarked the other day. Well, Julian, I'm glad we shall leave together, anyhow. Come and have some tea."

Julian went to his friend's room. The fag brought the tea and toast, and they spent a merry evening, chatting over the speeches, and the way in which the day had gone off. At lock-up, Julian went to write some letters, and then feeling the melancholy thought of future days stealing over him, he plunged into a book of poems till it was bed-time, being disturbed a good deal, however, by the noisy mirth which resounded long after forbidden hours from Bruce's study overhead. Bruce was also to leave Harton in a month, and they were going up together to Saint Werner's College, Camford. But the difference was, that Bruce went up wealthy and popular; Julian, whose retiring disposition and refined tastes won him far fewer though truer friends, was going up as a sizar, with no prospect of remaining at the University unless he won himself the means of doing so by his own success. It was this thought that had made him sigh.

CHAPTER TWO

JULIAN HOME

"O thou goddess,
Thou divine Nature, how thyself thou blazon'st
In these two princely boys; they are as gentle
As zephyrs blowing beneath the violet,
Not wagging his sweet head; and yet as fierce,
Their royal blood enchafed, as the rud'st wind
That by the top doth take the mountain pine,
And makes him bow to the vale."

Cymbeline, Act 4, scene 2.

It was but recently, (as will be explained hereafter), that the circumstances had arisen which had rendered it necessary for Julian Home to enter Saint Werner's as a sizar and since that necessity had arisen, he had been far from happy. A peculiar sensitiveness had been from childhood the distinctive feature of his character. It rendered him doubly amenable to every emotion of pleasure and pain, and gave birth to a self-conscious spirit, which made his nature appear weaker, when a boy, than it really was. While he was at Harton, this self-consciousness made him keenly, almost tremblingly, alive to the opinions of others about himself. His self-depreciation arose from real humility, and there was in his heart so deep a fountain of love towards all his fellows, and so sympathising an admiration of all their good or brilliant qualities, that he was far too apt to suffer himself to be tormented by the indifference or dislike of those who were far his inferiors.

It was strange that such a boy should have had enemies, but he was sadly aware that in that light some regarded him. Had it been possible to conciliate them without any compromise in his line of action, he would have done so at any cost; but as their enmity arose from that vehement moral indignation which Julian both felt and expressed against the iniquities which he despised and disapproved, he knew that all union with them was out of his power. As a general rule, the best boys are by no means the most popular.

It was the great delight of Julian's detractors to compare him unfavourably with their hero, Bruce. Bruce, as a fair scholar and a good cricketer, with no very marked line of his own—as a fine-looking fellow, anxious to keep on good terms with everybody, and

7

with an apparently hearty "well met" for all the world—cut against the grain of no one's predilections, and had the voice of popular favour always on his side. While ambition made him work tolerably hard, as far as he could do so without attracting observation, the line he took was to disparage industry, and ally himself with the merely cricketing set, with some of whom he might be seen strolling arm-in-arm, in loud conversation, at every possible opportunity. Julian, on the other hand, though a fair cricketer, soon grew weary of the "shop" about that game, which for three months formed the main staple of conversation among the boys; and while his countenance was too expressive to conceal this fact, he in his turn found himself unable to enlist more than a few in any interest for those intellectual pursuits which were the chief joy of his own life.

"Home, I've been watching you for the last half-hour," said Bruce, one day at dinner, "and you haven't opened your lips."

"I've had nothing to say."

"Why not?"

"Because, since we came in, not one word has been said about any human subject but cricket, cricket, cricket; it's been the same for the last two months; and as I haven't been playing this morning—"

"Well, no one wants you to talk," interrupted Brogten, one of the eleven, Julian's especial foe. "I say, Bruce, did you see—"

"I was only going to add," said Julian, with perfect good-humour, heedless of the interruption, "that I couldn't discuss a game I didn't see."

"Nobody asked you, sir, she said," retorted Brogten rudely; "if it had been some sentimental humbug, I dare say you'd have mooned about it long enough."

"Better, at any rate, than some of your low stories, Brogten," said Lillyston, firing up on his friend's behalf.

"I don't know. I like something manly."

"Vice and manliness being identical, then, according to your notions?" said Lillyston.

Brogten muttered an angry reply, in which the only audible words were "confound" and "milksops."

"Well spoken, advocate of sin and shame;
Known by thy bleating, Ignorance thy name,"

thought Julian; but he did not condescend to make any further answer.

"I hate that kind of fellow," said Brogten, loud enough for the friends to hear, as they rose from the table; "fellows who think

8

themselves everybody's superiors, and walk with their noses in the air."

"I wonder that you will still be talking, Brogten; nobody marks you," said Lillyston, treating with the profoundest indifference a stupid calumny. But poisoned arrows like these quivered long and rankled painfully in Julian's heart.

Yet no sensible boy would have given Julian's reputation in exchange for that of Bruce; for in all except the mean and coarse minority, Julian excited either affection or esteem, and he had the rare inestimable treasure of some real and noble-hearted friends; while Bruce was too vain, too shallow, and too fickle to inspire any higher feeling than a mere transient admiration.

Latterly it had become known to the boys that Julian was going up to Saint Werner's as a sizar, and being ignorant of the reasons which decided him, they had been much surprised. But the little clique of his enemies made this an additional subject of annoyance, and there were not wanting those who had the amazing bad taste to repeat to him some of their speeches. There are some who seem to think that a man must rather enjoy hearing all the low tittle-tattle of envious backbiters.

"I knew he must be some tailor's son or other," remarked Brogten.

"I say, Bruce, we shall have to cut him at Saint Werner's," observed an exquisite young exclusive.

Such things—the mere lispings of malicious folly—Julian could not help hearing; and they galled him so much that he determined to have a talk on the subject with his tutor, who was a Saint Werner's man. It was his tutor's custom to devote the hour before lock-up on every half-holiday to seeing any of his pupils who cared to come and visit him; but as on the rich summer evenings few were to be tempted from the joyous sounds of the cricket-field, Julian found him sitting alone in his study, reading.

"Ha, Julian!" he exclaimed, rising at once, with a frank and cordial greeting. "Here's a triumph! A boy actually enticed from bats and balls to pay me a visit!"

Julian smiled. "The fact is, sir," he said, "I've come to ask you about something. But am I disturbing you? If so, I'll go and 'pursue vagrant pieces of leather again,' as Mr Stokes says when he wants to dismiss us to cricket."

"Not in the least. I rather enjoy being disturbed during this hour. But what do you say to a turn in the open air? One can talk so much better walking than sitting down on opposite sides of a fireplace with no fire in it."

Julian readily assented, and Mr. Carden took his arm as they bent their way down to the cricket-field. There they stopped involuntarily for a time, to gaze at the house match which was going on, and the master entered with the utmost vivacity into the keen yet harmless "chaff" which was being interchanged between the partisans of the rival houses.

"What a charming place this field is," he said, "on a summer evening, while the sunset lets fall upon it the last innocuous arrows of its golden sheaf. When I am wearied to death with work or vexation—which, alas! is too often—I always run down here, and it gives me a fresh lease of life."

Julian smiled at his tutor's metaphorical style of speech, which he knew was in him the natural expressions of a glowing and poetic heart, that saw no reason to be ashamed of its own warm feelings and changeful fancies; and Mr Carden, wrapped in the scene before him, and the sensations it excited, murmured to himself some of his favourite lines—

> "Alas that one
> Should use the days of summer but to live,
> And breathe but as the needful element
> The strange superfluous glory of the air
> Nor rather stand in awe apart, beside
> The untouched time, and murmuring o'er and o'er
> In awe and wonder, 'These are summer days!'"

"Shall we stroll across the fields, sir, before lock-up?" said Julian, as a triumphant shout proclaimed that the game was over, and the Parkites had defeated the Grovians.

"Yes, do. By the bye, what was it that you had to ask me about?"

"Oh, sir, I don't think I've told you before; but I'm going up to Saint Werner's as a sub-sizar."

Mr Carden looked surprised. "Indeed! Is that necessary?"

"Yes, sir; it's a choice between that and not going at all. And what I wanted to ask you was, whether it will subject me to much annoyance or contempt; because, if so—"

"Contempt, my dear fellow!" said Mr Carden quickly. "Yes," he added, after a pause, "the contempt of the contemptible—certainly of no one else."

"But do you think that any Harton fellows will cut me?"

"Unquestionably not; at least, if any of them do, it will be such a proof of their own absolute worthlessness, that you will be well rid of such acquaintances."

Julian seemed but little reassured by this summary way of viewing the matter.

"But I hope," he said, "that no one, (even if they don't cut me), will regard my society as a matter of mere tolerance, or try an air of condescension."

"Look here, Julian," said the master; "a sub-sizar means merely a poor scholar, for whom the college has set apart certain means of assistance. From this body have come some of the most distinguished men whom Saint Werner's has ever produced; and many of the Fellows, (indeed quite a disproportionate number), began their college career in this manner. Now tell me—should you care the snap of a finger for the opinion or the acquaintance of a man who could be such an ineffable fool as to drop intercourse with you because you are merely less rich than he? Don't you remember those grand old words, Julian—

"Lives there for honest poverty,
Who hangs his head and a' that?
The coward slave we pass him by,
And dare be poor for a' that."

"And yet, sir, half the distinctions of modern society rest upon accidents of this kind."

"True, true! quite true; but what is the use of education if it does not teach us to look on man as man, and judge by a nobler and more real standard than the superficial distinctions of society? But answer my question."

"Well, sir, I confess that I should think very lightly of the man who treated me in that way; still I should be annoyed very much by his conduct."

"I really think, Julian," replied Mr Carden, "that the necessity which compels you to go up as a sizar will be good for you in many ways. Poverty, self-denial, the bearing of the yoke in youth, are the highest forms of discipline for a brave and godly manhood. The hero and the prophet are rarely found in soft clothing or kingly houses; they are never chosen from the palaces of Mammon or the gardens of Belial."

They talked a little longer on the subject, and Mr Carden pointed out how, at the universities more than anywhere, the aristocracy of intellect and character are almost solely recognised, and those patents of nobility honoured which come direct from God. "After a single term, Julian, depend upon it you will smile at the sensitiveness which now makes you shrink from entering on this position. At least, I assume that even by that time your name will be

11

honourably known, as it will be if you work hard. You must never forget that 'Virtus vera nobilitas' is the noble motto of your own college."

"Well, I will work at any rate," said Julian; "indeed I must."

"But may I ask why you have determined on going up as sizar?"

"Oh yes, sir. I am far too grateful for all your many kindnesses to me, not to tell you freely of my circumstances."

And so, as they walked on that beautiful summer evening over the green fields, Julian, happy in the quiet sympathising attention of one who was not only a master, but a true, earnest, and affectionate friend, told him some of the facts to which we shall allude in the retrospect of the next chapter.

CHAPTER THREE

A RETROSPECT

"Give me the man that is not Passion's slave,
And I will wear him in my own heart's core,
Yea, in my heart of hearts."

Shakespeare

Julian's father was Rector of Ildown, a beautiful village on the Devonshire coast. As younger son, his private means were very small, and the more so as his family had lost in various unfortunate speculations a large portion of the wealth which had once been the inheritance of his ancient and honourable house. Mr. Home regretted this but little; contentment of mind and simplicity of tastes were to him a far deeper source of happiness than the advantages of fortune. Immediately after his university career he had taken holy orders, and devoted to the genial duties of his profession all the energies of a vigorous intellect and a generous heart.

During his first curacy he was happy enough to be placed in the diocese of a bishop, whose least merit was the rare conscientiousness with which he distributed the patronage at his disposal. Whenever a living was vacant, the Bishop of Elford used deliberately to pass in mental review all the clergy under his jurisdiction, and single out from amongst them the ablest and the best. He was never influenced by the spirit of nepotism; he was never deceived by shallow declaimers, or ignorant bigots, who had thrust themselves into the notoriety of a noisy and orthodox reputation. The ordinary Honourable and Reverend, whose only distinction was his title or his wealth, had to look for preferment elsewhere; but often would some curate, haply sighing at the thought that obscurity and poverty were his lot for this life, and meekly bearing both for the honour of his Master's work, be made deservedly happy by at last attaining the rewards he had never sought. Few, indeed, were the dioceses in which the clergy worked in a more hopeful spirit, in the certainty that the good bishop never suffered merit to pass unrecognised; and for talent and industry, no body of rectors could be compared to those whom Bishop Morris had chosen from the most deserving of the curates who were under his pastoral care.

Mr. Home, after five years' hard work, had been promoted by the bishop to a small living, where he soon succeeded in winning the warmest affection of all his parishioners, and among others, of his squire and church-warden, the Earl of Raynes, who, from a feeling of sincere gratitude, procured for him, on the first opportunity, the rectory of Ildown.

Here, at the age of thirty, he settled down, with every intention of making it his home for life; and here he shortly after wooed and won the daughter of a neighbouring clergyman, whose only dower was the beauty of a countenance which but dimly reflected the inner beauty of her heart.

Very tranquil was their wedded life; very perfect was the peacefulness of their home. Under her hands the rectory garden became a many-coloured Eden, and the eye could rest delightedly on its lawns and flower-beds, even amid that glorious environment of woods and cliffs, free moors and open sea, which gave to the vicinity of Ildown such a nameless charm. But the beauty without was surpassed by the rarer sunshine of the life within and when children were born to them—when little steps began to patter along the hall, and young faces to shine beside the fire, and little strains of silvery laughter to ring through every room—there was a happiness in that bright family, for the sake of which an emperor might have been content to abdicate his throne. Oh that the river of human life could flow on for ever with such sparkling waters, and its margin be embroidered for ever with flowers like these.

Julian was their eldest son, and it added to the intensity of each parent's love for him to find that he seemed to have inherited the best qualities of them both. Their next child was Violet, and then, after two years' interval, came Cyril and Frank. The four children were educated at home, without even the assistance of tutor or governess, until Julian was thirteen years old; and during all that time scarcely one domestic sorrow occurred to chequer the unclouded serenity of their peace. Even without the esteem and respect of all their neighbours, rich and poor, the love of parents and children, brothers and sister, was enough for each heart there.

But the day of separation must come at last, however long we may delay it, and after Julian's thirteenth birthday it was decided that he must go to school. In making this determination, his father knew what he was about. He knew that in sending his son among a multitude of boys he was exposing him to a world of temptation, and placing him amid many dangers. Yet he never hesitated about it, and when his wife spoke with trembling anxiety of the things which she had heard and read about school-life, he calmly replied that without danger there can be no courage, and without temptation no real virtue or tried strength.

"Poor Julian," said Mrs Home, "but won't he be bullied dreadfully?"

"No, dear; the days of those atrocities about which you read in books are gone by for ever. At no respectable school, except under very rare and peculiar circumstances, are boys exposed to any worse difficulties in the way of cruelty than they can very easily prevent or overcome."

"But then those dreadful moral temptations," pleaded the mother.

"They are very serious, love. But is it not better that our boy should learn, by their means, (as thousands do), to substitute the manliness of self-restraint for the innocence of ignorance—even on the very false supposition that such an innocence can be preserved? And remember that he does not escape these temptations by avoiding them; from the little I have seen, it is my sincere conviction that for after-life, (even in this aspect alone, without alluding to the innumerable other arguments which must be considered), the education of a public school is a far sounder preparation than the shelter of home. I cannot persuade our neighbour Mrs Hazlet of this, but I should tremble to bring up Julian with no wider experience than she allows to her boy."

So Julian went to Harton, and, after a time, thoroughly enjoyed his life there, and was unharmed by the trials which must come to every schoolboy; so that when he came back for his first holidays, the mother saw with joy and pride that her jewel was not flawed, and remained undimmed in lustre. Who knows how much

14

had been contributed to that glad result by the daily and nightly prayer which ever ascended for him from his parents' lips, "Lead him not into temptation, but deliver him from evil."

For when he first went to school, Julian was all the more dangerously circumstanced, from the fact that he was an attractive and engaging boy. With his bright eyes, beaming with innocence and trustfulness, the healthy glow of his clear and ingenuous countenance, and the noble look and manners which were the fruit of a noble mind, he could never be one of those who pass unknown and unnoticed in the common throng. And since to these advantages of personal appearance he superadded a quick intelligence, and no little activity and liveliness, he was sure to meet with flattery and observation. But there was something in Julian's nature which, by God's grace, seemed to secure him from evil, as though he were surrounded by an atmosphere impermeable to base and wicked hearts. He passed through school-life not only unscathed by, but almost ignorant of, the sins into which others fell; and the account which his contemporaries might have given of their schoolboy days was widely different from his own. He was one of those of whom the grace of God took early hold, and in whom "reason and religion ran together like warp and woof," to form the web of a wise and holy life. Such happy natures—such excellent hearts there are; though they are few and far between.

To Hugh Lillyston Julian owed no little of his happiness. They had been in the same forms together since Julian came, and the friendship between them was never broken. When Lillyston first saw the new boy, he longed to speak to him at once, but respected him too much to thrust himself rudely into his acquaintance. During the first day or two they exchanged only a few shy words; for Julian, too, was pleased and taken with Lillyston's manly, honest look. But both had wisely determined to let their knowledge of each other grow up naturally and gradually, without any first-sight vows of eternal friendship, generally destined to be broken in the following week.

Lillyston had observed, not without disgust, that two thoroughly bad fellows were beginning to notice the newcomer, and determined at all hazards to tell Julian his opinion of them. So one day as they left the school-room together, he said—

"Do you know Brant and Jeffrey?"

"Yes; a little," answered Julian.

"Did you know them before you came, or anything?"

"No; but they will wait for me every now and then at the door of the fourth-form room when I'm coming out and I'm sure I don't

15

want them, but one doesn't wish to seem uncivil, and I don't know how to get rid of them."

"H'm! well, I wouldn't see too much of them if I were you."

"No? but why?"

"Well, never mind—only I thought I'd tell you;" and Lillyston, half-ashamed at having taken this step, and half-afraid that Julian might misconstrue it, ran away. Julian, who was little pleased with the coarse adulation of Brant and Jeffrey, took his friend's advice, and from that time he and Lillyston became more and more closely united. They were constantly together, and never tired of each other's society; and at last, when their tutor, observing and thoroughly approving of the friendship, put them both in the same room, the school began in fun to call them Achilles and Patroclus, Damon and Pythias, Orestes and Pylades, David and Jonathan, Theseus and Pirithous, and as many other names of paria amicorum as they could remember.

Yet there was many a Harton boy who would have said, "Utinam in tali amicitia tertius ascriberer!" for each friend communicated to the other something at least of his own excellences. Lillyston instructed Julian in the mysteries of fives, racquets, football, and cricket, until he became an adept at them all; and Julian, in return, gave Lillyston very efficient help in work, and inspired him with intellectual tastes for which he felt no little gratitude in after days. The desire of getting his remove with Julian worked so much with him that he began to rise many places in the examinations; and while Julian was generally among the first few, Lillyston managed to be placed, at any rate, far above the ranks of the undistinguished herd.

So, form by form, Lillyston and Julian Home mounted up the school side by side, and illustrated the noblest and holiest uses of friendship by adding to each other's happiness and advantage in every way. I am glad to dwell on such a picture, knowing, O holy Friendship, how awfully a schoolboy can sometimes desecrate thy name!

Three years had passed, and they were now no longer little boys, but in the upper fifth form together, and Julian was in his sixteenth year. It was one March morning, when, shortly after they entered the school-room, the school "Custos" came in and handed to the master a letter—

"It's for Mister Home, sir, by telegraph."

The master called Julian, (whose heart beat quick when he heard his name), and said to him—

"Perhaps you had better take it out of the room, Home, before you read it, as it may contain something important."

With a grateful look for this considerate kindness, Julian took the hint, and leaving the room, tore open the message, which was from his mother—

"Dear Julian—Come home instantly; your father is most dangerously ill. I cannot add more."

The boys heard a cry, and the master made a sign to Lillyston, who had already started to his feet. Springing out of the unclosed door, he found Julian half-fainting; for his home affections were the very mainsprings of his life. He read the message, helped Julian down-stairs, flung a little cold water over his face, and then led him to their own study, where he immediately began, without a word, to pack up for him such things as he thought he would require.

Lillyston made all the necessary arrangements, and did not leave his friend until he had seen him into the railway carriage, and pressed his hand with a silent farewell. He watched the train till it was out of sight.

Then first did Julian's anguish find vent in tears. Passionately he longed at least to know the worst, and would have given anything to speed the progress of the train, far too slow for his impatient misery. He was tormented by remembering the unusually solemn look and tone with which his father had parted from him a month before, and by the presentiment which at that moment had flashed across him with uncontrollable vividness, that they should never meet again. At last, at last they reached Ildown late in the evening, just as the flushed glare of crimson told the death-struggle of an angry sunset with the dull and heavy clouds. The station was a mile from the town, and it was a raw, gusty, foggy evening. There was no conveyance at the station, but leaving with the porter a hasty direction about his luggage, Julian flew along the road heedless of observation, reached the cliff, and at length stood before the rectory door. He was wet, hungry, and exhausted, for since morning he had tasted nothing, and his run had spattered him with mud from head to heel. It was too dark to judge what had happened from the appearance of the house, and half-frantic as he was with fear and eagerness, he had yet not dared to give a loud summons at the door, lest he should disturb his father's slumber or excite his nerves.

Ah! Julian, you need not restrain your impetuous dread from that cause now—

The door opened very quietly, and in reply to Julian's incoherent question, the good old servant only shook her head, and turned away to brush off with her apron the tears which she vainly struggled to repress. But the boy burst into the study where he knew that the rest would be, and in another moment his arm was round his mother's neck, while Cyril and Violet and little Frank drew close

17

and wept silently beside them both. But still Julian knew not or would not know the full truth, and at last he drew up courage to ask the question which had been so long trembling on his lips—

"Is there no hope, mother, no hope?"

"Don't you know then, my boy? Your father is—"

"Not dead," said Julian, in a hollow voice. "Oh, mother, mother, mother."

His head drooped on her shoulder the news fell on him like a horrible blow, and, stunned as he was with weariness and anxiety, all sense and life flowed from him for a time.

The necessity for action and the consolation of others are God's blessed remedies to lull, during the first intolerable moments, the poignancy of bereavement. Mrs Home had to soothe her children, and to see that they took needful food and rest; and she watched by the bedside of her younger boys till the silken swathe of a soft boyish sleep fell on their eyes, red and swollen with many tears. Then she saw Violet to bed, and at last sat down alone with her eldest son, who by a great prayerful effort aroused himself at last to a sense of his position.

He took her hand in his, and said in a low whisper, "Mother, let me see him?"

"Not now, dearest Julian; wait till to-morrow, for our sakes."

"What was the cause of death, mother?"

"Disease of the heart;" and once more the widow's strength seemed likely to give way. But this time it was Julian's turn to whisper, "God's will be done."

Next morning Mrs Home, with Julian and Violet, entered the room of death. Flowers were scattered on the bed, and on that face, calm as marble yet soft as life, the happy wondering smile had not yet even died away. And there Julian received from his mother a slip of paper, on which his father's dying hand had traced the last messages of undying love and when they had left him there alone, he opened and read these words, written with weak and wavering pen—

"My own dearest boy, in this world we shall never meet again. But I die happy, Julian, for my trust is in God, who cares for the widow and the fatherless. And you, Julian, will take my place with Violet, Cyril, and dear Frankie—I need say nothing of a mother to such a son. God bless you, my own boy. Be brave, and honest, and pure, and God will be with you. Your dying father,

"Henry Home."

18

The last part was almost illegible, but Julian bent reverently over his father's corpse, and it seemed that the smile brightened on those dead lips as he bowed his young head in prayer.

Reader, for many reasons we must not linger there. But I had to tell you of that death and of those dying words which Julian knew by heart through life, and which he kept always with him as the amulet against temptation. He never forgot them; and oh! how often in the hours of trial did it seem as if that dying message was whispered in his ear, "Be brave, and honest, and pure, and God will be with you."

The concluding arrangements were soon made. The family left the rectory, but continued to reside at Ildown, a spot which they loved, and where they were known and loved. Mr. Home had insured his life for a sum, not large indeed, but sufficient to save them from absolute penury, and had besides laid by sufficient to continue Julian's education. It was determined that he should return to Harton, and there try for the Newry scholarship in time. If he should be successful in getting this, there would be no further difficulty in his going to college, for it was expected that a wealthy aunt of his would assist him. His guardians, however, were kind enough to determine that, even in case of his failing to obtain the Newry, they would provide for his university expenses, although they did not conceal from him the great importance of his earnestly studying with a view to gain this pecuniary aid. Cyril was sent to Marlby, and Frank, who was but ten years old, remained for the present at Ildown grammar school.

After the funeral Julian returned to Harton with a sadder and wiser heart. Though never an idle boy, he had not as yet realised the necessity of throwing himself fully into the studies of the place, but had rather given the reins to his fancy, and luxuriated in the gorgeous day-dreams of poetry and romance. Henceforward, he became a most earnest and diligent student, and day by day felt that his intellectual powers grew stronger and more developed by this healthier nourishment. At the end of that quarter he gained his first head-remove, and Mr Carden rejoiced heartily in the success of his favourite pupil.

"Why, Julian, you will beat us all if you go on at this rate," said he, after reading over the trial verses which Julian asked him to criticise after the examination. "You always showed taste, but here we have vigour too; and for a wonder, you haven't made any mistakes."

"I'm afraid I shall be 'stumped' in the Greek 'Iambi,' sir, as Mr Clarke calls them."

19

"Ah! well, you must take pains. You've improved, though, since you had to translate Milton's—

> "Smoothing the raven down
> Of darkness, till it smiled;

"when, you remember, I gave you a literal version of your 'Iambi,' which meant 'pounding a pea-green fog.' Eh?"

"Oh, yes," said Julian, "I remember too that I rendered 'the moon-beams' by 'the moon's rafters.'"

"Never mind," said Mr Carden, laughing, "improve in them as much as you have in Latin verse, and we shall see you Newry scholar yet."

A thrill of joy went through the boy's heart as he heard these words.

CHAPTER FOUR

HOW JULIAN LOST A FORTUNE

> "Most like a step-dame or a dowager
> Long withering out a young man's revenue."
>
> *Shakespeare*

I must not chronicle Julian's school-life, much as I should have to tell about him, and strong as the temptation is, but another event happened during his stay at Harton which affected so materially his future years that I must proceed to narrate it now.

Julian's father had a sister much older than himself, who many years before had married a baronet-farmer, Sir Thomas Vinsear of Lonstead Abbey. It was certainly not a love match on the lady's side, for the baronet was twenty years her senior, and his tastes in no respect resembled hers. But she was already of "a certain age," and despairing of a lover, accepted the good old country squire, and was located for the rest of her life as mistress of Lonstead Abbey.

As long as he lived all was well; Lady Vinsear, like a sensible wife, conformed herself to all his wishes and peculiarities, and won in no slight degree his gratitude and affection. But he did not long survive his marriage, and after a few years the lady found herself alone and childless in the solitary grandeur of her husband's home.

Her brother Henry, the Rector of Ildown, had always been her special favourite, and she looked to his frequent visits to enliven her loneliness. But she was piqued by his having married without consulting her, and behaved so uncourteously to Mrs Home, that for a long time the intercourse between them was broken.

One day, however, shortly before his death, she had written to announce an intended visit, and in due time her carriage stood before the rectory door. It so happened that it was Julian's holiday-time, and he was at home. Changed as the old lady had become by years and disappointment, and the ennui of an aimless widowhood, little relieved by the unceasing attendance of a confidante, yet Lady Vinsear's childless and withered heart seemed to be touched to life again when she gazed on her brother's beautiful and modest boy. Courteous without subservience, and attentive without servility, Julian, by his graceful and unselfish demeanour, won her complete affection, and she dropped to the family no ambiguous hints, that, for Julian's sake, she should renew her intercourse with them, and make him her heir. Circumstanced as he was, Mr. Home could not but rejoice in this determination, and the more so from his proud consciousness that not even the vilest detractor could charge him with having courted his rich sister's favour by open or secret arts. From Julian he would have concealed Lady Vinsear's intention, but she had herself made him tolerably aware of it, after a fit of violent spleen against Miss Sprong, her confidante, who, seeing how the wind lay, had tried to drop little malicious hints against the favourite nephew, until the old lady had cut them short, by a peremptory order that Miss Sprong should leave the room. That little rebuff the lady never forgot and never forgave, and, under the guise of admiration, she nursed her enmity against the unconscious Julian until due opportunity should have occurred to give it vent.

Every now and then, Julian, when wearied with study, would be tempted to think in his secret heart, "What does it matter my working so hard, when I shall be master of Lonstead Abbey some day?" And then perhaps would follow a rather inconsistent fit of idleness, till Mr Carden, or some other master, applied the spur again.

"I can't make you out, Julian," said Lillyston; "sometimes you grind away for a month like—like beans, and then you're as idle again for a week as the dog that laid his head against a wall to bark."

"Well, shall I tell you, Hugh?" answered Julian, who had often

21

felt that it would be a relief to put his friend in possession of the secret. And he told Lillyston that he was the acknowledged heir of his aunt's property.

"Oh, well then," said Lillyston, "I don't see why I should work either, seeing as how Lillyston Court will probably come to me some day. I say, Julian, I vote we both try for lag next trials. It'd save lots of grind."

All this was brought out very archly, and instantly recalled to Julian's mind the many arguments which he had used to his friend, especially since his father's death, to prove that, under any circumstances, diligence was a duty which secured its own reward; indeed, he used to maintain that, even on selfish grounds it was best, for in the long run the idlest boys, with their punishments and extras, got far the most work to do—to say nothing of the lassitude that usurps the realm of neglected duty, and that disgraceful ignorance which is the nemesis of wasted time.

He burst out laughing. "You have me on the hip, Hugh, and I give in. In proof whereof, here goes the novel I'm reading; and I'll at once set to work on my next set of verses;" whereon Julian pitched his green novel to the top of an inaccessible cupboard, got down his Elegiacs for the next day, and had no immediate recurrence of what Lillyston christened the "pudding theory of work."

It was during his last year at Harton that Lady Vinsear, in consequence of one of her sudden whims, wrote to invite him to Lonstead, with both his brothers; for she never took any notice of either Violet or Mrs Home. The time she mentioned was ten days before the Harton holidays began. So that Frank and Cyril, (who came back from Marlby just in time), had to go alone, rather to their disgust; Julian, however, promising to join them directly after he returned from school. The wilful old lady, urged on by the confidante, took considerable umbrage at this, and wrote that "she was quite sure the Doctor would not have put any obstacles in the way of Julian's coming had he been informed of her wishes. And as for trials, (the Harton word for examination), which Julian had pleaded in excuse, he had better take care that, in attending to the imaginary trials of Harton, he didn't increase his own real trials."

This sentence made Julian laugh immoderately, both from his aunt's notion of the universal autocracy of her will, and from her obvious bewilderment at the technical word "Trials," which had betrayed her unconsciously into a pun, which, of all things, she abhorred. However, he wrote back politely—explained what he meant by "Trials"—begged to be excused for a neglect of her wishes, which was inevitable—and reiterated his promise of joining his brothers, as early as was feasible, under her hospitable roof.

It was not without inward misgiving that Cyril and Frank found themselves deposited in the hall of their glum old aunt's large and lonely house, the very size and emptiness of which had tended not a little to increase the poor lady's vapours. However, they were naturally graceful and well-bred, so that, in spite of the patronising empire assumed over them by the vulgar and half-educated Miss Sprong—which Cyril especially was very much inclined to resent— the first day or two passed by with tolerable equanimity.

But this dull routine soon proved unendurable to the two lively boys. They found it impossible to sit still the whole evening, looking over sacred prints; and this was the only amusement which Miss Sprong suggested to Lady Vinsear for them. Of late the dowager had taken what she considered to be a religious turn; but unhappily the supposed religion was as different from real piety as light from darkness, and consisted mainly in making herself and all around her miserable by a semi-ascetic puritanism of observances, and a style of conversation fit to drive her little nephews into a lunatic asylum.

Though they both felt a species of terror at their ungracious aunt, and the ever-detonating Miss Sprong, the long-pent spirit of fun at times grew too strong in them, and they would call down sharp rebukes by romping in the drawing-room, so as to disturb the two ladies while they read to each other, for hours together, the charming treatises of their favourite moderate divine.

The boys were seated on two stools, in the silence of despair, and at last Cyril, who had been twirling his thumbs for half an hour, and listening to a dissertation on Armageddon, gave a yawn so portentous and prolonged that Frank suddenly exploded in a little burst of laughter, which was at once checked, when Miss Sprong observed—

"I think it would be profitable if your ladyship,"—Miss Sprong never omitted the title—"would set your nephews some of Watts' hymns to learn."

The nephews protested with one voice and much rebellion, but at last their irate aunt quenched the unseemly levity, and they were fairly set to work at Dr Watts—Frank getting for his share "The little busy bee." But instead of learning it, they got together, and Cyril began drawing pictures of cruet-stands and other impieties, whereby Frank was kept in fits of laughter, and when called up to say his hymn, knew nothing at all about it. Cyril sat by him, and when Frank had exhausted his stock of acquirements by saying, in a tone of disgust—

"How doth the little busy bee—"

23

Cyril suggested—

"Delight to bark and bite."

"Oh, yes—

"How doth the little busy bee
Delight to bark and bite—

"How does it go on, Cyril?" said Frank.

"To gather honey all the day,
And eat it all the night,"

whispered the audacious brother, conjuring into memory the schoolboy version of that celebrated poem.

Frank, who was far too much engrossed in his own difficulties to think of what he was saying, artlessly repeated the words, and opened his large eyes in amazement, when he was greeted by a shout of laughter from Cyril, and a little shriek of indignation from Miss Sprong, which combined sounds started Lady Vinsear from the doze into which she had fallen, and ended in the summary ejectment of the young offenders.

The next day, to their own great relief and delight, they were sent home in disgrace; and knowing that their mother would not be angry with them for a piece of childish gaiety under such trying circumstances, they were surprised and pained to see how grave she and Violet looked when they told their story. But Mrs Home's thoughts had reverted to Julian, and she knew Miss Sprong too well not to be aware that she had designs on Lady Vinsear's property, and would excite against Julian any ill-will she could.

That her fears were not unfounded was proved by the fact that, in the middle of trial-week, Julian received an altogether intolerable epistle from Miss Sprong, written, she said, "at the express request and dictation of his esteemed aunt," calling him to account for this little incident in a way that, (to use Lillyston's expression), instantly "put him on his hind legs." He read a part of this letter to Lillyston, and, with his own comments, it ran thus:—

"*Lady Vinsear desires me to say,*" (Hem! I doubt that very much), "*that the rudeness of those two little boys, to say nothing of their great immorality and impiety,*" (I say, that's coming it too strong, or rather too Sprong), "*is such as to reflect great discredit on the influences to which they have been lately—*"

"By Jove! this is too bad," said Julian, passionately; "when she

24

adds innuendoes against my mother to her other malice—I won't stand it," and, without reading farther, he tossed the letter into the fire, watching with vindictive eyes its complete consumption—

"There goes the squire—revered, illustrious spark!
And there—no less illustrious—goes the clerk!"

he said, as he watched the little red streams flickering out of the black paper ashes. "And now for the answer! Bother the woman for plaguing me, (for I know it's none of my aunt's handiwork), in the middle of trial-week."

"I say, Julian, don't be too fiery in your answer, you know, for you really ought to appease the poor old lady. Only think of that impudent little brother of yours! I must make the young rogue's acquaintance some day."

But Julian had seized a sheet of note-paper, and wrote to his aunt, not condescending to notice even by a message her obnoxious amanuensis:—

"My Dear Aunt—I cannot believe that the letter I received to-day really emanated from you, at least not in the language in which it was couched.

"I have neither time nor inclination," ('Hoity, toity, how grand we are!') "to attend to the foolish trifle to which your amanuensis," ('Meaning me!' screamed the irrepressible Sprong), "alludes; but I am quite sure that, on reflection, you will not be inclined to judge too hardly a mere piece of fun and thoughtless liveliness; for that Frankie meant to be rude, I don't for a moment believe. I shall only add, that if I were not convinced that you can never have sanctioned the expressions which the lady," (Julian had first written 'person,' but altered it afterwards), "who wrote for you presumed to apply to my brothers, and above all, to my mother, I should have good reason to be offended; but feeling sure that they are not attributable to you, I pass them over with indifference. I am obliged to write in great haste, so here I must conclude.

"Believe me, my dear Aunt, your affectionate nephew,
"Julian Home."

Lady Vinsear was secretly pleased with the spirit which this letter showed, and was not sorry for the snubbing which it gave to her lady-companion; but she determined to exercise a little tyranny, and fancied that Julian would be too much frightened to resent it. Accustomed to the legacy-hunting spirit of many parasites, the old lady thought that Julian would be like the rest, and hoped to enjoy the sight of him reduced to submission and obedience, in the hopes of future advantage; not that she would exult in his humiliation, but she was glad of any pretext to bring the noble boy before her as a suppliant for her favour. Accordingly, setting aside her first and better impulses, she wrote back a sharp reply, abusing Cyril and Frank in round and severe terms, and adding some bitter innuendoes about the poverty of the family, and their supposed expectations at her decease. Miss Sprong lent all the venom of her malicious ingenuity to this precious performance, which fortunately did not reach Julian until trials were nearly over. Tired with excitement and hard work, the boy could ill endure these galling allusions, and wrote back a short and fiery reply:—

"My Dear Aunt—If any one has persuaded you that I am eager to purchase your good-will at any sacrifice, and that in consideration of 'supposed advantages' hereafter to be derived from you—I shall be willing to endure unkindly language or groundless insinuations about my other relatives—then they have very seriously misled you as to my real character. This is really the only reply of which your letter admits. I shall always be ready, as in duty bound, to bestow on you such respect and affection as our relationship demands and your own kindness may elicit, but I would scorn to win your favour at the expense of a subservience at once ungenerous and unjust.
"Believe me to remain, your affectionate nephew,
"Julian Home."

This letter decided the matter. Lady Vinsear wrote back, that as he obviously cared nothing about her, and did not even treat her with ordinary deference, she had that day altered her will. Poor old lady! Julian's angry letter cost her many a pang; and that night, as she sat in her bedroom by her lonely hearth, and thought over her dead brother and this gallant high-souled boy of his, the tears coursed each other down her furrowed cheeks, and she could get no rest. At last she had taken her desk, and, with trembling hands, written:—

"Dearest Julian—Forgive an old woman's whim, and come to me and comfort my old age. All I have is yours, Julian; and I love you, though I wrote to you so bitterly.—Your loving aunt,
"Caroline Vinsear."

But when morning came, Sprong resumed her ascendency, and by raking up and blowing the cooled embers of her patroness'

26

wrath, succeeded once more in fanning them to the old red heat, after which she poured vinegar upon them, and they exploded in the pungent fumes of the note which told our hero that he was not to hope, for the future, to be one day owner of a handsome fortune.

Of course, at first he was a little downcast; and in talking to Lillyston, compared himself to Gautier sans avoir, and "Wilfred the disinherited."

"Never mind, Julian; it matters very little to you," said Lillyston proudly.

"Anyhow I must have no more fits of idleness," answered Julian.

And indeed the only pain it caused him arose from the now necessary decision that he must go to Saint Werner's College as a sizar, or not at all. But for all that he went home with a light heart, and had once more gained the proud distinction of head-remove—one for which, at that time, I very much doubt whether he would have exchanged the prospect of a rich inheritance.

And the misfortune proved an advantage to Cyril too, as we shall see.

"So here's the little rogue who has lost me a thousand a year," said Julian laughingly, when he got home, and took Cyril on his knee by the fireside after dinner. The next moment he was very sorry he had said it, for Cyril hung his head, and seemed quite disconcerted; but his brother laughed away his sorrow, as he thought, and no further allusion to the subject was made.

But that night, as Julian looked into his brother's bedroom before he went to bed, he found Cyril crying, and his pillow wet with tears.

"Cyril, what's the matter, my boy?—you're not ill, are you?"

Cyril sat up, his eyes still swimming, and threw his arms round his brother's neck. "I've ruined you, Julian," he said.

"My dear child, what nonsense! Nay, my foolish little fellow," answered Julian, "this is really a mistake of yours. Aunt Vinsear was angry with me for my letters,—not with you. Don't cry so, Cyril, for I really don't care a rush about it; but I shall care if it vexes you. But shall I tell you why you ought to know of it, Cyril?"

"Why?"

"Because, my boy, it affects you too. You know, Cyril, that we are very poor now. Well, you see we shall have to support ourselves hereafter, and mother and Violet depend on us so you must work hard, Cyril, will you? and don't be idle at Marlby, as I'm afraid you have been. Eh, my boy?"

The boy promised faithfully, and performed the promise well

in after days; but that night Julian did not leave him until he was fast asleep.

We shall tell only one more scene of Julian's Harton life, and that very briefly.

It is a glorious summer afternoon; four o'clock bell is just over, and it is expected that in a few minutes the examiner, (an old Hartonian and senior classic), will read out the list which shall give the result of many weeks' hard work. The Newry scholarship is to be announced at the same time: Bruce and Home are the favourite names.

A crowd of boys throng round the steps, but Julian is not among them; he is leaning over the rails of the churchyard, under the elm-trees by Peachey's tomb, filled with a trembling and almost sickening anxiety. Bruce, confident of victory, is playing racquets, just below the schoolyard.

The Examiner suddenly appears from the speech-room door. There is a breathless silence while he reads the list, and then announces, in an emphatic voice—

"The Newry scholarship is adjudged to Julian Home!"

Off darts Lillyston, bounds up the hill into the churchyard, and has informed the happy Julian of his good fortune long before the "three cheers for Mr Burton," and "three cheers for Home," have died away.

CHAPTER FIVE

SAINT WERNER'S

"So soon the boy a youth, the youth a man,
Eager to run the race his fathers ran."

Rogers' Human Life

The last day at Harton came; the last chapel-service in that fair school fabric; the last sermon, "Arise, let us go hence;" the last look at the churchyard and the fourth-form room; the last "Speecher," and delivering up of the monitor's keys; the last farewells to Mr Carden and the other masters, and the Doctor, and

28

their schoolfellows and fags; and then with swelling hearts Julian and Lillyston got into the special train, thronged with its laughing and noisy passengers, and during the twenty minutes which were occupied by their transit to London, were filled with the melancholy thought that the days of boyhood were over for ever.

"Good-bye, Frank," said Julian—"To-morrow, to fresh fields and pastures new."

"Good-bye, Julian. We must meet next at Saint Werner's."

"Mind you write meanwhile."

"All right. You shall hear in a week. Good-bye." And Lillyston nodded from the cab window his last farewell to Julian Home, the Harton boy.

But if there were partings, what glorious meetings there were too, during those twenty-four hours. Ah! they must be felt, not written of: but I am sure that no family felt a keener joy that day, than Julian's mother, and sister, and brothers, when they saw him again, and learnt with pride that he had won a scholarship of 100 pounds a year; even Will and Mary, the faithful servants, seemed, when they heard it, to look up to their young master with even more honour than before.

Bruce spent the first part of his holidays in shooting, and the latter weeks in all the gaieties of a wealthy London family. He was naturally self-indulgent, and as no one urged him to make good use of his time, he devoted it to every possible amusement which riches could procure. Both he and his parents had a boundless belief in his natural abilities, and these, he thought, would be quite sufficient to gain him such honours as should be a graceful addition to the public reputation which he intended to win. A week or two before the Camford term commenced, he engaged some splendid lodgings, the most expensive which he heard of, and, turning out the furniture which was usually let with them, gave an almost unlimited order to a fashionable upholsterer to see them fitted out with due luxury and taste. When he came up as a freshman, which he deferred doing until the last possible moment, he was himself amazed to see how literally his orders had been obeyed. The rooms were refulgent with splendour: glossy tables, velvet-cushioned chairs, Turkey carpets, rich curtains, and an abundance of mirrors, made them, as the tradesman remarked "fit for a lord;" and Bruce took possession, with no little pride and self-satisfaction at finding himself his own master in so brilliant an abode.

Meanwhile, the holidays had passed by with Julian very differently, but very happily. Without tiring himself, or harassing his attention by study, he made a rule of devoting to work some portion, at least, of every day. Long strolls with his mother and sister in the bright summer evenings, bathes and boating excursions with Cyril and Frank, and happy, lonely rambles on the beach, kept him in health and spirits, and he looked forward with eager ambition to the arena which he was so soon to enter.

"The Harton boys have gone back by this time, haven't they?" asked Violet, as she sat with her mother and brother on the lawn one afternoon. "Don't you wish you were there again with them, Julian?"

"No," said Julian, "I wouldn't exchange Saint Werner's man even for Harton boy."

"How soon shall you have to go up to Saint Werner's?" said Mrs Home.

"On October 15th; in about a fortnight's time. I mean to go up a day or two beforehand to get settled. You and Violet must come with me, mother."

"But is that usual? Won't you get laughed at as though you were coming up under female escort?" asked Violet.

"Pooh! you don't suppose I care for that," said Julian, "even supposing it were likely to be true; besides—" He said no more, but his proud look at his sister's face seemed to imply that he expected rather to be envied than laughed at.

Accordingly, they went up together, and, as the train drew nearer and nearer to Camford, all three grew silent and thoughtful. They were rightly conscious that on the years to be spent in college life depended no small part of Julian's future happiness and prosperity. Three years at least would be spent there; years wealthy with all blessing, or prolific of evil and regret.

It was night when they arrived, and in the dimly-lighted streets there was not enough visible to gratify Julian's eager curiosity. The omnibus was crowded with undergraduates, who were chiefly freshmen, but apparently anxious to seem very much at home. At the station, the piles of luggage seemed interminable, and Mrs. Home and Violet were not sorry to escape from the unusual confusion to the quiet of their hotel.

Next morning, directly after an impatient breakfast, Julian started to call on his tutor.

"Which is the way to Saint Werner's College?" he asked of the waiter.

"Straight along, sir," was the reply, and off he started down King's Parade. In his hurry to make the first acquaintance with his new college, Julian hardly stopped to admire the smooth green quadrangle and lofty turrets of King Henry's College, or Saint Mary's, or the Senate House and Library, but strode on to the gate of Saint Werner's. Entering, he gazed eagerly at the famous great court, with its chapel, hall, fountain, and Master's lodge; and then made his way through the cloisters of Warwick's Court to his tutor's rooms.

On entering, he found himself in a room, luxuriously furnished, and full of books. In a large armchair before the fire sat a clergyman, whom Julian at once conjectured to be Mr Grayson, the tutor on whose "side" he was entered. He was a tall, grave-looking man, of about forty, and rose to greet his pupil with a formal bow.

"How do you do, Mr —? I did not quite catch the name."

"Home, sir," said Julian, advancing to shake hands in a cordial and confiding manner; but the tutor contented himself with a very cold shake, and seemed at a loss how to proceed.

Julian was burning with curiosity and eagerness. He longed to ask a hundred questions; at such a moment—a moment when he first felt how completely he had passed over the boundary which divides boyhood from manhood, he yearned for a word of advice, of encouragement, of sympathy. He expected, at least, something which should resemble a welcome, or a direction what to do. Nothing of the kind, however, came. While Julian was awaiting some remark, the tutor shuffled, hemmed, and looked ill at ease, as though at a loss how to begin the conversation.

At last Julian, in despair, asked, "Whereabouts are my rooms, sir?"

"Oh, the porter will show you; you'll find no difficulty about them," said the tutor.

"Have you anything further to ask me, Mr. Home?" he inquired, after another little pause.

"Nothing whatever, sir," said Julian, a little indignantly, for he began to feel much like what a volcano may be supposed to do when its crater is filled with snow. "Have you anything to tell me, sir?"

"No, Mr. Home. I hope you'll—that is—I hope—good morning," he said, as Julian, to relieve him from an unprofitable commonplace, backed towards the door, and made a formal bow.

"Humph," thought Julian. "What an icicle; not much good to be got out of that quarter. An intolerably cold reception. It's odd, too, for the man must have heard all about me from Mr Carden."

As we shall have very little to do with Mr Grayson, we may here allow him a cordial word of apology. What was to Julian the commencement of an epoch, was, be it remembered, to the tutor a commonplace and almost everyday event. The whole of that week he had been occupied in receiving visits from "the early fathers," who came up in charge of their sons, and all of whom seemed to expect that he would show the liveliest and tenderest interest in

31

their respective prodigies. Other freshmen had visited him unaccompanied, and some of them seemed rather inclined to patronise him than otherwise. He was a shy man, and always had a painful suspicion at heart that people were laughing at him. Having lived the life of a student, he had never acquired the polished ease of a man of the world, and had a nervous dread of strangers. His manners were but an icy shield of self-defence against ridicule, and they suited his somewhat sensitive dignity. He persuaded himself, too, that the "men" on his side were "men" in years and discretion as well as name, and that they must stand or fall unaided, since the years of boyish discipline and school constraint were gone by. It never occurred to him that a word spoken in due season might be of incalculable benefit to many of his charge. Being a man of slow sensibilities, he could not sympathise with the enthusiastic temperament of youths like Julian, nor did he ever single out one of his pupils either for partiality or dislike. Yet he was thoroughly kind-hearted, and many remembered his good deeds with generous gratitude. Nor was he wholly wrong in his theory that a tutor often does as much harm by meddling interference as he does by distance and neglect.

When a boy goes to college, eager, quick, impetuous, rejoicing as a giant to run his course, he is generally filled with noble resolutions and elevating thoughts. There is a touch of flame and of romance in his disposition; he feels himself to be the member of a brotherhood, and longs to be a distinguished and worthy one; he is anxious for all that is grand and right, and yearns for a little sympathy to support his determination and enliven his hopes. Some there may be so dull and sensual, so swallowed up in selfishness and conceit, so chill to every generous sentiment, and callous to every stirring impulse, that they experience none of this; their sole aim is, on the one hand to succeed, or on the other, to amuse and gratify themselves, to cultivate all their animal propensities, and drown in the mud-honey of premature independence the last relics of their childish aspirations. With men like this, to dress showily, to drive tandem and give champagne breakfasts, comes as a matter of course; while their supremest delight is to wander back to their old school, in fawn-coloured dittos, and with a cigar in their mouths, to show their superiority to all sense of decency and good taste. But these are the rare exceptions. However much they may conceal their own emotions, however dead and cynical, and contemptible they may grow in after days, there are few men of ordinary uprightness who do not feel a thrill of genuine enthusiasm when they first enter the walls of their college, and who will not own it without a blush.

Now Julian was an enthusiast by nature and temperament; all the sentiments which we have been describing he felt with more than ordinary intensity. It gave a grandeur to his hopes, and a distinct sense of ennobling pleasure to remember that he was treading the courts which generations of the good and wise had trodden before him, and holding in his hand the torch which they had handed down to him. Their memory still lingered there, and he trusted that his name too might in after days be not wholly unremembered. At least he would strive, with a godlike energy, to fail in no duty, and to leave no effort unfulfilled. If he viewed his coming life too much in its poetical aspect, at least his glowing aspirations and golden dreams were tempered with a deep humility and a childlike faith.

After fuming a little at the icy reception which his tutor had given him, he walked up and down the court, thinking of his position, and his intentions—of the past, the present, and the future—until proud tears glistened in his eyes. It was clear to him that now he would have to stand alone amid life's trials, and alone face life's temptations. And he was ready for the struggle. With God's help he would not miss the meaning of his life, but take the tide of opportunity while it was at the flood.

Before rejoining his mother, he determined to call on one of the junior fellows, the only one with whom he had any acquaintance, the Reverend N Admer. He only knew him from a casual introduction; but Mr Admer had asked him to call, on his arrival at Saint Werner's, and Julian hoped both to get some information from him to dissipate the painful feeling of strangeness and novelty, and also partially to do away with the effect of Mr Grayson's coldness.

Although it was now past ten in the morning, he found Mr Admer only just beginning breakfast, and looking tired and lazy. He was received with a patronising and supercilious tone, and the Fellow not only went on with his breakfast, but occasionally glanced at a newspaper while he talked. Not that Mr Admer at all meant to be unkind or rude, but he hated enthusiasm in every shape; he did not believe in it, and it wearied him—hence freshmen during their first few days were his profound abhorrence.

After a few commonplace remarks, Julian ventured on a question or two as to the purchases which he would immediately require, the hours of lecture and hall, and the thousand-and-one trifles of which a newcomer is necessarily ignorant. Mr Admer seemed to think this a great bore, and answered languidly enough, advising Julian not to be "more fresh" than he could help. It requires very small self-denial to make a person at home by supplying him with a little information; but small as the effort would have been, it was greater than the Reverend N Admer could afford to make, and his answers were so little encouraging that Julian, making ample allowance for the ennuyé condition of the young Fellow, relapsed into silence.

"And what do you think of Saint Werner's?" asked Mr Admer, taking the initiative, with a yawn.

Julian's face lighted up. "Think of it! I feel uncommonly proud already of being a Saint Werner's man."

"Genius loci, and all that sort of thing, eh?"

The sneering way in which this was said left room for no reply, so Mr Admer continued.

"Ah you'll soon find all that sort of twaddle wear off."

"I hope not," said Julian.

"Of course you intend to be senior classic, or senior wrangler, or something of that sort?"

"I expect simply nothing; but if I were inclined to soar, one might have a still higher ambition than that."

"Oh, I see; an embryo Newton,—all that sort of thing."

"I didn't mean quite 'all that sort of thing,' since you seem fond of the phrase," said Julian, "but really I think my aspirations, whatever they are, would only tire you. Good morning."

"Good morning," said Mr Admer, nodding. "We don't shake hands up here. I shall come and call on you soon."

"The later the better," thought Julian, as he descended the narrow stairs. "Good heavens! is that a fair specimen of a don, I wonder. If so, I shall certainly confine my acquaintance to the undergraduates."

No, Julian, not a fair specimen of a don altogether, but in some of his aspects a fair specimen of a certain class of university men, who profess to admire nothing, hope for nothing, love nothing; who think warmth of heart a folly, and sentiment a crime; who would not display an interest in any thing more important than a boat-race or a game of bowls, to save their lives; who are very fond of the phrase, "all that sort of nonsense," to express everything that rises above the dead level of their own dead mediocrity in intelligence and life. If you would not grovel in spirit; if you would not lose every tear that sparkles, and every sigh that burns; if you would not ossify the very power of passion; if you would not turn your soul into a mass of shapeless lead, avoid those despicable cynics, who never leave their discussion of the merits of beer, or the powers of stroke oars, unless it be to carp at acknowledged eminence, and jeer at genuine emotion. How often in such company have I seen men relapse into stupid silence, because, if they ventured on any expression of lively interest, one of the throng, amid the scornful indifference of the rest, would give the only acknowledgment of his remark, by taking the pipe out of his mouth, to give vent to a low guttural laugh.

After this it was lucky for Julian that he had brought his mother and sister with him, and that a moment after leaving Mr Admer he caught sight of Hugh Lillyston. With a joyful expression of surprise, they grasped each other's hands, and interchanged so friendly a greeting that Julian in an instant had scattered to the winds the gloomy impression which was beginning to creep over him.

"How long have you been here, Hugh?"

"I came yesterday."

"Have you seen your rooms yet?"

"No; I am just going to look for them."

"Well, come along; I know where they are."

"But stop," said Julian, "I must go to the Eagle first for my people. They'll be expecting me."

"Really. So Mrs. Home's here?" asked Lillyston.

"Yes, and my sister. If you've nothing to do, come and be introduced."

"How immensely jolly. I wish my mother and sister had taken the trouble to come with me, I know."

They went to the hotel, and Lillyston was able to gratify the curiosity he had long felt to see his friend's relations.

"Whom do you think I've brought back with me, mother? guess," said Julian, as he entered the room beaming with pleasure. "Here, Hugh, come along. My mother—my sister—Mr Lillyston."

"What! is this the Mr Lillyston of whom we've heard so much?" asked Mrs Home, with a cordial shake of the hand, while Violet looked up with a quick glance of curiosity and pleasure.

"No other," said Hugh, laughing; "and really I feel as if I were an old friend already."

"You are so, I assure you," said Mrs Home, "and I hope we shall often meet now." Lillyston hoped the same, as he looked at Violet.

It was arranged that they should all four go at once to Julian's rooms, and help in the grand operation of unpacking. The rooms were very pleasant attics in the great court, looking out on the Fellows' bowling-green, and the Iscam flowing beyond it. The furniture, most of which Julian was going to take from the previous possessor, was neat and comfortable, and when the book shelves began to glitter with his Harton prizes and gift-books, Julian was delighted beyond measure with the appearance of his new home.

35

For some hours the unpacking continued vigorously, only interrupted by an excursion for lunch to the hotel, since Julian had as yet purchased no plates and received no commons.

On their return they found an old lady in the room—

"A charred and wrinkled piece of womanhood;"

who, in a voice like the grating of a blunt saw, informed Julian that she was to be his bedmaker, and asked him whether he intended "to tea" in his rooms that evening. (The verb "to tea" is the property of bedmakers, and, with beautiful elasticity, it even admits of a perfect tense—as "have you tea'd?")

"By all means," said Julian; "lay the table for four this evening at eight o'clock, and get me some bread and butter. You'll stay, Hugh, won't you?"

"I should like to, very much. But won't it be your last evening with your mother and Miss Home?"

"Yes; but never mind that."

Lillyston shook his head, and bidding the ladies a warm good-bye, left them to enjoy with Julian his first quiet evening in Saint Werner's, Camford.

"I must hang my pictures before you go, Violet. I shall want your advice."

"Well, let me see," said Violet. "The water-colour likenesses of Cyril and Frankie ought to go here, one on each side of Mr Vere; at least, I suppose, you mean to put Mr Vere in the place of honour?"

"Oh, certainly," said Julian; "every time I look on that noble face, so full of strength and love, and so marked with those 'divine hieroglyphics of sorrow,' I shall learn fresh lessons of endurance and wisdom."

"People will certainly call you a heretic, if you do," laughed Violet.

"People!" said Julian scornfully.

"Of whom to be dispraised were no small praise.

"Let them yelp."

Mr. Vere was an eminent clergyman, who had been an intimate friend of Mr. Home before his death. Julian had only heard him preach, and met him occasionally; but he had read some of his works, and had received from him so much sympathising kindness and intellectual aid, that he regarded him with a love and reverence little short of devotion—as a man distinguished above all others for his gentleness, his eloquence, his honesty, his learning, and his love.

This likeness had belonged to Mr. Home, and Julian had asked leave to carry it with him whenever he should go to the University.

"Yes, the place of honour for Mr Vere."

"And where shall we hang this?" said Julian, taking up a photograph of Van Dyck's great painting of Jacob's Dream: the Hebrew boy is sleeping on the ground, and his long, dark curls, falling off his forehead, mingle with the rich foliage of the surrounding plants, fanned by the waving of mysterious wings; a cherub is lightly raising the embroidered cap that partially shades his face, and at his feet, blessing him with uplifted hand, stands a majestic angel, on whose flowing robes of white gleams a celestial radiance from the vista, alight with heavenly faces, that opens over his head. A happy and holy slumber seems to breathe from the lad's countenance, and yet you can tell that the light of dreams has dawned under his "closed eyelids," and that the inward eye has caught full sight of that Beatific Epiphany.

"We must hang this in your bedroom, Julian," said Mrs Home. "I shall love to think of you lying under the outstretched hand of this heavenly watcher."

So they hung it there, and the task was over, and they spent a happy happy evening together. Next morning Julian accompanied them to the train, and walked back to the matriculation examination.

CHAPTER SIX

RENCONTRES

"A boy—no better—with his rosy cheeks
Angelical, keen eye, courageous look,
And conscious step of purity and pride."

Wordsworth's Prelude

A public school man is by no means lonely when he first enters the university. He finds many of his old school-fellows accompanying him, and many who have gone up before him, and he feels united to them all by a bond of fellowship, which at once creates for him a circle of friends. Had Julian merely kept up his

Harton acquaintances, he would have known as many Camford men as were at all necessary for the purposes of society.

But although with most or all of the Hartonians Julian remained on pleasant and friendly terms, there were others whom he saw quite as much, and whose society he enjoyed all the more thoroughly because their previous associations and experiences were different from his own. And on looking back in aftertimes, what a delight it was to remember the noble hearts which, during those years of college life, had always beaten in unison with his own. Few enjoyments were more keen than that social equality and unconventional intercourse common among all undergraduates, which might at any time ripen into an earnest and invaluable friendship, or merely stop at the stage of an agreeable acquaintanceship. A great, and not the least useful portion of University education consisted in the intimate knowledge of character and the many-sided sympathies which were thus insensibly acquired.

During the first few weeks of college life, of course, a good deal of time was spent in receiving and returning the visits of acquaintances, old and new. Of the latter, there was one with whom Julian and Lillyston were equally charmed, and who soon became their constant companion. His name was Kennedy, and Julian first got to know him by sitting next him in lecture-room. His lively remarks, his keen and vivid sense of the ludicrous, the quick yet kindly notice he took of men's peculiarities, his ardent appreciation of the books which occupied their time, and the pleasant, rapid way in which he would dash off a caricature, soon attracted notice, and he rapidly became popular, both among undergraduates and dons. He was known, too, by the warm eulogy of his fellow-Marlbeians, who were never tired of singing his praises among themselves.

"Splendid!" whispered he to Julian warmly, after Julian had just finished construing a difficult clause in the Agamemnon, which he had done with a spirit and fire which even kindled a spark of admiration in the cold breast of Mr Grayson. "Splendidly done, Home! I say, how very reserved you are. Here have I been longing to know you for the last ten days, and we have hardly got beyond a nod to each other yet. Do come in to tea at my rooms to-night at eight. I want to introduce you to a friend of mine—Owen of Roslyn school."

"With pleasure," said Julian. "That dark-haired fellow is Owen, is it not? I hear he's going to do great things!"

"Oh yes! booked for a Fellow and a double-first; so you ought to know him, you know."

"Silence, gentlemen," said Mr Grayson, turning his stony gaze on Kennedy, whose bright face instantly assumed a demure expression of deep attention, while the light of laughter which still danced in his eyes might have betrayed to a careful observer the fact that the notes on which he appeared to be so assiduously occupied mainly consisted of replications of Mr Grayson's placid physiognomy and Roman nose.

"I've brought an umbra with me, Kennedy, in the person of Mr Lillyston, who sits next to me at lectures, and wanted to be introduced to you," said Owen, as he came in to Kennedy's room that evening.

"I'm delighted," said Kennedy. "Mr Lillyston, let me introduce you to Mr. Home."

"We hardly need an introduction, Hugh, at this time of day; do we?" said Julian, laughing; and the four were soon as much at home as it was possible for men to be. There was no lack of conversation. I think the rooms of a Camford undergraduate are about the last place where conversation ever flags; and when men like Kennedy, Owen, Julian, and Lillyston meet, it is perhaps more genuinely earnest and interesting than in any other time or place.

The next day, as Kennedy was sitting in Julian's rooms, glancing over the Aeschylus with him, in strutted Hazlet, whom we have incidentally mentioned as having been the son of a widow lady living at Ildown. He had come up to Camford straight from home, and as he had only received a home-education everything was strangely bewildering to him, and Julian was almost the only friend he knew. Nor was he likely to attract many friends; his manner was strangely self-confident, and his language dictatorial and dogmatic. In his mother's house he had long been the centre of religious tea-parties, before which he was often called upon to read and even to expound the Scriptures. "At the tip of his subduing tongue" were a number of fantastic phrases, originally misapplied, and long since worn bare of meaning, and the test of his orthodoxy was the universality with which he could reiterate proofs of heresy against every man of genius, honesty, and depth—who loved truth better than he loved the oracles of the prevalent idols. Hazlet practised the duty of Christian charity by dealing indiscriminate condemnation against all except those who belonged to his own exclusive and somewhat ignorant school of religious intolerance. His face was the reflex of his mind; his lank black hair stuck down in stiff dry straightness over a contracted forehead and an ill-shaped head; his spectacles gave additional glassiness to a lack-lustre eye, and the manner in which he carried his chin in the air seemed like an acted representation of "I am holier than thou."

Far be it from me to hold up to ridicule any body of earnest and honest men, to whatever party they may belong. I am writing of

Hazlet, not of those who hold the same opinions as he did. That man must have been unfortunate in life who has not many friends, and friends whom he holds in deep affection, among the adherents of opinions most entirely antagonistic to his own. Hazlet's repulsiveness was due to a very mistaken education, developing a very foolish idiosyncrasy, and especially to the pernicious system of encouraging sentiments and expressions which in a boy's mind could not be other than sickly exotics. He had to be taught his own hypocrisy by the painful progress of events, and, above all, he had to learn that religious shibboleths may be no proof of sanctification, and that religious intolerance is usually the hybrid offspring of ignorance and conceit. In many essential matters he held the truth,—but he held it in unrighteousness.

It may be imagined that Hazlet was no favourite companion of Julian Home. But Julian loved and honoured to the utmost of his power the good points of all; he had a deep and real veneration for humanity, and rarely allowed himself an unkind expression, or a look which indicated ennui, even to those associates by whose presence he was most unspeakably bored. Hazlet mistook his courteous manner for a deferential agreement, and was, too often, in Julian's presence more than usually insufferable in his Pharisaical tendencies.

"Good heavens!" said Kennedy, who saw Hazlet coming across the court. "Who's this, Home? He looks as if he had been just presiding at three conventicles and a meeting at Philadelphus Hall. Surely he can't be coming here."

"Oh, yes," said Julian, "that's a compatriot of mine named Hazlet; a very good fellow, I believe, though rather obtrusive perhaps."

"Good morning, Home," said Hazlet, in a measured and sanctified tone, as he entered the room and sat down.

Kennedy glanced impatiently at the Aeschylus.

"Ah! I see you're engaged on that heathen poet. It often strikes me, Home, that we may be wrong after all in spending so much time on these works of men, who, as Saint Paul tells us, were 'wholly given to idolatry.' I have just come from a most refreshing meeting at—"

"I say, Home," cut in Kennedy hastily, "shall I go? I suppose you won't do over any more of the Agamemnon this morning."

"I don't know," said Julian; "perhaps Hazlet will join us in our construe."

"No, I think not," said Hazlet, with a compassionate sigh. "I have looked at it; but some of it appeared to me so pagan in its sentiments that I contented myself with praying that I might not be put on. But you haven't told me what you think about what I was saying."

"Botheration," said Kennedy; "so your theory is that Christianity was intended to put an extinguisher over the light of heaven-born genius, and that the power and passion and wisdom of Aeschylus came from himself or the devil, and not from God? Surely, without any further argument on such an absurd proposition, it ought to be sufficient for you that this kind of learning forms a part of your immediate duty."

"I find other duties more paramount—now prayer, for instance, and talk with sound friends."

"Phew!!!" whistled Kennedy, thoroughly disgusted at language which was as new to him as it was distasteful; and, to relieve his feelings, he abandoned the conversation to Julian, and began to turn over the books on the table. Julian, however, seemed quite disinclined to enter into the question, and after a pause, Hazlet, gracefully waiving his little triumph, asked him with a peculiar unction—

"And how goes it, my dear Home, with your immortal soul?"

"My soul!" said Julian carelessly. "Oh! it's all right."

Hazlet then began to look at Julian's pictures.

"Ah," he observed with a deep sigh, "I'm sorry to see that you have the portrait of so unsound, so dangerous a man as Mr Vere."

"We'll drop that topic, please, Hazlet," said Julian, "as we're not likely to agree upon it."

"Have you ever read one word that Mr Vere ever wrote?" asked Kennedy.

"Well, yes; at least no, not exactly: but still one may judge, you know; besides, I've seen extracts of his works."

"Extracts!" answered Kennedy scornfully; "extracts which often attribute to him the very sentiments which he is opposing. But it isn't worth arguing with one of your school, who have the dishonesty to condemn writers whom you are incapable of understanding, on the faith of extracts which they haven't even read."

The wrathful purpling of Hazlet's sallow countenance portended an explosion of orthodox spleen, but Julian gently interposed in time to save the devoted Kennedy from a few unmeasured anathemas.

"Hush!" he said, "none of the odium theologicum, please, lest the mighty shade of Aeschylus smile at you in scorn. Do drop the subject, Hazlet."

"Very well, if you like, Home; but I must deliver my

41

conscience, you know. But really, Julian, you are not very Christian in your other pictures."

This was too much even for Julian's politeness, and he joined in the shout of laughter with which Kennedy greeted this appeal.

"Fools make a mock at sin," said Hazlet austerely. "I trust that you will both be brought to a better state of mind. Good morning!"

Kennedy flung himself into an armchair, and after finishing his laugh, exclaimed, "My dear Home, where did you pick up that intolerable hypocrite?"

"Hush, Kennedy, hush! Don't call him a hypocrite. His mode of religion may be very offensive to us, and yet it may be sincere."

"Faugh! the idea of asking you, 'How's your soul?' It reminds me of a friend of mine who was suddenly asked by a minister in a train 'if he didn't feel an aching void?' 'An aching void? Where?' said Jones, in a tone of alarm, for he was an unimaginative person. 'Within, sir, within!' said the stranger. Jones felt anxiously to find whether one of his ribs was accidentally protruding, but finding them all safe, set down the minister for a lunatic, and moved to the further end of the carriage."

Julian smiled; he was more accustomed to this kind of phraseology than his friend, and knew that outrageous as it was to good taste under the circumstances, it yet might spring from a sincere and honourable motive, or at best must be regarded as the natural result of innate vulgarity and mistaken training.

"Surely at best," continued Kennedy, "it's a most unwarrantable impertinence for a fellow like that to want to dabble his ignorant and coarse hand in the hallowed secrets of the microcosm. Not to one's nearest and dearest friend, not to one's mother or brother would one babble promiscuously on such awful themes; and to have the soul's sublime and eternal emotions, its sacred and unspoken communings, lugged out into farcical prominence by such conversational cant as that, is to dry up the very fountain of true religion, and put a premium on the successful grin of an offensive hypocrisy."

Kennedy seemed quite agitated, and as usual found relief in striding up and down the room. His religious feelings were deep and real—none the less so for being hidden—and Hazlet's language and manner had given him a rude shock.

"Another hour in that fellow's company would make me an infidel," he exclaimed with quivering lip. "Pray for me, indeed, with some of his 'sound and congenial friends.' Faugh! 'sound!' how does he dare to judge whether his superiors are 'sound' or not? and why must he borrow a metaphor from Stilton cheeses when he's talking of religious convictions."

42

"Why really, Kennedy," said Julian, "to see the contempt written in your face, one would think you were an archangel looking at a black beetle, as a learned judge once observed. If you won't regard Hazlet as a man and a brother, at least remember that he's a vertebrate animal."

But Kennedy was not to be joked out of his indignation, so Julian continued. "I wish you knew more of Lillyston. At one time, I should have been nearly as much bothered by Hazlet as you, but Lillyston's kind, genial good-humour with every one, and the genuine respectful sympathy which he shows even for things he can least understand, have made me much happier than I should have been. Now, he might have done Hazlet some good, whereas your opposition, my dear fellow, will only make him more rampant than ever. Ah, here Lillyston comes."

"What an honest open face," said Kennedy.

"Like the soul which looks through it, sans peur et sans reproche," said Julian warmly.

"Rather a contrast to the last comer," murmured Kennedy, as he picked up his cap and gown to walk to the lecture-room.

"There, don't think of Hazlet any more," said Julian.

"'He prayeth best who loveth best
All things both great and small,
For the dear God who loveth us,
He made and loveth all.'

"A capital good motto that; isn't it, Hugh?"

"I must love Hazlet as one of the very small things, then," said the incorrigible Kennedy as he left the room with the other two.

Hazlet was put on to construe during the lecture, and if anything could have shaken the brazen tower of his self-confidence, it would have been the egregious display of incapacity which followed; but Hazlet rather piqued himself on his indifference to the poor blind heathen poets, on whose names he usually dealt reprobation broadcast. "Like lions that die of an ass's kick," those wronged great souls lay prostrate before Hazlet's wrathful heels.

43

Chapter Seven

The Scorn of Scorn

"And not a man, for being simply man,
Hath any honour, but honour for those honours
That are without him—as place, riches, favour,
Prizes of accident as oft as merit."

Shakespeare

Very different in all respects were Julian's rencontres with others of his old schoolfellows. There were some, indeed, among them who had left Harton while they were still in low forms, and some whose tastes and pursuits were so entirely different from his own, that it was hardly likely that he should maintain any other intercourse with them than such as was demanded by a slight acquaintance. But of Bruce, at any rate, it might have been expected that he would see rather more than proved to be the case. Bruce, as having been head of the school during the period when Julian was a monitor, had been thrown daily into his company, and, as inmates of the same house, they had acted together in the thousand little scenes which diversify the bright and free monotony of a schoolboy's life.

But the first fortnight passed by, and Bruce had not called on Julian, and as they were on different "sides," they had not chanced to meet, either in lecture-room or elsewhere. Julian, not knowing whether his position as sizar would make any difference in Bruce's estimation of him, had naturally left him to take the initiative in calling; while Bruce, on the other hand, always a little jealous of his brilliant contemporary, and not too anxious to be familiar with a sizar, pretended to himself that it was as much Julian's place as his to be first in calling. Hence it was that, for the first fortnight, the two did not happen to come across each other.

Meanwhile Bruce also had made many fresh acquaintances. His reputation for immense wealth and considerable talent—his dashing easy manner—his handsome person and elaborate style of dress, attracted notice, and very soon threw him into the circle of all the young fashionables of Saint Werner's. His style of life cannot be better described than by saying that he affected the fine gentleman. Hardly a day had passed during which he had not been at some large breakfast or wine-party, or formed one of a select little body of

44

supping aristocrats. He did very little work, and pretended to do none, (for Bruce was a first-rate specimen of the never-open-a-book genus), although at unexpected hours he took care to get up the lecture-room subjects sufficiently well to make a display when he was put on. Even in this he was unsuccessful, for scholarship cannot be acquired per saltum, and Mr Serjeant, the lecturer on his side, looked on him with profound contempt as a puppy who was all the more offensive from pretending to some knowledge. He told him that he might distinguish himself by hard steady work, but would never do so without infinitely more pains than he took the trouble to apply. His quiet and caustic strictures, and the easy sarcasm with which he would allow Bruce to flourish his way through a passage, and then go through it himself, pointing out how utterly Bruce had "hopped with airy and fastidious levity" above all the nicer shades of meaning, and slurred over his ignorance of a difficulty by some piece of sonorous nonsense, made him peculiarly the object of the young man's disgust. But though Mr Serjeant wounded his vanity, the irony of "a musty old don," as Bruce contemptuously called him, was amply atoned for by the compliments of the fast young admirers whom Bruce soon gathered round him, and some of whom were always to be found after hall-time sipping his claret or lounging in his gorgeous rooms. To them Bruce's genius was incontestably proved by the faultless evenness with which he parted his hair behind, the dapperness of his boots, and the merit of his spotless shirts.

Sir Rollo Bruce, Vyvyan's father, was a man of no particular family, who had been knighted on a deputation, and contrived to glitter in the most splendid circles of London society. His magnificent entertainments, his exquisite appointments, his apparently fabulous resources, were a sufficient passport into the saloons of dukes; and, although ostensibly Sir Rollo had nothing to live on but his salary as the chairman of a bank, nobody who had the entrée of his house cared particularly to inquire into the sources of his wealth. Vyvyan imitated his father in his expensive tastes, and cultivated, with vulgar assiduity, the society of the noblemen at his college. In a short time he knew them all, and all of them had been at his rooms except a young Lord De Vayne, of whom we shall hear more hereafter, and whose retiring manners made him shrink with dislike from Bruce's fawning familiarity.

The sizars at Saint Werner's do not dine at the same hour as the rest of the undergraduates, but the hour after, and their dinner consists of the dishes which have previously figured on the Fellows' table. It seems to me that the time may come when the authorities of that royal foundation will see reason to regret so unnecessary an arrangement, the relic of a long, obsolete, and always undesirable system. Many of Saint Werner's most distinguished alumni have themselves sat at the sizars' table, and if any of them were blessed or cursed with sensitive dispositions, they will not be dead to the justice of these remarks. The sizars are, by birth and education, invariably, so far as I know, the sons of gentlemen, and perhaps most often of clergymen whose means prevent them from bearing unassisted the heavy burden of University expenses. After a short time many of these sizars become scholars, and eventually a large number of them win for themselves the honours of a fellowship. Why put on these young students a gratuitous indignity? Why subject them to the unpleasant remarks which some are quite coarse enough to make on the subject? The authorities of Saint Werner's are full of real courtesy and kindness, and that the arrangement is not intended as an indignity I am well aware; it is, as I have said, the accidental fragment of an obsolete period—a period when scholars dined on "a penny piece of beef," and slept two or three in a room at the foot of the Fellows' beds. All honour to Saint Werner's; all honour to the great, and the wise, and the learned, and the noble whom she has sent forth into all lands; all honour to the bravery and the truthfulness of her sons; all honour to the profound scholars, and able teachers, and eloquent orators who preside at her councils; she is a Queen of colleges, and may wield her sceptre with a strong hand and a proud. But are there not some among her subjects who are deaf to the sounds of calm advice?—some who are so blind as to love her faults and prop up her abuses?—some who daub her walls with the untempered mortar of their blind prejudice, and treat every one as an enemy who would aid in removing here and there a bent pillar, and here and there a crumbling stone? (These words were written some time ago. I trust that since then all causes of offence, if they ever existed, have long been forgiven and forgotten.)

And now let all defenders of present institutions, however bad they may be—let all violent supporters of their old mumpsimus against any new sumpsimus whatever, listen to a conversation among some undergraduates. It may convince them, or it may not— I cannot tell; but I know that it had a powerful influence on me.

Bruce was standing in the Butteries, where he had just been joined by Lord Fitzurse and Sir John D'Acres, who by virtue of their titles—certainly not by any other virtue—sat among reverend Professors and learned Doctors at the high table, far removed from the herd of common undergraduates. With the three were Mr. Boodle and Mr. Tulk, (the "Mister" is given them in the college-lists out of respect for the long purses which have purchased them, the

46

privilege of fellow-commoners or ballantiogennaioi), who enjoyed the same enviable distinction and happy privilege. By the screens were four or five sizars; a few more were scattered about in the passage waiting, whilst the servants hurriedly placed the dishes on the table set apart for them; and Julian was chatting to Lillyston, who chanced at the moment to have been passing by.

"Who is that table for?" asked D'Acres, pointing through the open door of the hall.

"Oh, that's for the sizars," tittered the feeble-minded Boodle, who tittered at everything.

"S–s–sizars!" stammered Lord Fitzurse. "What's that mean? Are they v–v–very big f–f–fellows?"

"Ha! ha! ha!" said Bruce. "No; they're sons of gyps and that kind of thing, who feed on the semese fragments of the high table."

"They must be g–g–ghouls!" said his lordship, shudderingly.

"Hush," said D'Acres, who was a thorough gentleman, "some of the sizars may be here;" and he dropped Bruce's arm.

"Pooh! they'll feel flattered," said Bruce carelessly, as D'Acres walked off.

"Indeed!" said Julian, striding indignantly forward, for the conversation was so loud that he had heard every word of it. "Flattered to be the butt for the insolence of puppyism and every fool who is coarse enough to insult them publicly."

"Who the d–d–d–deuce are you?" said Lord Fitzurse, "for you're coming it r–r–rather strong."

"Who is he?" said Lillyston, breaking in, "your equal, sir, in birth, as he is your superior in intellect, and in every moral quality. Gentlemen," he continued, "let me warn you not to have the impertinence to talk in this way again."

"Warn us!" said Bruce, trying to hide under bravado his crestfallen temper; "why, what'll you do if we choose to continue?"

"Make a few counter-remarks to begin with, Bruce, on parasites and parvenus, tuft-hunting freshmen, and the tenth transmitters of a foolish face," retorted Lillyston, glowing with honest indignation.

"And turn you out of the butteries by the shoulders," said a strong undergraduate, who had chanced to be a witness of the scene. "A somewhat boyish proceeding, perhaps, but exactly suited to some capacities."

Bruce and his friends, seeing that they were beginning to have the worst of it, thought it about time to swagger off, and for the future learnt to confine their remarks to a more exclusive circle.

There had been another silent spectator of the scene in the person of Lord De Vayne. He was a young viscount whose estate bordered on the grounds of Lonstead Abbey, and he had known Julian since both of them were little boys. He had been entirely educated at home with an excellent tutor, who had filled his mind with all wise and generous sentiments; but his widowed mother lived in such complete seclusion that he had rarely entered the society of any of his own age, and was consequently timid and bashful. Meeting sometimes with Julian, he had conceived a warm admiration for his genius and character, and at one time had earnestly wished to join him at Harton. But his mother was so distressed at the proposition that he at once abandoned it, while he eagerly looked forward to the time when he should meet his friend at Saint Werner's, on the books of which college he had entered his name partly for this very reason. He had not been an undergraduate many days before he called on Julian, who had received him indeed very kindly, but who seemed rather shy of being much in his company for fear of the remarks which he had not yet learnt entirely to disregard. This was a great source of vexation to De Vayne, though the reason of it was partly explained after the remarks which he had just overheard.

"Home," he whispered, "I wish you'd come into my rooms after hall, I should so much like to have a talk. Do," he said, as he saw that Julian hesitated, "I assure you I have felt quite lonely here."

Accordingly, after hall, Julian strolled into Warwick's Court, and found his way to Lord De Vayne's rooms.

"I am so glad to see you, Julian, at last. As I have told you," he said, with a glistening eye, "I have been very lonely. I have never left home before, and have made no friend here as yet;" and he heaved a deep sigh.

Julian felt his heart full of friendliness for the gentle boy whose total inexperience made him seem younger than he really was. He glanced round the rooms; they were richly furnished, but full of memorials of home, that gave them a melancholy aspect. Over the fireplace was a water-colour likeness of his lady-mother in her widow's weeds, and on the opposite side of the room another picture of a beautiful young child—De Vayne's only brother, who had died in infancy. The handsomely-bound books on the shelves had been transferred from their well-known places in the library of Uther Hall, and the regal antlers which were fastened over the door had once graced the dining-room. Thousands would have envied Lord De Vayne's position; but he had caught the shadow of his mother's sadness, his relations were few, at Saint Werner's as yet he had found none to lean upon, and he felt unhappy and alone.

"I was so ashamed, Julian," he said, "so utterly and

48

unspeakably ashamed to hear the rudeness of these men as we came out of hall. I'm afraid you must have felt deeply hurt."

"Yes, for the moment; but I'm sorry that I took even a moment's notice of it. Why should one be ruffled because others are unfeeling and impertinent; it is their misfortune, not ours."

"But why did you come up as a sizar, Julian? Surely with Lonstead Abbey as your inheritance—"

"No," said Julian with a smile; "I am lord of my leisure, and no land beside."

"Really! I had always looked on you as a future neighbour and helper."

He was too delicate to make any inquiries on the subject, but while a bright airy vision rose for an instant before Julian's fancy, and then died away, his friend said, with ingenuous embarrassment:

"You know, Home, I am very rich. In truth, I have far more money than I know what to do with. It only troubles me. I wish—"

"Oh, dear no!" said Julian hastily; "I got the Newry scholarship, you know, at Harton, and I really need no assistance whatever."

"I hope I haven't offended you; how unlucky I am," said De Vayne blushing.

"Not a whit, De Vayne; I know your kind heart."

"Well, do let me see something of you. Won't you come a walk sometimes, or let me come in of an evening when you're taking tea, and not at work?"

"Do," said Julian, and they agreed to meet at his rooms on the following Sunday evening.

Sunday at Camford was a happy day for Julian Home. It was a day of perfect leisure and rest; the time not spent at church or in the society of others, he generally occupied in taking a longer walk than usual, or in the luxuries of solemn and quiet thought. But the greatest enjoyment was to revel freely in books, and devote himself unrestrained to the gorgeous scenes of poetry, or the passionate pages of eloquent men; on that day he drank deeply of pure streams that refreshed him for his weekly work; nor did he forget some hour of commune, in the secrecy of his chamber and the silence of his heart, with that God and Father in whom alone he trusted, and to whom alone he looked for deliverance from difficulty, and guidance under temptation. Of all hours his happiest and strongest were those in which he was alone—alone except for a heavenly presence, sitting at the feet of a Friend, and looking face to face upon himself.

He had been reading Wordsworth since hall-time, when the ringing of the chapel-bell summoned him to put on his surplice, and walk quietly down to chapel. As there was plenty of time, he took a

49

stroll or two across the court before going in. While doing so, he met De Vayne, and in his company suddenly found himself vis-à-vis with his old enemy Brogten.

"Hm!" whispered Brogten to his companion; "the sizars are getting on. A sizar and a viscount arm-in-arm!"

Julian only heard enough of this sentence to be aware that it was highly insolent; and the flush on De Vayne's cheek showed that he too had caught something of its meaning.

"Never mind that boor's rudeness," he said. "I feel more than honoured to be in the sizar's company. How admirably quiet you are, Julian, under such conduct!"

"I try to be; not always with success, though," he answered, as his breast swelled, and his lip quivered with indignation

"Scorn!—to be scorned by one that I scorn:
Is that a matter to make me fret?
Is that a matter to cause regret?
Stop! let's come into chapel."

They went into chapel together. De Vayne walked into the noblemen's seats, and Julian, hot and angry, and with the words, "Scorn!—to be scorned by one that I scorn," still ringing in his ears, strode up the whole length of the chapel to the obscure corner set apart—is it not very needlessly set apart?—for the sizars' use.

Saint Werner's chapel on a Sunday evening is a moving sight. Five hundred men in surplices thronging the chapel from end to end—the very flower of English youth, in manly beauty, in strength, in race, in courage, in mind—all kneeling side by side, bound together in a common bond of union by the grand historic associations of that noble place—all mingling their voices together with the trebles of the choir and the thunder-music of the organ. This is a spectacle not often equalled; and to take a share in it, as one for whose sake in part it has been established, is a privilege not to be forgotten. The music, the devotion, the spirit of the place, smoothed the swelling thoughts of Julian's troubled heart. "Are we not all brethren? Hath not one Father begotten us?" Such began to be the burden of his thoughts, rather than the old "Scorn!—to be scorned by one that I scorn." And when the glorious tones of the anthem ceased, and the calm steady voice of the chaplain was heard alone, uttering in the sudden hush the grand overture to the noble prayer—

"O Lord, our heavenly Father, high and mighty, King of Kings, Lord of Lords, the only Ruler of princes, who dost from thy throne behold all the dwellers upon earth."

50

Then the last demon of wrath was exorcised, and Julian thought to himself—

"No; from henceforth I scorn no one, and am indifferent alike to the proud man's scorn and the base man's sneer."

The two incidents that we have narrated made Julian fear that his position as a sizar would be one of continual annoyance. He afterwards gratefully acknowledged that in such a supposition he was quite mistaken. Never again while he remained a sizar did he hear the slightest unkind allusions to the circumstance, and but for the external regulations imposed by the college, he might even have forgotten the fact. Those regulations, especially the hall arrangements, were indeed sufficiently disagreeable at times. It could not be pleasant to dine in a hall which had just been left by hundreds of men, and to make the meal amid the prospect of slovenly servants employed in the emptying of wine-glasses and the ligurrition of dishes, sometimes even in passages of coquetry or noisy civilities, on the interchange of which the presence of these undergraduates seemed to impose but little check. These things may be better now, and in spite of them Julian felt hearty reason to be grateful for the real kindness of the Saint Werner's authorities. In other respects he found that the fact of his being a sizar made no sort of difference in his position; he found that the majority of men either knew or cared nothing about it, and sought his society on terms of the most unquestioned equality, for the sake of the pleasure which his company afforded them, and the thoughts which it enabled them to ventilate or interchange.

CHAPTER EIGHT

STUDY AND IDLENESS

"Then what golden hours were for us,
While we sate together there!
How the white vests of the chorus
Seemed to wave up a live air.
How the cothurns trod majestic,
Down the deep iambic lines,
And the rolling anapaestic
Curled like vapour over shrines!"

E Barrett Browning

The incentives which lead young men to work are as various as the influences which tend to make them idle. One toils on, however hopelessly, from a sense of duty, from a desire to please his parents, and satisfy the requirements of the place; another because he has been well trained into habits of work, and has a notion of educating the mind; a third because he has set his heart on a fellowship; a fourth, because he is intensely ambitious, and looks on a good degree as the stepping-stone to literary or political honours. The fewest perhaps pursue learning for her own sake, and study out of a simple eagerness to know what may be known, as the best means of cultivating their intellectual powers for the attainment of at least a personal solution of those great problems, the existence of which they have already begun to realise. But of this rare class was Julian Home. He studied with an ardour and a passion, before which difficulties vanished, and in consequence of which, he seemed to progress not the less surely, because it was with great strides. For the first time in his life, Julian found himself entirely alone in the great wide realm of literature—alone, to wander at his own will, almost without a guide. And joyously did that brave young spirit pursue its way—now resting in some fragrant glen, and by some fountain mirror, where the boughs which bent over him were bright with blossom, and rich with fruit—now plunging into some deep thicket, where at every step he had to push aside the heavy branches and tangled weeds—and now climbing with toilful progress some steep and rocky hill, on whose summit, hardly attained, he could rest at last, and gaze back over perils surmounted, and precipices passed, and mark the thunder rolling over the valleys, or gaze on kingdoms full of peace and beauty, slumbering in the broad sunshine beneath his feet.

Julian read for the sake of knowledge, and because he intensely enjoyed the great authors, whose thoughts he studied. He had read parts of Homer, parts of Thucydides, parts of Tacitus, parts of the tragedians, at school, but now he had it in his power to study a great author entire, and as a whole. Never before did he fully appreciate the "thunderous lilt" of Greek epic, the touching and voluptuous tenderness of Latin elegy, the regal pomp of history, the gorgeous and philosophic mystery of the old dramatic fables. Never before had he learnt to gaze on "the bright countenance of truth, in the mild and dewy air of delightful studies." Those who decry classical education, do so from inexperience of its real character and value, and can hardly conceive the sense of strength and freedom which a young and ingenuous intellect acquires in all literature, and in all thought, by the laborious and successful endeavour to enter into that noble heritage which has been left us by the wisdom of bygone generations. Those hours were the happiest of Julian's life; often would he be beguiled by his studies into the "wee small" hours of night; and in the grand old company of eloquent men, and profound philosophers, he would forget everything in the sense of intellectual advance. Then first he began to understand Milton's noble exclamation—

"How charming is divine philosophy!
Not harsh and rugged as dull fools suppose,
But musical as is Apollo's lute,
And a perpetual feast of nectared sweets,
Where no crude surfeit reigns."

He studied accurately, yet with appreciation; sometimes the two ways of study are not combined, and while one man will be content with a cold and barren estimate of ge's and pon's derived from wading through the unutterable tedium of interminable German notes, of which the last always contradicted all the rest; another will content himself with eviscerating the general meaning of a passage, without any attempt to feel the finer pulses of emotion, or discriminate the nicer shades of thought. Eschewing commentators as much as he could, Julian would first carefully go over a long passage, solely with a view to the clear comprehension of the author's language, and would then re-read the whole for the purpose of enjoying and appreciating the thoughts which the words enshrined; and finally, when he had finished a book or a poem,

53

would run through it again as a whole, with all the glow and enthusiasm of a perfect comprehension.

Sometimes Kennedy, or Owen, or Lord De Vayne, would read with him. This was always in lighter and easier authors, read chiefly for practice, and for the sake of the poetry or the story, which lent them their attraction. It was necessary to pursue in solitude all the severer paths of study; but he found these evenings, spent at once in society and yet over books, full both of profit and enjoyment. Lillyston, although not a first-rate classic, often formed one of the party; Owen and Julian contributed the requisite scholarship and the accurate knowledge, while Lillyston and De Vayne would often throw out some literary illustration or historical parallel, and Kennedy gave life and brightness to them all, by the flow and sparkle of his gaiety and wit. But it must be admitted that Kennedy was the least studious element in the party, and was too often the cause of digressions, and conversations which led them to abandon altogether the immediate object of their evening's work.

Kennedy had a tendency to idleness, which was developed by the freedom with which he plunged into society of all kinds. His company was so agreeable, and his bright young face was so happy an addition to all parties, that he was in a round of constant engagements—breakfast parties, wines, supper parties, and dinners—that encroached far too much on the hours of work. At school the perpetual examinations kept alive an emulous spirit, which counteracted his fondness for mental vagrancy; but at college the examinations—at least those of any importance—are few and far between; and he always flattered himself that he meant soon to make up for lost time, for three years looks an immense period to a young man at the entrance of his university career. It was nearly as necessary, (even in a pecuniary point of view), for him as for Julian to make the best use of his time; for although he was an only son, he was not destined to inherit a fortune sufficient for his support.

"Just look at these cards," he said to Julian one day; "there is not one of them which hasn't an invitation scribbled on it. These engagements really leave one no time for work. What a bore it is! How do you manage to escape them?"

"Well—first, I haven't such a large acquaintance as you; that makes a great deal of difference. But, besides, I make a point of leaving breakfast parties at ten, and wines at chapel-time—so that I really don't find them any serious hindrance. No hindrance, I mean, in comparison with the delight and profit of the society itself."

"I wish I could make the same resolution," said Kennedy; "but the fact is, I find company so thoroughly amusing, that I'm always tempted to stay."

"But why not decline sometimes?"

"I don't know—it looks uncivil. Here, which of these shall I cut?" he said, tossing three or four notes and cards to Julian.

"This for one," said Julian, as he read the first:—

"*Dear Kennedy—Come to supper and cards at ten. Bruce wants to be introduced to you. Yours,*
"*'C Brogten.'*"

"Yes, I think I shall. I don't like that fellow Brogten, who is always thrusting himself in my way," said Kennedy. "Heigh ho!" and Kennedy leant his head on his arm, and fell into a reverie, thinking that after all his three years at college might be over almost before he was aware of how much time he lost.

"I hope you don't play cards much," said Julian.

"Why? I hear Hazlet has been denouncing them in hall with unctuous fervour, and I do think it was that which led me to join in a game which was instantly proposed by some of the men who sat near."

"I don't say that there's anything diabolical," said Julian, smiling, "in paint and pasteboard, or that I should have the least objection to play them myself if I wanted amusement, but I think them—except very occasionally, and in moderation—a waste of time; and if you play for money I don't think it does you any good."

"Well, I've never played for money yet. By the bye, do you know Bruce? He has the character and manner of a very gentlemanly fellow."

"Yes, I know him," said Julian, who made a point of holding his tongue about a man when he had nothing favourable to say.

"Oh, ay, I forgot; of course; he's a Hartonian. But didn't you think him gentlemanly?"

"He has an easy manner, and is accustomed to good society, which is usually all that is intended by the word," said Julian.

"I think I must go just this one evening. I like to see a variety of men; one learns something from it."

Kennedy went. The supper took place in Brogten's rooms, and the party then adjourned to Bruce's, where they immediately began a game at whist for half-a-crown points, and then "unlimited loo." Kennedy was induced to play "just to see what it was like." As the game proceeded he became more and more excited; the others were accustomed to the thing, and concealed their eagerness; but Kennedy, who was younger and more inexperienced than any of them, threw himself into the game, and drank heedlessly of the wine that freely circulated. Surely if guardian spirits attend the footsteps

55

of youth, one angel must have wept that evening "tears such as angels weep" to see him with his flushed face and sparkling eyes, eagerly seizing the sums he won, or, with clenched hand and contracted brow, anxiously awaiting the result of some adverse turn in the chances of the game. I remember once to have accidentally entered a scene like this in going to borrow something from a neighbour's room; and I shall never forget the almost tiger-like eagerness and haggard anxiety depicted on the countenances of the men who were playing for sums far too extravagant for an undergraduate's purse.

How Kennedy got home he never knew, but next morning he awoke headachy and feverish, and the first thing he saw on his table was a slip of paper on which was written, "Kennedy admonished by the senior Dean for being out after twelve o'clock." The notice annoyed and ashamed him. He lay in bed till late, was absent from lecture, and got up to an unrelished breakfast, at which he was disturbed by the entrance of Bruce, to congratulate him on his winnings of the evening before.

While Bruce was talking to him, Lillyston also strolled in on his way from lecture to ask what had kept Kennedy away. He was surprised to see the pale and weary look on his face, and catching sight of Bruce seated in the armchair by the fire, he merely made some commonplace remarks and left the room. But he met Julian in the court, and told him that Kennedy didn't seem to be well.

"I'm not surprised," said Julian; "he supped with Brogten, and then went to play cards with Bruce, and I hear that Bruce's card parties are not very steady proceedings."

"Can't we manage to keep him out of that set, Julian? It will be the ruin of his reading."

"Ay, and worse, Hugh. But what can one say? It will hardly do to read homilies to one's fellow undergraduates."

"You might at least give him a hint."

"I will. I suppose he'll come and do some Euripides to-night."

He did come, and when they had read some three hundred lines, and the rest were separating, he proposed to Julian a turn in the great court.

The stars were crowding in their bright myriads, and the clear silvery moonlight bathed the court, except where the hall and chapel flung fantastic and mysterious shadows across the green smooth-mown lawns of the quadrangle. The soft light, the cool exhilarating night air were provocative of thought, and they walked up and down for a time in silence.

Many thoughts were evidently working in Kennedy's mind, and they did not all seem to be bright or beautiful as the thoughts of

56

youth should be. Julian's brain was busy, too; and as they paced up and down, arm in arm, the many-coloured images of hope and fancy were flitting thick and fast across his vision. He was thinking of his own future and of Kennedy's, whom he was beginning to love as a brother, and for whose moral weakness he sometimes feared.

"Julian," said Kennedy, suddenly breaking the silence; "were you ever seized by an uncontrollable, unaccountable, irresistible presentiment of coming evil,—a feeling as if a sudden gulf of blackness and horror yawned before you—a dreadful something haunting you, you knew not what, but only knew that it was there?"

"I have had presentiments, certainly; though hardly of the kind you describe."

"Well, Julian, I have such a presentiment now, overshadowing me with the sense of guilt, of which I was never guilty; as though it were the shadow of some crime committed in a previous state of existence, forgotten yet unforgotten, incurred yet unavenged."

"Probably the mere result of a headache this morning, and the night air now," said Julian, smiling at the energetic description, yet pained by the intensity of Kennedy's tone of voice.

"Hush, Julian! I hate all that stupid materialism. Depend upon it, some evil thing is over me. I wonder whether crimes of the future can throw their crimson shadow back over the past. My life, thank God, has been an innocent one, yet now I feel like the guiltiest thing alive."

"One oughtn't to yield to such feelings, or to be the victim of a heated imagination, Kennedy. In my own case at least, half the feelings I have fancied to be presentiments have turned out false in the end—presentiments, I mean, which have been suggested, as perhaps this has, by passing circumstances."

"God grant this may be false," said Kennedy, "but something makes me feel uneasy."

"It will be a lying prophet, if you so determine, Kennedy. The only enemy who has real power to hurt us is ourselves. Why should you be agitated by an idle forecast of uncertain calamity? Be brave, and honest, and pure, and God will be with you."

"Don't be surprised," continued Julian, "if you've heard me say the same words before; they were my father's dying bequest to his eldest son."

"Be brave, and honest, and pure—" repeated Kennedy; "yes, you must be right, Julian. Look what a glorious sky, and what numberless 'patines of bright gold.'"

Julian looked up, and at that moment a meteor shot across the heaven, plunging as though from the galaxy into the darkness, and after the white and dazzling lustre of the trail had disappeared, seeming to leave behind the glory of it a deeper gloom. It gave too true a type of many a young man's destiny.

Kennedy said nothing, but although it is not the Camford custom to shake hands, he shook Julian's hand that night with one of those warm and loving grasps, which are not soon forgotten. And each walked slowly back to his own room.

CHAPTER NINE

THE BOAT-RACE

"And caught once more the distant shout,
The measured pulse of racing oars
Between the willows."

In Memoriam

The banks of "silvery-winding Iscam" were thronged with men; between the hours of two and four the sculls were to be tried for, and some 800 of the thousand undergraduates poured out of their colleges by twos and threes to watch the result from the banks on each side.

The first and second guns had been fired, and the scullers in their boats, each some ten yards apart from the other, are anxiously waiting the firing of the third, which is the signal for starting. That strong splendid-looking young man, whose arms are bared to the shoulder, and "the muscles all a-ripple on his back," is almost quivering with anxious expectation. The very instant the sound of the gun reaches his ear, those oar-blades will flash like lightning into the water, and "smite the sounding furrows" with marvellous regularity and speed. He is the favourite, and there are some heavy bets on his success; Bruce and Brogten and Lord Fitzurse will be richer or poorer by some twenty pounds each from the result of this quarter of an hour.

The three are standing together on the towing-path opposite that little inn where the river suddenly makes a wide bend, and where, if the rush of men were not certain to sweep them forward,

58

they might see a very considerable piece of the race. But directly the signal is given, and the boats start, everybody will run impetuously at full speed along the banks to keep up with the boats, and cheer on their own men, and it will be necessary for our trio to make the best possible use of their legs, before the living cataract pours down upon them. Indeed, they would not have been on the towing-path at all, but among the rather questionable occupants of the grass plot before the inn on the other side of the river, were it not for their desire to run along with the boats, and inspirit the rowers on whom they have betted.

But what is this? A great odious slow-trailing barge looms into sight, nearly as broad as the river itself, black as the ferrugineous ferryboat of Charon, and slowly dragged down the stream by two stout cart horses, beside which a young bargee is plodding along in stolid independence.

"Hi! hi! you clodhopper there, stop that infernal barge," shouted Bruce at the top of his voice, knowing that if the barge once passed the winning posts, the race would be utterly spoilt.

"St–t–t–topp there, you cl–l–lown, w–w–will you," stuttered Fitzurse more incoherent than usual, with indignation.

The young bargee either didn't hear these apostrophes, or didn't choose to attend to them, when they were urged in that kind of way; and besides this, as the men were entirely concealed from his view by the curve of the river, he wasn't aware of the coming race, and therefore saw no reason to obey such imperious mandates.

"Confound the grimy idiot; doesn't he hear?" said Bruce, turning red and pale with excitement as he thought of the money he had at stake, and remembered that the skiff on which all his hopes lay was first in order, and would therefore be most likely to suffer by any momentary confusion. "Come, Brogten, let's stop him somehow before it's too late."

"Let's cut the scoundrel's ropes," said Brogten between his teeth; and at once the three darted forward at full speed, at the very instant that the sharp crack of the final signal-gun was heard.

It so happened that Julian and Lillyston had started rather late for the races, and had come up with the barge just as it had first neglected the summons of Bruce and Fitzurse.

"Come, bargee," said Lillyston good-humouredly, "out of the way with the barge as quick as ever you can; there's a boat-race, and you'll spoil the fun."

"Oh, it's a race, be it?" said the man, as he instantly helped Lillyston to back the horses. "If them young jackanapes had only toald me, 'stead of blusterin' that way—"

His speech was interrupted by Bruce, who, with his friends, had instantly sprung at the ropes, and cut them in half a dozen places, while the great heavy horses, frightened out of their propriety, turned tail and bolted away at a terrifically heavy trot.

"You big hulking blackguard," roared Brogten, who had been the first to use his knife, "why the devil didn't you move when we told you? What business have louts like you to come blundering up the river, and spoil our races?" And Fitzurse, confident in superior numbers, gave emphasis to the question by knocking off the man's cap.

The bargee was a strongly-built, stupid, healthy-looking young man, of some twenty-three years old, who, from being slow of passion was all the more terrible when aroused. Not finding any vent for his anger in words, he suddenly seized Bruce, (who of the three stood nearest him), by the collar of his boating jersey, shook him as he might have done a baby, and almost before he was aware, pitched him into the river. Instantly swinging round, he gave Lord Fitzurse a butt with his elbow, which sent his lordship tottering into the ditch on the other side, and while his wrath was still blazing, received in one eye a blow from Brogten's strong fist, which for an instant made him reel.

But it was only for an instant, and then he repaid Brogten with a cuff which felled him to the ground. Brogten was mad with fury. At that moment the men were running round the corner, at the bend of the Iscam, in full career, and hundreds on both sides of the river must have seen him sprawl before the man's blow. He sprang to his feet, and, blind with rage, lifted the clasp-knife with which he had cut the ropes. A second more, and it would have been buried to the handle in the right arm which, quick as lightning, the bargee raised to shield his face, when Brogten's arm was seized from behind by Lillyston, who wrested the knife from him, and pitched it into the river.

Brogten turned round, still unconscious what he was about. Julian stood nearest him, and he thought it was Julian who had disarmed him. Old hatred was suddenly joined to outrageous passion, and clenching his fist, he struck Julian in the face. Julian started back just in time to evade the full force of the blow, and fearing a second attack, suddenly tripped his aggressor as he once more rushed towards him.

But now the full tide of men had reached the spot; the barge had drifted helplessly lengthwise across the stream, and an angry circle closed round the chief actors in the scene we have described, while a hundred hasty voices demanded what was the row, and what

60

the bargee meant by "stopping the race in that stupid way?" Meanwhile Bruce, wet and muddy, was declaiming on one side, and Fitzurse, bruised and dirty, on the other, was stammering his uncomprehended oaths; while a dozen men were holding Brogten, who, foiled a second time, and now in a dreadfully ungovernable passion, was struggling with the men who held him, and vowing murder against Julian and the bargee.

It was no time for deliberation, nor are excited, hasty, and disappointed boys the most impartial of jurors. Julian and Lillyston were rapidly explaining the true state of the case to the few who were calm enough to listen; but all that appeared to most of the bystanders was, that a bargee had spoiled the event of the day, and assaulted two or three undergraduates. A cry arose to duck the fellow in the muddiest angle of the Iscam, and twenty hands were laid on his shoulder, to drag him off to his fate. But a sense of injustice, joined to strength and passion, are all but irresistible when their opponents are but half in earnest; and violently exerting his formidable muscles, the man shook himself free with a determination, agility, and pluck which, by a visible logic, showed the men how cruel and cowardly it was to punish him before they knew anything of the rights of the case. Lillyston's voice, too, began to be loudly heard, and several dons among the crowd exerted themselves to restore order out of the hubbub.

There is nothing like a touch of manliness. A feeble, and fussy, and finicking little proctor, who happened to be on the bank, was pompously endeavouring to assert his dignity, and make himself attended to. He was just beginning to get indignant at the laughing contempt with which his impotent efforts were received, and was asking men for their names and colleges, in a futile sort of way, when a tall and stately tutor in the crowd raised his voice above the uproar, and said, "Silence, gentlemen, if you please, for a moment." He was recognised and respected, and the men made room for him into the centre of the throng.

"Now, my man, just tell us what's the matter." The man was beginning to tell them how wantonly his ropes had been cut, and he himself insulted, when Bruce broke in, "That's a lie, you beggar; we asked you to move, and you wouldn't. I'll have you in prison yet, my fine fellow, you'll see."

"And if I don't make you pay for they ropes, you young pink-and-white monkey, my name ain't Jem—that's all."

"Did anybody see what really took place?" asked the don, cutting short the altercation.

"Yes, I did," said Lillyston instantly; "the fellow was civil enough, and began to back his horses the moment I told him there was a race, when these gentlemen ran up, abused him, struck him, and cut the ropes."

"Ay, it's all very fine for you gentlefolk," said the man with bitter scorn, "to take away a poor man's living for your pleasure. How do you think I'm to pay for them ropes? Am I to take the bread out of the children's mouths, let alone being kicked and speered at? Hang you all, I ain't afeard o' none o' you; come on, the whole lot o' you to one. I ain't afeard—not I," he said again, glaring round like a bull at bay, and stripping an arm of iron strength.

"I never cut your ropes, you brute," said Bruce, between his teeth, "though you wouldn't move when we asked you civilly."

"What's that, then?" said the man, pointing to a bit of rope two inches long which Bruce still held dangling in his hand.

"I'm afraid you forget the facts, Bruce, in your excitement," said Lillyston, very sternly.

"Facts or not, I'll have you up for assault," said Bruce affectedly, wringing the mud out of his wet sleeve.

"Have me up for assault," mimicked the man, trying to mince his broad rough accents into Bruce's delicate tones; and he condescended to add no more, but turned round to catch his horses, which had trotted through the open gate of a neighbouring field, and were now quietly grazing.

"I hope, gentleman," said Brogten, bluntly, "that you're not going to believe that blackguard's word against ours."

"You forget, sir," said Mr Norton, the tall don, "that what the blackguard, (as you are pleased to call him), said is confirmed by a gentleman here."

"And impugned by three gentlemen," said Bruce, who felt how thoroughly he was in disgrace.

"Do you mean to deny, Bruce, that you swore at the man first, and then cut his ropes, when he was already stopping his barge?" asked Lillyston.

"I mean to say he wouldn't move when we told him."

"I appeal to Home," said Lillyston; "didn't the man instantly stop when he understood why we wanted him to do so?"

"Yes," said Julian, who, still dizzy with Brogten's blow, was standing a little apart, "I am bound to say that the man was entirely in the right."

"I am inclined to think so," said Mr Norton, with scorn in his eye; and so saying, he took the little proctor's arm, and strode away, while the crowd of undergraduates also broke up, and streamed off in twos and threes.

"Do you mean to pay that fellow for his rope, Bruce?" asked Lillyston; "if not, I do."

"Pay!" said Brogten, with an explosion of oaths; "I'll pay you and your sizar friend there for this, depend upon it."

"We're not afraid," said Lillyston, quietly. Julian only answered the threat by a bow, and the two walked off to the bargee, who, in despair and anger, was knotting together the cut pieces of his rope.

Lillyston slipped a sovereign into his hand, and told him how sorry he was for what had happened.

"Thank you, sir," said the man, humbly; "it's a hard thing for a poor chap to be treated as I've been; but you're a rale gentleman."

"Well, do me one favour, then. Promise not to say a word to, or take any notice of, those three fellows as they pass you."

The man promised; but there was no need to have done so, for furious as Brogten was, he and his companions were too crestfallen to take any notice of the bargee in passing, except by contemptuous looks, which he returned with interest. On the whole, it struck them that they would not make a particularly creditable display in hall that evening, and therefore they partook instead of a sumptuous repast in the rooms of Lord Fitzurse, who made up for the dirt which they had been eating by the splendour of his entertainment.

"I'll be even yet with that fellow Home," muttered Brogten, as they were parting.

"He's not w—w—worth it," said the host. "He's one of the g—g—ghouls; eh, Bruce—ha! ha! ha!"

CHAPTER TEN

CONTRASTS

"And here was Labour his own bond slave; Hope
That never set the pains against the prize;
Idleness halting with his weary clog,
And poor misguided Shame and witless Fear
And simple Pleasure foraging for Death."

Wordsworth. The Prelude

Although Julian did not immediately feel, and had not particular reason to dread, the results of Brogten's displeasure, yet it was very annoying to be on the same stair-case with him. It was a constant reminder that there was one person, and he near at hand, who regarded him as an enemy. For a time, indeed, Brogten tried a few practical jokes on his neighbour and quondam school-fellow, which gratified for the moment his desire for revenge. Thus he would empty the little jug of milk which stood every day before Julian's door into the great earthenware pitcher of water which was usually to be found in the same position or he would make a surreptitious entry into his rooms, and amuse himself by upturning chairs and tables, turning pictures with their faces to the wall, and doing sometimes considerable ,damage and mischief. Once Julian, on preparing to get into bed, found a neat little garden laid out for his reception, between the sheets—flower-beds and gravel walks, all complete. This course of petty annoyance he bore, though not without a great struggle, in dignified and contemptuous silence. He looked Brogten firmly in the face, whenever they chanced to meet, and never gave him the triumph of perceiving that his small arts of vexation had taken the slightest effect. He merely smiled when the hot-headed Kennedy suggested retaliation, and would not allow Lillyston to try the effect of remonstrance. It was not long before Brogten became thoroughly ashamed that his malice should be tried and despised, and he would have proceeded to more overt acts of hatred had he not been one day informed by Lillyston that the Hartonians generally had heard of his proceedings, and that if he continued them he would be universally cut. For, indeed, such practical jokes as Brogten attempted are now almost unknown at Camford, and every man's room is considered sacred in his absence. But although he desisted from this kind of malice, it was not long before Brogten was generally shunned by his former schoolfellows. He developed into such a thorough blackguard that, had it not been for his merits as an oarsman and a cricketer, even the countenance of Bruce and Lord Fitzurse would have been insufficient to prevent him from being deserted by all the undergraduates of Saint Werner's, except that small and wretched class who take refuge from vacuity in the society of cads, dog-fanciers, and grooms.

Yet Brogten's Harton education, idle as he had been, sufficed to make him see that he was sinking lower and lower, not only in the world's estimation, but in his own. Unable to make the mental effort which the least approach to study would have required, he suffered his few intellectual faculties to grow more and more gross and stolid, and spent his mornings in smoking, drinking beer, or lounging in the rooms of some one as idle and discontented as himself. It was sad to see the change which even in his first term came over his face; it was not the change from boyhood to youth which gave a manlier beauty to the almost feminine delicacy of Julian's features, but it was a look in which effrontery supplied the place of self-dependence, and coarseness was the substitute for strength. Beer in the morning, and brandy in the evening, cards, and low company, and vice, made him sink into a degradation from which he was only redeemed by the still lingering ambition to excel in athletic sports, and by the manly exercises which rescued him for a time from such dissipation as would have incapacitated him from shining in the boat or in the field.

Lillyston was a singular contrast with Brogten; originally they were about equal in ability, position, and strength. They had entered school in the same form, and, until Julian came, they had generally been placed near each other in the quarterly examinations. Both of them were strong and active, and without being clever or brilliant they were both possessed of respectable powers of mind. Both of them had been in the Harton eleven, and now each of them was already in the second boat of their respective clubs; but with all these similarities Lillyston was beginning to be one of the men most liked and respected among all the best sets of his own year, and was reading for honours with a fair chance of ultimate success, while Brogten was looked on as a low and stupid fellow, whose company was discreditable, and whose doings were a disgrace to his old school.

The two presented much the same contrast as was also visible between Julian and Bruce. While Julian and Lillyston had mutually influenced each other for good, while they had been growing up together in warm and honourable friendship, thinking whatsoever things are pure and true and of good report, the other two had only fostered each other's vanity, and rather encouraged than checked each other's failings. At school they were always exchanging the grossest flattery, and the lessons and tendencies which each had derived from the other's society were lessons of weakness and sin alone. And now Bruce was looked on at Saint Werner's as a vain, empty fellow, living on a reputation for cleverness which he had never justified,—low, dressy, and extravagant, despised by the reading men, (whose society he affected to avoid), for his weakness and want of resolution; by the real athletes for his deficiency in strength and pluck, and by the aristocrats, (whose rooms he most frequented), for the ill-concealed obscurity of his father's origin, and the ill-understood source of his wealth. Since he first astonished the men of his year by the brilliancy of his entertainments and the gorgeousness of his rooms, he had steadily declined in general estimation among all whose regard was most really valuable, and he would have found few among his immense acquaintance who cared as much for him as they did for his good dinners and recherché wines. Julian, on the other hand, who knew far fewer men, could count among his new and old companions some real friends— friends who would cling to him in adversity as well as in prosperity, and who loved him for his own sake, whether his fortunes were in sunshine or in cloud. First among these newly-acquired friends he counted the names of Owen and Kennedy, among the old ones of Lillyston and De Vayne. But, besides these, he had been sought out by all the most distinguished men among the Saint Werner's undergraduates, while Mr Admer, who improved immensely on acquaintance, had introduced him to some of the most genial and least exclusive dons. Even Mr Grayson used to address him with something approaching to warmth, and so high was his general reputation, that he had no difficulty in making the acquaintance of every man of his college, whom he in the least cared to see or know.

Brogten was one of those who perceived these contrasts, and the bitter intense malice with which they filled him was one of the evil feelings which helped to drag him down from following out his occasional resolutions for better things.

Strange that a few weeks could produce such differences but so it was. At the end of those few weeks Bruce went back to take part in his mother's splendid theatricals and routs, with a consciousness of neglected opportunities and wasted times even if his conscience laid no worse sins to his charge. Brogten went back, cursing himself and all around him, with the violent self-accusations of a reprobate obstinacy, a man in vice, though hardly more than a boy in years. Kennedy went back happy on the whole, happy above all in the certainty that he had made in Julian one noble friend. Lillyston went back happy, well-pleased with the sense of duty done, and the prime of life well and innocently enjoyed. And Julian went back in the same train with De Vayne, happy too, with a mind strengthened and expanded, with knowledge deepened and widened, with an honourable ambition opening before him, and friends and a fair position already won. All these results had sprung from those few and swiftly-gliding weeks.

The Christmas time passed very pleasantly for the Homes. They had few relations, and Lady Vinsear had dropped all intercourse with them, but they were happy in themselves. Violet, too, had the pleasure of forming an acquaintance with Kennedy's sister Eva, who, with her aunt, happened to be paying a short visit to a family in the neighbourhood. Frank and Cyril were at home for their holidays, and the house and garden at Ildown rang all day long with their merry voices and incessant games. Old Christmas observances were not yet obsolete in Ildown, and Yule logs and royal feasts were the order of the day. The bright, clear, frosty air— the sparkling sea and freshening wind—a lovely country, a united and cheerful family, and the delights of moderate study, made the weeks speed by in pure enjoyment. With his mother, his brothers, and Violet, Julian felt the need of no other society, but he corresponded with Kennedy and other college friends, and saw a great deal of Lord De Vayne, who continually rode over to pass the Sunday with them at Ildown, and sometimes persuaded all the Homes to come and spend the day with him and his mother in the beautiful but lonely grounds of Other Hall.

Whenever they accepted the invitation, the young and pensive viscount seemed another man. He would join in the boys' mirth with the most joyous alacrity, and talked to Violet with such vivacity that none who saw him would believe what a shade of melancholy usually hung over his mind. His life had been spent in seclusion, and he had never yet seen any to whom his heart turned with such affection as he felt for Julian and Violet. His mother observed it, and often thought that if she saw in Violet Home the future Lady De Vayne, a source of happiness was laid up for her only son, which would fulfil, and more than fulfil, her fondest prayers. It never occurred to her to think that he would do better to choose a bride among the noblest and wealthiest houses of England, rather than in the orphan family of a poor and unknown clergyman. What she sought for him was goodness and usefulness, not grandeur or riches; a lonely and sorrowful life had taught her at how slight a value rank and wealth are to be reckoned in any high or true estimate of the meaning of human life; nor did it add greatly to her desire for such a match that Violet, with her bright hair, and soft eyes, and graceful figure—with her sweet musical voice, and the rippling silver of her laugh, and the rich imagery which filled her fancy—might well have fulfilled the ideal of a poet's dream. But Violet was still very young, and none of Lady De Vayne's hopes had ever for an instant crossed her mind.

Julian was at this time, and had been for some months, intensely occupied with the thought and desire of winning the Clerkland scholarship, a university scholarship of 60 pounds a year, open to general competition among all the undergraduates of less than one year's standing. This scholarship was the favourite success of Camford life. It stamped at once a man's position as one of the most prominent scholars of his year, and as the names of many remarkable men were found in the list of those who had already obtained it, it gave a strong prestige of future distinction and success. Julian had a peculiar reason for longing to gain it, because, with his Harton scholarship, it would not only enable him at once to enter his name as a pensioner, instead of a sizar, at Saint Werner's, but even make him independent of all help from his family and guardians. There would have been reasons sufficient to account for his passionate desire for this particular distinction, even independently of his natural wish to justify the general opinion of his abilities, and the eager ambition caused by the formidable numbers of the other competitors. In short, at this time, to obtain the Clerkland scholarship was the most prominent personal desire in Julian's heart, and could some genius have suddenly offered him the fulfilment of any one wish, this would undoubtedly have been the first to spring to his lips. He looked with emulation, almost with envy, on those who had won it before him; he almost knew by heart the list of Clerkland scholars; and when he returned to Camford, constantly discussed the chances of success in favour of the different candidates. Do not blame him; his motives were all high and blameless, although he at length turned over this thought so often in his mind as to recur to it with almost selfish iteration, and to regard success in this particular struggle as the one thing wanting to complete, or even to create his happiness.

He could not refrain from mentioning it at home, although, for the sake of preventing disappointment, he generally avoided dwelling on any of his school or college struggles. Deprecating his own abilities, it made him doubly anxious to find that not only did his Saint Werner's contemporaries regard him as the favourite candidate, and bet upon him in the sporting circles, (although Brogten furiously took the largest odds against him), but, what was worse, his own family, always proud of him, seemed to regard his triumph as certain. Thus circumstanced, and most fondly avoiding every possibility of causing pain or disappointment to that thrice-loved circle, of which he regarded himself as the natural protector and head, he was more than ever determined to do his very utmost to prevent failure, and give them the lasting pride and pleasure which they would all receive by seeing his name in the public papers as Clerkland scholar.

"Come, Julian, and let's have a row or a sail," said Cyril one morning to him, as he sat at work. "Frank and I have nothing to do to-day."

"Not to-day, Cyril, my boy. I really must do some work; you know De Vayne made me ride with him yesterday, and I've done very little the last day or two."

"I wish I liked work as you do, Julian."

"It isn't only that I like work, (though I do)," said Julian; "but you know a good deal depends on it."

"Oh! I know!" said Cyril; "you mean the Clerkland scholarship; but never mind, Julian, Lord De Vayne told me you were sure of that."

"Did he?" said Julian, a little anxiously; "then for goodness' sake, don't believe him. It's very kind of him to say so—but he's quite mistaken."

"Ah, you always say so beforehand, you know. You used to say that about the Harton scholarship, Julian, and yet you see? Do come."

"Well, I'll come," said Julian, smiling a little sadly. "But, Cyril, don't, pray, say anything of that kind to mother or to Violet, for if I should fail it would make me doubly sad."

Cyril, thanking Julian, and still laughingly prophesying success, ran out to tell Frank; and, when he had gone, Julian stamped his foot passionately on the ground, and said half-aloud, "I will get this Clerkland, I will get it, I must get it."

He paused a moment, and then, raising his eyes and hands to heaven, prayed that "God would do for him that which was best for his highest welfare;" but even as he prayed, he secretly determined that obtaining the Clerkland scholarship was, and must necessarily be, the best piece of worldly prosperity that could possibly happen to him.

CHAPTER ELEVEN

SCREWED IN

Reader, if the latter part of the preceding chapter has been dull to you, it is because you have never entered into the devouring ambition which, in a matter of this kind, actuates a young man's heart when he is aiming at his first grand distinction—an ambition which, if selfishly encouraged, becomes dangerous both to health and peace, and works powerfully, perhaps by a merciful provision, to the defeat of its own darling hope.

As long as Julian had been at home, a thousand objects helped to divert his thoughts from their one cherished desire; but when he returned to Camford, finding the Clerkland a frequent subject of discussion among the men, even in hall, and constantly meeting others who were as absorbed in the thought of the approaching examination as himself, he once more fell into the vortex, and thought comparatively of little else.

As yet he had had no means of measuring himself with others, except so far as the lecture-room enabled him to judge of the abilities of some few in his own college. Under these circumstances all conjecture must have seemed to be idle; but somehow or other at Camford, by a sort of intuition, the exact place a man will ultimately take is often prophesied from the first with wonderful accuracy. Saint Werner's, being by far the largest college at Camford, supplied the majority of the candidates, and Julian, Owen, and Kennedy were all three mentioned as likely to be first; but the rival ranks of Saint Margaret's boasted their champions also, and almost every small college nursed some prodigy of its own, for which it vehemently predicted an easy and indisputable success.

Owen was the competitor whom Julian most really feared; educated at Roslyn, a comparatively small school, his scholarship was not so ready and polished as that acquired by the training of Marlby and Harton, but, on the other hand, he had improved greatly in the short time he had been at Saint Werner's, and besides his sound knowledge he had a strong-headed common sense, and a clearness and steadiness of purpose, more valuable than a quick fancy and refined taste. In composition, and in all the lighter and more graceful requirements of a classical examination, Julian had an undoubted superiority, but Owen was his equal, if not his master, in the power of unravelling intricacies and understanding logic; and, besides this, Owen was a better mathematician, and, although

70

classics had considerable preponderance, yet one mathematical paper always formed part of the Clerkland examination. Kennedy who, if he had properly employed his time, would have been no mean rival to either of them, had unfortunately been so idle, and continued to be so gay and idle even for the weeks immediately preceding the examination, that they all felt his chance to be gone. He acknowledged the fact himself, with something between a laugh and sigh, and only threatening to catch them both up in the classical tripos, he resigned all hope for himself, and threw all his wishes into the scale of Julian's endeavours. And although Owen was liked and respected, there was no doubt that Julian was regarded throughout the University as the popular candidate; the Hartonians especially, who had carried off the prize for several years, were confident that he would win them another victory.

As the time drew near, Julian became more and more feverish with eagerness, and his friends feared that he would hinder, by over reading, his real probability of success. Kennedy felt this most strongly, but being himself engaged in the competition, was afraid that any attempt to divert Julian's thoughts would not have a disinterested look. Lillyston and De Vayne, unrestrained by such motives, did all they could to take him from his books, and amuse him by turning his attention to other subjects; but with such strong reasons for exertion, and so much depending on success or failure, the Clerkland scholarship continued ever the prominent subject of Julian's thoughts.

At last the long looked for week arrived. After chapel, on the Sunday morning, De Vayne invited himself to breakfast with Julian, and continued in his company the greater part of the day, going with him to the University sermon. He entirely forbade Julian even to allude more than once to the coming examination, and managed in the evening to get him to come to his rooms, where, with some other Hartonians and Kennedy, they spent a very pleasant evening.

"Good-night," he said to Julian, as he strolled with him to his stair-case across the starlight court; "don't stay up to-night. In quietness and confidence shall be your strength."

The examination was to last a week, and Julian rose for it refreshed and cheerful on Monday morning. The papers suited him excellently, and his hopes rose higher and higher as he felt that in each paper he had done to the utmost of his knowledge and ability. He had not been able to afford a private tutor during the term, with whom he might have discussed the papers, but he sent his Iambics and Latin verse to Mr Carden at Harton, who wrote back a most favourable and encouraging judgment of them, and seemed to regard Julian's success as certain. Julian had implicit confidence in his opinion, for Mr Carden entered very warmly into all his hopes and wishes, and kept up with him an affectionate correspondence, which had helped him out of many intellectual difficulties, and lessened the force of many a temptation.

The papers usually lasted from nine till twelve in the morning, and from two to four in the afternoon. It was on the Friday morning, when only three more papers remained, that Julian found Mr Carden's kind and hopeful letter lying on his breakfast-table at eight o'clock; he read it with a glow of pleasure, because he knew that he could rely thoroughly on the accuracy and truth of his old tutor's judgment, and as he read and re-read it, his hopes rose higher and higher. Finishing breakfast, he began to build castles in the air, and to imagine to himself the delight it would be to write and tell the Doctor and Mr Carden of this new leaf to the Harton laurels. Never before had he a more reasonable ground for favourable expectation, and he began almost to run over in his mind the sort of letter he would write, and the kind of things he would say. Leaning over his window-sill, he enjoyed the cool feeling of the early spring breeze on his brow and hair, and then, finding by his watch that it was time to start, he took his cap and gown, and prepared to sally out to the senate-house.

It was the custom of the gyp, when he had laid breakfast, and put the kettle on the fire, to go away and "sport the oak," (i e, shut the outer door), so as to prevent any one from coming into the rooms until their owner was awake and dressed. Julian therefore was not surprised to see his door "sported," but was surprised to find that, when he lifted the latch, the door did not open to his touch. He pushed it with some force, and then kicked it with his foot to see if some stone or coal had not caught against it, but the door still remained obstinately closed; he put his shoulder against it, fancying that some heavy weight like the coal-box or water-pitcher might have been placed outside,—but all in vain; the thick door did not even stir, and then there flashed upon Julian the bitter truth that he had been screwed in. He understood now the stifled titter which he fancied he had heard after one of his most violent efforts to get out.

In one instant, before he had time to think, a fit of blind, passionate, uncontrollable fury had clouded and overpowered Julian's whole mind. Almost unconscious of what he was doing, he kicked the door with all his might, and beat on it savagely with his clenched fists until his knuckles streamed with blood; he forgot everything but the one burning determination to get out at all hazards, and to wreak on Brogten, whom he felt to be the author of his calamity, some desperate and terrible revenge. But the thick oak

72

door, screwed evidently with much care; and in many places, resisted all his efforts, and no one came to help him from outside. The gyp, who was usually about, happened to have gone on an errand; the stair-case was one of the most secluded in the college; the Fellow who was Julian's nearest neighbour had "gone down" for a few days, and it was improbable that any one ever heard him except Brogten, to whom, he thought, every sound of his angry violence would be perfect music.

All was useless, and Julian, as he strode up and down the room, clenched his hands, and bit his lips in passionate excitement. Suddenly it struck him that he would escape by the window; but looking out for the purpose, he found that, when he had jumped on the sloping roof below him, he was still thirty feet above the ground, which, in that place, was not the turf of the bowling-green, but a hard gravel road. Giving up the attempt in despair he sat down, and covered his face with his hands; but instantly the picture of the senate-house, with the sixty candidates who were trying for the scholarship, all writing at some new paper—while he was thus cut off, (as he thought), from the long-desired accomplishment of all his hopes—rose before his eyes, and springing up once more he seized the poker, and raising it over his shoulder like a hammer, brought down the heavy iron knob with a crash on the oaken panels. He struck again and again, but, by a shower of fierce blows, could only succeed in covering the door with deep round dents. Finally he seized the heaviest chair in the room, and dashed it savagely with one heavy drive against the unyielding oak; a second blow shivered the chair to splinters, and Julian, a compulsory prisoner at that excited moment, flung himself on the sofa, furious and weary, with something that sounded like a fierce imprecation.

Full twenty minutes had been occupied by his futile and frantic efforts, and for a few moments longer he sat still in a stupor of grief and rage. Meanwhile, several of the other competitors for the Clerkland had noticed his absence in the senate-house, and Owen and Kennedy kept directing anxious glances to the door, and dreading that he was ill. At last half an hour had elapsed, and Kennedy, unable any longer to endure the suspense, went up to the examiner and said—

"One of the candidates is absent, sir. Would you allow me to go and inquire the reason?"

"Who is it?" asked the examiner.

"Home, sir."

"Indeed. But I am afraid I cannot allow you to leave the senate-house; the rules, you know, on this subject are necessarily very strict."

"Then, sir, I will merely show up what I have written, for I am sure there must be some unusual reason for Home's absence."

"Oh, no, Mr Kennedy, pray don't do so," said the examiner, who knew how well Kennedy had been doing; "I will send the University marshal to inquire for Mr. Home; it is a very unusual compliment to pay him, but I think it may be as well to do so."

It so happened that, as the marshal crossed the court to Julian's rooms, Lillyston and De Vayne, who were strolling towards the grounds, caught sight of him, and went with much curiosity to inquire the object of his errand.

"Home not in the senate-house," said Lillyston, on hearing the marshal's answer. "Good heavens, what can be the matter?" and without waiting to hear more, he darted to Julian's door, and called his name.

"What do you want?" said Julian in a fretful and angry voice.

"Why are you sported? And why aren't you in for the Clerkland?"

"Can't you see, then?"

"What! So you are screwed in," said Lillyston in deep surprise; "wait three minutes, Julian, three minutes, and I will let you out."

He sprang down-stairs, four steps at a time, borrowed a screwdriver at the porter's lodge, was back in a moment, and then with quick and skilful hand he drew out, one after another, the screws which had been driven deep into the door.

Julian lifted the latch inside, and Lillyston saw with surprise and pain his scared and wild glance. Julian said not a word, but rushed past his friend, and burst furiously into Brogten's room. Fortunately Brogten was not in, for the moment he heard steps approaching, he had purposely gone out; but Lillyston followed Julian, and said—

"Come, this is folly, Julian; you have not a moment to lose. You will be already nearly an hour late, and remember that the Clerkland may depend upon it."

He suffered himself to be led, but as he walked he was still silent, and seemed as though he were trying to gulp down some hard knot that rose in his throat. His expression was something totally different from anything that Lillyston had ever observed in him, even from a boy, and his feet seemed to waver under him as he walked.

De Vayne joined them in the court, and was quite startled to see Julian looking so ill. He saw that it was no time to trouble him with idle inquiries, and merely pressed him to come into his rooms and take some wine before going to do the paper. Julian silently complied. The kind-hearted young viscount took out a bottle of wine, of which Julian swallowed off a tumblerful, and then, without speaking a word, strode off to the senate-house, which he reached pale and agitated, attracting, as he entered, the notice and commiseration of all present.

The examiner, with a kind word of encouragement, and an inquiry as to the cause of his delay, which Julian left unanswered, promised to allow him in the evening as much additional time for doing the paper as he had already lost. Julian bowed, and walked to his place.

And now that he was seated, with the paper before him, he found himself in a condition to do nothing. His mind was in a tumult of wrath and sorrow. Bitter sorrow that his hopes should be shattered; fiery wrath that any one should have treated him with such malignant cruelty. His brain swam giddily, and his head throbbed with violent pain. His hands were still raw and bleeding with his efforts to burst open the door; and the consciousness that his whole appearance was wild, and that several eyes were upon him, unnerved him so completely, that he was quite unable to collect or control his scattered senses. He made but little progress. The clock of Saint Mary's told the passing hours, and at twelve Julian found himself with nothing written except a few half-finished and incoherent sentences which he was ashamed to show up. Dashing the nib of his pen on the desk, he split it to pieces; and then, tearing up his papers, was hurrying out, when the voice of the examiner suddenly recalled him.

"You have not shown me up any papers, Mr. Home."

"No, sir," he answered sullenly.

"Indeed! But why?"

"I have not done any, sir."

"Really. I am sorry for that. It is a serious matter, for you have been doing remarkably well, and— Are you not feeling well?"

"No, sir, not exactly."

"Hum! Well, it is a great pity; a great pity; a very great pity. However—"

There seemed to be no more to say, and as Julian's mind was in too turbulent a state to allow of his being communicative, he did not trust himself to make any remark, and left the room.

Kennedy, who came up with him as he went out, asked what was the matter; but as he only answered with an impatient gesture, and evidently seemed to wish to be alone, Kennedy left him and went to inquire of Lillyston what had happened, while Julian hastened to the solitude of his own room, and breaking with his poker one of the outer hinges of his door, to secure himself from a second imprisonment, flung himself on a chair, and pressed his hands to his burning forehead. In his bitterness of soul he half determined to abandon all further attempt to gain the Clerkland, and dwelt, with galling recurrence, on the anguish of defeated aims. But the sound of the clock striking the hour of examination started him into sudden effort, and almost mechanically he seized his cap and gown, and went out without food and unrefreshed.

Although he endeavoured, with all his might, to shake off all thought of the morning's insult and misfortune, he only partially succeeded, and when he folded up his papers, he felt that the fire and energy which had shone so conspicuously during the earlier days of the examination, and had imparted such strength and brilliancy to his efforts, were utterly extinguished, and had left him wandering and weak. When the time was over, he went to De Vayne's rooms, and said abruptly—

"De Vayne, will you lend me your riding-whip?"

"Certainly," said De Vayne, starting up to meet him.

"Are you going to have a ride? I wish you would ride my horse; I'll hire another, and come with you."

"No; I don't want a ride."

"What do you want the whip for, then?" said De Vayne uneasily.

"Nothing. Let me go; it must be time for you to go to hall."

"I'm not going to dine in hall to-day," said De Vayne. "Dining at the high table, with none but dons to talk to, is dull work for an undergraduate. Stop! you shall dine with me here, Julian. I know you won't care to go to hall to-day. Nay, you shall," he said, putting his back against the door; "I shall be as dull as night without you."

He made Julian stay, for it happened that at that moment his gyp brought up dinner, and Julian, hungry and weary, was tempted to sit down. De Vayne, who only too well divined his reason for borrowing the whip, was delighted at having succeeded in detaining him, for he knew that the only time when Julian would be likely to meet Brogten was immediately after hall.

Wiling away the time with exquisite tact—talking to him without pressing him to talk much in reply—turning his thoughts to indifferent subjects, until he had succeeded in arousing his interest—the young viscount detained his guest till evening, and then persuaded him to have tea. Lord De Vayne played well on the piano, and knowing Julian's passion for music, was rewarded for his unselfish efforts by complete success in rousing his attention. He played some of the finest passages of a recent and beautiful oratorio, until Julian almost forgot his troubles, and was ready to talk with more freedom and in a kindlier mood.

"You surely won't want the whip now," said De Vayne in some dismay, as Julian picked it up on saying good-night.

"Yes, I shall," answered Julian. "Good-night!"

CHAPTER TWELVE

A GUST OF THE SOUL

"Once more will the wronger, at this last of all.
Dare to say 'I did wrong,' rising in his fall?"

Browning

The story of Brogten's practical joke, and the circumstances which made it so unusually disgraceful, spread with lightning-like rapidity through Saint Werner's College; and when he swaggered into hall with his usual self-confident air, he was surprised to find himself met with cold and even with frowning looks. Snatches of conversation which went on around him soon showed him the reason of the general disapprobation; and when he learnt how violently the current of popular opinion was beginning to set against him, and how unfavourable a view was taken of his conduct, he began seriously to regret that he had given the reins to his malice.

"I shouldn't wonder now if Home were to lose the Clerkland; he was sure of it before this morning," said one.

"What a cursed shame!" echoed another. "I never in my life heard a more blackguard trick. That fellow Brogten has lost the Hartonians the scholarship; lucky if he hasn't lost it to Saint Werner's too. Perhaps that Benedict man will get it."

"I say, Kennedy," said a third, "if I were you or Lillyston, or any other of Home's particular friends, I'd duck Brogten."

"Let's wait till we see whether Home does lose the scholarship first," said Lillyston. "If he does, Brogten deserves anything; but I have strong hopes yet."

"I know Home," said Kennedy, "and he would never forgive such an interference, or I declare I should be inclined to do it."

"I should like to see you do it," thundered Brogten, from a farther end of the table.

"I have just given my reasons for not seeing fit to do it," said Kennedy, with a curl of the lip. "By the bye, Mr Brogten," he continued sarcastically, "I hope that you don't, after this, expect to be paid any of the bets you have made against Home's getting the Clerkland?"

"There's my betting-book," replied Brogten, flinging it at Kennedy, whom it struck in the face, and who took no further notice of the insult than to pick up the book, and throw it into the great brazier, full of glowing charcoal, which stands in the centre of Saint Werner's hall.

"Don't do that, confound you!" cried Brogten, springing up. "Do you think there are no bets in it but those about the Clerkland?"

"Keep your missiles to yourself, then," said Kennedy, while Brogten burnt his fingers in the vain attempt to rescue his book.

"I hope you've at least hedged, or behaved as judiciously in the case of your other bets as in those about the Clerkland," suggested one of his sporting friends.

This last sneer and insinuation was too much, and it galled the proud man to the quick to hear the laugh of scorn which followed it. He turned round, seized his cap, and flinging at Kennedy a look of intense and concentrated hatred, left the hall, and rushed up to his rooms.

To do Brogten justice, he had never intended for a moment to affect Julian's chance of ultimate success, when he enjoyed the mean satisfaction of screwing up his door. He had regarded him with indeed dislike, which received a tinge of deeper intensity from the envy, and even admiration, with which it was largely mingled. But although he had calculated that his trick might be more telling and offensive if done at this particular opportunity, and although he had quite sufficient grudge against his former school-fellow to wish him a deep annoyance, yet he would never have dreamed of wilfully thwarting his most cherished aims, or materially affecting his prospects and position. So vile a malice would have been intolerable to any one, and the thought of it was thoroughly intolerable to Brogten, in whom all gleams of honourable feeling were by no means extinguished, however dormant they might seem. It had never entered into his thoughts to anticipate the violent consequences which his act had produced; and when told of Julian's passion and suffering, he had felt such real remorse that he had even half intended to wait for him as he went to hall, and there, (in a quasi-public manner, since some men were sure to be standing about on the hall steps), to endure the mortification of expressing his regret to the man whom he had chosen to treat as his enemy. But when he found himself cut and jeered at—when he was even met by the suggestion that he had intended basely to serve his own pecuniary interests at Julian's expense—a method of swindling which he had never for one instant contemplated—all his softer and better feelings vanished at once, and created a brutal hardness in his heart, which now once more he was striving in solitude to mollify or remove.

And he succeeded so far that, while brooding savagely over the venomous shafts of sarcasm and ridicule with which Kennedy had wounded him, he gradually softened his feelings towards Julian, by transferring them in tenfold virulence against Julian's nearest friend. Home and he had been school-fellows after all, and Julian had never done him any wrong; on the contrary, he liked the boy; he remembered distinctly how the first seeds of ill-will against him had been sown, by the reserve with which Julian, as a school-fellow, had received his advances. Without being rude and uncivil, he had yet managed to hold aloof from him, and as Brogten was in some repute at Harton, when Home came, and was moreover an Hartonian of much longer standing, his sensitive pride had been stung by the fact that the "new fellow," whose pleasant face and manners had attracted his notice, did not at once and gratefully embrace his proffered friendship. Circumstances had tended to widen the breach between them, but secretly he liked Home still, and would have gladly been his friend. "And, after all," he thought, "Home has never once retaliated any injury which I have undoubtedly done him; he has never done me any harm. Even in the affair at the boats, he only did what was quite justifiable, and I was far more in the wrong than he was when I struck him. And now they all say I shall have prevented him from getting this confounded Clerkland. And I know how he longed for it, and how much all his hopes and wishes were fixed upon it. Upon my word, when I come to think of it, it was a very blackguard thing of me to do, and I wish I had been at the bottom of the sea before I did it. I think—yes—I think I'll go and see Home, and ask his pardon; yes, upon my word I need his forgiveness, and would give a good deal to get it. He's a grand fellow after all. I wish he'd take me as a friend. I should be infinitely better for it; and I will be better, too." And as he thus reasoned with himself, Brogten began to yearn for better things, and for Julian's friendship as a means of helping him to higher aims; and he remembered the lines—

> "I would we were boys as of old,
> In the field, by the fold;
> His outrage. God's patience, man's scorn,
> Were so easily borne."

So his thoughts ran on, but when it occurred to him that no such humiliation on his part would perhaps go very far to mend the general disgust with which he had been greeted, he began to waver again. "What business had they to assume that I meant the worst? I may be a bad fellow, but," (and a mental oath followed), "I'm not a black-leg after all. That fellow Kennedy—curse him!—I'll be even with him yet. I swear that he shall rue it. I'll be a very fiend in the vengeance I take—curse him, curse him!" And stamping his heel furiously on the floor, he swallowed some raw brandy, and began to pace up and down his room.

The conflict of his thoughts lasted, almost without intermission, till evening. Finally, however, his heart softened towards Julian, as he ran over in his mind all the circumstances of the day. Cheating his conscience with the fancy that he was conquering his feelings of revenge and hate, while he was only displacing them with others of a deeper dye, he at last determined to go up at once to Julian's room, ask his pardon openly, honestly, and unreservedly, confess his past unworthy malice, and obtain, if possible, at least, Julian's forgiveness, perhaps even his friendship, in return for so great a victory over himself.

It was a victory over himself, and no slight one. For at least five years he had been nursing into dislike an inward feeling of respect for his enemy, and now to humble himself so completely before him, required a struggle of which he had hardly supposed himself capable, and of which he was secretly a little proud. It inspired him with better hopes for the future, and gave him a pledge of combating successfully other vicious propensities which had gained an ascendency over him.

Hesitatingly he went up to Julian's rooms; he saw the broken door, and it made him waver. All was silence inside, but still he hoped that Julian was in, because he felt sure that he should never persuade his natural pride to consent to such a sacrifice again. But yet, what should he say? He had been thinking of a thousand set forms of apology, but they all vanished, as, with beating heart, he knocked, a little loudly, at the door.

Julian, too, had been brooding on the events of the day, and fanning every now and then into fierce bursts of flame the dying embers of his morning's indignation. He took the worst view, and had every reason to take the worst view, of Brogten's intentions. He had received at his hands many wrongs, and an incivility as unvarying as it was undeserved. Of course he could not tell that this rudeness was but the cover of a real desire for cordiality between them, and now he fully believed that Brogten had intentionally, deliberately, and with malice prepense, formed a deep laid scheme to dash from his lips the cup of happiness as he was in the very act of tasting it. The success which had seemed in his very grasp would have removed the poverty, which had been one of the severest trials, not to himself only, but to those whom he most dearly loved; it was the thing—the one thing—of which he had thought, and for which he had prayed. "And now it was wrenched from him," so he thought, "by this mean and dastardly villain."

He had determined to horse-whip Brogten, at all hazards, though he knew that Brogten was far stronger than himself. De Vayne's manoeuvre had disconcerted his intention, for he could not carry it out in cold blood; but even now he felt by no means sure that he was right to take passively an insult which, if unresented, might, he thought, be repeated, some other time, and which, if frequently repeated would render college life wholly intolerable. All this was floating through his mind, when there came a loud—he took it for an insolent—knock at the door, and his enemy stood before him.

His enemy stood before him, humbled and remorseful, with the words of apology on his lips, and his heart full of such emotions as might have enabled Julian to convert him from an enemy into a lasting and grateful friend. But when he saw him, in one instant furious, unreasoning, headlong anger had again seized Julian's mind—the more easily because he had already yielded to it once. Without stopping to hear a word—without catching the gentler tone of Brogten's rough voice—without noticing his downcast expression of countenance—Julian sprang up, assumed that Brogten had come to ridicule or even insult him, glared at him, clenched his teeth, and then seizing De Vayne's riding-whip, laid it without mercy about Brogten's shoulders.

During the first few blows, Brogten was disarmed by intense surprise. Of all receptions, this was the only one which it had never occurred to him to contemplate. He had imagined Julian bitter, sarcastic, cold; he had prepared himself for a torrent of passionate and overwhelming invective; he had thought how to behave if Julian remained silent, or rejected with simple contempt his stammered apology; but to be horse-whipped by one so much weaker than himself—by one whom he remembered to have pitied and patronised when he came to Harton, a delicate rosy-cheeked boy—this he had certainly never thought of. Julian had almost expended his rage in half a dozen wild blows before Brogten was startled from his surprise into a consciousness of his position.

But when he did realise it all the demon took possession of his heart. He seized Julian by the collar, wrenched the whip out of his hand, and raised the silver knob at the end of the handle. What fearful hurt Julian might have received from so heavy a weapon in so powerful a hand, or how far Brogten's fury might have transported him, none can tell; but at that very moment he heard a step on the stairs, which arrested his violence, and the moment after Lillyston entered.

"What!" said Lillyston indignantly, as he caught the almost diabolical expression of Brogten's face. "Not content with doing your best to ruin Home, you are using personal violence to one not so strong as yourself. Come, sir, you have felt what I can do before. Drop that whip, or take the consequences."

"Stop, Hugh," said Julian sullenly; "I horse-whipped him first."

"You!" said Lillyston.

"Yes," answered Brogten slowly, while his voice shook with passion; "yes, he did horse-whip me, and I took it. Note that, you Lillyston, and don't think I'm afraid of you. And as for you, Home, listen to me. I came here solely to tell you that though I screwed you in, I never dreamt that such results would follow. I never dreamt—so help me, God!—of doing more than causing you ten minutes' annoyance; and now, when I was told how it had hindered you in the examination, I was heartily sorry and ashamed of what I had done, and,"—he began to speak lower and faster, as the remembrance of a better mood came over him—"and I came here, Home, to ask your forgiveness. Yes; I to beg pardon of you, and humbly and honestly too. And now you see how you have received me. Yes," he continued fiercely; "no word between us from henceforth. You have horse-whipped me, sir, and I, who never took a blow from man yet without returning it, have taken your horse-whipping. Take your whip," he said, flinging it to the end of the room; "and after that never dare to say that all accounts are not squared between us."

Lillyston made room for him to pass. With a lowering countenance he turned from them, and they continued silent till they had heard his last heavy footfall as he went down the echoing stairs.

Lillyston sat on the sofa, and Julian kept his eyes fixed on the floor. There seemed nothing to talk about, so Lillyston merely said, "Good-night, Julian. I came to advise you to go to bed early, and so get a good night's rest, that you may be yourself to-morrow. You have not been yourself to-day. Good-night."

But a worse evil had happened to Julian that day than hindrance in his career of ambition and hope. He had lost a golden opportunity for an act of Christian forgiveness which might have had the noblest influence on the life of an erring human soul. He had lost a golden opportunity of doing lasting good, and that, too, to one who hated him. Alas, it is too seldom that we have power in life to raise up them that fall! Julian felt bitterly, he felt even with poignancy, Brogten's closing words; but it was too late now to offer the forgiveness which would have been invaluable to his persecutor, and would have had a healing effect on his own troubled thoughts so short a time before. All this gave deeper vexation to Julian's heart as he went moodily to bed.

And Brogten? He sat sullenly over his fire till the last spark died from its ashes, and his lamp flickered out, and he shivered with cold. "It is of no use to conquer myself," he thought; "it is of no use to do better or be better if this comes of it. Horse-whipped, and by him!" But, as he had said, he no longer grieved over Julian's injury. That was wiped off by the horse-whipping, and he had now made himself understand that his inward respect for Home was deeper than the long superficial quarrel that had existed between them. It was against Kennedy that the current of his anger now swept this ever-growing temptation for revenge. His craving, often yielded to, became terrible in its virulence, and from this day forward there was in Brogten's character a marked change for the worse. He ever watched for his opportunity, certain that it would come in time; and this encouragement of one bad passion opened the floodgates for a hundred more. And so on this evening he went on selling himself more and more completely to the devil, till the anger within him burned with a red heat, and as he went to bed the last words he muttered to himself were, "That fellow Kennedy shall rue it; curse him, he shall rue it to his dying day."

CHAPTER THIRTEEN

THE CLERKLAND SCHOLARSHIP

How different our smaller trials look, when they are seen from the distance of a quiet and refreshful rest. Utterly wearied, Julian slept deeply, and when the servant awoke him next morning, he determined that as the errors of yesterday were irreparable, he would at least save the chances of to-day.

He rose at once, and read during breakfast the letter from

home, which came to him from one of his family nearly every day. This morning it was from Violet, and he could see well how anxiously they were awaiting the result of his present examination, and yet how sure they were that he would succeed. Unwilling to trouble them by the painful circumstances of the day before, he determined not to write home again until the decision was made known.

This morning's paper was to be the last, and Julian applied to it the utmost vigour of his powers. After the first few moments, he had utterly banished every sorrowful reflection, and when the clock struck twelve, he felt that once more he had done himself justice. He answered with a smiling assent, the examiner's expressed hope, that his health was better than it had been the day before, and joining Owen as he left the senate-house, found, on comparing notes, that he had done the paper at least as well as his dreaded but friendly rival.

His spirits rose, and his hopes revived in full. Shaking off examination reminiscences, he proposed to De Vayne, Kennedy, and Lillyston a bathe in the Iscam, and then a long run across the country. They started at once, laughing and talking incessantly on every subject, except the Clerkland, which was tabooed. Ten minutes' run brought them to a green bend of the Iscam, where a bathing-shed had been built, and after enjoying the bathe as only the first bathe in a season can be enjoyed, they struck off over the fields towards some neighbouring villages, which De Vayne had often wanted to visit, because their old churches contained some quaint specimens of early architecture. On the way they passed through Barton Wood, and there found some fine specimens of herb Paris, with large bright purple berries resting on its topmost trifoliations, one of which Julian eagerly seized, saying that his sister had long wanted one for her collection of dried plants.

"I suppose you want the one you have gathered, De Vayne, for some botanist," said Lillyston.

"No—yes—at least I meant it for a lady, too; but it's of no use now," he said stammering.

"For a lady—of no use now," said Kennedy laughing; "what do you mean?"

"Oh, never mind," said Julian, as he noticed De Vayne's blush, and divined that he had meant the plant for Violet, but without knowing how much he was vexed by losing the opportunity of doing something for her.

They had a beautiful walk; De Vayne made little sketches of the windows and gargoyles of the village churches, and they all returned in the evening to a dinner which Lillyston had ordered in his own rooms, and which gave the rest an agreeable surprise when they got in.

"Julian," whispered De Vayne as they went away, "would you mind my sending that herb Paris to Vi— I beg pardon, to Miss Home, to your sister."

"Oh dear, yes, if you like," said Julian carelessly, surprised at the earnestness of his manner about such a trifle.

"It's only, you know, because Miss Home had heard that they were to be found near Camford, and asked me to get her one for her herbarium."

"Oh, very well, send it by all means. I shouldn't like you to break a promise."

"Thank you," said De Vayne; "and I suppose that Miss Home wouldn't mind my sending it in a letter."

"Certainly not," said Julian, laughing; "I've no doubt she'll be highly flattered. Here's the plant. Good-night."

"What could he have meant," thought he, "by making such a fuss about the trifolium, and by blushing so when Kennedy chaffed him? He surely can't have fallen in love with my dear little Vi." Now he thought of it, many indications seemed to show that such was really the case, and Julian contemplated the thought with singular pleasure. It did him good by diverting his attention from all harassing topics, and knowing that Violet was well worthy of Lord De Vayne, and could make him truly happy, while his high character and cultivated intellect rendered him well suited for her, he hoped in his secret heart that some day might see them united.

But Lord De Vayne, full of delight, took the plant, dressed it carefully, cut it to the size of an envelope, and then with a thrill of exquisite emotion sat down to write his letter to Violet Home.

"Dear Violet," he wrote, after having chosen a good sheet of note-paper and a first-rate pen, "you remember that I promised to find you a—"

"Dear Violet—no, that won't quite do," he said, as he read over what he had written, "at least not yet. How pretty it looks! What a charming name it is! I wish I might leave it, it does look so happy. I wonder whether it would do to call her Violet? No, I suppose not; at least not yet—not yet!" and the young viscount let his fancy wander away to Other Hall, and there by the grand old fireplace in the drawing-room he placed in imagination a slight graceful figure with soft fair hair, and a smile that lighted up an angel face,—and by her side he sat down, and let his thoughts wander through a vista of golden years.

Waking from his reverie, he found that his letter would be too late for the post, so he deferred it till Monday, and then wrote—

"Dear Miss Home—I enclose you a specimen of the herb Paris, which I promised to procure for you, if I could find one in Barton Wood. Julian was the actual discoverer, but has kindly allowed me to send it in fulfilment of my promise; he is quite well, and we are all hoping that you may hear in a day or two that he has got the Clerkland scholarship. With kindest remembrances to Mrs Home and your brothers, I remain, dear Miss Home, very truly yours, De Vayne."

Little did Violet dream that this commonplace note had given its author such deep pleasure, and that before he despatched it he had kissed it a thousand times for her sake, and because it was destined for her hand.

De Vayne would not have added the allusion to the Clerkland, but that rumours were already gaining ground in Julian's favour. The universal brilliancy of his earlier papers had already attracted considerable attention, and from mysterious hints at the high table, De Vayne began to gather almost with certainty that Julian was the successful candidate. Similar reports from various quarters were rife among the undergraduates, and were supposed to be traceable to competent authorities.

Wednesday evening came, and next morning the result was to be made known. As certainty approached, and suspense was nearly terminated, Julian awaited his fate with sickening, almost with trembling anxiety. At nine o'clock he knew that the paper on which was written the name of the Clerkland scholar would be affixed to the senate-house door, but he did not venture to go and read it. He knew that, if he were successful, a hundred men would be eager to rush up to his rooms with the joyful intelligence; if unsuccessful, he still trusted that he had one or two friends sufficiently sincere to put an end to his painful anxiety by telling him the news.

Nine o'clock struck. Oh, for the sound of some footstep on the stairs! Many must know the result by this time. Julian's hopes were still high, and he could not fail to hear of the numerous and seemingly authoritative reports which had ascribed success to him. He pressed his hands hard together, as he prayed that what was most for his welfare might be granted to him, and thought what boundless delight success would bring with it. What a joy it would be, above all, to write home, and gladden their hearts by the news of his triumph.

Every moment his suspense made him more feverish, and now the clock struck a quarter past nine, and he feared that in this case no news must be bad news. He leaned out of the window, and at this moment Mr Grayson strolled across the bowling-green. Then he heard another don, who was following him, call out—

"I say, do you know that the Clerkland is out?"

"Is it?" said Mr Grayson, with unusual show of interest.

"Yes. Who do you think has got it?"

"A Saint Werner's man, I hope."

"Yes."

"Well, who is it?"

What was the answer—Owen or Home?—at that distance the names sounded exactly alike.

"Oh, then, I am very sorry for—" Again Julian could not, with his utmost effort, catch the name with certainty; and, unable any longer to endure this state of doubt, he seized his cap and gown, when the sound of a slow footstep stopped him.

But it was Brogten's step, and Julian heard him pass into his own room.

A moment of breathless silence, and then another step, or rather the steps of two men; he detected by the sound that they were Lillyston and De Vayne. In one moment he would know the— Was it the best or the worst? He stood with his hand on the handle of the door; but it seemed as if they would never get to the top of the stairs. Why on earth were they so slow?

"Well," said Julian, as they came in sight, "is the Clerkland out?" He knew it was, but would not ask them the result.

"Yes," they both said; and Lillyston added, in a sorrowful tone of voice, "I am sorry for you, Julian, but Owen has got it."

Julian grew very pale, and for one second reeled as if he would faint. Lord De Vayne caught him as he staggered, and added eagerly, "But you are most honourably mentioned, Julian, 'proxime accessit,' and an allusion to your illness during one paper."

"Nothing, nothing," muttered Julian; "please leave me by myself." They were unwilling to leave him, and both lingered, but he entreated them to go, and respecting his desire for solitude they left him alone.

Julian found relief in a burst of passionate tears. He flung himself on the ground and cursed his birth, and his hard fate, and above all he cursed Brogten, who, as was clear, had been the cause, the sole cause, as Julian obstinately said, of his heavy misfortune. "Here I am," he murmured, "a sizar, an orphan, poor, without relations, with others depending on me, with my own way to make in the world, and now he has lost me the one thing I longed for, the one thing which would have made me happy," and as Julian kept brooding on this, on the loss of reputation, of help, of hope, his eyes grew red and swollen, and his temples throbbed with pain. He was

87

far from strong, and the shock of news that shattered all his hopes, and dashed rudely to the ground his long, long cherished desires, came more heavily upon him, because his constitution, naturally delicate, had suffered much during the last week from study and over anxiety. The necessity of writing home haunted him,—to his mother and sister, whose pride in him was so great, and who hoped so much for the honours which they thought him so sure to win,—to his brothers who had seen his diligence, and who would be deeply sorry to know that it had been in vain; to them at least he would be forced to announce the humiliating intelligence of defeat. He might leave his other friends to learn it from accidental sources, but oh, the bitterness of being obliged to announce it for himself, to those to whose disappointment he was most painfully alive, and oh, the intolerable plague of receiving letters of commiseration.

He could not do anything, he could not read, or write, or even think, except of the one blow which had thus laid him prostrate. He leaned over his window-sill, and stared stupidly at the great stone bears carved on the portals of Saint Margaret's; his eyes wandered listlessly over the smooth turf of the Fellows' bowling-green, and the trim parterres full of crocus and anemone and violet which fringed it; he watched the boats skim past him on the winding gleams of the Iscam, and shoot among the water-lilies by the bridge and then he stared upwards at the sun, trying to think of nothing until his eyes watered, and then the sight of a don in the garden below made him shrink back, to avoid observation, into his own room.

Some of the Saint Werner's men would be coming soon to condole with him. What a nuisance it would be! He got up and sported the door. This action recalled in all their intensity his bitterest and angriest feelings, and he flung the door open again, and threw himself full length on the sofa, until a sort of painful stupor came over him, and he became unconscious of how the time went by.

At length a slight sound awoke him, and he saw De Vayne standing by him. De Vayne was so gentle in heart and manner, so full of sympathy and kindness, that of all others he was the one whom at that moment Julian could best endure to see.

"I am afraid," he said, "that you will think me very foolish, De Vayne. But to me everything almost depended on this scholarship, and you can hardly tell how absolutely it had engrossed my hopes."

"It is very natural that you should feel it, Julian. But I came to ask if you would like me to save you the trouble of writing home to-day. I could say more, you know, than you could," he added with a pleasant smile, "of the splendid manner in which you acquitted yourself, of which I have heard a great deal that I will tell you some day."

"Thanks, De Vayne. I should be really and truly grateful if you would. They will expect to hear by to-morrow, and I know that if I write now, I shall be saying something bitter and hasty."

"Very well, I will. Are you inclined for a stroll now?"

"No, thank you," said Julian, unwilling to encounter the many eyes which he knew would look on him with curiosity to see how he bore his loss.

"Good morning then; I shall come again soon."

"Do, I shall like to see you," said Julian; and De Vayne went away, thinking with some happiness, that if he had won Julian's affection, that would be something towards helping him to win Violet's too.

Julian had no intention that any strange eye should see how much he had felt his disappointment, so when Mr Admer came to see him, he gave no sign of vexation, and they talked indifferently for a few minutes, till Mr Admer said—

"Well, Home, I'm sorry you haven't got this scholarship. Not that it makes the least difference, you know, really. No sensible man would have thought one atom the better of you for getting it, and even your reputation stands just as high as before.

"Ah, I see you take it to heart rather; all very natural, but when you're my age you'll think less of these things. There are higher successes in the world than these small University affairs."

"But they aren't small to me," said Julian. "Not to men up here," said Mr Admer.

> "'They think the rustic cackle of their body
> The murmur of the world.'"

"Perhaps, after all, if you had got it, it would only have helped to make you as fussy, as foolish, and as self-important as Jones, and Brown, and Robinson, who, because they are dons, think themselves the most important people in England, when really they are only conspicuous for empty-headedness and conceit; or as the senior Wrangler, who entering the theatre at the same moment as the queen, bowed graciously on all sides in acknowledgment of the acclamations. As it is, Home, you are a man who ought to do something in the world."

Julian could not help smiling at Mr Admer's usual style, and would have found some relief in arguing with him, had not Hazlet entered, whose very appearance put Mr Admer to a precipitate flight. There could not have been any human being less likely to give

89

Julian any effectual consolation at such a moment, and he could not help sighing as Mr. Admer left him to his persecutor.

"Fugit improbus ac me sub cultro linquit," he said appealingly, secure in Hazlet's ignorance of the Latin tongue; but Mr Admer only shook his head significantly, and disappeared.

With his black shining hair brushed down in unusual lankiness over his receding forehead, and with an expression of sleek resignation unusually sanctimonious, Hazlet sat down, and gave a half groan.

"I am sorry," he said, "dear Julian—"

"Home, if you please, Hazlet," interrupted Julian.

Hazlet was a little taken aback, but he said—

"Well, dear Home—"

"Home only, if you please," said Julian still more abruptly.

"Ah! I see you are in a rebellious—excuse me, dear—I mean Home,—a rebellious spirit. I feared it would be so when I saw that godless young clergyman with you."

Julian relieved his disgust by an expression of impatience.

"I have no doubt, dear Ju—, I mean Home—I have no doubt," he continued, with a gusto infinitely annoying, "that you needed this rod. I am afraid that you are as yet unconverted; that you have as yet no saving, no vital sense of Christianity. Some sin, perhaps, needs correction; some—"

"Confound your intolerable impudence and cant!" said Julian, starting from his seat, aroused by his hypocritical prate into unwonted intolerance; and he suddenly observed, by the cowering attitude which Hazlet assumed, that the worthy youth was afraid of receiving at his head the water-bottle, on which Julian's hand was resting. Julian thought it best to avoid the temptation, and hoping Hazlet would take the hint, he said, "Forgive my rudeness, Hazlet, but I am very tired and annoyed just now; in fact, I am hardly in a condition to talk with, as you see, and you are really quite incapable of saying anything to help me."

But Hazlet had come prepared to say his say, and did not attempt to move.

"Ah," he said, with a sigh which seemed to express satisfaction—(some people always sigh when they thank God)—"I am afraid you are unprepared for the consolations of religion."

"Of such a religion as yours, most certainly," interrupted Julian, with haughty vehemence.

"The natural man, you see—" He stopped as he saw Julian's hand fidgeting towards the water-bottle. "Ah! well, you will have still to sit at the sizars' table, and dine on the Fellows' leavings; perhaps it might inscrutably be good for you to bear the yoke—"

90

Had the fellow come to insult him? Was he there on purpose to gratify his malice at another's misfortune, under the pretext of pious reflections? Half-a-dozen times Julian had thought so, and thought so correctly. Hazlet's very little and very ignorant mind had been fed into self-complacency by the cheering belief that he and his friends formed a select party whose future welfare was secure, while "the world" was very wicked, and destined to everlasting burning; and in proportion to his gross conceit, was he nettled with the evident manner in which Julian, though without any rudeness, avoided his company even at Ildown, where he reigned with undisputed sway among his own admiring circle of gynaikazia. (Excuse the word, gentle reader; it is Saint Paul's—not mine.) Hazlet had come there, though in the depth of his hypocrisy he hardly knew it himself, to enjoy a little triumph over Julian's pride, and to pour a little vinegar, in the guise of a good Samaritan, on wounds which he knew to be bleeding still.

In saying the last sentence, in which he cut Julian to the very quick, Hazlet had seemed to his victim's excited imagination to be actually smacking his lips with undisguised delight. "Ah, you will have still to dine at the sizars' table on the Fellows' leavings." Julian knew that the form of the sentence made it most maliciously and odiously false;—and that this hypocritical son of Belial should address him at such a moment in such a way was so revolting to his own generous spirit, that he could endure it no longer.

"What did you say?" he asked sharply.

"Of course, my dear Ju—, Home, I mean—poverty is no disgrace to you, you know. Some of the sizars are pious men, I have no doubt, and I dare say the Fellows leave—"

"I swear this is too much," said Julian, using the only oath that ever in all his life-time crossed his lips. "You canting and mean— Pshaw! you are beneath my abuse. Sizar indeed! there, take that, and begone." He had meant to empty the tumbler in his face, but his hand shook with passion, and the glass flew out of it, and after cutting the top of Hazlet's head, fell broken on the floor.

With a howl of dismay Hazlet fled to his own rooms, where, having satisfied himself that the cut had done little other harm than leaving some red streaks upon his damp and lanky hair, he put over it some strips of plaster as large as he conveniently could, and then with a lugubrious expression went to hall, and gratified his malice by buzzing and babbling among his fellows all sorts of lies and exaggerations about Julian's conduct and state of mind. When Kennedy came in, however, he put an abrupt end to Hazlet's calumnies by handling his own tumbler with so significant a glance, that Hazlet assumed a look of terror, and, amid shouts of laughter, retired with all speed out of reach of the danger.

Lillyston, always a firm and faithful friend, was grieved to the soul to hear of Julian's condition; for, without believing half that Hazlet said, it was at least clear that Julian had shown some violence, and, if Hazlet was to be trusted, "had sworn at him in a manner perfectly awful." What had come over Julian of late? Since that fit of uncontrollable and lasting passion which had overpowered him when he was screwed in, he did not seem to have recovered that noble moral strength and equilibrium which was usually conspicuous in his character. The restlessness which had prevented him from doing the paper, the half sullen silence through the day, the horse-whipping of Brogten, the second outburst of unchecked feeling at the loss of the scholarship, and finally, this treatment of Hazlet, caused Lillyston a deep regret that his friend should have strayed so widely from his usual calm and manly course. It was as if one staggering blow had loosened all the joints of his moral armour, and left room for successive wounds. He determined to go and see him before chapel, and, if possible, get him to come and spend the evening quietly with him; he was only prevented from going at once by supposing that Julian would be dining by himself to avoid meeting any one in hall, and he did not wish to disturb him at his lonely meal.

Julian's head was aching with mortification, passion, and fatigue; it seemed as if he had but one thought to which he could turn, and that this was a thought of weariness and pain. He dwelt much less on his own defeat than on the disappointment which he knew it would cause to Violet and his young brothers. He knew well that Mrs Home would bear it with equanimity, because she regarded all the events of life, however painful, with the same quiet resignation, and trusted ever in the gentle dealing and loving purposes of His hand who guides them all. Poor Julian longed to be able to regard it in this light too, but he had suffered the angry part of his nature to gain the victory, and his human reason was now being torn by his lion heart.

Unable to endure the notion of going to hall, which would be a painful reminder that the opportunity to which he had long looked for emancipation from his sizarship had passed by, he determined to take some wine, in the hope that it would support him till the evening. He could not of course afford to give wine parties, but he always kept a few bottles in his rooms for medicinal purposes, or to offer to any stranger who might come to visit him. Taking out a decanter, he sat down in his armchair, and drank a glass or two. The wine exhilarated him; as he had scarcely tasted anything all day, it got rapidly into his head, and in a few minutes his thoughts seemed in a tumult of delirious emotion. Pride and passion triumphed over every other feeling; after all, what was the scholarship to him? Tush! he looked for better things in life than scholarships. He would discard the petty successes of pedantry, and would seek a loftier greatness. He had been a fool to trouble himself about such trifles. And as these arrogant mists clouded his fancy, he broke out into irregular snatches of unmeaning song.

It was a saint's-day evening, and consequently chapel was at a quarter past six instead of six, and the undergraduates wore surplices in chapel instead of their ordinary gowns. On saints'-days there is always a choral service at Saint Werner's College, and the excellence of the choir generally attracted a large congregation. To Julian, who was fond of music, these saint's-day services had a peculiar interest; and now while his brain was swimming with the fumes of wine, he determined to go to chapel, and imagined to himself the pleasure he should feel in striding haughtily through the throng of men up the long aisle to the sizar's seat, to show by his look and manner that his courage was undaunted, and that his self-confidence rose superior to defeat. Although the chapel-bell had not yet begun to ring, he put out his cap and surplice, and sat down to drink more wine.

Just as the clock struck six, Lillyston knocked at Julian's door.

"Aha! old fellow," said Julian, "you are just in time to have a glass of wine before chapel."

"No, thank you," said Lillyston coldly, sick at heart to see a fresh proof of his friend's unworthy excitement, but without realising as yet his true condition.

"Tush! you think I care about that trumpery Clerkland? Not I! Won't you have some wine?—no? well, I shall, and then I'm going to chapel."

His flushed countenance, and excited manner, joined to the harsh tones of his generally pleasant and musical voice, produced on Lillyston's mind a feeling of deep pain and shame, and when with unsteady hand, Julian endeavoured to pour out for himself a fresh glass, and in doing so spilt the wine in great streams over the table, Lillyston saw that he was in an utterly unfit state to go to chapel, and that the attempt to do so would certainly draw upon him exposure and disgrace.

"Julian," he said gently; "you are not in a condition to go to chapel; you must not think of it."

"What do you mean?" said Julian with a stupid stare.

"I mean," he replied slowly, "that the wine has got into your head."

A laugh, half hysterical, half defiant, was the only answer, and Julian began to put on his surplice, wrong side out.

"Julian, I beg of you to stay here as you would avoid ruin."

"Pooh! I am not a child, as you seem to think. You are—Yes, you are a fool, Lillyston."

Pained to the very heart, Lillyston wavered for a moment, but a glance at Julian decided him. Five years of happy uninterrupted friendship, five years during which he had regarded his friend's stainless character with ever-growing pride and affection, determined him at all hazards to save him from the effects of this temporary possession. Firmly, but quietly, he planted his back against the door, and said—

"Dear Julian, I beseech you not to go."

The tone of voice, the mention of his own name recalled Julian for a moment, but the sound of the chapel-bell renewed his determination, and he answered, "Nonsense. Come, make room."

"You shall not go, Julian."

"But I will," shouted he angrily; "how dare you prevent me; stand aside."

Lillyston did not stir, and rendered furious by opposition, Julian grappled with him. It required all Lillyston's strength to retain his position against this wild assault, but he managed to do so without inflicting any hurt; and when Julian paused, Lillyston noticed with a sense of relief that the chapel-bell had ceased to ring.

"I WILL go," said Julian, madly renewing the struggle. But with all his efforts he could not stir Lillyston from the door, and only succeeded in tearing his surplice from the neck downwards. He paused, and, baffled of his intention, glared at his opponent.

"The clock has now struck," said Lillyston calmly, "and the doors will be shut. You are too late to get in." Julian stamped impatiently on the floor, and prepared to close with Lillyston again, but now Lillyston stepped from the door, and as he slowly went out, turned round and said—

"Julian, do you call this being brave or strong? Can you let one disappointment unman you so utterly?"

"Be brave, and honest, and pure, and God will be with you." The words flashed into light from the folded pages of Julian's memory, and with them the dim image of a dead face, and the dying echo of a father's voice.

CHAPTER FOURTEEN

MR. CARDEN

"Pol pudere quam pigere proestat totidem literis."

Plautus Trinum, Two, 2

Who has not felt, who does not know, that one sin yielded to, that one passion uncontrolled, too often brings with it a train of other sins, and betrays the drawbridge of the citadel to a thousand enemies beside?

It had been so with Julian Home, and in proportion to the true strength and beauty of his character, was the poignancy of his bitterness when he awoke the next morning, and calmly reviewed the few last excited, prayerless, and unworthy days. Surely after so many proofs of weakness, surely after emotions and acts so violently inadequate to the circumstances which had caused them, his best friends must despise him as utterly as he despised himself.

He arose that morning strong out of weakness. He determined that he would be checked no longer by unavailing regrets, and that his repentance should be open and manly, as his prostration had been conspicuous. Fortified by the humiliating experience of his own want of strength he sought for help in resolute determination and earnest prayer. After breakfast, his first step was to call on Owen, and congratulate him with hearty and unaffected simplicity on his success—a success which Owen generously acknowledged to be due solely to Julian's misfortune. It was much more difficult to call on Hazlet, but this, too, Julian felt to be his duty; and distasteful as it was, he would not shrink from performing it. Hazlet received him with a ludicrous air of offended dignity, and was barely overcome into a tone of magnanimous forgiveness by Julian's frank apology. On the whole, Julian decided that it would be best not to call on Brogten, lest, by so doing, he should seem to be reminding him of the consequences of his enmity under the appearance of expressing a regret. It only remained therefore to see Lillyston, and to this visit Julian looked with unmitigated joy.

"Forgive me, Hugh," he said, as he entered the room; "from this time forward I shall owe you a new debt of gratitude; you have saved me from I know not what disgrace."

Lillyston was delighted to see him look like his old self once more. The thunder-cloud which had been hanging on his brow was dissipated, and the sullen expression had wholly passed.

"Don't talk of debt, Julian," he said; "between friends, you know, there are no obligations—they are merged in the friendship itself."

"I am amazed at my own intolerable folly, Hugh. I hope this is the last time that I shall yield to such storms of passion. I have much to be ashamed of."

"Well, Julian," said Lillyston, changing the subject, "you mustn't think any more of this Clerkland, for potentially you got it, as everybody acknowledges; dynamei you were successful, if not ezgo."

"I don't mean to let it discourage me," said Julian, "though the potential is mightily different from the actual." Nor did he suffer it to discourage him, or weaken his endeavours. His life soon began to flow once more in its usual, even, and quiet course. It did not take him long to discover that it was possible to live happily without the Clerkland, and he wondered in himself at the intensity of the desire to obtain it, which he had suffered to overpower him. He felt no touch of envy towards Owen, whose friendship he began to value more and more, and who voluntarily told him, from information that he had derived from the examiners themselves, that the decision had long hung in a doubtful scale. In fact, the scholarship would have been divided between both of them but for one of the examiners, who hardly appreciated Julian's merits. It was so well understood that Julian must have been the successful candidate but for the one fatal paper on Monday morning, that he rather gained than lost in reputation from the result of the competition.

It was a few days after these events that Julian received from Mr Carden a pressing invitation to spend a Sunday with him at Harton. Glad of a change, he easily obtained an exeat, and went down on the Saturday morning. Even the half-year since he had left had made a perceptible change in the old place. There were many new faces, and many old ones had disappeared, so that, already, he began to feel himself half a stranger among the familiar scenes. But alike from boys and masters he received a kindly greeting, and Mr Carden entertained him with a pleasant and genial hospitality. The only thing which pained him was the obvious change for the worse in Mr Carden's health. He wore a sadder expression than of old, and though he made no remark about his health, yet every now and then his face seemed to be suddenly contracted by a throb of pain.

On the Monday morning, when it was necessary for Julian to return to Camford, Mr Carden called him into his study after breakfast, and asked him to choose any book he liked, as a farewell present, from the shelves.

"But why a farewell present, Mr Carden?" asked Julian, laughing. "Aren't you ever going to ask me to Harton again?"

"No," said Mr Carden with a sad smile, "never again.

"I resign my mastership at the end of this term," he continued, in answer to Julian's inquiring look; "my health is so uncertain that I feel unequal any longer to these most arduous, most responsible duties. Perhaps, too," he added, "I may be a little disappointed in the result of my labours; but, at any rate, though as yet few are aware of it, this is my last month at Harton—so choose one of my books, Julian, as a farewell present."

Julian expressed his real sorrow at Mr Carden's failing health. "If you go away," he said, "it will seem as if the chief tie which bound me to dear old Harton was suddenly snapped." He chose as his memento a small volume of sermons which Mr Carden had published in former days, and asked him to write his name on the title-page.

"Yes," said the master, "you shall have that book if you like; but I mean you to have also a more substantial memorial of my library. Here, Julian, this book I always destined to be yours some day; you may as well have it now."

He took down from the shelves a richly bound copy of Coleridge's works, in ten volumes, which Julian knew to be the one book of his library which he most deeply prized. His marginal comments enriched almost every page, and Julian was ashamed to take what he knew that the owner so highly valued.

"But I thought you told me once that you were thinking of publishing a biography of Coleridge, and an edition of his writings," said Julian. "Surely, sir, you will want these manuscript notes, won't you?"

"Ah, Julian! that is one of the many plans which have floated through my mind unfulfilled. My life, I fear, will have been an incomplete one. Thank God that there is no such thing as a necessary man—il n'y a point d'hommes nécessaires; others will be found to do a thousandfold better the work which I had purposed to do." And then he murmured half to himself—

"Till, in due time, one by one,
Some with lives that came to nothing, some with deeds as well undone,
Death came suddenly, and took them where men never see the sun."

His eyes filled with tears. "No," he said, "take the book, Julian. If it does you all the good it has done me, it will have been more useful than I could ever have made it. And when you hang on the eloquent and earnest words of the great poet philosopher, mingle his teachings with some few memories of me; it will be like a drop of myrrh, perhaps, in the cup, but I should like," he added, with faltering voice, "to leave at least one to think of me with affection."

He turned away as his old pupil grasped his hand; and Julian, as he went back in the train to Camford, could not help a feeling of real pity that one so generous and upright in heart and life should be destined to so lonely and sorrowful a lot.

As he had said, he resigned his Harton mastership at the end of the term, and sailed to Madeira for his health. He begged Julian to continue his correspondence with him, and to tell him all about his old Harton and Camford friends.

During Easter week, while Julian was at Ildown, he received from him a letter to the following effect:—

"Dear Julian—I was not mistaken in hinting, while you were at Harton, that we should never meet again. I am on my death-bed; and, in all probability, the rapid decline which is now wasting my powers, and which, while I write, shakes me with painful fits of coughing, will have terminated my life before this letter reaches your hands.

"I leave life, I hope, with simple resignation; and although I have left undone much which I hoped to have accomplished, yet I die trusting in God. My friends in this world have been few, and my fortune have not been bright, yet happiness has largely preponderated even in my destiny, and I look on the death which is approaching as the commencement, not as the end, of true existence.

"But I did not write to you, dear Julian, to tell you of the frame of mind in which death finds me. I wrote to bid you farewell, and to tell you of something which concerns you—I mean my intention, recently adopted, of leaving you my small private fortune, and the added earnings which my labours have procured. Together, they amount only to ten thousand pounds, but I hope that they may be of real service to you. Had you still been the heir to your aunt's property, perhaps even if you had got the Clerkland, I should have disposed of this money in some other way; but as these events have been ordered otherwise, and as I have no relations of my own who need the legacy, nor any friend in whose welfare I take deeper interest than in yours, it gives me a gleam of real satisfaction to be able to place at your disposal this little sum.

"Good-bye, my dear Julian. When these words meet your eye, I expect to be in that state where even your prayers can benefit me no more. But I know your affectionate and grateful

heart, and I know that you will sometimes recur with a thought of kindness to the memory of your affectionate friend, Henry Carden."

The next mail brought the news of Mr Carden's death. It caused many a sorrowing heart both at Harton and at Camford. Mr Carden was a man whose impetuous and enthusiastic disposition had caused him to commit many serious errors in life, and these had been a barrier to the success which must otherwise have rewarded his energy and talent. But even among those who were envious of his ability, and offended by his eccentricities, they were few who did not do justice to the rectitude of his motives, and none who did not admit the warmth of his affections. There were more to mourn over his untimely death than there had been to forgive the mistakes he made, and by wise and friendly counsel to raise him to that height which he might easily have obtained. And among the crowd who had known him, and the many who honoured him, there were some who loved him with no ordinary love, and who were not too proud to admit the obligation of a permanent gratitude. It was one of the great happinesses of Mr Carden's life that of this number was Julian Home.

With a clear 300 pounds a year of his own, it was of course unnecessary for Julian to return to Saint Werner's as a sizar, and he at once wrote to his tutor to beg that his name might be removed from the list. There was one respect in which he found this a very material addition to his comfort and happiness. As the sizars dined an hour later than the other men, and at a separate table, he had been by this means cut off from the society of many of his friends in hall, where men have more opportunities of meeting and becoming intimate than anywhere else. It was no slight addition to his happiness to sit perpetually with the group of friends he valued most.

"I've got a magnificent plan for the Long, Julian," said Kennedy to him one day, as they left the hall. "My father is going to Switzerland for three months, with my sister Eva and me. Eva goes under the wing of an aunt of mine, Mrs Dudley, whom I think you met at Ildown once. Won't you come with us?"

The proposal was very tempting, the more so as Julian had never been abroad. He mentioned it in his next letter home, and asked if it would be possible for any of them to accompany him, without which he gave up all intention of making the tour. In reply, Mrs Home proposed that Violet should go, (if Mrs Dudley would kindly chaperon her), because the trip would be of great advantage to her in many ways; and that Cyril should go, as a reward for his industry and success at Marlby. "As for Frankie and me," she continued, "we will stay at home to take care of Ildown in your absence. Frank is too young to enjoy travelling, and I have but little desire for it; we two will stay behind, and I daresay we shall be very happy, especially if you write us long accounts of all your proceedings."

So this most delightful plan was definitely adopted, and all concerned were full of the happiest anticipations. Kennedy and Julian looked forward to it with the utmost eagerness; Violet, who had already grown fond of Mrs Dudley and Eva, was charmed at the prospect, and Cyril, with all a boy's eagerness for novelty, was well-nigh wild with joy.

But as yet six weeks were to elapse before the Long commenced.

CHAPTER FIFTEEN

KENNEDY'S DISHONOUR

"I fancied Cuthbert's reddening face
Beneath its garniture of curly gold,
Dear fellow, till I almost felt him fold
An arm in mine, to fix me to the place.
That way he used, ... Alas! one hour's disgrace!"

Robert Browning. Childe Roland

"I am very doubtful, after all, Julian, whether I shall be one of the Switzerland party," said Kennedy, with a sigh, as he and Julian were walking round the Saint Werner's gardens one bright evening of the May term. The limes and chestnuts were unfolding their tender sprays of spring-tide emerald, the willows shivered as their green buds made ripples in the water, and the soft light of sunset streamed over towers and colleges, giving a rich glow to the broad windows of the library, and bathing in its rosy tinge the white plumage of the swans upon the river. The friends were returning from a walk, during which they had thoroughly enjoyed the blue and golden weather. Up to this time Kennedy had seemed to be in the

100

highest spirits, and Julian was astonished at the melancholy tone in which the words were spoken.

"Doubtful? Why?" said Julian, quickly.

"Because my father has made it conditional on my getting a first class in the May examination."

"But, my dear fellow, there is not the ghost of a doubt of your doing that."

"I don't feel so sure."

"Why, there are often thirty in the first class in the freshman's year; and just as if you wouldn't be among them!"

"All very well; I know that anybody can do it who works, but I am ashamed to say that I haven't read one of the books yet."

"Haven't you, really? Well then, for goodness' sake, lose no more time."

"But there's only a fortnight to the examination."

"My dear Kennedy, what have you been doing to be so idle?"

"Somehow or other the time manages to slip away. Heigh ho!" said Kennedy, "my first year at college nearly over, and nothing done—nothing done! How quickly the time has gone!"

"Yes," said Julian;

> "ptezugas gaz epoomaduas phezai
> Kampes bzadutezoi ta poteemena syllabein,

"as Theocritus prettily observes."

Seized with the strong determination not only to pass the examination, but even to excel in it, Kennedy devoted the next fortnight to unremitted study for the first time since he had been an undergraduate. But the more he read the more painfully he became aware of his own deficiencies, and the more bitterly he deplored the waste of time. He seemed to be toiling in vain after the opportunities he had lost. He knew that the examination, though limited in subjects, was searching in character, and he found it impossible to acquire, by a sudden impulse, what he should have learned by continuous diligence. As the time drew nearer, he grew more and more nervous. He had set his heart on the Swiss tour, and it now seemed to him painfully probable that he would fail in fulfilling the condition which his father had exacted, and without which he well knew that Mr Kennedy would insist on his spending the vacation either at Camford or at home.

Of the three main subjects for examination he had succeeded by desperate effort, aided by natural ability, in very quickly mastering two sufficiently well to secure a creditable result; but the third subject, the Agamemnon of Aeschylus, remained nearly

101

untouched, and Kennedy was too good and accurate a scholar not to be aware that the most careful and elaborate study was indispensable to an even tolerable understanding of that masterpiece of Grecian tragedy. Besides this, he had a hatred of slovenly and superficial work, and he therefore determined to leave the Aeschylus untouched, while, at the same time, he was quite conscious that if he did so, all chance of distinction, and even all chance of a first class were out of the question. With some shame he reflected over this proof, that, for all purposes of study, a third of his academical life had been utterly and wholly lost.

As he had decided on giving up the Aeschylus, it became more imperative to make sure of the Tacitus and Demosthenes, and he therefore went to Mr Grayson's rooms to get a library order which should entitle him to take from the Saint Werner's library any books that would be most likely to give him effectual help.

At the moment of his arrival, Mr Grayson was engaged, and he was shown into another room until he should be ready. This room was the tutor's library, and like many of the rooms in Camford, it opened into an inner and smaller study, the door of which was partly open.

Kennedy sat down, and after a few minutes, as there seemed to be no signs that he would be summoned immediately, he began to grow very restless. He tried some of the books on the table, but they were all unspeakably dull; he looked at the pictures on the wall, but they were most of them the likenesses of Camford celebrities which he already knew by heart; he looked out of the window, but the court was empty, and there was nothing to see. Reflecting that the only thing which can really induce ennui in a sensible man, is to be kept waiting when he is very busy for an indefinite period, which may terminate at any moment, and may last for almost any length of time, Kennedy, vexed at the interruption of his work, chose the most comfortable armchair in the room, and settled himself in it with a yawn.

At this moment, as ill fate would have it, his eye caught sight of a book lying on Mr Grayson's reading-desk. Lazily rising to see what it was, he found it to be an Aeschylus, and turned over the leaves with a feeling of listless indifference. Between two of the leaves lay a written paper, and suddenly, after reading two or three lines, he observed it to be a manuscript copy of the much-dreaded Agamemnon paper for the May examination.

Temptation had surprised him with sudden and unexpected violence. He little knew that on this idle weary moment rested the destiny of many years.

As when in a hostile country one has laid aside his armour,

and from unregarded ambush the enemy leaps on him, and, though he be strong and noble, stabs him with a festering wound, so this temptation to a base act sprang on poor Kennedy when he was unarmed and unprepared. In the gaieties of life, and the brightnesses of hope, and the securities of unbroken enjoyment, he had long been trusting in himself only, in his own high principle, his own generous impulses, his own unstained honour. But these were never sufficient for any human being yet, and they snapped in an instant under this unhappy boy.

The only honourable thing to do, the thing which at another moment Kennedy might have done, and which any man would have done, whose right instincts and high character had the reliable support of higher principles than mere personal self-confidence and pride, would have been to shut the book instantly, inform Mr Grayson that he had accidentally read one of the questions, and beg him to change it before the examination. This Kennedy knew well; it flashed before him in an instant as the only proper course but at the same instant he passionately obliterated the suggestion from his mind, fiercely stifled the impulse to do right, choked the rebukes of honour and principle, and blindly willed to save his reputation as a scholar, and his chance of enjoyment for the vacation by reading through the entire number of the questions. This mental struggle did not last an instant, for the emotions of the spirit belong only to eternity, and the guilt of human actions is not commensurate with the length of time they occupy. But in the intense wish to see what the examination would be like, and to secure his first class, Kennedy repressed altogether by one blow the moral element of his being, and concentrated his whole intellect on the paper before him. To read it through was the work of a minute; when it was read through, it was too late to wish the act undone, and without suffering himself to dwell, or even to recur in thought to the nature of his proceedings, Kennedy deliberately read through the whole paper a second time.

But this imperious effort of the will was not exercised without visible effects. Absorbed as he was in seizing every prominent subject in the questions, his forehead contracted, his hand shook, his knees trembled, and his heart palpitated with violence. He observed nothing; he did not notice the shadow that chequered the sunlight streaming from the door of the inner room; he did not hear the light step which passed over the carpet; he did not feel the breath of a man who stood behind him, looked over his shoulder, watched his eager determination to secure the unfair advantage, smiled at his agitation, and then slipped back again into the inner room, unnoticed as before.

It was done. Not a question but was printed indelibly on Kennedy's memory. Quickly, fearfully, he shut the book, and glided back to the armchair, in the vain attempt to look and feel at ease.

At ease! No, now the tumult broke. Now Kennedy hated himself; called himself mean, vile, contemptible, a reptile, a cheat. Now his insulted honour began to vindicate its rights, and his trampled sense of truth to spring up with a menacing bound, and his conscience to speak out calmly and clearly the language of self-condemnation and contempt. Good heavens! how could he have sunk so low; fancy if Julian had seen him, or could know his meanness. Fancy if anybody had seen him. Hazlet, or Fitzurse, or Brogten himself, could hardly have been guilty of a more dishonourable act.

You miserable souls, that do not know what honour is, or what torments rend a truly noble heart, if ever it be led to commit an act which to your seared consciences and muddy intelligence appears a trivial sin, or even no sin at all; you, the mean men to whom an offence like this is so common, that, unless it were discovered, it would not trouble your recollections with a feather's weight of remorse,—for you, I scorn to write, and I scorn from my inmost being the sneer with which you will regard the agony that Kennedy suffered from his fall. But to the high and the generous, who have erred and have bewailed their error in secret,—to them I appeal to imagine the anguish of self-reproach, the bitterness of humiliation, which stung him in those few moments after his first dishonour. It is the lofty tower that falls with the heaviest crash; it is the stately soul that suffers the deepest abasement; it is the white scutcheon on which the dark stain seems to wear its darkest hue.

He had not sat there for many minutes—though to him they seemed like hours—when a step on the stairs told him that his tutor's visitor had departed, and the gyp blandly entering, observed—

"Now, sir, Mr Grayson can see you."

"Oh! very well," said Kennedy, rising and assuming, with a painful effort, his most indifferent look and tone.

"Pardon me, Mr Kennedy, my turn first; I have been waiting longest," said a harsh voice behind him, that sounded mockingly to his excited ear. He turned sharply round, and with a low bow and a curl on the protruding lip, and a little guttural laugh, Brogten came from the inner room, and passed before him into Mr Grayson's presence.

If a thunderbolt had suddenly fallen before Kennedy's feet and cloven its sulphurous passage into the abyss, he could hardly have been more startled or more alarmed. Without a word he sat down half stupefied. Was any one else in the inner room? For very shame he dare not look. Had Brogten seen him? If so, would he at once tell Mr Grayson? What would be done in that case? Dare he deny the fact? Passionately he spurned the hateful suggestion. Would Brogten tell all the Saint Werner's men? Brogten of all others, whom he had publicly insulted and branded with dishonour! Ah me, there is no anguish so keen, so deadly, as the anguish of awakened shame!

With unspeakable anxiety Kennedy awaited Brogten's departure. Why should he be so long? Surely he must be telling Mr Grayson.

At last the heavy step was heard, the door opened, and the gyp once more announced that Mr Grayson was disengaged.

Pale and almost breathless, Kennedy went into the room.

"Good morning, Mr Kennedy."

"Good morning, sir."

He quite expected that Mr Grayson was about at once to address him on the subject of the paper, and, expecting this, totally forgot the purpose for which he had come. The tutor's cold eye was upon him, and after a pause he said—

"Well, Mr Kennedy?"

"Well, sir?" he replied, with a start.

"Do you want anything?"

"Oh, I came for— Really, sir, I must beg your pardon, but I have forgotten what it was."

"To look at an examination-paper," were the words which, in his embarrassment, sprang to his lips, but he checked them just in time.

"Really, Mr Kennedy, you appear to be strangely absent this morning," said Mr Grayson, in a tone the reverse of encouraging.

"Oh, I remember now," he replied, desperately; "it was a library order I wanted."

Mr Grayson wrote him the order. Kennedy took it, and, without even shaking the cold hand which the tutor proffered, hurried out of the room, relieved at least by the conviction that Brogten, if he had seen him look at the paper, had not, as yet at any rate, revealed it to the examiner.

"After all," he reflected, "he was hardly likely to do that. But had he told the men?"

Kennedy did not go to the library; he could not bear to meet anybody, and hastened to bury himself in his own rooms. His walk, usually so erect and gay as he went across the court—the tune he used to hum so merrily in the sunshine—and the bright open glance of recognition with which he passed his acquaintances and friends, were gone to-day. He shuffled silently along the cloisters with downcast eyes.

Hall-time would be the time to know whether Brogten had seen him and betrayed him. And if he had seen him, surely there could be no doubt he would tell of him. What a sweet revenge it would be for that malicious heart! How completely it would turn the tables on Kennedy for the day when he had sarcastically alluded to Brogten's bets! How amply it would fulfil the promise of which that parting scowl of hatred had been full.

He went to hall rather late on purpose; and instead of sitting in his usual place near Julian, he chose a vacant place at another table. Half a minute sufficed to show him that there was no difference in his reception; the same frequent nods and smiles from all sides still gave him the frank greeting of which, as a popular man, he was always sure. He looked round for Brogten, but could make nothing of his face; it simply wore a somewhat slight smile when their eyes met, and Kennedy's fell. Kennedy began to convince himself that Brogten could not have seen what he had done in Mr Grayson's room.

The thought rolled away a great load—a heavy, intolerable load from his heart. It was not that with him, as with so many thousands, the fear of discovery constituted the sense of sin, but young as he was, and high as his character had stood hitherto in man's estimation, he prayed for any chastisement rather than that of detection, any stroke in preference to open shame. This was the one thing which he felt he could not bear.

Even now, as conscience strongly suggested, he might make, by private confession to his tutor, or at any rate by not using the knowledge he had thus acquired, the only reparation which was still in his power. But it was a hard thing for conscience to ask—too hard for poor Kennedy's weakness. Much of the paper, as he saw at once, he could very easily have answered from his previous general knowledge and scholarship; so easily, that he now felt convinced that he might have done quite enough of it to secure his first class. His sin then had been useless, quite useless, worse than useless to him. Was he obliged also to make it positively injurious? was he to put himself in a worse position than if he had never committed it? After all the punishment which the sin had brought with it, was he also to lose, in consequence of it, the very advantage, the very enjoyment, for the sake of which he had harboured the temptation? It was too much—too much to expect.

The night before the Aeschylus examination he began to read up the general information on the subject, and he intended to do it quite as if he were unaware of what the actual questions were to be.

But it was the merest self-deception. Each question was branded in fiery letters on his recollection, and he found that, as he read, he was skipping involuntarily every topic which he knew had not been touched on in Mr Grayson's paper.

Oh, the sense of hypocrisy with which he eagerly seized the paper next morning, and read it over as though unaware of its contents.

Julian could not help observing that, during the last few days, Kennedy's spirits had suffered a change. His old mirth came only in fitful bursts, and he was often moody and silent; but Julian attributed it to anxiety for the result of the examination, and doubt whether he should be allowed by his father to make one of the long-anticipated party in the foreign tour.

Kennedy dared not admit any one into his confidence, but the last evening, before they went down, he turned the conversation, as he sat at tea in Owen's room, to the topic of character, and the faults of great men, and the aberrations of the good.

"Tell me, Owen," he said, "as you're a philosopher—tell me what difference the faults of good men make in our estimate of them?"

"In our real estimate," said Owen, "I fancy we often adopt, half unconsciously, the maxim, that 'the king can do no wrong'— that the true hero is all heroic."

"Yes," said Kennedy; "but when some one calls your attention to the fact of their failings, and makes you look at them—what then?"

"Why, in nine cases out of ten the faults are grossly exaggerated and misrepresented, and I should try to prove that such is the fact; and for the rest,—why, no man is perfect."

"You shirk the question, though," said Lillyston; "for you have to make very tremendous allowance indeed for some of the very best of men."

As, for instance?

"As, for instance, king David."

"Oh, don't take Scripture instances," said Suton, an excellent fellow whom they all liked, though he took very different views of things from their own.

"Why not, in heaven's name?" said Kennedy; "if they suit, they are good because so thoroughly familiar."

"Yes, but somehow one judges them differently."

"I daresay you do,—in fact I know you do; but you've no business to. I maintain that even according to Moses, king David deserved a felon's death. Murder and adultery were crimes every bit as heinous then as they are now. Yet David, this most human of heroes, was the man after God's own heart. Solve me the problem."

"Practically," said Lillyston; "I believe one follows a genuine instinct in determining not to look at the spots, however wide or dark they are, upon the sun."

"And in accepting theoretically old Strabo's grand dictum, ouch oion agathon genesthai poieeteen mee pzotezon geneethenta anoza agathon. Eh?"

"As Coleridge was so fond of doing," said Julian.

"Ay, he needed the theory," said Suton.

"Hush!" said Julian, "I can't stand any such Philadelphus hints about Coleridge. By the bye, Owen, you might have quoted a still more apt illustration from Seneca, who criticises Livy for saying 'Vir ingenii magni magis quam boni' with the remark, 'Non potest illud separari; aut et bonum erit aut nec magnum.'"

Mr Admer, who was one of the circle, chuckled inwardly at the discussion. "I was once," he said, "at a party where a lady sang one of Byron's Hebrew melodies. At the close of it a young clergyman sighed deeply, and with an air of intense self-satisfaction, observed, 'Ah! I was wondering where poor Byron is now!' What should you have all said to that?"

"Detesting Byron's personal character, I should have said that the very wonder was a piece of idle and meddling presumption," said Owen.

"And I should have answered that the Judge will do right," said Suton reverently.

"Or if he wanted a text, 'Who art thou that judgest another?'" said Lillyston contemptuously.

"And I," said Julian, should have said,—

> "Let feeble hands iniquitously just,
> Rake up the relics of the sinful dust,
> Let Ignorance mock the pang it cannot heal,
> And Malice brand what Mercy would conceal;—
> It matters not!"

"And I," said Kennedy, "should have been vehemently inclined to tweak the man's nose."

"But what did you say, Mr Admer?" asked Lillyston.

"I answered a fool according to his folly. I threw up my eyes and said, 'Ah, where, indeed! What a good thing it is that you and I, sir, are not as that publican.'"

"I should think he skewered you with a glance, didn't he?" said Kennedy.

"No, he was going to bore me with an argument, which I declined."

"But you've all cut the question: tell me now, supposing you had known king David, should you have thought worse of him, should you have been cool to him—in a word, should you have cut him after his fall?"

"I think not—I mean, I shouldn't have cut him," said Owen.

"And yet you would have treated so any ordinary friend."

"Not necessarily. But remember that the two best things happened to David which could possibly happen to a man who has committed a crime."

"Namely?"

"Speedy detection," said Lillyston.

"And prompt punishment," added Julian; "but for these there's no knowing what would have become of him."

Unsatisfactory as the discussion had been, yet those words rang hauntingly in Kennedy's ears; he could not forget them. During all those first days of happy travel they were with him; with him as they strolled down the gay and lighted Boulevards of Paris; with him beside the quaint fountains of Berne; and the green rushing of the Rhine at Basle; with him amid the scent of pine-cones, and under the dark green umbrage of forest boughs; with him when he caught his first glimpse of the everlasting mountains, and plunged into the clear brightness of the sapphire lake—the thought of speedy detection and prompt punishment. It was no small pleasure to partake in Violet's happiness, and mark the ever fresh delight that lent such a bright look to Cyril's face; but before Kennedy in the midst of enjoyment, the memory of a dishonourable act started like a spectre, and threw a sudden shadow on his brow. He felt its presence when he saw the sun rise from Rigi; it stood by him amid the wreathing mists of Pilatus; it even checked his enthusiasm as they gazed together on the unequalled glories spread beneath the green summit of Monterone, and as their graceful boat made ripples on the moonlit waves of Orta and Lugans. In a word, the conviction of weakness was the only alloying influence to the pleasure of his tour, the one absinthe-drop that lent bitterness to the honeyed wine. It was not only the consciousness of the wrong act and its possible results, but horror at the instability of moral principle which it showed, and a deep fear lest the same weakness should prove a snare and a ruin to him in the course of future life.

CHAPTER SIXTEEN

A DAY OF WONDER

> "Flowers are lovely. Love is flowerlike,
> Friendship is a sheltering tree;
> O the joys that came down showerlike
> With virtue, truth, and liberty,
> When I was young."

> *Coleridge*

"To-morrow, then, we are all to ascend the Schilthorn," said Mr Kennedy, as he bade good-night to the merry party assembled in the salle à manger of the chalet inn at Mürrem.

"Or as high as we ladies can get," said Mrs Dudley.

"Oh, we'll get you up, aunt," said Kennedy; "if Julian and my father and I can't get you and Miss Home and Eva up, we're not worth much."

"To say nothing of me" said Cyril, putting his arms akimbo, with a look of immense importance.

"Breakfast, then, at five to-morrow morning, young people," said Mr Kennedy, retiring; and full of happy anticipations they went off to bed.

Punctually at five they were all seated round the breakfast-table, eagerly discussing the prospects of the day.

"I say, did any of you see the first sunbeam tip the Jungfrau this morning?" said Kennedy. "It looked like—like—what did it look like, Miss Home?"

"Like the golden rim of a crown of pearls," said Violet, smiling. "And did you see the morning star, shining above the orange-coloured line of morning light, over the hills behind us, Eva? What did that remind you of?"

"Oh, I can't invent poetic similes," answered Eva. "I must take refuge in Wordsworth's—

> "'Sweet as a star when only one
> Is shining in the sky.'"

"Yes," said Julian; "or Browning's—

"'One star—the chrysolite!'"

"Hum!" said Cyril, who had been standing impatiently at the door during the colloquy; "when you young ladies and people have done poetising, etcetera, the guide's quite ready."

"Come along, then; we're soon equipped," said Violet, adjusting at the looking-glass her pretty straw hat, with its drooping feather, and the blue veil tied round it.

"I say, Miss Kennedy—bother take it though, I can't always be saying Miss Kennedy—it's too long. I shall call you Eva—may I?" said Cyril.

"By all means, if you like."

"Well, then, Eva, the guide is such a rum fellow; he looks like a revived mummy out of—out of Palmyra," said he, blundering a little in his geography.

"Mummy or no," said Julian, "he'll carry all our provisions and plaids to-day up to the top, which is more than most of your A Cs would do."

"A C—what does that mean?" asked Violet. "One sees it constantly in the visitors' books."

"Don't you know, Vi?" said Cyril. "It stands for athletic climber."

"Alpine Club, you little monkey," said Kennedy, throwing a fir-cone at him. "You'll be qualified for the Alpine Club, Miss Home, before the day's over, I've no doubt."

"No," said Julian, "they want 13,000 feet, I believe, and the Schilthorn is only 9,000."

"Nearly three times higher than Snowdon; only fancy!" said Cyril.

Meanwhile the party had started with fair weather, and in high spirits. The guide, with the gentlemen's plaids strapped together, led the way cheerily, occasionally talking his vile patois with Julian and Mr Kennedy, or laughing heartily at Cyril's "bad language"—for Cyril, not being strong in German, exercised a delightful ingenuity in making a very few words go a very long way. Kennedy walked generally with Eva and Violet, while Julian often joined them, and Cyril, always with some new scheme in hand, or some new fancy darting through his brain, ran chattering, from one group to another, plucking bilberries and wild strawberries in handfuls, and trying the merits of his alpenstock as a leaping-pole.

The light of morning flowed down in an ever-broadening river, and peak after peak flashed first into rose, then into crimson, and then into golden light, as the sun fell on their fields of snow; high overhead rose Alp after Alp of snow-white and luminous cloud, but the flowing curves of the hills themselves stood unveiled, with their crests cut clearly on the pale, divine, lustrous blue of heaven, and our happy band of travellers gazed untired on that glorious panorama of glistering heights from the towering cones of the Eiger and the Moench to the crowding precipices of the Ebenen-fluen and the Silberhorn. Deep below them, in the valley, "like handfuls of pearl in a goblet of emerald," the quiet châlets clustered over their pastures of vivid grass, and gave that touch of human interest which alone was wanting to complete the loveliness of the scene.

Every step brought them some new object to gaze upon with loving admiration; now the gaunt spurs of some noble pine that had thrust his gnarled roots into the crevices of rock to look down in safety on the torrent roaring far below him, and now the track of a chamois, or the bright black eyes of some little marmot peering from his burrow on the side of a sunny bank, and whistling a quick alarm to his comrades at their play.

"What an extraordinary howl," said Cyril, laughing, as the guide whooped back a sort of jodel in answer to a salute from the other side of the valley.

"It's very harmonious—is it not?" said Violet.

"Yes, that's one of the varieties of the Ranz des Vaches," said Kennedy.

"And why do they shout at each other in that way?"

"Because the mountains are lonely, Cyril, and the shepherds don't see human faces too often; so men begin to feel like brothers, and are glad to greet each other in these silent hills."

"Did you hear how the mountain echoed back his cry?" said Eva; "it sounded like a band of elves mocking at him."

"Yes, you'll hear something finer directly; the guide told me he was going to borrow an alpen-horn at one of these châlets, and then you'll discover for the first time what echo can do."

In a few minutes the guide appeared with the horn, and blew. Heavens! what a melody of replications! How in the hollows of the hills every harsh tone died away, and all the softer notes flowed to and fro in tenderest music, and fainted in distant reverberations more and more exquisite, more and more exquisitely low. Can it be a mere echo of those rude blasts? It seemed as though some choir of spirits had caught each tone as it came from the peasant's horn, and had deified it there among the clouds, and had repeated it over and over with divinest variations, to show man how crabbed were the sounds which he produced, and yet how ravishing they might one day become, when to the symphony of silver strings they rang out amid the seraph harps and choral harmonies of heaven. All the party stood still in rapturous attention, and even Cyril forgot for ten minutes his frolicsome and noisy mirth.

Reader, have you ever seen an Alpine pasture in warm July at early morning? If not, you can hardly conceive the glorious carpet over which the feet of the wanderer in Switzerland press during summer tours. Around them as they passed the soft mosses glowed with gold and crimson, and the edges of the lady's-mantle shimmered with such diamonds and pearls as never adorned a lady's mantle yet. Everywhere the grass was vivid with a many-coloured tissue of dew-dropped flowers: pale crocuses, and the bright crimson-lake carnation, and monk's-hood, and crane's-bill, and aster alpinus, and the lovely myosotis, and thousands of yellow and purple flowers, nameless or lovelier than their names, were the tapestry on which they trod; and it was interwoven through warp and woof with the blue gleam of a myriad harebells. At last they came to the cold region of those delicate nurslings of the hills, the gentianellas and gentians. Kennedy, who had been keenly on the look out, was the first of the party to find the true Alpine gentian, and instantly recognising it, ran with it to Violet and his sister.

"There," he said, "the first Alpine gentian you ever saw. Did you ever know real blue in a flower before? Doesn't it actually seem to shed a blue radiation round it?"

"How perfectly beautiful!" said Violet; "see, Eva, how intense blue and green seem to be shot into each other, or to play together like the waters of a shoaling sea."

"Shall I take a root or two?" said Kennedy.

"Not the slightest use," said Julian; "they only grow at certain elevations, and would be dead before you got down."

"Isn't it strange, Violet, that Nature should fling such a tender and exquisite gem so high up among these awful hills, where so few eyes see them?"

"Just look," said Julian, "how the moss and the grass seem to be illuminated with them, as though the heavens were golden, and stars in it were of blue."

While they talked, Cyril dashed past them with all the ardour of a young entomologist in full chase of a little mountain-ringlet, which he soon caught and pinned on the top of his straw hat. In a few minutes more he had added a great fritillery to his collection, and it gave him no trouble to pick out the finest of the superb lazy-flying Apollos, which quickly shared the same fate.

"Here's another for you, Cyril," said Eva, pointing to a gorgeous peacock-butterfly which had settled amicably by a bee on the pink-and-downy coronet of a great thistle.

113

"Oh, I don't want that; one can get it any day in England; here though, look at this lovely burnet-moth," he cried, as the blue-and-red-winged little creature settled on the same thistle-head.

"What a shame to disturb that beautiful Psyche," said Julian, as Cyril dashed his cap over the prey, and the peacock fluttered off; "it was enjoying itself so intensely in the sunshine, opening and shutting its wings in unmitigated contentment." But Cyril had secured his moth without heeding the remark, and was now twenty yards ahead.

A sudden roar of sound stopped him, and he waited to ask the rest, "if they had heard the thunder?"

"It wasn't thunder, but the rush of an avalanche," said Kennedy; "there, you may see it still on the side of the Jungfrau."

"What, those little white streaks, which look like a mountain torrent?"

"Yes."

"And can those threads of snow make all that row?"

"You must remember that the threads of snow are five miles off, and are perhaps thousands of tons in weight."

By this time they had reached the part of the mountain where the climb became really toilsome, and they settled down into the steady pace, which the Swiss guides always adopt because they know that it is the quickest in the long run. And at this point Mr Kennedy and Mrs Dudley left them, preferring, like sensible old people, to stroll back in quiet, and avoid an exertion which they found too fatiguing. They knew that they could safely entrust the party to the care of Julian and the guide. The ladies often needed help, and there seemed to be something very pleasant to Kennedy in the light touch of Violet's hand, for he lent her his arm or his alpenstock oftener than was absolutely required. They only stopped once more to quench their thirst at a streamlet which was rushing impetuously down the rocks, and a little below them foamed over the precipice into a white and noisy cataract.

"I never noticed water before falling from such a height," said Julian; "it looks exactly like a succession of white comets plunging through the sky in a crowd."

"Or a throng of white-sheeted ghosts hurrying deliriously through the one too-narrow entrance of the lower world," said Kennedy. "Doesn't it remind one of Schiller's line—

"'Und es wallet und liedet und brauset und Pikcht?'"

"I admire the rainbow most, which over-arches the fall, and plays into light, or dies away as the sunbeams touch the foam," said Violet.

"Doesn't it remind you of Al-Sirat's arch, Miss Home?" asked Kennedy.

"Haven't the pleasure of that gentleman's acquaintance," observed Cyril.

"Nor I," said Kennedy; "but Al-Sirat's arch is the bridge—narrow as the edge of a razor, or the thread of an attenuated spider—which is supposed to span the fiery abyss, over which the good skate into Paradise, while the bad topple over it. Don't you remember Byron's lines about it in the Giaour?

> "'Yea, Soul, and should our prophet say
> That form was nought but breathing clay,
> By Alla! I would answer nay;
> Though on Al-Sirat's arch I stood,
> That topples o'er the fiery flood,
> With Paradise within my view,
> And all its Houris beckoning through.'

"Pretty nearly the only lines of Byron I know." Somehow Kennedy was looking at Violet while he repeated the lines.

A few minutes more brought them on to the great field of snow, through which they toiled along laboriously, treading as much as possible in the footsteps of the guide.

"This isn't a glacier, is it?" asked Cyril.

"Oh dear, no! If it were, you wouldn't find it such easy walking, for it would be full of hidden crevasses, and we should have to march much more carefully, occasionally poking our feet through the snow that lightly covers a fathomless depth."

"Yes, you must have read in Murray that eerie story of the guide that actually tumbled, though not very deep, into the centre of the glacier, and found his way back to light down the bed of a sub-glacial torrent, with no worse result than a broken arm."

"There is a still eerier story, though, of two brothers," said Kennedy, "of whom one fell into a crevasse, and was caught on a ledge some fifty feet down, where he could be actually seen and heard."

"Did he ever get out?" asked Violet.

"Yes; the guide went back four hours' walk, and brought ropes and assistance just before dark, and meanwhile the other brother waited anxiously by the side of the crevasse, talking, and letting down brandy and other things to keep the poor fellow alive. He did escape, but not without considerable risk of being frozen to death."

Beguiling the way with talk, they at last got over the tedious climb, and reached the summit. Eva and Violet were very tired, but the difficult and eager air of the icy mountain-top was exhilarating as new wine, and the provisions they had brought with them reinvigorated them completely. To hungry and thirsty climbers black bread and vin ordinaire taste like nectar and ambrosia. The day was cloudless, the view unspeakably magnificent, and Cyril's high spirits were contagious. They lingered long before they began the descent, and laughingly pooh-poohed the guide's repeated suggestion that it was getting late.

"I bet you Kennedy has been writing poetry," said Cyril; "do make him read it, Julian."

"Hear, hear!" said all in chorus, and Julian with playful force possessed himself of the pocket-book, while Kennedy, only asseverating that the verses were addressed to nobody in particular, fled from the sound of his own lyrics, which Julian proceeded to read.

> "Rose-opals of the sunlit hills
>   Are flashing round my lonely way,
> And cataracts dash the rushing rills
>   To plumes of glimmering spray.
> But mountain-streams and sunny gleams
>   Are not so dear to me,
> As dawning of the golden love
>   My spirit feels for thee!
>
> "Their diamond crowns and giant forms,
>   The lordly hills upraise;
> Nor rushing winds nor shattering storms
>   Can shake their solid base:
> Though Europe rests beneath their crests,
>   And empires sleep secure,
> Less firm their bases than my love,
>   Their snow less brightly pure."

"There, rubbish enough," said Kennedy, returning and snatching away the pocket-book before Julian could read another verse. "'Like coffee made without trouble, drunk without regret,' as the Monday Oracle, with its usual exquisite urbanity, observed of a recent poet."

"Of course addressed quite to an imaginary object, Eddy," said Eva, while Violet looked towards the hills, and hoped that the glow which covered her fair face might be taken for a reflection of the faint tinge that already began to fall over the distant ridges of pale snow.

116

"We really must come away," said Julian; "it'll be sunset very soon, and then we shall have to climb down nearly in the dark."

So they left the ridge, and while Kennedy and Cyril, amid shouts of laughter, glissaded gallantly over the slopes of snow, Julian and the guide conducted the girls by a method less rapid, but more secure. Arrived at the rocks, Cyril went forward with the guide, Julian followed with Eva, and Kennedy with Violet led up the rear.

Why did they linger so long? Violet was tired, no doubt, but could she not have walked as fast as Eva, or was Kennedy's arm less stout than Julian's? She lingered, it seemed, with something of a conscious pleasure, now to pluck a flower or a fern, now to look at some yellow lichens on the purple crags; and once, when Julian looked back, the two were some way behind the rest of the party. They were standing on a rock gazing on the fading splendour of the mountains in front of them, while the light wind that had risen during the sunset, flung back his hair from his forehead, and played with one golden tress which had strayed down Violet's neck. He shouted to them to make haste, and they waved their hands to him with a gay salute. Thinking that they would soon overtake him, he pressed forward with Eva, and did not look back again.

While Kennedy walked on with Violet in silence more sweet than speech, they fell into a dreamy mood, and wandered on half-oblivious of things around them, while deeper and deeper the shades of twilight began to cast their gloom over the hills.

"Look, Violet, I mean Miss Home; the moon is in crescent, and we shall have a pleasant night to walk in; won't it be delightful?"

"Yes," she murmured; but neither of them observed that the clouds were gathering thick and fast, and obscured all except a few struggling glimpses of scattered stars.

They came to a sort of stile formed by two logs of wood laid across the gap in a stone wall, and Kennedy vaulting over it, gave her his hand.

"Surely," she said, stopping timidly for a moment, "we did not pass over this in coming, did we?"

Kennedy looked back. "No," he said, "I don't remember it; but no doubt it has been put up merely for the night to prevent the cattle from going astray."

They went forward, but a deeper and deeper misgiving filled Violet's mind that they had chosen a wrong road.

"I think," she said with a fluttered voice, "that the path looks much narrower than it did this morning. Do you see the others?"

They both strained their eyes through the gloom, now

117

rendered more thick than ever by the dark driving clouds, but they could see no trace of their companions, and though they listened intently, not the faintest sound of voices reached their eager ears.

They spoke no word, but a few steps farther brought them to a towering rock around the base of which the path turned, and then seemed to cease abruptly in a mass of loose shale. It was too clear now. They had lost their road and turned, whilst they were indulging those golden fancies, into a mere cattle-path worn by the numerous herds of goats and oxen, the music of whose jangling bells still came to them now and then in low sweet snatches from the pastures of the valley and hill.

What was to be done? They were alone amid the all but unbroken silence, and the eternal solitudes of the now terrible mountain. The darkness began to brood heavily above them; no one was in sight, and when Kennedy shouted there was no answer, but only an idle echo of his voice. Sheets of mist were sweeping round them, and at length the gusts of wind drove into their faces cold swirls of plashing rain.

"Oh, Mr Kennedy, what can we do? Do shout again."

Once more Kennedy sent his voice ringing through the mist and darkness, and once more there was no answer, except that to their now excited senses it seemed as if a scream of mocking laughter was carried back to them upon the wind. And clinging tightly to his arm, as he wrapped her in his plaid to shelter her from the wet, she again cried, "Oh, Edward, what must we do?"

Even in that fearful situation—alone on the mountain, in the storm,—he felt within him a thrill of strength and pleasure that she called him Edward, and that she clung so confidingly upon his arm.

"Dare you stay here, Violet," he asked, "while I run forward and try to catch some glimpse of a light?"

"Oh, I dare not, I dare not," she cried; "you might miss your way in coming back to me, and I should be alone."

He saw that she loved him; he had read the secret of her heart, and he was happy. Passionately he drew her towards him, and on her soft fragrant cheek—on which the pallor of dread had not yet extinguished the glow which had been kindled by the mountain wind—he printed a lover's kiss; but in maidenly reserve she drew back, and was afraid to have revealed her secret, and once more she said, "Oh, Mr Kennedy, we shall die if we stay here unsheltered in this storm."

As though to confirm her words, the thunder began to growl, and while the sounds of it were beaten back with long loud hollow buffetings from the rocks on every side, the blue and winged flash of lightning glittered before their eyes, cleaving a rift with dazzling and vivid intensity amid the purple gloom.

"Stay here but one instant, Violet—Miss Home,"—he said; "I will climb this rock to see if any light is near, and will be with you again in a moment."

He bounded actively up the rock, reckless of danger, and gazed from the summit into the night. For a second, another flash of lightning half blinded him with its lurid glare, but when he was again accustomed to the darkness, he saw a dull glimmer in the distance, and supposing it to come from the hotel, sprang down the rock again to Violet's side.

"This way," he said, "dear Violet; I see a light, and from the direction of it I think it must be from our hotel. Keep up courage, and we shall soon reach it."

Dangerous as it was to hurry over the wet and slippery shale, and down the steep sides of the rugged hill, Kennedy half drew, half-carried her along with swift steps towards the place from which the dim light still seemed to allure them by its wavering and uncertain flicker.

CHAPTER SEVENTEEN

A NIGHT OF TERROR

"For the strength of the hills we bless Thee,
Our God, our Father's God;
Thou hast made our spirits mighty,
By the touch of the mountain sod!"

Hemans

"Here you all are, then," said the cheerful voice of Mr Kennedy, as Julian, Eva, and Cyril, followed by the guide, entered the little Mürrem Inn.

"Here are three of us," answered Julian; "haven't Edward and Violet arrived? Not having seen them for the last half-hour, I fancied they must have got before us by some short cut."

"No, they've not come yet. Fortunately for you, Eva, Aunt

119

Dudley is very tired and has gone to bed," he said laughing, "otherwise you would have got a scolding for not taking better care of Violet."

"Oh, then, they must be close behind somewhere for certain," said Julian; "they could not have missed the path—it lay straight before us the whole way."

"Well, I hope they'll be in soon, for it begins to look lowering. I've ordered tea for you; make haste and come down to it. You're ready for tea, Cyril, I have no doubt."

"Rather!" said Cyril, reviving; for fatigue had made him very quiet during the last half-hour. And, indeed, the tempting-looking display on the table, the bright teapot, and substantial meal, and amber-coloured honey, would have allured a more fastidious appetite.

They ran up-stairs to make themselves comfortable before having tea and retiring to bed, and on re-entering the warm and glowing room, their first question was, "Have they come?"

"No," said Mr Kennedy, anxiously, and even the boy's face grew grave and thoughtful as Julian rose from the tea-table and said, "I must go and search for them."

He seized his straw hat, put on his boots again, and ran out, calling on the guide to accompany him. They took out with them a lighted torch, but it was instantly extinguished by the streaming rain. Julian and the guide shouted at the top of their voices, but heard no sound in reply; and the darkness was now so intense, that it was madness to proceed farther amid that howling storm.

They ran back to the inn, where the rest sat round the table, pale and trembling with excessive fear. In reply to their hasty questions, Julian could only shake his head sorrowfully.

"The guide says that in all probability they must have been overtaken by the storm, and have run to some chalet for refuge. If so, they will be safe and well-treated till the morning."

"You children had better go to bed," said Mr Kennedy to Eva and Cyril, who reluctantly obeyed. "You cannot be of any help, and directly the storm begins to abate, Julian and I will go and find the others."

"Oh, papa," sobbed Eva; "poor Eddy and Violet! What will become of them? Perhaps they have been struck by the lightning."

"They are in God's hand, dearest," he said, tenderly kissing her tearful face, "as we all are. In His hand they are as safe as we."

"In God's hand, dear Eva," said Julian, as he bade her good-night. "Go to sleep, and no doubt they will be here safe before you awake."

"I shall not sleep, Julian," she whispered; "I shall go and pray for their safety. Dear, dear Eddy and Violet."

Cyril lingered in the room.

"Do let me stay up with you, Julian. I couldn't sleep—indeed, I couldn't; and I might be of some use when morning comes, and when you go to look for them. Do let me stay, Julian."

Julian could not resist his brother's wish, though Mr Kennedy thought it best that the boy should go to bed.

So they compromised matters by getting him to lie down on the sofa, while they sat up, and stared out of the windows silently into the rain. How wearily the time goes by when you dread a danger which no action can avert.

Meanwhile the objects of their anxiety had hurried up to the light, and found that it came from the ragged windows of an old tumble-down tenement, built of pine-boards which the sun had dried and charred, until they looked black and stained and forbidding. Going up the rotten wooden steps to the door, and looking through the broken windows, Kennedy saw two men seated, smoking, with a flaring tallow candle between them.

"Must we go in there?" asked Violet; and Kennedy observed how her arm and the tones of her voice were trembling with agitation.

"Isn't it better than staying out in this dreadful storm?" said Kennedy. "The Swiss are an honest people, and I daresay these are herdsmen who will gladly give us food and shelter."

Their voices had roused the inmates of the châlet, and both the men jumped up from their seats, while a large and fierce mastiff also shook himself from sleep, and gave a low deep growl.

Kennedy knocked at the door. A gruff voice bade him enter; and as he stepped over the threshold, the dog flew at him with an angry bark. Violet uttered a cry of fear, and Kennedy struck the dog a furious blow with the knobbed end of his alpenstock, which for the moment stunned the animal, while it drew down on the heads of the tired and fainting travellers a volley of brutal German oaths.

"Can you give us shelter?" said Kennedy, who spoke German with tolerable fluency. "We have lost our way, and cannot stay out in this storm."

The man snarled an affirmative, and Violet observed with a shudder that he was an ill-looking, one-eyed fellow, with villainy stamped legibly on every feature. The other peasant looked merely stolid and dirty, and seemed to be little better than a cretin, as he sat heavily in his place without offering to stir.

"Can't you give us some food, or at any rate some milk?—we have been to the top of the Schilthorn, and are very tired."

The man brought out a huge coarse wooden bowl of goat's milk, and some sour bread; and feeling in real need of food, they

121

tried to eat and drink. While doing so, Kennedy noticed that Violet gave a perceptible start and looking up, observed the one eye of their grim entertainer intently fixed on the gold watch-chain which hung over his silk jersey. He stared the man full in the face, finished his meal, and then asked for a candle to show the lady to her room.

"No light but this," said the Cyclops, as Kennedy mentally named him.

"Then you must lend me this."

And taking it without more ado, he went first to the cupboard from which the milk had been produced, where seeing another dip, he coolly took it, lighted it, and pushed open the creaking door which opened on the close, damp closet which the man had indicated as the only place where Violet could sleep.

This room opened on another rather larger; and here, putting the candle on the floor, for the room, (if room it could be called), was destitute of all furniture, he spread his plaid on the ground over some straw, and said—

"Try to sleep here, Miss Home, till morning. I will keep watch in the outer room."

He shut the door, went back to the two men, looked full at them both, and leaving them their candle, returned to the closet, where, fastening the door with his invaluable alpenstock, he sat on the ground by the entrance of Violet's room. He heard her murmuring words of prayer, and knew well that she could not sleep in such a situation; but he himself determined to sit in perfect silence, to keep watch, and to commend himself and her, whom he now knew that he loved more than himself, in inward supplication to the merciful protection of their God and Father.

He felt a conviction that they had fallen into bad hands. The man's anger had first been stirred by the severe wound which Kennedy had in self-defence inflicted on the dog, and now there was too much reason to dread that his cupidity had been excited by the sight of the gold chain, and by Violet's ornaments, which gave promise that he might by this accident gain a wealthy prize.

After an interval of silence, during which he perceived that they listened at his door, and were deceived by his measured breathing into a notion that he was asleep, he noticed that they put out the candle, and continued to whisper in low thick voices. He was very very weary, his head nodded many times, and more than once he was afraid that sleep would overcome him, especially as he dared not stir or change his position; but the thought of Violet's danger, and the blaze of the lightning mingled with the yell of the wind kept him watchful, and he spent the interminable moments in thinking how to act when the attack came.

122

At last, about an hour and a half after he had retired, he heard the men stir, and with a thrill of horror he detected the sound of guns being loaded. Violet's candle was yet burning, as he perceived by the faint light under her door, so he wrote on a leaf of his pocketbook in the dark, "Don't be afraid, Violet, whatever you may hear; trust in God," and noiselessly pushed it under the crevice of the door into her room.

The muffled footsteps approached, but he never varied the sound of his regular breathing. At last came a push at the door, followed by silence, and then the whisper, "he has fastened it." Still he did not stir, till he observed that they were both close against the door, and were preparing to force it open. Then guided by a swift instinctive resolution, he determined to trust to the effects of an unexpected alarm. Noiselessly moving his alpenstock, he suddenly and with all his force, dashed the door open, shouted aloud, and with his utmost violence swung round the heavy iron spike. A flash, the report of a gun, and a yell of anguish instantly followed; and as Violet in terror and excitement threw open her door, the light which streamed from it showed Kennedy in a moment that the foremost villain, startled by the sudden opposition, had accidentally fired off his gun, of which the whole contents had lodged themselves in the shoulder of his comrade.

This second man had also armed himself with a chamois-gun, which slipped out of his hands as he fell wounded to the ground. Springing forward Kennedy wrenched it out of his relaxing grasp, and presented it full at the head of the other, who, half-stunned with the blow he had received from the heavy iron-shod point of the ashen alpenstock, was crouching for concealment in the corner of the chalet.

"Violet," he said, "all is now safe. These wretches are disarmed; if you like to take shelter here till the morning, I can secure you from any further attack. If you stir but an inch," he continued, addressing the unwounded man, "I will shoot you dead. Lay down your gun."

The man's one eye glared with rage and hatred, but Kennedy still held the loaded gun at his head, and he was forced sullenly to obey. Kennedy put his foot upon the gun, and was in perplexity what to do next, fearing that the wounded murderer, who was moaning heavily, might nevertheless spring at him from behind, and also momentarily dreading an attack from the mastiff, who kept up a sullen growl.

"Let us leave this dreadful place," said Violet, who, pale but undaunted at the horrors of the scene, had taken refuge by Kennedy's side.

"Dare you pick up and carry the gun?" he asked. "It would be dangerous to leave it in their hands."

Violet picked it up, where it lay under his feet, and then glided rapidly out of the châlet, while Kennedy slowly followed, never once taking his eye from his crouching antagonist. Before he stepped into the open air, he said to the men, "If I hear but one footstep in pursuit of us, I will shoot one of you dead."

"Oh, what a relief to be on the mountain-turf once more!" said Violet in a low and broken whisper, as she grasped Kennedy's arm, and he cautiously led her down a rude path, which was faintly marked a few hundred yards from the lonely cottage where they had been. "Are we safe now, do you think?"

"Yes, quite safe, Violet, I trust. They will not dare pursue me, now that their guns are gone, and I have this loaded one in my hand."

"Dear brave Mr Kennedy. How shall I ever thank you enough for having saved my life so nobly? If you had not been so strong and watchful, we should both have now been killed."

"I would die a thousand deaths," he whispered, "to save you from the least harm, Violet. But you are tired, you must rest here till the dawn. Sit under this rock, dearest, and cover yourself with my plaid. I will keep watch still."

She sat down wearily, and her head sank upon the rock. The storm was over: the thunder was still muttering like a baffled enemy in the distance, but the wind after its late fury was sobbing gently and fitfully like a repentant child. The rock gave her shelter, and after her fatigue and agitation she was sleeping peacefully, while Kennedy bowed down his head, and thanked God for the merciful protection which He had extended to them.

He had not been seated long when his eye caught the light of torches, being waved at a distance in the direction of the hotel. In an instant, he felt sure that Julian was come out to search for them, and gently awakening Violet, he told her with a thrill of joy that help was at hand. The torches drew nearer the place where they were seated, and he raised a joyous shout. As yet they were too far off to hear him, but suddenly it occurred to him to fire his gun. The flash and echoing report attracted their notice; the torches grew rapidly nearer; he could almost see the dark figures of those who carried them; and now in answer to his second shout came the hurried sound of familiar voices, and in five minutes more Julian and his father had grasped him by the hands, and Cyril had flung his arms round Violet's neck.

And now at last Kennedy gave way to his emotion, and his highly-wrought feelings found relief in a burst of passionate tears. It

124

was no time for questionings. Julian passed his arm round his sister's waist, and, aided by Mr Kennedy, half-carried her to their hotel. Kennedy leaned heavily on the guide's arm; the honest landlord, who accompanied the searching party, carried the plaid, the alpenstock, and one of the guns, and Cyril, impressed by the strange scene, carried the other gun, full of wondering conjecture what Kennedy could have been doing with it, and from whence it could have come.

And when Violet reached Eva's room, in which she slept, she could only say, as they sat locked in a long embrace:—

"Dearest Eva, it is only through Edward that my life has been saved."

Eva had never before heard Violet call her brother by his name, and she was glad at heart.

CHAPTER EIGHTEEN

THE ALPEN-GLUHEN

"And, last of all,
Love, like an Alpine harebell, hung with tears,
By some cold morning glacier."

The Princess

Violet's fluttered nerves and wearied frame rendered it necessary for the party of English travellers to stay for a few days at Mürrem, and afterwards it was decided that they should all go down to Grindelwald, and spend there the remainder of the time which they had set apart for the Swiss tour. The landlord of the Jungfrau treated them with the utmost consideration, and amused Kennedy by paying him as much deference as if he had been Tell or Arnold himself. Leaving in his hands all endeavours to discover the two scoundrels, who had entirely decamped, Kennedy gave him one of the guns, while he carried with him the other to keep as a trophy in his rooms at Camford.

There are few sights more pleasant than that of two families bound together by the ties of friendship and affection, and living together as though they were all brothers and sisters of a common

125

home. For long years afterwards the Homes and the Kennedys looked back on those days at Grindelwald as among the happiest of their lives, and, indeed, they glided by like a dream of unbroken pleasure. How is it that there can be such a thing as ennui, or that people ever can be at a loss what to do? In the morning they took short excursions to the glaciers or the roots of the great mountains, and Cyril made adventurous expeditions with his fishing-rod to the mountain-streams. And at evening they sat in the long twilight in the balcony of their room, while Eva and Violet sang them sweet, simple English songs, which rang so softly through the air, that the crowd of guides and porters which always hang about a Swiss hotel used to gather in the streets to listen, and the English visitors collected in the garden to catch the familiar tones. Julian and Kennedy always gave some hours every day to their books, and Cyril, though he could be persuaded to do little else, spent some of his unemployed time on his much-abused holiday task for the ensuing quarter at Marlby.

And when the candles were lit, the girls would sketch or work, and Julian or Kennedy would read or translate to them aloud. Sometimes they spent what Mr Kennedy used to call "an evening with the immortals," and taking some volume of the poets, would each choose a favourite passage to read aloud in turn. This was Mr Kennedy's great delight, and he got quite enthusiastic when the well-remembered lines came back to him with fresh beauty, borne on the pleasant voices of Eva, Julian, or Cyril, like an old jewel when new facets are cut on its lustrous surface.

"Stop there; that's an immortal, lad—an immortal," he would say to Cyril, when the boy seemed to be passing over some flower of poetic thought without sufficient admiration; and then he would repeat the passage from memory with such just emphasis, that on these evenings all felt that they were laying up precious thoughts for happy future hours.

"Now, Mrs Dudley, and you young ladies, we're going to translate you part of a Greek novel to-night," said Julian.

"A Greek novel!" said Cyril, with a touch of incredulous suspicion. "Those old creatures didn't write novels, did they?"

"Only the best novel that ever was written, Cyril."

"What's it called?"

"The Odyssey."

"Oh, what a chouse! You don't mean to call that a novel, do you?"

"Well, let the ladies decide."

So he read to them how Ulysses returned in the guise of a beggar, after twenty years of war and wandering to his own palace-door, and saw the haughty suitors revelling in his halls; and how, as he reached the door, Argus, the hunting-dog, now old and neglected, and full of fleas, recollected him, when all had forgotten him, and fawned upon him, and licked his hand and died; and how the suitors insulted him, and one of them threw a foot-stool at him, which by one quick move he avoided, and said nothing, and another flung a shin-bone at his head, which he caught in his hand, and said nothing, but only smiled grimly in his heart—ever so little, a grim, sardonic smile and how the old nurse recognised him by the scar of the boar's tusk on his leg, but he quickly repressed the exclamation of wonderment which sprang to her lips; and how he sat, ragged but princely, by the fire in his hall, and the red light flickered over him, and he spake to the suitors words of solemn warning; and how, when Agelaus warned them, a strange foreboding seized their souls, and they looked at each other with great eyes, and smiled with alien lips, and burst into quenchless laughter, though their eyes were filled with tears; and how Ulysses drew his own mighty bow, which not one of them could use, and how he handled it, and twanged the string till it sang like a swallow in his ear, and sent the arrow flying with a whiz through the twelve iron rings of the line of axes; and then, lastly, how, like to a god, he leapt on his own threshold with a shout, and gathered his rags about him, and aided by the young Telemachus and the divine Swineherd, sent hurtling into the band of wine-stained rioters the swift arrows of inevitable death.

Pleased with the tale, which the girls decided, in spite of Cyril's veto, to be a genuine novel, they asked for a new Greek romance, and Julian read to them from Herodotus about the rise and fall of empires, and "Strange stories of the deaths of kings." One of his stories was the famous one of Croesus, and the irony of his fate, and the warning words of Solon, all of which, rendered into quaint rich English, struck Cyril so much, that, mingling up the tale with reminiscences of Longfellow's "Blind Bartimeus," he produced, with much modesty at the breakfast-table next morning, the following very creditable boyish imitation:—

"Speak Grecia's wisest, thou, 'tis said,
Full deeply in Life's page hast read,
And many a clime hath known my tread;
    Tis pantoon olbiotatos?

"The monarch raised his eager eye,
Gazed on the sage exultingly,
And slow came forth the calm reply
    Tellos ho Atheenaios.

"Upon his funeral pyre he lay
Crownless, his sceptre passed away,
The shade of Solon seem to say,
    oudeis toon zoontoon holbios.

"How little thought that Grecian sage
Those words should live from aye to aye,
    Tis pantoon olbiotatos?
    Tellos ho Atheenaios,
    oudeis toon zoontoon holbios."[1]

In a manner such as this the summer hours glided happily away. But all things, happy or mournful, must come to an end, lest we should forget God in our prosperity, or curse Him in our despair. Too quickly for all their wishes their last Sunday in Switzerland had come. Most of them had spent the day in thoughtful retirement or quiet occupations, and both morning and evening they assembled together in their pleasant sitting-room for matins and evensong. Their thoughts were full of the coming separation, and it gave a deep interest to these last services; for the Homes, unwilling to leave their mother and Frank so long alone at Ildown, were to start for England on the following day, and the Kennedys intended to visit Chamounix for two weeks more.

On the Sunday evening they strolled down to the glacier to look once again, for the last time, into its crevices, and wonder at its fairy caverns, fringed with icicles, like rows of silver daggers, and ceiled with translucent sapphire, beneath whose blue fretwork the stray sunbeams lost their way amid ice-blocks of luminous green, and pillars of lapis-lazuli and crystal. They sat on a huge boulder of granite, which some avalanche had torn down, and tumbled from the mountain's side, and there enjoyed the icy wind which tempered the warm evening air, as it swept over the leaping waves of the glacier stream.

"What a mixture of terror and beauty these monstrous glaciers are," said Julian; "crawling down the valleys, and shearing away the solid rocks before them like gigantic ploughshares."

"Yes," said Eva. "When you look up at the tumbled pinnacles of those séracs, does it not seem as if Summer had rent in anger with some great ice-axe the huge enemy whom she could not quite destroy?"

"And see," said Mr Kennedy, "how Nature gets out of these terrible heaps of shattered ice both use and beauty; and since she

---

[1] These verses were really written by a boy of fourteen.

128

must leave them as the eternal fountains of her rivers, see how she tinges them with her loveliest blue."

They talked on until it was time to return, but Violet and Kennedy still lingered, sitting on the vast boulder, under pretence of seeing the sunset.

"Well, don't get lost again, that's all," said Cyril sagely.

"Oh no, we shall be back very soon," answered Violet, but she felt instinctively that the "very soon" in time might measure an eternity of emotion.

Need we say that Kennedy and Violet had, since that night of wild adventure, loved each other, hour by hour, with deeper affection? He was young, and brave, and light-hearted, and of a pleasant countenance; and she was a young, and confiding, and graceful, and lovely girl, and they were drawn to one another with a love which absorbed all other thoughts, and overpowered all other considerations; and it was unspeakable happiness for each to know how lovely were all their acts, and how dear were all their words in the other's eyes. And now that the time was come to declare the love in words, and ratify it by a plighted troth, there was something in the act so solemn as almost to disturb their dream of a lover's paradise.

They sat silent on the rock until the sun had set behind the peaks of snow, and their eyes were filled with idle yet delicious tears. Ripples of luminous sunshine, and banks of primrose-coloured cloud still lingered on the path which the sun had traversed, and, when even these began to fade, there stole along the hill crests above them a film of tender colour, flinging a veil of the softest carnation over their cold grey rocks, and untrodden fields of perpetual snow.

"Look, Violet, at that rose-colour on the hills; does it not seem as it rests on those chill ledges, as though Nature had said that her last act to-day should be a triumph of glory, and her last thought a thought of love?"

Violet murmured an assent.

"Oh, Violet," he continued, "you know that I love you, and I know that you love me;—is it not so, Violet?"

He hardly heard the "Yes," which came half like a sigh from her lips.

"Violet, dear Violet, we part to-morrow; let me hear you say 'Yes' more clearly still."

"You know I love you, Edward—did you not save my life?"

"I know you love me," he repeated slowly, "but, oh Violet, I am not worthy of you—I am not all you think me." There passed over his fair forehead the expression of humiliation and pain which she had seen there with wonder once or twice before.

129

"You are good and noble, Edward," she answered; "I see you to be good and noble, or I could not love you as I do."

"No," he said, "alas! not good, not noble, Violet—in no wise worthy of one so pure, and bright, and beautiful as you are." He bent his face over her hand, and his warm tears fell fast upon it. "But," he continued, "I will strive to be so hereafter, Violet, for your sweet sake. Oh, can you take me as I am? Will you make me good and noble, Violet, as Julian is? Can you let the sunshine of your life fall on the shadow of mine?"

She did not understand his passion as he raised to her his face, not bright and laughing as it generally was, but stained with the traces of many tears; she only knew that he had won her whole heart, and for one moment she let her hand rest in the curls of the head which he had bent once more.

"Oh, Violet," he said, looking up again, "I can be anything if you love me." In an instant the cloud had passed away from his face, and the old sunshine brightened his blue eyes. For one instant their eyes met with that lustrous and dewy love-gleam that only lovers know, but during that instant it seemed as if their souls had flowed together into a common fount. With a happy look she suffered him to take her hand, and draw off from her finger a sapphire ring; this he put on his own finger, while on hers he replaced it by the gold-set ruby, his mother's gift, which he usually wore.

The crescent moon had risen as they walked home, and they found the rest of the party seated in the hotel garden, under her soft silver light; but nobody seemed to be much in a mood for talking, until that little monkey Cyril, who observed everything, exclaimed—

"Why, Julian, do look; Violet has got Kennedy's ring on, and—well, I declare if he hasn't got hers."

"Let us all come up-stairs," said Kennedy hastily and then, before them all, he drew Violet to his side, and said—

"Julian, Violet and I are betrothed to each other."

"As I thought," said Julian with a smile, as a rush of sudden emotion made his eyes glisten, and he warmly grasped Kennedy's hand.

"And as I hoped, Julian," said Mr Kennedy, as he turned away to wipe his spectacles, which somehow had grown dim.

The moonlight streamed over them as the two stood there together, young, happy, hopeful, beautiful, and while Cyril held Kennedy's hand, Eva and Violet exchanged a sister's kiss.

And Julian looked on with a glow of happiness—happiness that had one drawback only—a passing shadow of sorrow for the possible feelings of De Vayne.

130

CHAPTER NINETEEN

ONLY A BLUSH

"Erubuit! salva res est!"

Plautus

Back from the glistening snow-fields, where every separate crystal flashes with a separate gleam of light—back from the Alpine pastures, embroidered with their tissue of innumerable flowers, over which, like winged flowers, the butterflies flutter continually—back from the sunlit silver mantle of the everlasting hills, and the thunder of the avalanche, and the wild leap of the hissing cataract—back to the cold grey flats and ancient towers of Camford, and the lazy windings of the muddy Iscam, and the strife and struggle of a university career.

Kennedy arrived at Camford at mid-day, and as but few men had yet come up, he beguiled the time by going out to make the usual formal call on his tutor. As he passed the door of the room where temptation had brought on him so many heavy hours, he could hardly repress an involuntary shudder; but on the whole, he was in high spirits, and Mr Grayson received him with something almost approaching to cordiality.

"You did very well in the examination, Mr Kennedy; very well indeed. With diligence you might have been head of your year—as it was, you were in the first ten."

"Was Owen head of the year, sir?"

"No, Home was head; his brilliant composition, and thorough knowledge of the books, brought him to the top. Either he or Owen were first in all the papers except one."

"Which was that, sir?"

"The Aeschylus paper, in which you were first, Mr Kennedy; you did it remarkably accurately. If you had seen the paper, you could hardly have done it better."

"Indeed! Would you give me a library order, sir?" said Kennedy, rising abruptly, to change the subject. Mr Grayson was offended at this sudden change of subject, and, silently writing the order, bade Kennedy a cold "good morning." All that Kennedy hoped was that he would not tell others as well as himself, the odious fact of his success.

The thought damped his spirits, but he shook it off. The novelty of returning as a junior soph, the pleasure of meeting the familiar faces once more, the consciousness of that bright change of existence, which, during the past vacation, had bound the golden thread of Violet's destiny with his, filled him with inward exultation. And then there was real delight in the warmth with which he was greeted by all alike.

He found himself, very unexpectedly, a hero in the general estimation. The romantic adventure on the Schilthorn had been rumoured about among the numerous English visitors to the Valley of Lauterbrunnen, until it had reached the editor of a local paper, and so had flowed through Galignani into the general stream of the English journals. True, the names had been suppressed, but all the Saint Werner's men knew who was intended by "Mr K dash y," and as he entered the hall there was a murmur of applause.

He was greeted on all sides with eager questions.

"I say, Mr K dash y," said one, "did the fellow whom you shot die of his wound?"

"It was rather a chouse to shoot a cretin, though," said another, in chaff.

"I didn't shoot him," said Kennedy.

"No, you very leerily managed to make the other fellow shoot him. Preserve me from my friends, must have been his secret reflections."

"Have you kept the guns, Kennedy? You must let me have a look after hall."

While this kind of talk was going on, Brogten, who was nearly opposite to Kennedy, sat silent, and watched him.

He did not join in the remarks about the night adventure in Switzerland, but when there was a slight pause in the fire of questions, he turned the conversation to the subject of the May examination.

"Those are not your only triumphs, Kennedy, it appears. You seem to have been doing uncommonly well in the examination, too."

"Oh aye, you were in the first ten," said Suton; "Mr Grayson told me so."

"Who was first?" asked Lillyston.

"Oh, Home of course; except in one paper, and Kennedy was first in that."

"I believe that was the Aeschylus paper," said Brogten, throwing the slightest unusual emphasis into his tone; "you were first in that, weren't you, Kennedy?"

The men were surprised to hear Brogten address him with such careless familiarity, knowing the old quarrel that existed between them; and they were still more surprised to hear Brogten interest himself about a topic usually so indifferent to him as the

132

result of an examination. It seemed particularly strange that he should give himself any trouble to inquire about the present list, because he himself had been posted, in company with Hazlet and Lord Fitzurse, i e, their names had been written up below the eighth class, as "unworthy to be classed."

"Was I?" said Kennedy in the most careless tone he could assume.

"Yes—really, didn't you know it? You did it so well that Grayson said, you couldn't have done the paper better if you had seen it beforehand."

"I say, Kennedy, you must have come out swell, then," said D'Acres, "for Grayson said just the same thing to me."

"How very odd," said Brogten, affectedly. "You didn't see the papers beforehand, Kennedy—did you?"

The last few moments had been torture to Kennedy; he had moved uneasily; the bright look of gratified triumph, which the allusions to his courage had called forth, had gone out the moment the examination was mentioned, and it was only by a painful and violent exercise of the will that he was able to keep back the blood which had begun to rush towards his cheeks. In the endeavour to check or suppress the blush, he had grown ashy pale; but now that Brogten's dark and cruel eye was upon him—now that the protruding underlip curled with a sneer that left no more room to doubt that he was master of Kennedy's guilty secret—the effort was useless, and spite of will, the burning crimson of an uncontrollable shame burst and flashed over Kennedy's usually clear and open face. It was no ordinary blush—no common passage of colour over the cheeks. Over face, and neck, and brow the guilty blood seemed to be crowding tumultuously, and when it had filled every vein and fibre till it swelled, then the rich scarlet seemed to linger there as though it would never die away again, and if for an instant it began to fade, then the hidden thought sent new waves of hot agony in fresh pulses to supply its place. And all the while the conscious victim made matters worse by his attempts to seem unconcerned, until his forehead was wet with heavy perspiration. By that time the men had turned to other topics, and were talking about Bruce's laziness, and the utter manner in which he must have fallen off for his name to appear, as it had done, in the second class; and, in course of time, Kennedy's face was as pale and cold as it before had burned and glowed.

And all this while, though he would not look—though he looked at his plate, and at the busts over his head, and the long portraits of Saint Werner's worthies on the walls, and on this side and on that—Kennedy knew full well that Brogten's eye had been on him from beginning to end, and that Brogten was enjoying, with devilish malignity, the sense of power which he had gained from the knowledge of another's sin. The thought was intolerable to him, and, finishing his dinner with hasty gulps, he left the hall.

"Brogten, how rude you were to Kennedy," said Lillyston.

"Was I?" said Brogten, in a tone of sarcasm and defiance.

"No wonder he blushed at your coarse insinuations."

"No wonder," said Brogten, in the same tone; "am I the only person who makes coarse insinuations, as you call them?"

"It is just like you to do so."

"Is it? Oh well, I shall have to make some more, perhaps, before I have done."

"Well, you'd better look out what you say to Kennedy, at any rate. He is a fiery subject."

"Thank you, I will."

This wrangling was very unprofitable, and Lillyston gladly dropped it, not however without feeling somewhat puzzled at the air which Brogten assumed.

That night Kennedy was sitting miserably in his room alone; he had refused all invitations, and had asked nobody to take tea with him. He was just making tea for himself, when Brogten came to see him.

"May I stay to tea?" he asked, in mock humility.

"If you like," said Kennedy.

He stayed to tea, and talked about all kinds of subjects rather than the one which was prominent in the thoughts of both. He told Kennedy old Harton stories, and asked him about Marlby; he turned the subject to Home, and really interested Kennedy by telling him what kind of a boy Julian had been, and what inseparable friends he had always been with Lillyston, and how admirably he had recited on speech-day, and how stainless his whole life had been, and how vice and temptation seemed to skulk away at his very look.

"You are reconciled to him, then," said Kennedy in surprise.

"Oh, yes. At heart, I always respected him. He wasn't a fellow to take the worst view of one's character, you know, or to make nasty innuendoes—" He stopped, and eyed Kennedy as a parrot eyes a finger put into his cage, which he could peck if he would. "He wasn't, you know, a kind of fellow who would force you to leave the table by sneering at you in hall—" He still continued to eye Kennedy, but in vain, for Kennedy kept his moody glance on the table and was silent, and would not look at him or speak to him. Brogten could not help being struck with his appearance as he sat there motionless,— the noble and perfectly formed head, the well-cut features, the

134

cheek a little pale now, so boyishly smooth and round, the latent powers of fire and sarcasm and strength in the bright eye and beautiful lip. It was a base source of triumph that made Brogten exult in the knowledge that this youth was in his power; that he held for a time at least the strings of his happiness or misery; that at any time by a word in any public place he could bring on his fine features that hue of shame; that for his own purposes he could at any time ruin his reputation, and put an end to his popularity.

Not that he intended to do so. He had the power, but unless provoked, he did not wish or mean to use it. It was far more luxurious to keep it to himself, and use it as occasion might serve. Everybody's secret is nobody's secret, and it was enough for Brogten to enjoy privately the triumph he had longed for, and which accident had put into his hands.

"Come, come, Kennedy," he said, "this is nonsense; we understand each other. I saw you coolly read over the whole examination-paper, you know, which wasn't the most honourable thing in the world to do—"

He paused and half relented as he saw a solitary tear on Kennedy's cheek, which was indignantly brushed away almost as soon as it had started.

"Come," he said, "cheer up, man. I'm not going to tell of you; neither Grayson nor any of the men shall know it, and at present not a soul has a suspicion of such a thing except ourselves. Come—I've had my triumph over you, for your sharp words in hall last term, before all the men, and that's all I wanted. Don't let's be enemies any longer. Good-night."

But Kennedy sat there passively, and when Brogten had gone away whistling "The Rat-catcher's Daughter," he leant his head upon his hand, and his thoughts wandered away to Violet Home.

O holy, ennobling, purifying love! He felt that if he had known Violet before, he should not now have been in Brogten's power. He fancied that the secret had oozed out; he fancied that men eyed him sometimes with strange glances; he pictured to himself the degradation he should feel if Julian, or De Vayne, or Lillyston ever knew of what weakness he was capable. This one error rode like a night-mare on his breast.

But none of his gloomy presentiments on the score of detection were fulfilled. Except to Bruce, and that under pledge of secrecy, Brogten never betrayed what he knew, and the only immediate way in which he exercised the influence which his knowledge gave him, was by claiming with Kennedy a tone of familiarity, and asking him to card parties, suppers, and idle riots of all kinds, in which Bruce and Fitzurse were frequent visitors.

135

CHAPTER TWENTY

BRUCE THE TEMPTER

"Oui autrefois; mais nous avons changé tout cela."

Molière

Bruce was disgusted with his second class in the Saint Werner's May examination. He had quite flattered himself that he could not fail to be among the somewhat large number who annually obtained the pleasant and easy distinction of a first. He had not been nearly so idle as men supposed, although he had managed to waste a large amount of time; and if he could have foreseen that his name would only appear in the Second class, he would have endeavoured to be lower still, so as to make it appear that he had not condescended to give a thought to the subject. As it was, he hoped that if he got a first, men would remark, "Clever fellow that Bruce! Never opened a book, and yet got a first class;" whereas now he knew that the general judgment would be, "Bruce can't be half such a swell as one fancied. He's only taken a second."

His vanity was wounded, and he determined to throw up reading altogether. "What good would it do him to grind? His father was rolling in money, and of course he should cut a very good figure in London when he had left Camford, which was a mere place for crammers and crammed, etcetera."

So Bruce became more and more confirmed as a trifler and an idler, and he suffered that terrible ennui, which dogs the shadow of wasted time. Associating habitually with men who were his inferiors in ability, and whose tastes were lower than his own, the vacuity of mind and lassitude of body, which at times crept over him, were the natural assistants of every temptation to extravagance, frivolity, and sin.

An accidental conversation gave a mischievous turn to his idle propensities. Coming into hall one evening, he found himself seated next to Suton, and observing from the goose on the table, and the audit ale which was circling in the loving cup that it was a feast, he turned to his neighbour, and asked:—

"Is it a saint's-day to-day?"

"Yes," said Suton, "and the most memorable of them all—All Saints' Day."

"Oh, really," said Bruce with an expression of half

136

contemptuous interest, "then I suppose chapel's at a quarter past six, and we shall have one of those long winded choral services."

"Don't you like them?"

"Like them? I should think not! Since one's forced to do a certain amount of chapels, the shorter they are the better."

"Of course, if you regard it in the light of 'doing' so many chapels, you won't find it pleasant."

"Do you mean to tell me now," said Bruce, turning round and looking full at Suton, "that you regard chapels as anything but an unmitigated nuisance?"

"Most certainly I do mean to tell you so, if you ask me."

"Ah! I see—a Sim!" said Bruce, with the slightest possible shrug of the shoulders.

"I don't know what you mean by a 'Sim,' Mr Bruce," said Suton, slightly colouring; "but whether a Sim or not, I at least expect to be treated as a gentleman."

"Oh, I beg pardon," said Bruce; "but I couldn't help recognising the usual style of—"

"Of cant, I suppose you would say. Thank you. You must find it a cold faith to disbelieve in all sincerity."

"Well, I don't know. At any rate, I don't believe that all your saints put together were really a bit better than their neighbours; so I can't get up an annual enthusiasm in their honour. All men are really alike at the bottom."

"Nero's belief," said Owen, who had overheard the conversation.

"It doesn't matter whether it was Nero's or Neri's or Neander's," answered Bruce; "experience proves it to be true."

Suton had finished dinner, and as he did not relish Bruce's off-hand and patronising manner, he left the discussion in Owen's hand. But between Owen and Bruce there was an implacable dissimilarity, and neither of them cared to pursue the subject.

Bruce, who went to wine with D'Acres, repeated there the subject of the conversation, and found that most of his audience affected to agree with him. In fact, he had himself set the fashion of a semi-professed infidelity; and amid his most intimate associates there were many to adopt with readiness a theory which saved them from the trouble and expense of a scrupulous conscience. With Bruce this infidelity was rather the decay of faith than the growth of positive disbelief. He had dipped with a kind of wilful curiosity into Strauss's Life of Jesus, and other books of a similar description, together with such portions of current literature as were most clever in sneering at Christianity, or most undisguised in rejecting it.

Such reading—harmless, or even desirable, as it might have

been to a strong mind sincere in its search for truth, and furnished with that calm capacity for impartial thought which is the best antidote against error—was fatal to one whose superficial knowledge and irregular life gave him already a powerful bias towards getting rid of everything which stood in the way of his tendencies and pursuits. Bruce was not in earnest in the desire for knowledge and wisdom: he grasped with avidity at a popular objection, or a sceptical argument, without desiring to understand or master the principles which rendered them nugatory; and he was ignorant and untaught enough to fancy that the very foundations of religion were shaken if he could attack the authenticity of some Jewish miracle, or impugn the genuineness of some Old Testament book.

When all belief was shaken down in his shallow and somewhat feeble understanding, the structure of his moral convictions was but a baseless fabric. Error in itself is not fatal to the inner sense of right; but Bruce's error was not honest doubt, it was wilful self-deception, blindness of heart, first deliberately induced, then penally permitted.

In Bruce's character there was not only the error in intellectu, but also the pertinacia in voluntate. All sense of honour, all delicacy of principle, all perception of sin and righteousness, all the landmarks of right and wrong, were obliterated in the muddy inundation of flippant irreverence and ignorant disbelief.

> "For when we in our viciousness grow hard,
> O, misery on't! the wise gods seal our eyes:
> In our own filth drop our clear judgments, make us
> Adore our errors, laugh at us while we strut
> To our confusion."

"I'm sometimes half inclined to agree with what you were saying about would-be saints," said Brogten, as they left D'Acres' wine-party.

"What fun it would be to try the experiment of a saint's peccability on some living subject," said Bruce.

"Rather! Suppose you try on that fellow Hazlet?"

"Oh, you mean the lank party who snuffles the responses with such oleaginous sanctimony. Well, I bet you 2 to 1 in ponies that I have him roaring drunk before a month's over."

"I won't take the bet," said Brogten, "because I believe you'll succeed."

"I'll t–t–take it for the fun," said Fitzurse.

"Done, then!" said Bruce.

138

So Bruce, pour passer le temps, deliberately undertook the corruption of a human soul. That soul might have been low enough already; for Hazlet was, as we have seen, mean-hearted and malicious, and in him, although unknown to himself, the garb of the Pharisee but concealed the breast of the hypocrite. But yet Hazlet was free, and if Bruce had not undertaken the devil's work, might have been free to his life's end, from all gross forms of transgression—from all the more flagrant and open delinquencies that lay waste the inner sanctities of a fallen human soul.

He was an easy subject for Bruce's machinations, and those machinations were conceived and carried on with consummate and characteristic cleverness. Bruce did not spread his net in the sight of the bird, but set to work with wariness and caution. He determined to try the arts of fascination, not of force. The thought of the desperate wickedness involved in his attempt either never crossed his mind, or, if it did, was rejected as the feeble suggestion of an over-scrupulous conscience. Bruce pretended at least to fancy that the basis of all men's characters was identical, and that, as they only differed in external manifestations, it made very little difference whether Hazlet became "fast" or continued "slow." "Fast" and "slow" were the mild euphemisms with which Bruce expressed the slight distinction between a vicious and a virtuous life.

At hall—the grand place for rencontres—he managed to get a seat next to his victim, and began at once to treat him with that appearance of easy and well-bred familiarity which he had learnt in London circles. He threw a gentle expression of interest into his face and voice, he listened with deference to Hazlet's remarks, he addressed several questions to him, thanked him politely for all his information, and then adroitly introduced some delicate compliments on the agreeableness of Hazlet's society. His bait took completely; Hazlet, whom most men snubbed, was quite flustered with gratified vanity at the condescending notice of so unexceptionable a man of fashion as the handsome and noted Vyvyan Bruce. "At last," thought Hazlet, "men are beginning to appreciate my intellectual powers."

After continuing this process for some days, until Hazlet was unalterably convinced that he must be a vastly agreeable and attractive person, Bruce asked him to come to breakfast, and invited Brogten and Fitzurse to meet him. He calculated justly that Hazlet, accustomed only to the very quiet neighbourhood of a country village, would be duly impressed with the presence and acquaintance of a live lord; and he instructed both his guests in the manner in which they should treat the subject of their experiment. Hazlet thought he had never enjoyed a breakfast party so much.

There was a delicious spice of worldliness in the topics of conversation which was quite refreshing to him, accustomed as he was to the somewhat droning moralisms of his "congenial friends." Nothing which could deeply shock his prejudices was ever alluded to, but the discussions which were introduced came to him with all the charm of novelty and awakened curiosity.

Hazlet never could endure being a silent or inactive listener while a conversation was going forward. No matter how complete his ignorance of the subject, he generally managed to hazard some remarks. Bruce talked a good deal about actors and theatres, and Hazlet had never seen a theatre in his life. He did not like, however, to confess this fact, and, after a little hesitation, began to talk as if he were an habitué. The dramatic criticisms, which he occasionally saw in the papers, furnished him with just materials enough to amuse Bruce and the others at his assumption of "savoir vivre," and to furnish a laugh at his expense the moment he was gone; but of this he was blissfully unconscious, and he rather plumed himself on his knowledge of the world. He had yet to learn the lesson that consistency alone can secure respect. He had indeed ventured at first to remark, "Don't you think the stage a little—just a little—objectionable?"

"Objectionable," said Bruce, with a bland smile; "oh, my dear fellow, what can you mean? Why, the stage is a mirror of the world, and to show virtue her own image is one of its main objects."

"Yes," said Hazlet, "I am inclined to think so. I should like to see a theatre, I confess."

He had let slip unintentionally the implied admission that he had never been to a theatre; but when Fitzurse asked in astonishment, "What, have you never been to a theatre?" he merely replied, "Well, I can hardly say I have; at least not for a long time."

"Oh, then we must all run down to London some night very soon," said Bruce, "and we'll go together to the Regent."

"But I've no friend in London, except—except a clergyman or two, who perhaps might object, you know."

"Oh, never mind the clergymen," said Bruce; "you shall all come and stay with me at Vyvyan House."

Here was a triumph!—to go to the celebrated Vyvyan House, and that in company with a lord, and to be a partaker of Bruce's hospitality! Of course it would be very rude and wrong to refuse so eligible an invitation. How pleasant it would be to remark casually at hall-time, "I'm just going to run down for the Sunday to Vyvyan House with Bruce and Lord Fitzurse!"

"Let me see," said Bruce, "to-day's Monday; supposing you

140

come to wine with me on Thursday, and then we'll see if we can't manage to get to London from Saturday to Monday."

"Thursday—I'm afraid I've an engagement on Thursday to—"

"To what?" asked Bruce.

The more Hazlet coloured and hung back, the more Bruce, in his agreeable way, pressed to know, till at last Hazlet, unable to escape such genial importunity, reluctantly confessed that it was to a prayer-meeting in a friend's rooms.

"Oh," said Bruce, with the least little laugh, "tea and hassocks, eh?" He said no more, but the little, scornful laugh, and the few scornful words had done their work more effectually than a volume of ridicule. It need not be added that Hazlet came, not to the prayer-meeting, but to the wine-party. Cards were introduced in the evening, and one of the players was Kennedy. Kennedy played often now, but he certainly did feel a qualm of intense and irrepressible disgust as, with great surprise, he found himself vis à vis with the spectacled visage of Jedediah Hazlet.

"But how shall I get my exeat to go to London?" said Hazlet.

"Oh, say a particular friend has invited you to spend the Sunday with him. Say you want to hear Starfish preach."

Mr Norton, Hazlet's tutor, who did not expect him to fall into mischief, and thought that very likely Mr Starfish's eloquence might be the operating attraction, granted him the exeat without any difficulty, and on Saturday Hazlet was reclining in a first-class carriage, with Bruce, Brogten, and Fitzurse, on his way to Vyvyan House. A change was observable in his dress. Bruce had hinted to him that his usual garb might look a little formal and odd at a theatre, and had persuaded him to come to his own egregious Camford tailor, Mr Fitfop, who, as a particular favour to his customer Bruce, produced with suspicious celerity the cut-away coat and mauve-coloured pegtops, in which unwonted splendour Hazlet was now arrayed. It was a pity that his ears were so obturated with vanity as not to have heard the shrieks of half-stifled laughter created by his first public appearance in this fashionable guise, which only required to be completed by the death's-head pin with which Bruce presented him, (and which therefore he was obliged to wear), to make it perfect.

The sumptuous and voluptuous richness of all the appointments in Vyvyan House introduced Hazlet to a new world. Sir Rollo and Lady Bruce were not in town, so that the four young men had the house entirely to themselves, and Bruce ordered about the servants with royal energy. Soon after their arrival they sat down to a choice dinner, and Bruce took care, although the champagne had been abundant at dinner, to pass pretty freely, at dessert, the best claret and amontillado of his father's cellars. Hazlet was not slow to follow the example which the others set him; he helped himself plentifully to everything, and after dinner, lolling in an easy attitude, copied from Fitzurse, he even ventured to exhibit his very recently acquired accomplishment of smoking a weed. Very soon he imagined that he had quite made an impression on the most fashionable members of the Saint Werner's world.

They went to the Regent, and between the acts, Bruce, who knew everything, introduced them behind the scenes. Hazlet, rather amazed at his own boldness, but in reality entirely ignorant which way to turn, necessarily followed his guides, and, exultant with the influence of mellow wine, imitated the others, and tried to look and feel at home. Within a month of Bruce's manipulation this excellent and gifted young man, this truly gracious light in the youthful band of confessors, was seated, talking to a fascinating young danseuse who wore a gossamer dress, behind the scenes of a petty London theatre. Bruce looked on with a smile, and hummed to himself—

"Jene Tänzerinn
Fliegt, mit leichtem Sinn
Und noch leichtern Kleide
Durch den Saal der Freude
Wie ein Zephyr bin, etcetera."

The head of Jedediah Hazlet was somewhat confused, when, after the play and an oyster supper in the cider cellars, it sank deep into the reposeful down of a spare chamber in the gay Sir Rollo Bruce's London house.

The next morning was Sunday. They none of them got up till twelve to a languid breakfast, and then read novels. Hazlet, who was rather shocked at this, did indeed faintly suggest going to church. "Oh yes," said Bruce, looking up with a smile from his Balzac, "we'll do that, or some other equally harmless amusement." The dinner hour, however, coincided with the time of evening service, so that it was impossible to go then, and finally they spent the evening in what they all agreed to call "a perfectly quiet game at cards."

CHAPTER TWENTY ONE

ONE OF THE SIMPLE ONES

"I tempted his blood and his flesh,
Hid in roses my mesh,
Choicest cates, and the flagon's best spilth."

Robert Browning

"Faugh," said Bruce, on his return to Camford, "that fellow Hazlet isn't worth making an experiment upon—in corpore vili truly; but the creature is so wicked at heart, that even his cherished traditions crumble at a touch. He's no game; he doesn't even run cunning."

"Then I hope you'll p–p–pay me my p–p–p–ponies," said Fitzurse.

"By no means; only I shall cut things short; he isn't worth playing; I shall haul him in at once."

Accordingly, Hazlet was invited once more to one of Bruce's parties—this time to a supper. It was one of the regular, reckless, uproarious affairs—D'Acres, Boodle, Tulk, Brogten, Fitzurse, were all there, and the élite of the fast fellow-commoners, and sporting men besides. Bruce had privately entreated them all not to snub Hazlet, as he wanted to have some fun. The supper was soon despatched, and the wine circled plentifully. It was followed by a game of cards, during which the punch-bowl stood in the centre of the table, rich, smoking, and crowned with a concoction of unprecedented strength. Hazlet was quite in his glory. When they had plied him sufficiently—which Bruce took care to do by repeatedly replenishing his cup on the sly, so that he might fancy himself to have taken much less than was really the case—they all drank his health with the usual honours:

"For he's a jolly good fe–el–low.
For he's a jolly good fe–el–low,
For he's a jolly good fe–el–l–ow—
Which nobody can deny,
Which nobody can deny;
For he's a jolly good fe–el–low," etcetera.

And so on, ad infinitum, followed by "Hip! hip! hip! hurrah! hurrah!! hurrah!!!" and then the general rattling of plates on the table, and breaking of wine-glass stems with knives of "boys who crashed the glass and beat the floor."

Hazlet was quite in the seventh heaven of exaltation, and made a feeble attempt at replying to the honour in a speech; but he was in so very oblivious and generally foolish a condition, that, being chiefly accustomed to Philadelphus oratory, he began to address them as "My Christian Friends;" and this produced such shouts of boisterous laughter, that he sat down with his purpose unaccomplished.

Before the evening was over, Bruce, in the opinion of all present, including Fitzurse himself, had fairly won his bet.

"I shan't mind p–p–paying a bit," said the excellent young nobleman; "it's been such r–r–rare f–f–fun."

Rare fun indeed! The miserable Hazlet, swilled with unwonted draughts, lay brutally comatose in a chair. His head rolled from side to side, his body and arms hung helpless and disjointed, his eyelids dropped—he was completely unconscious, and more than fulfilled the conditions of being "roaring drunk!"

Now for some jolly amusement—the opportunity's too good to be lost! What exhilaration there is on seeing a human soul imbruted and grovelling hopelessly in the dirt or rather to have a body before you, without a soul for the time being—a coarse animal mass, swinish as those whom the wand of Circe smote, but with the human intelligence quenched besides, and the charactery of reason wiped away. Here, some ochre and lamp-black, quick! There— plaster it well about the whiskers and eyelids, and put a few patches on the hair! Magnificent!—he looks like a Choctaw in his war-paint, after drinking fire-water.

Screams of irrepressible laughter—almost as ghastly, (if the cause of them be considered), as those that might have sounded round a witch's cauldron over diabolical orgies—accompanied the whole proceeding. So loud were they that all the men on the stair-case heard them, and fully expected the immediate apparition of some bulldog, dean, or proctor. It was nobody's affair, however, but Bruce's, and he must do as he liked. Suton, who "kept" near Bruce, was one of those whom the uproar puzzled and disturbed, as he sat down with sober pleasure to his evening's work. His window was opposite Bruce's, and across the narrow road he heard distinctly most of what was said. The perpetual and noisy repetition of Hazlet's name perplexed him extremely, and at last he could have no doubt that they were making Hazlet drunk, and then painting him; nor was it less clear that many of them were themselves half intoxicated.

It had of course been impossible for Suton and others of

similar character to avoid noticing the eccentricities of dress, and manner which had been the outward indications of Hazlet's recent course. When a man who has been accustomed to dress in black, and wear tail coats in the morning, suddenly comes out in gorgeous apparel, and begins to talk about cards, betting and theatres, his associates must be very blind, if they do not observe that his theories are undergoing a tolerably complete revolution. Suton saw with regret mingled with pity, Hazlet's contemptible weakness, and he had once or twice endeavoured to give him a hint of the ridicule which his metamorphosis occasioned; but Hazlet had met his remarks with such silly arrogance, nay, with such a patronising assumption of superiority, that he determined to leave him to his own experiences. This did not prevent Suton from feeling a strong and righteous indignation against the iniquity of those who were inveigling another to his ruin, and he felt convinced that, as at this moment Hazlet was being unfairly treated, it was his duty in some way to interfere.

He got up quietly, and walked over to Bruce's rooms. His knock produced instant silence, followed by a general scuffle as the men endeavoured to conceal the worst signs of their recent outrage. When Suton opened the door, he was greeted with a groan of derision.

"Confound you," said Bruce, "I thought it must be the senior proctor at the very least."

Without noticing his remark, Suton quietly said, "I see, Bruce, that you have been treating Hazlet in a very unwarrantable way; he is clearly not in a fit condition to be trifled with any more; you must help me to take him home."

"Ha! ha! rather a good joke. I shall merely shove him into the street, if I do anything. What business has he to make a beast of himself in my rooms?"

"What business have you to do the devil's work, and tempt others to sin? You will have a terrible reckoning for it, even if no dangerous consequences ensue," said Suton sternly.

"C–c–c–cant!" said Fitzurse.

"Yes—what you call cant, Fitzurse. You shall hear some more, and tremble, sir, while you hear it," replied Suton, turning towards him, and raising his hand with a powerful but natural gesture; "it is this 'Woe unto him that giveth his neighbour drink, that putteth thy bottle to him, and makest him drunken also—thou art filled with shame for glory.'"

"Bruce," said D'Acres, the least flushed of the party, "I really think we ought to take the fellow home. Just look at him."

Bruce looked, and was really alarmed at the grotesque yet

145

ghastly expression of that striped and sodden face, with the straight black hair, and the head lolling and rolling on the shoulder. Without a word, he took Hazlet by one arm, while Suton held the other, and D'Acres carried the legs, and as quickly as they could they hurried along with their lifeless burden to the gates of Saint Werner's. It was long past the usual hour for locking up, and the porter took down the names of all four as they entered. A large bribe which D'Acres offered was firmly, yet respectfully refused, and they knew that next day they would be called to account.

Having put Hazlet to bed they separated; Suton bade the others a stiff "Good-night;" and D'Acres as he left Bruce, said, "Bruce, we have been doing a very blackguard thing."

"Speak for yourself," said Bruce.

"Good," said D'Acres, "and allow me to add that I have entered your rooms for the last time."

Next morning Suton spoke privately to the porter, and told him that it would be best for many reasons not to report what had taken place the night before, beyond the bare fact of their having come into college late at night. The man knew Suton thoroughly and respected him; he knew him to be a man of genuine piety, and the most regular habits, and consented, though not without difficulty, to omit all mention of Hazlet's state. All four had of course to pay the usual gate fine, and D'Acres and Bruce were besides "admonished" by the senior Dean, but Suton and Hazlet were not even sent for. The Dean knew Suton well, and felt that his character was a sufficient guarantee that he had not been in any mischief; Hazlet had been irregular lately, but the Dean considered him a very steady man, and overlooked for the present this breach of rules.

Of course all Saint Werner's laughed over the story of Hazlet's escapade. He did not know how to avoid the storm of ridicule which his folly had stirred up. He had already begun to drop his "congenial friends" for the more brilliant society to which Bruce had introduced him, and so far from admitting that he felt any compunction, he professed to regard the whole matter merely as "an amusing lark." Bruce and the others hardly condescended to apologise, and at first Hazlet, who found it impossible at once to remove all traces of the paint, and who for a day or two felt thoroughly unwell, made a half-resolve to resent their coolness. But now, deserted by his former associates, and laughed at by the majority of men, he found the society of his tempters indispensable for his comfort, and even cringed to them for the notice which at first they felt inclined to withdraw.

"Wasn't that trick on Hazlet a disgraceful affair, Kennedy?" said Julian, a few days after. "Some one told me you were at the supper party; surely it can't be true."

"I was for about an hour," said Kennedy, blushing, "but I had left before this took place."

"May I say it, Kennedy?—a friend's, a brother's privilege, you know—but it surprises me that you care to tolerate such company as that."

"Believe me, Julian, I don't enjoy it."

"Then why do you frequent it?"

Kennedy sighed deeply and was silent for a time; then he said—

> "Not e'en the dearest heart, and next our own,
> Knows half the reasons why we smile or sigh."

"True," said Julian; for he had long observed that some heavy weight lay on Kennedy's mind, and with deep sorrow noticed that their intercourse was less cordial, less frequent, less intimate than before. Not that he loved Kennedy, or that Kennedy loved him less than of old, for, on the contrary, Kennedy yearned more than ever for the full cherished unreserve of their old friendship; but, alas there was not, there could not be complete confidence between them, and where there is not confidence, the pleasure of friendship grows dim and pale. And, besides this, new tastes were growing up in Edward Kennedy, and, by slow and fatal degrees, were developing into passions.

Hazlet had come to Camford not so much innocent as ignorant. He had never learnt to restrain and control the strong tendencies which, in the quiet shades of Ildown, had been sheltered from temptation. A few months before he would have heard with unmitigated horror the delinquencies which he now committed without a scruple, and defended without a blush. None are so precipitate in the career of sin and folly as backsliders; none so unchecked in the downward course as those to whom the mystery of iniquity is suddenly displayed when they have had none of the gradual training whereby men are armed to resist its seductions.

Who does not know from personal observation that the cycle of sins is bound together by a thousand invisible filaments, and that myriads of unknown connections unite them to one another? Hazlet, when he had once "forsaken the guide of his youth, and forgotten the covenant of his God," did not stop short at one or two temptations, and yield only to some favourite vice. With a rapidity as amazing as it was disastrous, he developed in the course of two or three months into one of the most shameless and dissipated of the worst Saint Werner's set. There was something characteristic in the way in which he frothed out his own shame, boasting of his

147

infamous liberty with an arrogance which resembled his former conceit in spiritual superiority.

Julian, who now saw less of him than ever, had no opportunity of speaking to him as to his course of life; but at last an incident happened which persuaded him that further silence would be a culpable neglect of his duty to his neighbour.

Montagu, of Roslyn School, came up to Camford to spend a Sunday with Owen, and Owen asked Julian and Lillyston to meet him. They liked each other very much, and Julian rapidly began to regard Montagu as a real friend. In order to see as much of each other as possible, they all agreed to take a four-oar on the Saturday morning, and row to Elnham; at Elnham they dined, and spent two pleasant hours in visiting the beautiful cathedral, so that they did not get back to Camford till eleven at night.

Their way from the boats to Saint Werner's lay through a bad part of the town, and they walked quickly, Owen and Montagu being a little way in front.

A few gas-lights were burning at long intervals in the narrow lane through which they had to pass, and as they walked under one of them they observed a group of four standing half in shadow. One of them Julian instantly recognised as the very vilest of the Saint Werner "fast men;" another was Hazlet; there could be no doubt as to the company in which he was.

For one second, Julian turned back to look in sheer astonishment,—he could hardly believe the testimony of his own eyes. The figure which he took to be Hazlet hastily retreated, and Julian half-persuaded himself that he was mistaken.

"Did you see who that was?" asked Lillyston sadly.

"Yes," said Julian; "one of the simple ones; 'but he knoweth not that the dead are there, and that her guests are in the depths of hell.'"

"You must speak to him, Julian."

"I will."

As Hazlet was out when he called, Julian wrote on his card, "Dear H, will you come to tea at 8? Yours ever, J Home."

At 8 o'clock accordingly Hazlet was seated, as he had not been for a very long time, by Julian's fireside. Julian's conversation interested him, and he could not help feeling a little humbled at the unworthiness which prevented him from more frequently enjoying it. It was not till after tea, when they had pulled their chairs to the fire, that Julian said, "Hazlet, I was sorry to see you in bad company last night."

"Me!" said Hazlet, feigning surprise.

"You!"

148

Hazlet saw that all attempt at concealment was useless. "For God's sake, don't tell my mother, or any of the Ildown people," he said, turning pale.

"Is it likely I should? Yet my doing so would be the very least harm that could happen to you, Hazlet, if you adopt these courses. I had rather see you afraid of the sin than of the detection."

Hazlet stammered out in self-defence one of those commonplaces which he had heard but too often in the society of those who "put evil for good and good for evil."

Julian very quietly tore the miserable sophism to shreds, and said, "There is but one way to describe these vices, Hazlet,—they are deadly, bitter, ruinous."

"Oh, they are very common. Lots of men—"

"Tush!" said Julian; "their commonness, if indeed it be so, does not diminish their deadliness. Not to put the question on the religious ground at all, I fully agree with Carlyle that, on the mere consideration of expedience and physical fact, nothing can be more fatal, more calamitous than 'to burn away in mad waste the divine aromas and celestial elements from our existence; to change our holy of holies into a place of riot; to make the soul itself hard, impious, barren.'"

Hazlet, ashamed and bewildered, confused his present position with old reminiscences, and muttered some balderdash about Carlyle "not being sound."

"Carlyle not sound?" said Julian; "good heavens! You can still retain the wretched babblements of your sectarianism while your courses are what they are!"

He was inclined to drop the conversation in sheer disgust, but Hazlet's pride was now aroused, and he began to bluster about the impertinence of interference on Julian's part, and his right to do what he chose.

"Certainly," said Julian, sternly, "the choice lies with yourself. Run, if you will, as a bird to the snare of the fowler, till a dart strike you through. But if you are dead and indifferent to your own miserable soul, think that in this sin you cannot sin alone; think that you are dragging down to the nethermost abyss others besides yourself. Remember the wretched victims of your infamous passions, and tremble while you desecrate and deface for ever God's image stamped on a fair human soul. Think of those whom your vileness dooms to a life of loathliness, a death of shame and anguish, perhaps an eternity of horrible despair. Learn something of the days they are forced to spend, that they may pander to the worst instincts of your degraded nature; days of squalor and drunkenness, disease and dirt; gin at morning, noon, and night; eating infection,

149

horrible madness, and sudden death at the end. Can you ever hope for salvation and the light of God's presence, while the cry of the souls of which you have been the murderer—yes, do not disguise it, the murderer, the cruel, willing, pitiless murderer—is ringing upwards from the depths of hell?"

"What do you mean by the murderer?" said Hazlet, with an attempt at misconception.

"I mean this, Hazlet; setting aside all considerations which affect your mere personal ruin—not mentioning the atrophy of spiritual life and the clinging sense of degradation which is involved in such a course as yours—I want you to see if you will be honest, that the fault is yet more deadly, because you involve other souls and other lives in your own destruction. Is it not a reminiscence sufficient to kill any man's hope, that but for his own brutality some who are now perhaps raving in the asylum might have been clasping their own children to their happy breasts, and wearing in unpolluted innocence the rose of matronly honour? Oh, Hazlet, I have heard you talk about missionary societies, and seen your name in subscription lists, but believe me you could not, by myriads of such conventional charities, cancel the direct and awful quota which you are now contributing to the aggregate of the world's misery and shame."

It took a great deal to abash a mind like Hazlet's. He said that he was going to be a clergyman, and that it was necessary for him to see something of life, or he would never acquire the requisite experience.

"Loathly experience!" said Julian with crushing scorn. "And do you ever hope, Hazlet, by centuries of preaching such as yours, to repair one millionth part of the damage done by your bad passions to a single fellow-creature? Such a hateful excuse is verily to carry the Urim with its oracular gems into the very sty of sensuality, and to debase your religion into 'a procuress to the lords of hell.' I have done; but let me say, Hazlet, that your self-justification is, if possible, more repulsive than your sin."

He pushed back his chair from the fire, and turned away, as Hazlet, with some incoherent sentences about "no business of his," left the room, and slammed the door behind him.

What are words but weak motions of vibrating air? Julian's words passed by the warped nature of Hazlet like the idle wind, and left no more trace upon him than the snow-flake when it has melted into the purpling sea. As the weeks went on, his ill-regulated passions grew more and more free from the control of reason or manliness, and he sank downwards, downwards, downwards, into the most shameful abysses of an idle, and evil, and dissipated life.

150

And the germ of that ruin was planted by the hand of the clever, and gay, and handsome Vyvyan Bruce.

CHAPTER TWENTY TWO

DE VAYNE'S TEMPTATION

"And felt how awful goodness is, and virtue
In her own shape how lovely."

Milton's Paradise Lost

Shall I confess it? Pitiable and melancholy as was Hazlet's course, I liked him so little as to feel for him far less than I otherwise should have done. His worst error never caused me half the pain of Kennedy's most venial fault. Must I then tell a sad tale of Kennedy too—my brave, bright, beautiful, light-hearted Kennedy, whom I always loved so well? May I not throw over the story of his college days the rosy colourings of romance and fancy, the warm sunshine of prosperity and hope? I wish I might. But I am writing of Camford—not of a divine Utopia or a sunken Atalantis.

Bruce, so far from being troubled by his own evil deeds, was proud of a success which supported a pet theory of his infidel opinions. He made no sort of secret of it, and laughed openly at the fool whom he had selected for his victim.

"But after all," said Brogten, who had plenty of common sense, "your triumph was very slight."

"How do you mean? I chose the most obtrusively religious man in Saint Werner's, and, in the course of a very short time, I had him, of his own will, roaring drunk."

"And what's the inference?"

"That what men call religion is half cant, half the accident of circumstances."

"Pardon me, you're out in your conclusion; it only shows that Hazlet was a hypocrite, or at the best a weak, vain, ignorant fellow. The very obtrusiveness and uncharitableness of his religion proved its unreality. Now I could name dozens of men who would see you dead on the floor rather than do as you have taught Hazlet to do—men, in fact, with whom you simply daren't try the experiment."

151

"Daren't! why not?"

"Why, simply because they breathe such a higher and better atmosphere than either you or I, that you would be abashed by their mere presence."

"Pooh! I don't believe it," said Bruce, with an uneasy laugh; "mention any such man."

"Well, Suton for instance, or Lord De Vayne."

"Suton is an unpleasant fellow, and I shouldn't choose to try him, because he's a bore. But I bet you what you like that I make De Vayne drunk before a month's over."

"Done! I bet you twenty pounds you don't."

Disgusting that the young, and pure-hearted, and amiable De Vayne should be made the butt of the machinations of such men as Bruce and Brogten! But so it was. So it was; I could not invent facts like these. They never could float across my imagination, or if they did, I should reject them as the monstrous chimeras of a heated brain. I can conceive a man's private wickedness,—the wickedness which he confines within his own heart, and only brings to bear upon others so far as is demanded by his own fancied interests; I can imagine, too, an open and willing partnership in villainy, where hand joins in hand, and face answereth to face. But that any knowing the plague of their own hearts, should deliberately endeavour to lead others into sin, coolly and deliberately, without even the blinding mist of passion to hide the path which they are treading,—this, if I had not known that it was so, I could not have conceived. The murderer who, atom by atom, continues the slow poisoning of a perishing body for many months, and dies amid the yell of a people's execration,—in sober earnest, before God, I believe he is less guilty than he who, drop by drop, pours into the soul of another the curdling venom of moral pollution, than he who feeds into full-sized fury the dormant monsters of another's evil heart. Surely the devil must welcome a human tempter with open arms.

Of course Bruce had to proceed with Lord De Vayne in a manner totally different from that which he had applied to Jedediah Hazlet. He felt himself that the task was far more difficult and delicate, especially as it was by no means easy to get access to De Vayne's company at all. Julian, Lillyston, Kennedy, and a few others, formed the circle of his only friends, and although he was constantly with them, he was rarely to be found in other society. But this was a difficulty which a man with so large an acquaintance as Bruce could easily surmount, and for the rest he trusted to the conviction which he had adopted, that there was no such thing as sincere godliness, and that men only differed in proportion to the weakness or intensity of the temptations which happened to assail them.

So Bruce managed, without any apparent manoeuvring, to see more of De Vayne at various men's rooms, and he generally made a point of sitting next to him when he could. He had naturally a most insinuating address and a suppleness of manner which enabled him to adapt himself with facility to the tastes and temperaments of the men among whom he was thrown. There were few who could make themselves more pleasant and plausible when it suited them than Vyvyan Bruce.

De Vayne soon got over the shrinking with which he had at first regarded him, and no longer shunned the acquaintance of which he seemed desirous. It was not until this stage that Bruce made any serious attempt to take some steps towards winning his wager. He asked De Vayne to a dessert, and took care that the wines should be of an insidious strength. But the young nobleman's abstemiousness wholly defeated and baffled him, as he rarely took more than a single glass.

"You pass the wine, De Vayne; don't do that."

"Thank you, I've had enough."

"Come, come; allow me," said Bruce, filling his glass for him.

De Vayne drank it out of politeness, and Bruce repeated the same process soon after.

"Come, De Vayne, no heel-taps," he said playfully, as he filled his glass for him.

"Thank you, I'd really rather not have any more."

"Why, you must have been lending your ears to—

"'Those budge doctors of the Stoic fur,
Praising the lean and sallow abstinence;'

"You take nothing. I shall abuse my wine-merchant."

"You certainly seem as anxious as Comus that I should drink, Bruce," said De Vayne, smiling; "but really I mean that I wish for no more."

Bruce saw that he had overstepped the bounds of politeness, and also made a mistake by going a little too far. He pressed De Vayne no longer, and the conversation passed to other subjects.

"Anything in the papers to-day?" asked Brogten.

"Yes, another case of wife-beating and wife-murder. What a dreadful increase of those crimes there has been lately," said De Vayne.

"Another proof," said Bruce, "of the gross absurdity of the marriage-theory."

De Vayne opened his eyes wide in astonishment. Knowing very little of Bruce, he was not aware that this was a very favourite

153

style of remark with him,—indeed, a not uncommon style with other clever young undergraduates. He delighted to startle men by something new, and dazzle them with a semblance of insight and reasoning. "The gross absurdity of the marriage-theory," thought De Vayne to himself; "I wonder what on earth he can mean?" Fancying he must have misheard, he said nothing; but Bruce, disappointed that his remark had fallen flat, (for the others were too much used to the kind of thing to take any notice of it), continued—

"How curious it is that the whole of the arguments should be against marriage, and yet that it should continue to be an institution. You never find a person to defend it."

"'At quis vituperavit?' as the man remarked, on hearing of a defence of Hercules," said De Vayne. "I should have thought that marriage, like the Bible, 'needed no apology.'"

"My dear fellow, it surely is an absurdity on the face of it? See how badly it succeeds."

Without choosing to enter on that question, De Vayne quietly remarked, "You ask why marriage exists. Don't you believe that it was originally appointed by divine providence, and afterwards sanctioned by divine lips?"

"Oh, if you come to that kind of ground, you know, and abandon the aspect of the question from the side of pure reason, you've so many preliminaries to prove; e g, the genuineness and authenticity of the Pentateuch and the Gospels; the credibility of the narrators; the possibility of their being deceived; the—"

"In fact," said De Vayne, "the evidences of Christianity. Well, I trust that I have studied them, and that they satisfy alike my reason and my conscience."

"Ah, yes! Well, it's no good entering on those questions, you know. I shouldn't like to shock your convictions, as I should have to do if I discussed with you. It's just as well after all—even in the nineteenth century—not to expose the exotic flower of men's belief to the rude winds of fair criticism. Picciola! it might be blighted, poor thing, which would be a pity. Perhaps one does more harm than good by exposing antiquated errors." And with a complacent shrug of the shoulders, and a slight smile of self-admiration, Bruce leant back in his armchair.

This was Bruce's usual way, and he found it the most successful. There were a great many minds on whom it created the impression of immense cleverness. "That kind of thing, you know, it's all exploded now," he would say among the circle of his admirers, and he would give a little wave of the hand, which was vastly effective—as if he "could an if he would" puff away the whole system of Christianity with quite a little breath of objection, but refrained from such tyrannous use of a giant's strength. "It's all very well, you know, for parsons—though, by the way, not half of the cleverest believe what they preach—but really for men of the world, and thinkers, and acute reasoners"—(oh, how agreeable it was to the Tulks and Boodles to be included in such a category)—"why, after such books as Frederic of Suabia 'De Tribus Impostoribus,' and Strauss' 'Leben Jesu,' and De Wette, and Feuerbach, and Van Bohlen, and Nork, one can't be expected, you know, to believe such a mass of traditionary rubbish." (Bruce always professed acquaintance with German writers, and generally quoted the titles of their books in the original; it sounded so much better; not that he had read one of them, of course.) And they did think him so clever when he talked in this way. Only think how wise he must be to know such profound truths!

But so far from Bruce's hardly-concealed contempt for the things which Christians hold sacred producing any effect on Lord De Vayne, he regarded it with a silent pity. "I hate," thought he, "when Vice can bolt her arguments, and Virtue has no tongue to check her pride." The annoying impertinence, so frequent in argument, which leads a man to speak as though, from the vantage-ground of great intellectual superiority to his opponent, the graceful affectation of dropping an argument out of respect for prejudices which the arguer despises, or an incapacity which the arguer implies—this merely personal consideration did not ruffle for a moment the gentle spirit of De Vayne. But that a young man—conceited, shallow, and ignorant—should profess to settle with a word the controversies which had agitated the profoundest reasons, and to settle with a sneer, the mysteries before which the mightiest thinkers had veiled their eyes in reverence and awe; that he should profess to set aside Christianity as a childish fable not worthy a wise man's acceptance, and triumph over it as a defeated and deserted cause; this indeed filled De Vayne's mind with sorrow and disgust. So far from being impressed or dazzled by Bruce's would-be cleverness, he sincerely grieved over his impudence and folly.

"Thank you, Bruce," he said, after a slight pause, and with some dignity, "thank you for your kind consideration of my mental inferiority, and for the pitying regard which you throw, from beside your nectar, on my delicate and trembling superstitions. But don't think, Bruce, that I admit your—may I call it?—impertinent assumption that all thinking men have thrown Christianity aside as an exploded error. Some shadow of proof, some fragment of reason, would be more satisfactory treatment of a truth which has regenerated the world, than foolish assertion or insolent contempt. Good-night."

155

There was something in the manner of De Vayne's reproof which effectually quelled Bruce, while it galled him; yet, at the same time, it was delivered with such quiet good taste, that to resent it was impossible. He saw, too, not without vexation, that it had told powerfully on the little knot of auditors. The wine-party soon broke up, for Bruce could neither give new life to the conversation, nor recover his chagrin.

"So-ho!" said Brogten, when they were left alone, "I shall win my bet."

"Hanged if you shall," said Bruce, with an oath of vexation. In fact, not only was he determined not to be foiled in proving his wisdom and power of reading men's characters, but he was wholly unable to afford any payment of the bet. Bruce could get unlimited credit for goods, on the reputation of his father's wealth, but money-dealers were very sharp-eyed people, and he found it much less easy to get his promissory-notes cashed. It was a matter of etiquette to pay at once "debts of honour," and his impetuous disposition led him to take bets so freely that his ready money was generally drained away very soon after his return. Not long before he had written to his father for a fresh supply, but, to his great surprise, the letter had only produced an angry and even indignant reproof. "Vyvyan," (his father had written—not even 'dear Vyvyan'), "I allow you 500 pounds a year, a sum totally out of proportion with your wants, and yet you are so shamefully extravagant as to write without a blush to ask me for more. Don't presume to do it again on pain of my heavy displeasure." This letter had so amazed him that he did not even answer it, nor, in spite of his mother's earnest, urgent, and almost heart-rending entreaties, post by post, would he even condescend to write home for many weeks. It was the natural result of the way in which at home they had pampered his vanity, and never checked his faults.

But, for these reasons, it was wholly out of Bruce's power to pay Brogten the bet, if he failed in trying to shake the temperance of De Vayne. He saw at once that he had mistaken his subject; he took De Vayne for a man whose goodness and humility would make him pliant to all designs.

A dark thought entered Bruce's mind.

He went alone into a druggist's shop, and said, with a languid air, "I have been suffering very much from sleeplessness lately, Mr Brent; I want you to give me a little laudanum."

"Very well, sir. You must be careful how you use it."

"Oh, of course. How many drops would make one drowsy, now?"

"Four or five, sir, I should think."

"Well, you must give me one of those little bottles full. I want to have some by me, to save trouble."

The chemist filled the bottle, and then said, "I'm afraid I'm out of my poison labels, sir. I'll just write a little ticket and tie it on."

"All right;" and putting it in his pocket, Bruce strolled away.

But how to see De Vayne again? He thought over their common acquaintances, and at last fixed on Kennedy as the likeliest man on whom he could depend to secure another meeting. Yet he hardly liked to suggest that Kennedy should give a wine-party, and ask De Vayne and himself; so that he was rather puzzled.

"I say, Brogten, how is it that we are always asking Kennedy to our rooms, and he so very seldom asks us?"

"I suppose because he isn't over-partial to our company."

"Why not?" said Bruce, who considered himself very fascinating, and quite a person whose society was to be courted; "and if so, why does he come to our rooms?"

Brogten might, perhaps, have thrown light on the subject had he chosen.

"Well," he said, "I'll give him a hint."

"Do; and get him to ask De Vayne."

Brogten did so; Kennedy assented to asking Bruce, though he listened to Brogten's hints, (which he instantly understood), with a sullenness which but a short time before had no existence, not even a prototype, in his bright and genial character. But when it came to asking De Vayne, he simply replied to Brogten's suggestion flatly:

"I will not."

"Won't you? but why?"

"Why? because I suspect you and that fellow Bruce of wishing to treat him as you treated Hazlet."

"I've no designs against him whatever."

"Well, I won't ask him,—that's flat."

"Whew–ew–ew–ew–ew!" Brogten began to whistle, and Kennedy relieved his feelings by digging the poker into the fire. And then there was a pause.

"I want you to ask De Vayne."

"And I tell you I won't ask him."

"Whew–w–w–w!" Another long whistle, during which Kennedy mashed and battered the black lumps that smouldered in the grate.

"Whew–ew–ew–ew! Oh, very well." Brogten left the room. At hall that day, Brogten took care to sit near Kennedy again, and the old scene was nearly re-enacted. He turned the conversation to the Christmas examination. "I suppose you'll be very high again, Kennedy."

"No," said he, curtly. "I've not read, and you know that as well as I do."

"Oh, but you hadn't read much last time, and you may do some particular paper very well, you know. I wish there was an Aeschylus paper; you might be first, you know, again."

Kennedy flung down his knife and fork with a curse, and left the hall. Men began to see clearly that there must have been some mystery attached to the Aeschylus paper, known to Brogten and Kennedy, and very discomfiting to the latter. But as Kennedy was concerned, they did not suspect the truth.

Brogten went straight from hall to Kennedy's rooms. He found the door sported, but knew as well as possible that Kennedy was in. He hammered and thumped at the door a long time with sundry imprecations, but Kennedy, moodily resolute, heard all the noise inside, and would not stir. Then Brogten took out a card and wrote on the back, "I think you'll ask De Vayne," and dropped it into the letter-box.

That evening he found in his own letter-box a slip of paper. "De Vayne is coming to wine with me to-morrow. Come, and the foul fiend take you. I have filled my decanters half-full of water, and won't bring out more than one bottle. E K."

Brogten read the note and chuckled,—partly with the thought of Kennedy, partly of Bruce, partly of De Vayne. Yet the chuckle ended in a very heavy sigh.

CHAPTER TWENTY THREE

KENNEDY'S WINE-PARTY, AND WHAT CAME OF IT

"Et je n'ai moi
Par la sang Dieu!
Ni foi, ni loi,
Ni jeu, ni lieu,
Ni roi, ni Dieu."
Victor Hugo, Notre Dame de Paris.
"Nay, that's certain but yet the pity of it,
Iago!—O Iago, the pity of it, Iago!"

Othello, Act 4, Scene 1.

"Are you going to Kennedy's, Julian?" asked De Vayne.
"No."
"I wish he'd asked you."
Julian a little wondered why he had not, but remembered, with a sigh, that there was something, he knew not what, between him and Kennedy. Yet Kennedy was engaged to Violet! The thought carried him back to the beautiful memories of Grindelwald and Mürrem,—perhaps of Eva Kennedy: I will not say.

As De Vayne glanced round at the men assembled at Kennedy's rooms, he felt a little vexation, and half wished he had not come. Why on earth did Kennedy see so much of these Bruces and Brogtens when he was so thoroughly unlike them? But De Vayne consoled himself with the reflection that the evening could not fail to be pleasant, as Kennedy was there; for he liked Kennedy both for Julian's sake and for his own. Happily for him he did not know as yet that Kennedy was affianced to Violet Home.

Kennedy sat at the end of the table with a gloomy cloud on his brow. "Here, De Vayne," he said; "I'm so really glad to see you at last. Sit by me—here's a chair."

De Vayne took the proffered seat, and Bruce immediately seated himself at his left hand. At first, as the wine was passed round, there seemed likely to be but little conversation, but suddenly some one started the subject of a "cause célèbre" which was then filling the papers, and Kennedy began at once to discuss it with some interest with De Vayne, who sat nearly facing him,

159

almost with his back turned to Bruce, who did not seem particularly anxious to attract De Vayne's attention.

"What execrable wash," said Brogten, emptying his glass.

De Vayne, surprised and disgusted at the rudeness of the remark, turned hastily round, and, while Bruce as hastily withdrew his hand, raised the wine-glass to his lips.

"Stop, stop, De Vayne," said Bruce eagerly; "there's a fly in your glass."

"I see no fly," said De Vayne, glancing at it, and immediately draining it, with the intention of saying something to smooth Kennedy's feelings, which he supposed would have been hurt by Brogten's want of common politeness.

"I think it very—" Why did his words fail, and what was the reason of that scared look with which he regarded the blank faces of the other undergraduates? And what is the meaning of that gasp, and the rapid dropping of the head upon the breast, and the deadly pallor that suddenly put out the fair colour in his cheeks? There was no fly—but, good heavens! was there death in the glass?

The whole party leapt up from their places, and gathered round him.

"What is the matter, De Vayne?" said Kennedy tenderly, as he knelt down and supported the young man in his arms. But there was no answer. "Here D'Acres, or somebody, for heaven's sake fetch a doctor; he must have been seized with a fit."

"What have you been doing, Bruce?" thundered Brogten.

"Bruce doing!" said Kennedy wildly, as he sprang to his feet. "By the God above us, if I thought this was any of your devilish machinations, I would strike you to the earth!"

"Doing? I?" stammered Bruce. "What do you mean?" He trembled in every limb, and his face was as pale as that of his victim; yet, though perhaps De Vayne's life depended on it, the young wretch would not say what he had done. He had meant but to put four or five drops into his glass, but De Vayne had turned round suddenly and startled him in the very act, and in the hurried agitation of the moment, his hand had slipped, and he had poured in all the contents of the bottle, with barely time to hurry it empty into his pocket, or to prevent the consequences of what he had done, when De Vayne lifted the glass to his lips.

The men all stood round De Vayne and Kennedy in a helpless crowd, and Kennedy said, "Here, fetch a doctor, somebody, and let all go except D'Acres; so many are only in the way."

The little group dispersed, and two of them ran off to find a doctor; but Bruce stood there still with open mouth, and a countenance as pale in its horror as that of the fainting viscount. He was anxious to tell the truth about the matter in order to avert worse consequences, and yet he dared not—the words died away upon his lips.

"Don't stand like that, Bruce," said Brogten indignantly, "the least you can do is to make yourself useful. Go and get the key of De Vayne's rooms from the porter's lodge. Stop, though! it will probably be in his pocket. Yes, here it is. Run and unlock his door, while we carry him to bed."

Bruce took the key with trembling hand, and shook so violently with nervous agitation that he could hardly make his way across the court. The others carried De Vayne to his bedroom as quickly as they could, and anxiously awaited the doctor's arrival. The livid face, with the dry foam upon the lips, filled them with alarm, but they had not any conception what to do, and fancied that De Vayne was in a fit.

It took Dr Masham a very short time to see that his patient was suffering from the influence of some poison, and when he discovered this, he cleared the room, and at once applied the proper remedies. But time had been lost already, and he was the less able to set to work at first from his complete ignorance of what had happened. He sat up all night with his patient, but was more than doubtful whether it was not too late to save his life.

The news that De Vayne had been seized with a fit at Kennedy's rooms soon changed into a darker rumour. Men had not forgotten the affair of Hazlet, and they suspected that some foul play had been practised on one whom all who knew him loved, and whom all, though personally unacquainted with him, heartily respected. That this was really the fact soon ceased to be a secret; but who was guilty, and what had been the manner or motives of the crime remained unknown, and this uncertainty left room for the wildest surmises.

The dons were not slow to hear of what had happened, and they regarded the matter in so serious a light, that they summoned a Seniority for its immediate investigation. Kennedy was obviously the first person of whom to make inquiries, and he told them exactly what had occurred, viz, that De Vayne after drinking a single glass of wine, fell back in his chair in the condition wherein he still continued. "Was anything the matter with the wine, Mr Kennedy?" asked Mr Norton, who, as one of the tutors, had a seat on the board.

"Nothing, sir; it was the same which we were all drinking."

"And without any bad effects?"

"Yes, sir."

"But, Mr Kennedy, there seems strong reason to believe that

some one drugged Lord De Vayne's wine. Were you privy to any such plan?"

"No, sir—not exactly," said Kennedy slowly, and with hesitation.

"Really, sir," said the Master of Saint Werner's, "such an answer is grossly to your discredit. Favour us by being more explicit; what do you mean by 'not exactly'?"

Kennedy's passionate and fiery pride, which had recently increased with the troubles and self-reprobation of his life, could ill brook such questioning as this, and he answered haughtily:

"I was not aware that anything of this kind was intended."

"Anything of this kind; you did then expect something to take place?"

"I thought I had taken sufficient precautions against it."

"Against it; against what?" asked Mr Norton.

Kennedy looked up at his questioner, as though he read in his face the decision as to whether he should speak or not. He would hardly have answered the Master or any of the others, but Mr Norton was his friend, and there was something so manly and noble about his look and character, that Kennedy was encouraged to proceed, and he said slowly:

"I suspected, sir, that there was some intention of attempting to make De Vayne drunk."

"You suspected that," said Mr Norton with astonishment and scorn, "and yet you lent your rooms for such a purpose. I am ashamed of you, Kennedy; heartily, and utterly ashamed."

Kennedy's spirit was roused by this bitter and public apostrophe. "I lent my rooms for no such purpose; on the contrary, if it existed, I did my best to defeat it."

"What made you suspect it?" asked Dr Rhodes, the Master.

"Because a similar attempt was practised on another."

"At which it seems that you were present?"

"I was not." Kennedy was too fiercely angry to answer in more words than were absolutely required.

"I am sorry to say, Mr Kennedy, you have not cleared yourself from the great disgrace of giving an invitation, though you supposed that it would be made the opportunity for perpetrating an infamous piece of mischief. Can you throw no more light on the subject?"

"None."

"Will you bring the decanter out of which Lord De Vayne drank?" said one of the seniors after a pause, and with an intense belief in the acuteness of the suggestion.

"I don't see what good it will do, but I will order my gyp to carry it here if you wish."

"Do so, sir. And let me add," said the Master, "that a little more respectfulness of manner would be becoming in your present position."

Kennedy's lip curled, and without answer he left the room to fetch the wine, grimly chuckling at the effect which the mixture would produce on Mr Norton's fastidious taste. When he reached his rooms, he stumbled against the table in his hurry, and upset a little glass dish which held his pencils, one of which rolled away under the fender. In lifting the fender to pick it up, a piece of paper caught his eye, which the bedmaker in cleaning the room had swept out of sight in the morning. He looked at it, and saw in legible characters, "Laudanum, Poison." It was the label which had been loosely tied on Bruce's phial, and which had slipped off as he hurried it into his pocket.

He read it, and as the horrid truth flashed across his mind, stood for a moment stupefied and dumb. His plan was instantly formed. Instead of returning to the conclave of Seniors he ran straight off to the chemist's, which was close by Saint Werner's.

"Do you know anything of this label?" he said, thrusting it into the chemist's hands.

"Yes," said the man, after looking at it for a moment; "it is the label of a bottle of laudanum which I sold yesterday morning to Mr Bruce of Saint Werner's."

Without a word, Kennedy snatched it from him, and rushed back to the Seniority, who were already beginning to wonder at his long absence. He threw down the piece of paper before. Mr Norton, who handed it to the Master.

"I found that, sir, on the floor of my room."

"And you know nothing of it?"

"Yes. It belongs to a bottle purchased yesterday by Bruce."

Amazement and horror seemed to struggle in the minds of the old clergymen and lecturers as they sat at the table.

"We must send instantly for this young man," said Mr Norton; and in ten minutes Bruce entered, pale indeed, but in a faultless costume, with a bow of easy grace, and a smile of polite recognition towards such of the board as he personally knew. He was totally unaware of what had been going on during Kennedy's cross-examination.

"Mr Bruce," said Mr Norton, to whom they all seemed gladly to resign the task of discovering the truth, "do you know anything of the cause of Lord De Vayne's sudden attack of illness last night?"

"I, sir? Certainly not."

"He sat next to you, did he not?"

"He did, I believe. Yes. I can't be quite sure—but I think he did."

"You know he did as well as I do," said Kennedy.

"Mr Kennedy, let me request you to be silent. Mr Bruce, had you any designs against Lord De Vayne?"

"Designs, sir? Excuse me, but I am at a loss to understand your meaning."

"You had no intention then of making him drunk?"

"Really, sir, you astonish me by such coarse imputations. Is it you," he said, turning angrily to Kennedy, "who have been saying such things of me?"

Kennedy deigned no reply.

"I should think the testimony of a man who doesn't scruple secretly to read examination-papers before they are set, ought not to stand for much." Brogten, as we have already mentioned, had revealed to him the secret of Kennedy's dishonour. This remark fell quite dead: Kennedy sat unmoved, and Mr Norton replied—

"Pray don't introduce your personal altercations here, Mr Bruce, on irrelevant topics. Mr Bruce," he continued, suddenly giving him the label, "have you ever seen that before?"

With a cry of agony, Bruce saw the paper, and struck his forehead with his hand. The sudden blow of shameful detection with all its train of consequences utterly unmanned him, and falling on his knees, he cried incoherently—

"Oh! I did it, I did it. I didn't mean to; my hand slipped: indeed, indeed it did. For God's sake forgive me, and let this not be known. I will give you thousands to hush it up—"

A general exclamation of indignation and disgust stopped his prayers, and the Master gave orders that he should be removed and watched. He was dragged away, tearing his hair and sobbing like a child. Kennedy, too, was ordered to retire.

It took the Seniors but a short time to deliberate, and then Bruce was summoned. He would have spoken, but the Master sternly ordered him to be silent, and said to him:

"Vyvyan Bruce, you are convicted by your own confession, extorted after deliberate falsehood, of having wished to drug the wine of a fellow-student for the purpose of entrapping him into a sin, to which you would otherwise have failed to tempt him. What fearful results may follow from your wickedness we cannot yet know, and you may have to answer for this crime before another tribunal. Be that as it may, it is hardly necessary to tell you that your time as a student at Saint Werner's has ended. You are expelled, and I now proceed to erase your name from the books." (Here the Master ran his pen two or three times through Bruce's signature in the college register). "Your rooms must be finally vacated to-morrow. You need say nothing in self-defence, and may go." As Bruce seemed determined to plead his own cause, they ordered the attendant to remove him immediately.

Kennedy was then sent for, and they could not help pitying him, for he was a favourite with them all.

"Mr Kennedy," said the senior Dean, "the Master desires me to admonish you for your very culpable connivance—for I have no other name for it—in the great folly and wickedness of which Bruce has been convicted—"

"I did not connive," said Kennedy.

"Silence, sir!"

"But I will not keep silence; you accuse me falsely."

"We shall be obliged to take further measures, Mr Kennedy, if you behave in this refractory way."

"I don't care what measures you take. I cannot listen in silence to an accusation which I loathe—of a crime of which I am wholly innocent."

"Why, sir, you confessed that you suspected some unfair design."

"But not this design. Proceed, sir; I will not interrupt you again; but let me say that I am totally indifferent to any blame which you throw on me for a brutality of which the whole responsibility rests on others."

The thread of the Dean's oration was quite broken by Kennedy's impetuous interruption, and he merely added—"Well, Mr Kennedy, I am sorry to see you so little penitent for the position in which you have placed yourself. You have disappointed the expectation of all your friends, and however you may brazen it out, your character has contracted a stain."

"You can say so, sir, if you choose," said Kennedy; and he left the room with a formal bow.

A few days after, Mr Grayson asked him to what Bruce had alluded in his insinuation about an examination-paper.

"He alludes, sir, to an event which happened some time ago."

Further questions were useless; nevertheless Kennedy saw that his tutor's suspicions were not only aroused, but that they had taken the true direction. Mr Grayson despised him, and in Saint Werner's he had lost caste.

That evening Bruce vanished from Camford, with the regrets of few except his tailors and his duns. To this day he has not paid his college debts or discharged the bill for the gorgeous furniture of his rooms. But we shall hear of him again.

CHAPTER TWENTY FOUR

DE VAYNE'S CHRISTMAS HOLIDAYS

"He that for love hath undergone
The worst that can befall,
Is happier thousandfold than one
Who never loved at all.
"A grace within his soul hath reigned,
Which nothing else can bring;
Thank God for all that I have gained
By that high suffering."

Moncton Manes

For many days Lord De Vayne seemed to be hovering between life and death. The depression of his spirits weighed upon his frame, and greatly retarded his recovery. That he, unconscious as he was of ever having made an enemy—good and gentle to all—with no desire but to love his neighbour as himself, and to devote such talents and such opportunities as had been vouchsafed him to God's glory and man's benefit;—that he should have been made the subject of a disgraceful wager, and the butt of an infamous experiment; that in endeavouring to carry out this nefarious plan, any one should have been so wickedly reckless, so criminally thoughtless;—this knowledge lay on his imagination with a depression as of coming death. De Vayne had been but little in Saint Werner's society, and had rarely seen any but his few chosen friends; and that such a calamity should have happened in the rooms and at the table of one of those friends,—that Kennedy, whom he so much loved and admired, should be suspected of being privy to it;—this fact was one which made De Vayne's heart sink within him with anguish and horror, and a weariness of life.

And in those troubled waters of painful thought floated the broken gleams of a golden phantasy, the rainbow-coloured memories of a secret love. They came like a light upon the darkened waves, yet a light too feeble to dissipate the under gloom. Like the phosphorescent flashes in the sea at midnight, which the lonely voyager, watching with interest as they glow in the white wake of the keel, guesses that they may be the heralds of a storm,—so these bright reminiscences of happier days only gave a weird beauty to the tumult of the sick boy's mind; and the mother, as she sat by him night and day during the crisis of his suffering, listened with a

166

deeper anxiety for future trouble to the delirious revelations of his love.

For Lady De Vayne had come from Other Hall to nurse her sick son. She slept on a sofa in his sitting-room, and nursed him with such tenderness as only a mother can. There was no immediate possibility of removing him; deep, unbroken quiet was his only chance of life. The silence of his sick-room was undisturbed save by the softest whispers and the lightest footfalls, and the very undergraduates hushed their voices, and checked their hasty steps as they passed in the echoing cloisters underneath, and remembered that the flame of life was flickering low in the golden vase.

De Vayne was much beloved, and nothing could exceed the delicacy of the attention shown him. Choice conservatory flowers were left almost daily at his door, and men procured rare and rich fruits from home or from London, not because De Vayne needed any such luxuries, which were easily at his command, but that they might show him their sympathy and distress. Several ladies more or less connected with Saint Werner's offered their services to Lady De Vayne, but she would not leave her son, in whose welfare and recovery her whole thoughts were absorbed.

And so, gloomily for the son and mother, the Christmas holidays came on, and Saint Werner's was deserted. Scarcely even a stray undergraduate lingered in the courts, and the chapel was closed; no sound of choir or organ came sweetly across the lawns at morning or evening; the ceaseless melancholy plash of the great fountain was almost the only sound that broke the stillness. Julian, Lillyston, and Owen had all gone down for the holidays, full of grief at the thought of leaving their friend in such a precarious state, but as yet not permitted to see or serve him. Lady De Vayne promised to write to Julian regular accounts of Arthur's health, and told him how often her son spoke of him, both in his wanderings, and in his clearer moments.

It was touching to see the stately and beautiful lady walking alone at evening about the deserted college, to gain a breath of the keen winter air, while her son had sunk for a few moments to fitful rest. She was pale with long watchings and deep anxiety, and in her whole countenance, and in her deep and often uplifted eyes, was that look of prayerfulness and holy communion with an unseen world which they acquire whose abode has long been in the house of mourning, and removed from the follies and frivolities of life.

Well-loved grounds of Saint Werner's by the quiet waves of the sedgy Iscam, with smooth green grass sloping down to the edge, and trim quaint gardens, and long avenues of chestnut and ancient limes! Though winter had long whirled away the last red and golden leaf, there was pleasure in the air of quiet and repose, which is always to be found in those memory-hallowed walks; and while Lady De Vayne could pace among them in solitude, she needed no other change, nor any rest from thinking over her sick son.

She was surprised one evening, very soon after the men had gone down, to see an undergraduate slowly approaching her down the long and silent avenue. He was tall and well made, and his face would have been a pleasant one, but for the deep look of sadness which clouded it. He hesitated and took off his cap as she came near, and returning his salute, she would have passed him, but he stopped her and said:

"Lady De Vayne."

Full of surprise she looked at him, and with his eyes fixed on the ground he continued, "You do not know my name; if I tell you, I fear you will hate me, because I fear you will have heard calumnies about me. But may I speak to you?"

"You are not Mr Bruce?" she said with a slight shudder.

"No; my name is Edward Kennedy. Ah, madam! do not look at me so reproachfully, I cannot endure it. Believe me, I would have died—I would indeed—rather than that this should have happened to Lord De Vayne."

"Nay, Mr Kennedy, I cannot believe that you were more than thoughtless. I have very often heard Julian Home speak of you, and I cannot believe that his chosen friend could be so vile as some reports would make you."

"They are false as calumny itself," he said passionately. "Oh, Lady De Vayne, none could have honoured and loved your son more than I did; I cannot explain to you the long story of my exculpation, but I implore you to believe my innocence."

"I forgive you, Mr Kennedy," she said, touched with pity, "if there be anything to forgive; and so will Arthur. A more forgiving spirit than his never filled any one I think. Excuse me, it is time for me to return to him."

"But will you not let me see him, and help you in nursing him? It was for this purpose alone that I stayed here when all the others went. Let me at least be near him, that I may feel myself to be making such poor reparation as my heedlessness requires."

She could hardly resist his earnest entreaty, and besides, she was won by compassion for his evident distress.

"You may come, Mr Kennedy, as often as you like; whenever Arthur is capable of seeing you, you shall visit his sick-room."

"Thank you," he said, and she perceived the tremble of deep emotion in his voice.

He came the next morning, and she allowed him to see De Vayne. He entered noiselessly, and gazed for a moment as he stood at the door on the pale wasted face, looking still paler in contrast with the long dark hair that flowed over the pillow. He was awake, but there was no consciousness in his dark dreamy eyes.

As De Vayne murmured to himself in low sentences, Kennedy heard repeatedly the name of Violet, and once of Violet Home. He sat still as death, and soon gathered from the young lord's broken words, his love, his deep love for Julian's sister.

And when Kennedy first recognised this fact, which had hitherto been quite unknown to him, for a moment a flood of jealousy and bitter envy filled his heart. What if Violet should give up her troth in favour of a wealthier, perhaps worthier lover? What if her family should think his own poor claims no barrier to the hope that Violet should one day wear a coronet? The image of Julian and Violet rose in his fancy, and with one more pang of self-reproach, he grew ashamed of his unworthy suspicions.

Yet the thought that De Vayne, too, had fixed his affections on Violet filled him with uneasiness and foreboding, and he determined, on some future occasion, to save pain to all parties, by getting Julian to break to De Vayne the secret of his sister's betrothal.

For several days he came to the sick-room, and a woman could hardly have been more thoughtful and tender than he was to his friend. It was on about the fourth evening that De Vayne awoke to complete consciousness. He became aware that some one besides his mother was seated in the room, and without asking he seemed slowly to recognise that it was Kennedy.

"Is that Kennedy?" he asked, in a weak voice.

"It is I," said Kennedy, but the patient did not answer, and seemed restless and uneasy and complained of cold.

When Kennedy went, De Vayne whispered to his mother, "Mother, I am very weak and foolish, but it troubles me somehow to see Kennedy sitting there; it shocks my nerves, and fills me with images of something dreadful happening. I had rather not see him, mother, till I am well."

"Very well, Arthur. Don't talk so much, love; I alone will nurse you. Soon I hope you will be able to return to Other."

"And leave this dreadful place," he said, "for ever."

"Hush, my boy; try to sleep again."

He soon slept, and then Lady De Vayne wrote to Kennedy a short note, in which she explained as kindly and considerately as she could, that Arthur was not yet strong enough to allow of any more visits to his sick-room.

"He shuns me," thought Kennedy, with a sigh, and packing up some books and clothes, he prepared to go home.

Of course he was to spend part of the vacation at Ildown. Violet wondered that he did not come at once; she was not exactly jealous of him, but she thought that he might have been more eager for her company than he seemed to be, and she would have liked it better had he come earlier. Poor Kennedy! his very self-denials turned against him for the sole reason why he kept away from Ildown, was, that he feared to disturb the freedom of Frank and Cyril by the presence of a stranger all the time of their holidays, and he hesitated to intrude on the united happiness which always characterised the Ildown circle.

Eva, too, was invited, and the brother and sister arrived at Ildown by a late train, and drove to the house. What a glowing welcome they received! Julian introduced them to Mrs Home, and Kennedy kissed affectionately the hand of his future mother. Frank and Cyril had gone to bed, but Frank was so determined to see Violet's lover that night, that he made Julian bring him into their bedroom, and he was more than satisfied with the first glimpse.

"And where is Violet?" asked Kennedy, in a matter-of-fact tone, for he well knew that she would not choose to meet him in the presence of others.

"In her own little room," said Julian, smiling; "I will show you the way." He led Kennedy up-stairs, and left him at the door; he well knew that her heart would be fluttering as much as his.

A light knock at the door, and a moment after they saw each other again.

She sat on the sofa, and the firelight flickered on the amethyst—his gift—which she wore on her white neck; and her bright eyes danced with tears and laughter, and her bosom heaved and fell as he clasped her to his breast and printed a long, long kiss upon her cheek.

In silence, more exquisite than speech, they gazed on each other; and as though her beauty were reflected on his own face, all trace of sorrow and shame fled like a cloud from his forehead; and who would not have said, looking upon the pair, that he was worthy of her, as she of him?

"My own Violet," he said, "you are beautiful as a vision to-night."

"Hush, flatterer!" and she placed her little hand upon his mouth:—no wonder that he seized and kissed it.

"And what a thrice-charming dress."

"Ah, I meant you to admire it," she said, laughing.

170

"'And thinking, this will please him best,
   She takes a ribbon or a rose,'"

he whispered to her.

"Come," she replied, "no ill-omened words, Edward. You know the sad context of those lines."

"No! no sadness to-night, my own Violet, my beautiful, beautiful Violet; you quite dazzle me, my child. I really can't sit by your side; come, let me sit on your foot-stool here, and look up in your face."

"Silly boy," she said, "come along, we shall keep them all waiting for supper."

While poor De Vayne languished on the bed of sickness, his sufferings were almost the only shadow which chequered the brightness of those weeks at Ildown. In the morning, Julian and Kennedy worked steadily; the afternoon and evening they devoted to amusement and social life. The Kennedys soon became great favourites among the Ildown people, and went out to many cheery Christmas parties; but they enjoyed more the quiet evenings at home when they all sat and talked after dinner round the dining-room fire, and while the two boys played at chess, and Violet and Eva worked or sketched, Julian and Kennedy would read aloud to them in turns. How often those evenings recurred to all their memories in future days.

Soon after the Kennedys had come, Julian received from Camford the Christmas college-list. He had again won a first class, but Kennedy's name, much to his vexation, appeared only in the third.

"How is it that Edward is only in the third class?" asked Violet of Julian—for, of course, she had seen the list. "He is very clever—is he not?"

"Very; one of the cleverest fellows in Saint Werner's."

"Then is he idle?"

"I'm afraid so, Vi. You must get him to work more."

So when he was seated by her on the sofa in her little boudoir, she said, "You must work more, Edward, at Camford, to please me."

"Ah, do not talk to me of Camford," he said, with a heavy sigh. "Let me enjoy unbroken happiness for a time, and leave the bitter future to itself."

"Bitter, Edward? but why bitter? Julian always seems to me so happy at Camford."

"Yes, Julian is, and so are all who deserve to be."

"Then you must be happy too, Edward."

171

His only answer was a sigh. "Ah, Violet, pray talk to me of anything but Camford."

The visit came to an end, as all things, whether happy or unhappy, must; and Julian rejoiced that confidence seemed restored between him and Kennedy once more. Of course, he told Violet none of the follies which had cost poor Kennedy the loss both of popularity and self-respect. Soon afterwards Lord De Vayne was brought back to Other Hall, and Violet and Julian were invited, with their mother, to stay there till the Camford term commenced. The boys had returned to school, so that they all acceded to Lady De Vayne's earnest request that they would come.

It was astonishing how rapidly the young viscount recovered when once Violet had come to Other Hall. Her presence seemed to fill him with fresh life, and he soon began to get down-stairs, and even to venture on a short walk in the park. His constitution had suffered a serious and permanent injury, but he was pronounced convalescent before the Homes finished their visit.

The last evening before their departure, he was seated with Violet on a rustic seat on the terrace, looking at the sun as it set behind the distant elms of the park, and at the deer as they grazed in lovely groups on the rich undulating slopes that swept down from the slight eminence on which his house was built. He felt that the time had come to speak his love.

"Violet," he said, as he looked earnestly at her, and took her hand, "you have, doubtless, seen that I love you. Can you ever return my love? I am ready to live and die for you, and to give you my whole affection." His voice was still low and weak through illness, and he could hardly speak the sentences which were to win for him a decision of his fate.

Violet was taken by surprise; she had known Lord De Vayne so long and so intimately, and their stations were so different, that the thought of his loving her had never entered her head. She regarded him familiarly as her brother's friend.

"Dear De Vayne," she said, "I shall always love you as a friend, as a brother. But did you not know that I have been for some months engaged?"

"Engaged?" he said, turning very pale.

"I am betrothed," she answered, "to Edward Kennedy. Nay, Arthur, dear Arthur," she continued, as he nearly fainted at her feet, "you must not suffer this disappointment to overcome you. Love me still as a sister; regard me as though I were married already, and let us enjoy a happy friendship for many years."

He was too weak to bear up, too weak to talk; only the tears coursed each other fast down his cheeks as he murmured, "Oh, forgive me, forgive me, Violet."

"Forgive you," she said kindly; "nay, you honour me too much. Marry one of your own high rank, and not the orphan of a poor clergyman. I am sure you will not yield to this sorrow, and suffer it to make you ill. Bear up, Arthur, for your mother's sake—for my sake; and let us be as if these words had never passed between us."

She lent him her arm as he walked faintly to his room, and as he turned round and stooped to kiss her hand, she felt it wet with many tears.

They went home next day, and soon after received a note from Lady De Vayne, informing them that Arthur was worse, and that they intended removing for some time to a seat of his in Scotland; after which they meant to travel on the Continent for another year, if his health permitted it. "But," she said, "I fear he has had a relapse, and his state is very precarious. Dear friends, think of us sometimes, and let us hope to meet again in happier days."

CHAPTER TWENTY FIVE

MEMORY THE BOOK OF GOD

"At Trompyngtoun, nat fer fra Cantebrigg,
Ther goth a brook, and over that a brigge,
Upon the whiche brook then stant a melle;
And this is verray sothe that I you telle."

Chaucer, The Reeve's Tale

There is little which admits of external record in Julian's life at this period of his university career. It was the usual uneventful, quiet life of a studious Camford undergraduate. Happy it was beyond any other time, except perhaps a few vernal days of boyhood, but it was unmarked by any incidents. He read, and rowed, and went to lectures, and worked at classics, mathematics, and philosophy, and dropped in sometimes to a debate or a private-business squabble at the Union, and played racquets, fives, and football, and talked eagerly in hall and men's rooms over the exciting topics of the day, and occasionally went to wine or to breakfast with a don, and, (absorbed in some grand old poet or historian), lingered by his lamp over the lettered page from chapel-time till the grey dawn, when he would retire to pure and refreshful sleep, humming a tune out of very cheerfulness.

Happy days, happy friendships, happy study, happy recreation, happy exemption from the cares of life! The bright visions of a scholar, the bright hilarity of a youth, the bright acquaintanceship with many united by a brotherly bond within those grey walls, were so many mingled influences that ran together "like warp and woof" in the web of a singularly enviable life. And every day he felt that he was knowing more, and acquiring a strength and power which should fit him hereafter for the more toilsome business and sterner struggles of common life. Well may old Cowley exclaim—

"O pulerae sine luxes aedes, vitaeque decore
Splendida paupertas ingenuusque pudor!"

All the reading men of his year were now anxiously occupied in working for the Saint Werner's scholarships. They were the blue ribbon of the place. In value they were not much more than 50 pounds a year, but as the scholars had an honourable distinctive seat both in hall and chapel, and as from their ranks alone the Fellows were selected, all the most intelligent and earnest men used their best efforts to obtain them on the earliest possible occasion. At the scholars' table were generally to be found the most distinguished among the alumni of Saint Werner's.

Julian still moved chiefly among his old friends, although he had a large acquaintance, and by no means confined himself to the society of particular classes. But De Vayne's illness made a sad gap in the circle of his most intimate associates, and he was not yet sufficiently recovered to attempt a correspondence. Among the dons, Julian began to like Mr Admer more and more, and found that his cynicism of manner was but the result of disappointed ambition and unsteady aims, while his heart was sound and right.

Kennedy, as well as Julian, had always hoped to gain a scholarship at his first trial, but now, with only one term left him to read in, his chance seemed to fade away to nothing. Poor fellow, he had returned with the strongest possible intention of working, and of abandoning at once and for ever all objectionable acquaintances and all dangerous ways. Hourly the sweet face of Violet looked in upon his silent thoughts, and filled him with shame as he thought of lost opportunities and wasted hours.

"Kennedy," said Mr Admer, "how can you be so intolerably

idle? I saw some of your Christmas papers, and they were wholly unworthy of your abilities."

"I know it well. But what could you expect? The Pindar I had read once over with a crib; the morality I had not looked at; the mathematics I did not touch."

"But what excuse have you? I really feel quite angry with you. You are wholly throwing away everything. What have you to show for your time and money? Only think, my dear fellow, that an opportunity like this comes only once in life, and soon your college days will be over with nothing to remember."

"True, too true."

"Well, I am glad that you see and own it. I began to fear that you were one of that contemptible would-be fine gentleman class that affects forsooth to despise work as a thing unworthy of their eminence."

"No, Mr Admer," said Kennedy, "my idleness springs from very different causes."

"And then these Brogtens and people, whom you are so often seen with; which of them do you think understands you, or can teach you anything worth knowing? and which of them do you think you will ever care to look back to as acquaintances in after days?"

"Not one of them. I hate the whole set."

"And then, my dear Kennedy—for I speak to you out of real good-will—I would say it with the utmost delicacy, but you must know that your name has suffered from the company you frequent."

"Can I not see it to be so?" he answered moodily; "no need to tell me that, when I read it in the faces of nearly every man I see. The men have not yet forgiven me De Vayne's absence, though really and truly that sin does not lie at my door. Except Julian and Lillyston there is hardly a man I respect, who does not look at me with averted eyes. Of course Grayson and the dons detest me to a man; but I don't care for them."

"Then, you mysterious fellow, seeing all this so clearly, why do you suffer it to be so?"

Kennedy only shook his head; already there had begun to creep over him a feeling of despair; already it seemed to him as though the gate of heaven were a lion-haunted portal guarded by a fiery sword.

For he had soon found that his intense resolutions to do right met with formidable checks. There are two stern facts—facts which it does us all good to remember—which generally lie in the path of repentance, and look like crouching lions to the remorseful soul. First, the fact that we become so entangled by habit and circumstance, so enslaved by association and custom, that the very atmosphere around us seems to have become impregnated with a poison which we cannot cease to breathe; secondly, the fact that "in the physical world there is no forgiveness of sins;" to abandon our evil courses is not to escape the punishment of them, and although we may have relinquished them wholly in the present, we cannot escape the consequences of the past. Remission of sin is not the remission of their results. The very monsters we dread, and the dread of which terrifies us into the consideration of our ways, glare upon us out of the future darkness, as large, as terrible, as irresistible, whether we approach them on the road to ruin, or whether we seem to fly from them through the hardly attained and narrow wicket of genuine repentance.

Both these difficulties acted with their full force on the mind of Kennedy. His error was its own punishment, and its heaviest punishment. The hours he had lost were lost so utterly, that he could never hope to recover them; the undesirable acquaintances he had formed were so far ripe as to render it no light task to abandon them; and above all, the fleck on his character, the connection of his name with the outrage on De Vayne, had injured his reputation in a manner which he never hoped, by future endeavours, to obviate or remove.

For instance, there was at once an objection to his dropping the society of the set to which Bruce and Brogten had introduced him. He owed them money, which at present he could not pay; his undischarged "debts of honour" hung like a millstone round his neck. To pay these seemed a necessary preliminary even to the possibility of commencing a new career.

But how to get the money? ah me! new temptations seemed springing up around like the crop of armed men from the furrows sown with the dragon's teeth.

There was but one way which suggested itself to his mind, by which he would be able at once to deliver himself in part by meeting the most exigent demands. Let me hurry over the struggle which it cost him, but finally he adopted it. It was this.

Mr Kennedy was most liberal in allowing his son everything which could possibly further his university studies, and the most important item in his quarterly expenses was the charge for private tuition. This sum was always paid by Kennedy himself, and it amounted at least to seven pounds a term. Now, what if he should not only ask his father to allow him this term a classical and a mathematical tutor, but also request permission to read double with them both i e, to go for an hour every day instead of every other day? This would at once procure him from his father the sum of twenty-eight pounds, and by means of this he could, with great economy, clear off all the most pressing of those pecuniary obligations which bound him to company, which he longed to shun, and exposed him to dangers which he had learnt to fear. Of course he would be obliged to forego all assistance from private tutors, and simply to appropriate the money, without his father's knowledge, to other ends. In a high point of view, it was simple embezzlement; it was little better than a form of swindling. But in this gross and repulsive shape, it never suggested itself to poor Kennedy's imagination. Somehow one's own sins never look so bad in our eyes as the same sins when committed by another. He argued that he would really be applying the money as his father intended, viz, to such purposes as should most advance the objects of his university career. He was committing a sin to save himself from temptation.

The near approach of the scholarship examination, and Kennedy's failure at Christmas, made his father all the more ready to give him every possible advantage that money could procure. Ignorant of the fact that to "read double" with a tutor was almost a thing unprecedented at Camford, and that to do so, both in classics and mathematics, was a thing wholly unknown, and indeed practically impossible, Mr Kennedy was only delighted at Edward's letter, as conveying a proof of his extreme and laudable eagerness to recover lost ground, and do his best. He very readily wrote the cheque for the sum required, and praised his son liberally for these indications of effort. How those praises cut Kennedy to the heart.

But he at once spent the money in the way which he had devised, and added thereby a new load of mental bitterness to the heavy weight which already oppressed him. The sum thus appropriated greatly lightened, although it did not remove, the pecuniary obligations which he had contracted at cards or in other ways to his set of "fast" companions; but it was at the cost of his peace of mind.

Externally he profited by the transaction. He was enabled in great measure, without the charge of meanness, to drop the most undesirable of his acquaintances, and awaking eagerly to the hope of at once redeeming his reputation and lessening his difficulties by gaining a scholarship, he began, for the first time since he had entered Saint Werner's, to work steadily with all his might.

He seemed to be living two lives in one, and often asked himself whether there was in his character some deeply-rooted hypocrisy. With Julian and Owen, and the men who resembled them, he could talk nobly of all that was honourable, and he powerfully upheld a chivalrous ideal of duty and virtue. And as his face lighted up, and the thoughts flowed in the full stream of eloquent language in reprobation of some mean act, or in glowing eulogium of some recorded heroism for the performance of what was right, who would have fancied, who would have believed, that Kennedy's own life had failed so egregiously in the commonest requirements of steadfastness and honesty?

None rejoiced more in the outward change of life than Julian Home; for Violet's sake now, as well as for Kennedy's, he felt a keen and brotherly interest in the progress and estimation of his friend. Once more they were to be found together as often as they had been in their freshman's year, and it was Julian's countenance and affection that tended more than anything else to repair Kennedy's damaged popularity, and remove the tarnish attaching to his name.

One evening they were taking the usual two-hours' constitutional—which is often the poor substitute for exercise in the case of reading men—and discussing together the chances of the coming scholarship examination, when they found themselves near a place called Gower's Mill, and heard a sudden cry for help. Pressing forwards they saw a boat floating upside down, and whirling about tumultuously in the racing and rain-swollen eddies of the mill-dam. A floating straw hat was already being sucked in by the gurgling rush of water that roared under the mighty circumference of the wheel, and for a moment they saw nothing more. But as they ran up, a black spot emerged from the stream, only a few yards from the mill, and they saw a man, evidently in the last stage of exhaustion, struggling feebly in the white and boiling waves.

The position was agonising. The man's utmost efforts only served to keep him stationary, and it was clear, from the frantic violence of his exertion, that he could not last an instant longer. Indeed, as they reached the bank, he began to sink and disappear— disappear as it seemed to the certainty of a most horrid death.

In one instant—without considering the danger and apparent hopelessness of the attempt, without looking at the wild force of the water, and the grinding roll of the big wheel, without even waiting to fling off their coats—Julian and Kennedy, actuated by the strong instinct to save a fellow-creature's life, had both plunged into the mill-dam, and at the same moment struck out for the sinking figure. It was not till then that they felt their terrific danger; in the swirl of those spumy and hissing waves it was all but impossible for them to make head against the current, and they felt it carry them nearer and nearer to the black, dripping mass, one blow of which would stun them, and one revolution of it mangle them with horrible mutilation. They reached the drowning wretch, and each seizing

178

him by the arm, shouted for assistance, and buffeted gallantly with the headstrong stream. The senseless burden which they supported clogged their efforts, and as they felt themselves gradually swept nearer, nearer, nearer to destruction, the passionate desire of self-preservation woke in both of them in all its wild agony;—yet they would not attempt to preserve themselves by letting go the man to save whose life they had so terribly endangered their own.

Meanwhile their repeated shouts and those of the swimmer, which had first attracted their own attention, had aroused the miller, who instantly, on hearing them, ran down with a rope to the water's side. He threw it skilfully; with a wild clutch Kennedy caught it, and in another moment, as from the very jaws of death, when they were almost touching the fatal wheel, they were drawn to shore, still carrying, or rather dragging, with them their insensible companion.

After a word of hurried thanks to the miller for saving their lives, they began to turn their whole attention to the half-drowned man, and to apply the well-known remedies for restoring extinct animation.

"Good heavens," said Julian, "it is Brogten!"

"Brogten?" said Kennedy; he looked on the face, and whispered half-aloud, "Thank God!"

They carried him into the mill, put him between the blankets in a warm bed, chafed his numb limbs, and sent off for the nearest doctor. Very soon he began to revive, and recovered his consciousness; immediately this was the case, Julian and Kennedy ran home as quickly as they could to change their wet clothes.

The next day the doctor ordered Brogten to lie in bed till after mid-day, and then allowed him, now thoroughly well and rested, to walk home to Saint Werner's. He had not yet learnt the names of his deliverers.

He reached the college in the evening, and after changing his boating dress, his first care was to try and learn to whom he was indebted for his life. Almost the first man he met told him that the men who had risked their safety for his were Home and Kennedy.

Home and Kennedy! Home, to whom he had caused the bitterest disappointment and done the most malicious injury which had ever happened to him in his life; Kennedy, whom he had tried but too successfully to corrupt and ruin, tempt from duty, and push from his good name!

Deeply, very deeply, was Brogten humiliated; he felt that his enemies had indeed heaped coals of fire upon his head.

He determined, as his first duty, to go and thank them both—Kennedy first, as the one against whom he had most wilfully sinned.

He found Kennedy sitting down to tea, and Julian, Owen, and Suton were with him.

"Kennedy," he said, "I have come to thank you and Home for a very gallant deed; I need not say how much I feel indebted to you for the risk you ran in saving my life."

Genuine tears rushed into his dark eyes as he spoke, and cordially grasped the hands which, without a word, they proffered. Community of danger, consciousness of obligation, blotted out all evil memories; and to have stood side by side together on the very brink of the precipice of death was a bond of union which could not be ignored or set aside. That night, in spite of bygones, the feeling of those three young men for each other was of the kindliest cast.

"Won't you stay to tea, Brogten?" said Kennedy.

He looked round, as though uncertain whether the others would like his company, but as they all seconded Kennedy's request, he gladly stayed. It was the first evening that he had regularly spent in the society of reading men, and he was both delighted and surprised at the rare pleasure he received from the vigour and liveliness of their conversation. These were the men whom he had despised as slow, yet what a contrast between their way of talking and the inanities of Fitzurse or the shallow flippancy of Bruce. As he sat there and listened, his very face became softer in its lines from the expression of a real and intelligent interest, and they all thought that he was a better fellow, on closer acquaintance, than they had been accustomed to suppose. Ah me! how often one remains unaware of the good side of those whom we dislike.

Oh, those Camford conversations—how impetuous, how interesting, how thoroughly hearty and unconventional they were! How utterly presumption and ignorance were scouted in them, and how completely they were free from the least shadow of insincerity or ennui. If I could but transfer to my page a true and vivid picture of one such evening, spent in the society of Saint Werner's friends—if I could write down but one such conversation, and at all express its vivacity, its quick flashes of thought and logic, its real desire for truth and knowledge, its friendly fearlessness, its felicitous illustrations, its unpremeditated wit, such a record, taken fresh from the life, would be worth all that I shall ever write. But youth flies, and as she flies all the bright colours fade from the wings of thought, and the bloom vanishes from the earnest eloquence of speech.

Yet, as I write, let me call to mind, if but for a moment, the remembrance of those happy evenings, when we would meet to read Shakespeare or the Poets in each other's rooms, and pleasant sympathies and pleasant differences of opinion freely discussed, called into genial life, friendships which we once hoped and believed would never have grown cold. Let the image of that bright social circle, picturesquely scattered in armchairs round the winter fire, rise up before my fancy once more, and let me recall what can never be again. Of the honoured and well-loved few who one night recorded their names and thoughts in one precious little book, two are dead though it is but five years back; C E B— is dead; and R H P— is dead; C E B— the chivalrous and gallant-hearted, the champion of the past, the "Tory whom Liberals loved;" and R H P—, the honest and noble, the eloquent speaker, and the brave actor, and the fearless thinker—he, too, is dead, nobly volunteering in works of danger and difficulty during the Indian Mutiny; but L—, and B—, and M—, and others are living yet, and to them I consecrate this page they will forgive the digression, and for their sakes I will venture to let it pass. We are scattered now, and our friendship is a silent one, but yet I know that to them, at least, changed or unchanged, my words will recall the fading memory of glorious days.

The conversation, (but do not suppose that I shall attempt, after what I have said, to reproduce it), happened to turn that evening on the phenomena of memory. It started thus:— They had been discussing some subject of the day, when Owen observed to Julian—

"Why, how grave you look, Julian."

"Do I? I was thinking of something odd. While you were talking—without the faintest apparent reason that I can discover, (and I was trying to hit upon one when you spoke)—a fact started up in my mind, which had no connection whatever with the subject, and yet which forced itself quite strongly and obtrusively on my notice."

"Just as one catches sight suddenly of some stray bit of seaweed floating in a great world of waters, which seems to have no business there," said Kennedy.

"Yes. But there must have been some reason for my thinking of it just then."

"The law of association, depend upon it," said Owen, "even if the connecting links were so subtle and swiftly moved that you failed to detect their presence."

"Are you of the Materialist school, Owen, about memory?" said Julian, "i e, do you go with Hobbes and Condillac, and make it a decaying sense or a transformed sensation?"

"Not a bit; I believe it to be a spiritual faculty, entirely independent of mere physical organisation."

181

"Wo-ho!" said Kennedy; "the physiologists will join issue with you there. How for instance do you account for such stories as that of the groom, who, getting a kick on a particular part of the head from a vicious horse, suffered no harm except in forgetting everything which had happened up to that time?"

"It isn't a bit conclusive. I don't say that the conscious exercise of memory mayn't be temporarily dependent on organisation, but I do believe that every fact ever imprinted on the memory, however long it may be latent, is of its very nature imperishable."

"Yes," said Suton. "Memory is the book of God. Did you see that story of the shipwreck the other day? One of the survivors, while floating alone on the dark midnight sea, suddenly heard a voice saying to him distinctly, 'Johnny, did you eat sister's grapes?' It was the revived memory of a long-forgotten childish theft. What have the Pineal-Gland-olaters to say to that?"

"What a profound touch that was of Themistocles," said Kennedy, "who rejected the offer of a Memoria Technicha, with the aspiration that some one could teach him to forget. Lethe is the grandest of rivers after all."

"I can illustrate what you are saying," said Brogten, "and I believe it to be true that nothing can be utterly forgotten. Yesterday when you saw me I had sunk twice, and when you rescued me I was insensible. Strange things happened to my memory then!"

"Tell us," said all of them eagerly.

"Well, I believe it's an old story, but I'll tell you. When the first agony of fear, and the sort of gulp of asphyxia was over, I felt as if I was sinking into a pleasant sleep, surrounded by the light of green fields—"

"Because the veins of the eye were bloodshot, and green is the complementary colour," interpolated Kennedy, whereat Owen gave a little incredulous guffaw; and Brogten continued—

"Well, then, it was that all my past life flashed before me, from the least forgotten venial fault of infancy to the worst passion of youth,—only they came to me clear and vivid, in retrograde order. The lies I told when I was a little boy, the wicked words I spoke, the cruel things I did, the first taint that polluted my mind, the faces of school-fellows whom I had irreparably injured, the stolen waters of manhood—all were dashed into my remorseful recollection; they started up like buried, menacing ghosts, without, or even against my will. I felt convinced that they were indestructible."

"That strain I heard was of a higher mood!" thought the auditors, for it was quite a new thing to hear Brogten talk like this, and in such a solemn, manly, sober voice.

"Fancy," said Kennedy, sighing, "an everlasting memory!"

The others went away, but Brogten still lingered in Kennedy's rooms, and, rising, took him by the hand. They both remembered another scene in these rooms, when they two were together,—the torturer and the tortured; but it was different now.

"The worst thing that haunted me, Kennedy, when you were saving my life, was the thought of my wickedness to you. I fear it can never be repaired; yet believe me, that from this day forth I have vowed before God to turn over a new leaf, and my whole effort will be to do all for you that ever may be in my power! Do you forgive me?"

"As I hope to be forgiven," he replied.

Yet it was part of Brogten's punishment in after days to remember that his hand had set the stone moving on the steep hill-side, which afterwards he had no power to stay. It would not come back to him for a wish, but leapt, and rushed, and bounded forward, splintering and splintered by the obstacles in its course, till at last— Could it be saved from being dashed to shivers among the smooth rocks of the valley and the brook?

CHAPTER TWENTY SIX

HAZLET'S VISION

"And ride on his breast, and trouble his rest
In the shape of his deadliest sin."

Anon

Before the scholarship, came the Little-go, so called in the language of men, but known to the gods as the Previous Examination. As it is an examination which all must pass, the standard required is of course very low, and the subjects are merely Paley's Evidences, a little Greek Testament, some easy classic, Scripture History, and a sprinkling of arithmetic and algebra.

The reading men simply regard it as a nuisance, interrupting their reading and wasting their time, i e, until the wisdom of maturer years shows them its necessity and use. But to the idle and the stupid, the name Little-go is fraught with terror. It begins to loom upon them from the commencement of their second year, and all their efforts must be concentrated to avoid the disgrace and hindrance of a pluck. There are regular tutors to cram Poll men for this necessary ordeal, and the processes applied to introduce the smallest possible modicum of information into the heads of the victims, the surgical operations necessary to inculcate into them the simplest facts, would, if narrated, form a curious chapter in morbid psychology. I suggest this merely as a pregnant hint for the future historian of Camford; personally I am only acquainted by report with the system resorted to.

Hazlet began to be in a fright about the Little-go from the very commencement of his second October. His mother well knew that the examination was approaching, and thought it quite impossible that her ingenuous and right-minded son could fall a victim to the malice of examiners. Hazlet was not so sure of this himself, and as the days had passed by when he could speak of the classics with a holy indignation against their vices and idolatry, he was wrought up by dread of the coming papers into a high state of nervous excitement.

I will not betray the mistakes he made, or dish up in this place the "crambe repétita" of those Little-go anecdotes, which at this period of the year awaken the laughter of combination-rooms, and dissipate the dulness of Camford life. Suffice it to say that Hazlet displayed an ignorance at once egregious and astounding; the ingenious perversity of his mistakes, the fatuous absurdity of his confusions, would be inconceivable to any who do not know by experience the extraordinary combinations of ignorance and conceit. The examiners were very lenient and forbearing, but Hazlet was plucked; plucked too in Scripture History, which astonished everybody, until it became known that he had attributed John the Baptist's death to his having "danced with Herodias's daughter"—traced a connection between the Old and New Testaments in the fact of Saint Peter's having cut off the ear of Malachi the last of the prophets—and stated that the substance of Saint Paul's sermon at Athens, was "crying vehemently about the space of two hours, Great is Diana of the Ephesians!"

It is a sad pity that such ludicrous associations should centre round the word "pluck." It is anything but a laughing matter to those who undergo the process; they have tried hard and worked diligently perhaps to pass the examination, and if they fail they see before them another long period of weary and dissatisfied effort, with the same probability of failure again and again repeated: for until the barrier of the Little-go is passed they can advance no further, and must simply stay at Camford until in some way or other they can succeed in getting up the requisite minimum of information. I have seen a strong man in the senate-house turn as white as a sheet, when a paper which he was unable to answer was placed before him. I fancy I see him now, and distinctly remember my strong feeling of compassion for his distress, and my earnest hope that he would not be "floored."

There was a general laugh in Saint Werner's when it was announced that Hazlet was plucked; and in Scripture History too! His follies and inconsistencies had unhappily made him a butt, but men little knew how heavily the misfortune would weigh upon him.

He happened at this time to be living on the same stair-case with Lillyston, and Lillyston, who was in the rooms below him, was quite amazed at the sounds which he heard proceeding from his rooms. For a long time there was a series of boo-hoos, long, loud, and wailing as of some animal in distress, and then there was an uproar as of some one running violently about, and throwing the furniture out of his way. Lillyston was just on the point of going to see what was the matter when the breathless bedmaker appeared at the door, and said—"Oh, Mr Lillyston, sir, do go and look at Mr Hazlet, sir; he's took very bad, he is."

"Took very bad—how do you mean?"

"Why, sir, it's the Little-go, sir, as done it. He's plucked, sir, and it's upset him like. So, when I asked him if he'd a-tea'd, and if I should take away the things, he begins a banging his chairs about, you see, sir, quite uncomfortable."

Lillyston immediately ran up-stairs. The violent fit seemed to have subsided, for Hazlet, peering out of a corner, with wandering, spectacled eyes, quite cowered when he saw him. Lillyston was shocked at the spectacle he presented. Hazlet was but half dressed, his hands kept up an uneasy and vague motion, his face was blank, and his whole appearance resembled that of an idiot.

"Why, Hazlet, my man, what's the matter with you?" said Lillyston, cheerily.

Hazlet trembled, and muttered something about a dog. It happened that just before coming back from the senate-house, a large Newfoundland had run against him, and his excited imagination had mingled this most recent impression with the vagaries of a temporary madness.

"The dog, my dear fellow; why, there's no dog here."

Hazlet only cowered farther into the corner.

"Here, won't you have some tea?" said Lillyston; "I'll make it for you. Come and help me."

He began to busy himself about setting the tea-things, and cutting the bread, while he occupied Hazlet in pouring out the water and attending to the kettle. Hazlet started violently every now and then, and looked with a terrified side-glance at Lillyston, as though apprehensive of some wrong.

At last Lillyston got him to sit down quietly, and gave him a cup of tea and some bread. He ate it in silence, except that every now and then he uttered a sort of wail, and looked up at Lillyston. The look didn't seem to satisfy him, for, after a few minutes, he seized his knife, and said, "I shall cut off your whiskers."

What put the grotesque fancy into his head, Lillyston did not know; probably some faint reminiscence of having been forced to shave after the trick which Bruce had played on him by painting his face with lamp-black and ochre.

Lillyston decidedly declined the proposition, and they both started up from their seats—Hazlet brandishing his knife with determined purpose, and looking at his companion with a strange savage glare under his spectacles.

After darting round the room once or twice to escape his attack, Lillyston managed with wonderful skill to clutch the wrist of Hazlet's right hand, and, being very strong, he held him with the grasp of a vice, while with his left hand he forced the knife out of his clutch, and dropped it on the floor. He held him tight for a minute or two, although Hazlet struggled so fiercely that it was no easy task, and then quietly forced him into a chair, and spoke to him in a firm authoritative voice—

"No mischief, Hazlet; we shan't allow it. Now listen to me: you must go to bed."

The tone of voice and the strength of will which characterised Lillyston's proceedings, awed Hazlet into submission. He cried a little, and then suffered Lillyston to see him into his rooms, and to put him into a fair way towards going to bed. Taking the precaution to remove his razor, Lillyston locked the door upon him, and determined at once to get medical advice. The doctor, however, could give very little help; it was, he said, a short fit of temporary madness, for which quiet and change of air were the only effectual remedies. He did not anticipate that there would be any other outbreak of violence, or anything more than a partial imbecility.

"Do come and help me to manage Hazlet," said Lillyston to Julian next morning; "his head has been turned by being plucked for the Little-go, and he's as mad as Hercules Furens."

Julian went, and they stayed in Hazlet's room till he had quietly breakfasted. He then appeared to be so calm that Lillyston agreed to leave Julian there for the morning, and to take the charge of Hazlet for the afternoon and evening. It seemed absolutely necessary that someone should take charge of him, and they thought it best to divide the labour.

Julian sorely felt the loss of time. He had a great deal to get through before the all-important scholarship examination, and the loss of every available hour fretted him, for since he had failed in the Clerkland, he was doubly anxious to gain a Saint Werner's scholarship at his first time of trial. Still he never wavered for a moment in the determination to fulfil the duty of taking care of his Ildown acquaintance, and he spent the whole tedious morning in trying to amuse him.

Hazlet's ceaseless allusions to "the dog," and the feeble terror which it seemed to cause him, made it necessary to talk to him incessantly, and to turn his attention, as far as possible, to other things. He had to be managed like a very wilful and stupid child, and when one of the five hours which Julian had to spend with him was finished, he was worn out with anxiety and fatigue. It is a dreadful thing to be alone in charge of a human being—a being in human shape, who is, either by accident or constitution, incapable alike of responsibility and thought. Hazlet had been able to play draughts pretty well, so Julian got out a board and challenged him to a game, but instead of playing, Hazlet only scrabbled on the board, and pushed the pieces about in a meaningless confusion, while every now and then the sullen glare came into his eye which showed Julian the necessity of being on his guard if self-defence should be needed. Then Julian tried to get him to draw, and showing him a picture, sketched a few strokes of outline, and said—

"Now, Hazlet, finish copying this picture for me."

Hazlet took the pencil between his unsteady fingers, and let it make futile scratches on the paper, and, when Julian repeated his words, wrote down in a slow painful hand—

"Finish copying pict–ure pict–."

What was to be done in such a case as this? Julian suggested a turn in the grounds, but Hazlet betrayed such dread at the thought of leaving his rooms, and encountering "the dog," that Julian was afraid, if he persisted, of driving him into a fit.

Just as the dilemma was becoming seriously unpleasant, Brogten came up to the rooms, and begged Julian to intrust Hazlet to his charge.

"Your time is valuable, Home—particularly just now. Mine is all but worthless. At any rate I have no special work as you have, and I can take care of poor Hazlet very well."

"Oh, no," said Julian; "I mustn't shrink from the duty I have undertaken, and besides you'll find it very dull and unpleasant work."

"Never mind that. I once had an idiot brother—dead now—

and I understand well how to manage any one in a case like this. Besides, Hazlet is one of the many I have injured. Let me stay."

"I really am afraid you won't like it."

"Nonsense, Home; I won't give in, depend upon it. I am quite in earnest, and am besides most anxious that you should get a scholarship this time. Don't refuse me the privilege of helping you."

Julian could refuse no longer, and went back to his rooms with perfect confidence that Brogten would do his work willingly and well. He looked in about mid-day to see how things were going on, and found that, after thoroughly succeeding in amusing his patient, Brogten had persuaded him to go to sleep, in the conviction that by the time he awoke he would be nearly well. Nor was he mistaken. The next day Hazlet was sufficiently recovered to go home for the Easter vacation.

It was a very bitter and humiliating trial to him; but misfortune, however frequently it causes reformation, is not invariably successful in changing a man's heart and life. Hazlet came back after the Easter vacation with recovered health, but damaged constitution, and in no respect either better or wiser for the misfortune he had undergone.

One peculiarity of his recent attack was a strong nervous excitability, which was induced by very slight causes, and Hazlet had not long returned to Saint Werner's when the dissipation of his life began once more to tell perniciously upon his state of health. It must not be imagined that because he was the easiest possible victim of temptation, he suffered no upbraidings of a terrified and remorseful conscience. Many a time they overwhelmed him with agony and a dread of the future, mingling with his slavish terrors of a material Gehenna, and stirring up his turbid thoughts until they drove him to the verge of madness. But the inward chimera of riotous passions was too fierce for the weak human reason, and while he hated himself he continued still to sin.

Late one night he was returning to his rooms from the foul haunts of squalid dissipation and living death, when the thought of his own intolerable condition pressed on him with a heavier than usual weight. It was a very cloudy night, and he had long exceeded the usual college hours. The wind tossed about his clothes, and dashed in his face a keen impalpable sleet, while nothing dispelled the darkness except the occasional gleam of a lamp struggling fitfully with the driving mist. Hazlet reached Saint Werner's wet and miserable; in returning he had lost his way, and wandered into the most disreputable and poverty-stricken streets, the very homes of thievery and dirt, where he seriously feared for his personal safety. By the time he got to the college gates he was drenched through and through, and while his body shivered with the cold air, the condition of his mind was agitated and terrified, and the sudden blaze of light that fell on him from the large college lamp, as the gates opened, dazzled his unaccustomed eyes.

Hastily running across the court to his own rooms, he groped his way—giddy and crapulous—giddy and crapulous—up the dark and narrow stair-case, and after some fumbling with his key opened the door.

Lillyston, who was just going to bed after a long evening of hard work, heard his footstep on the stairs, and thought with sorrow that he had not mended his old bad ways. He heard him open the door, and then a long wild shriek, followed by the sound of some one falling, rang through the buildings.

In an instant, Lillyston had darted up-stairs, and the other men who "kept" on the stair-case, jumped out of bed hastily, thrust on their slippers, and also ran out to see what was the matter. As Lillyston reached the threshold of Hazlet's rooms, he stumbled against something, and stooping down found that it was the senseless body of Hazlet himself stretched at full length upon the floor.

He looked up, but saw nothing to explain the mystery; the rooms were in darkness, except that a dull, blue flame, flickering over the black and red relics of the fire, threw fantastic gleams across the furniture and ceiling, and gave an odd, wild appearance to the cap and gown that hung beside the door.

Lillyston was filled with surprise, and lit the candle on the table. Lifting Hazlet on the sofa, he carefully looked at him to see if he was correct in his first surmise, that the unhappy man had swallowed poison, or committed suicide in some other way. But there was no trace of anything of the kind, and Hazlet merely appeared to have fainted and fallen suddenly.

Aided by Noel, one of those who had been alarmed by that piercing shriek, Lillyston took the proper means to revive Hazlet from his fainting fit, and put him to bed. He rapidly recovered his consciousness, but earnestly begged them not to press him on the subject of his alarm, respecting which he was unable or unwilling to give them any information.

The next morning he was very ill; excitement and anxiety brought on a brain fever, which kept him for many weary weeks in his sick-room, and from which he had not fully recovered until after a long stay at Ildown. As he lost, in consequence of this attack, the whole of the ensuing term, he was obliged to degrade, as it is called, i e to place his name on the list of the year below; and he did not return to Camford till the following October, where his somewhat insignificant individuality had been almost forgotten.

Let us anticipate a little to throw light on what we have narrated.

When Hazlet did come back to undergraduate life, he at once sought the alienated friends from whom he had been separated ever since the disastrous period of his acquaintanceship with Bruce. He came back to them penitent and humble, with those convictions now existing in his mind in their reality and genuineness, which before he had only simulated so successfully as to deceive himself. I will not say that he did not continue ignorant and bigoted, but he was no longer conceited and malicious. I will not say that he never showed himself dogmatic and ill-informed, but he was no longer obtrusive and uncharitable. His life was better than his dogmas, and the sincerity of his good intentions counteracted and nullified the ill effects of a narrow and unwholesome creed. There were no farther inconsistencies in his conduct, and he showed firmly, yet modestly, the line he meant to follow, and the side he meant to take. As his conscience had become scrupulous, and his life irreproachable, it mattered comparatively little that his intellectual character was tainted with fanaticism and gloom.

I would not be mistaken to mean that he found his penitence easy, or that he was, like Saint Paul, transformed as it were by a lightning flash—"a fusile Christian." I say, there were—after his two sicknesses and long suffering, and experiences bitter as wormwood—there were, I say, no more outward inconsistencies in his life; but I do not say that within there were no fierce, fearful struggles, so wearisome at times that it almost seemed better to yield than to feel the continued anguish of such mighty temptations. All this the man must always go through who has warmed in his bosom the viper whose poisoned fang has sent infection into his blood. But through God's grace Hazlet was victorious: and as, when the civilisation of some infant colony is advancing on the confines of a desert, the wild beasts retire before it, until they become rare, and their howling is only heard in the lonely night, and then even that sign of their fury is but a strange occurrence, until it is heard no more; so in Hazlet, the many-headed monsters, which breed in the slime of a fallen human heart, were one by one slain or driven backwards by watchfulness, and shame, and prayer.

Julian and Lillyston had never shunned his society, either when he breathed the odour of sanctity, or when he sank into the slough of wretchlessness. Both of them were sufficiently conscious of the heart's weakness to prevent them from the cold and melancholy presumption which leads weak and sinful men to desert and denounce those whom the good spirits have not yet deserted, and whom the good God has not finally condemned. As long as he sought their society, they were always open to his company, however distasteful; and the advice they gave him was tendered in simple good-will—not as though from the haughty vantage-ground of a superior excellence. Even when Hazlet was at the worst—when to be seen with him, after the publicity of his vices, involved something like a slur on a man's fair name—even in these his worst days neither Julian nor Lillyston would have refused, had he so desired it, to walk with him under the lime-tree avenue, or up and down the cloisters of Warwick's Court.

But they naturally met him more often when his manner of life was changed for the better, and were both glad to see that he had found the jewel which adversity possessed. It happened that he was with them one evening when the conversation turned on supernatural appearances, the possibility of which was maintained by Julian and Owen, while Lillyston in his genial way was pooh-poohing them altogether. Hazlet alone sat silent, but at last he said—

"I have never yet mentioned to any living soul what once happened to me, but I will do so now. Lillyston, you remember the night when I aroused you with a scream?"

"Well!" said Lillyston.

"That night I was returning in all the bitterness of remorse from places where, but for God's blessing, I might have perished utterly"—and Hazlet shuddered—"when from out of the storm and darkness I reached my room door. You know that a beam ran right across my ceiling. When I threw open the door to enter, I saw on that beam as clearly as I now see you—no, more clearly, far more clearly than I now see you, for your presence makes no special impression on me, and this was burnt into my very brain—I saw there written in letters of fire—

"'AND THIS IS HELL.'

"Struck dumb with horror, I stared at it; there could be no doubt about it, the letters burned and glared and reddened before my very eyes, and seemed to wave like the northern lights, and bicker into angrier flame as I looked at them. They fascinated me as I stood there dumb and stupefied, when suddenly I saw the dark and massive form of a hand, over which hung the skirt of a black robe, moving slowly away from the last letter. What more I might have seen I cannot tell;—it was then that I fell and fainted, and my shriek startled all the men on the stair-case."

Hazlet told his story with such deep solemnity, and such hollow pauses of emotion, that the listeners sat silent for a while.

"But yet," said Lillyston, "if you come to analyse this, it resolves itself into nothing. You were confessedly agitated, and almost hysterical that night; your body was unstrung; you were wet through, and it was doubtless the sudden passage from the darkness outside to the dim and uncertain glimmer of your own room, which acted so powerfully on your excited imagination, as to project your inward thoughts into a shape which you mistook for an external appearance. I remember noticing the aspect of your rooms myself that evening; the mysterious shadows, and the mingled effects of dull red firelight with black objects, together with the rustle of the red curtain in front of your window which you had left open, and the weird waving of your black gown in the draught, made such an impression even on me merely in consequence of the alarm your shriek had excited, that I could have fancied anything myself, if I wasn't pretty strong-headed, and rather prosaic. As it was, I did half fancy an unknown Presence in the room."

"Yes, but you say inward thoughts," replied Hazlet eagerly. "Now these weren't my inward thoughts; on the contrary they flashed on me like a revelation, and the strange word, 'And,' (for I read distinctly, 'And this is—') was to me like an awful copula connecting time and eternity for ever. I had always thought of quite another, quite a different hell; but this showed me for the first time that the state of sinfulness is the hell of sin. It was only the other day that I came across those lines of Milton—oh, how true they are—

"Which way I fly is hell, myself am hell,
And in the lowest deep a lower deep
Still gaping to devour me opens wide,
To which the hell I suffer seems a heaven."

"It was the truth conveyed in those lines which I then first discovered, and discovered, it seems to me, from without. I know very very little—I am shamefully ignorant, but I do think that the vision of that night taught me more than a thousand volumes of scholastic theology. And let me say too," he continued humbly, "that by it I was plucked like a brand from the burning; by it my conversion was brought about."

None of the others were in a mood to criticise the phraseology of Hazlet's religious convictions, and he clearly desired that the subject of his own immediate experiences, as being one full of awfulness for him, might be dropped.

"Apropos of your argument, I care very little, Hugh," said

Julian, "whether you make supernatural appearances objective or subjective. I mean I don't care whether you regard the appearance as a mere deception of the eye, wrought by the disordered workings of the brain, or as the actual presence of a supernatural phenomenon. The result, the effect, the reality of the appearance is just the same in either case. Whether the end is produced by an illusion of the senses, or an appeal to them, the end is produced, and the senses are impressed by something which is not in the ordinary course of human events, just as powerfully as if the ghost had flesh and blood, or the voice were a veritable pulsation of articulated air. The only thing that annoys me is a contemptuous and supercilious denial of the facts."

"I hold with you, Julian," said Owen. "Take for instance the innumerable recorded instances where intimation has been given of a friend's or relative's death by the simultaneous appearance of his image to some one far absent, and unconscious even of his illness. There are four ways of treating such stories—the first is to deny their truth, which is, to say the least, not only grossly uncharitable, but an absurd and impertinent caprice adopted in order to reject unpleasant evidence; the second is to account for them by an optical delusion, accidentally synchronising with the event, which seems to me a most monstrous ignoring of the law of chances; a third is to account for them by the existence of some exquisite faculty, (existing in different degrees of intensity, and in some people not existing at all), whereby physical impressions are invisibly conveyed by some mysterious sympathy of organisation a faculty of which it seems to me there are the most abundant traces, however much it may be sneered and jeered at by those shallow philosophers who believe nothing but what they can grasp with both hands: and a fourth is to suppose that spirits can, of their own will, or by superior permission, make themselves sometimes visible to human eyes."

"Or," said Julian, "so affect the senses as to produce the impression that they are present to human eyes."

"And to show you, Lillyston," said Owen, "how little I fear any natural explanations, and how much I think them beside the point, I'll tell you what happened to me only the other night, and which yet does not make me at all inclined to rationalise Hazlet's story. I had just put out the candle in my bedroom, when over my head I saw a handwriting on the wall in characters of light. I started out of bed, and for a moment fancied that I could read the words, and that somebody had been playing me a trick with phosphorus. But the next minute, I saw how it was; the moonlight was shining in through the little muslin folds of the lower blind, and as the folds were very symmetrical, the chequered reflection on the wall looked exactly like a series of words."

"Well, now, that would have made a capital ghost story," said Lillyston, "if you had been a little more imaginative and nervous. And still more if the illusion had only been partially optical, and partly the result of excited feelings."

"It matters nothing to me," said Hazlet, rising, "whether the characters I saw were written by the finger of a man's hand, or limned by spirits on the sensorium of the brain. All I know is that— thank God—they were there."

CHAPTER TWENTY SEVEN

JULIAN AND KENNEDY

"But there where I have garnered up my heart,
Where either I must live, or bear no life;
The fountain from the which my current runs
Or else dries up; to be discarded thence!
Patience, thou young and rose-lipped cherubim!
Aye there, look grim as hell!"

Othello, Act 4, scene 2

Saint Werner's clock, with "its male and female voice," has just told the university that it is nine o'clock.

A little crowd of Saint Wernerians is standing before the chapel door, and even the grass of the lawn in front of it is hardly sacred to-day from common feet. The throng composed of undergraduates, dons, bedmakers, and gyps, is broken into knots of people, who are chatting together according to their several kinds; but they are so quiet and expectant that the very pigeons hardly notice them, but flutter about and coo and peck up the scattered bread-crumbs, just as if nobody was there. If you look attentively round the court, you will see, too, that many of the windows are open, and you may detect faces half concealed among the window curtains. Clearly everybody is on the look out for something, though it is yet vacation time, and only a small section of the men are up.

194

The door opens, and out sail the Seniors, more than ever conscious of pride and power; they stream away in silk gowns, carrying on their faces the smile of knowledge even into their isolation, where no one can see it. For some reason or other they always meet in chapel, or, for all I know, it may be in the ante-chapel, to elect the Saint Werner's scholars.

And now the much talked of, much thought of, anxiously expected list, which is to make so many happy or miserable, is to be announced. On that little bit of paper, which the chapel-clerk holds in his hands as he stands on the chapel steps, are the names which everybody has been longing to conjecture. He comes out and reads. There are nine scholarships vacant, of which five will be given to the Third-year men, and four to Julian's year.

The five Third-year men are read first, and as each name is announced, off darts some messenger from the crowd to carry the happy intelligence to some expectant senior soph. The heads of listeners lean farther and farther out of the window, for the clerk speaks so loud as to make his voice heard right across the court; and the wires of the telegraph are instantly put into requisition to flash the news to many homes, which it will fill either with rejoicing or with sorrow.

And now for the four Second-year scholars, who have gained the honour of a scholarship their first time of trial, and whose success excites a still keener interest. They are read out in the accidental order of the first entering of their names in the college books.

Silence! the Second-year scholars are—**Dudley Charles Owen**, (for the names are always read out at full length, Christian names and all); **Julian Home; Albert Henry Suton**; and it is a very astonishing fact, but the fourth is Hugh James Lillyston.

Who would have believed it? Everybody expected Owen and Home to get scholarships their first time, and Suton was considered fairly safe of one; but that Kennedy should not have got one, and that Lillyston should, were facts perfectly amazing to all who heard them. Saint Werner's was full of surprise. But after all they might have expected it; Kennedy had been grossly idle, and Lillyston, who had been exceedingly industrious, was not only well-grounded at Harton in classics, but had recently developed a real and promising proficiency in mathematics; and it was this knowledge, joined to great good fortune in the examination, which had won for him the much-envied success.

But not Kennedy?

No. This result was enough most seriously to damp the

intense delight which Julian otherwise felt in his own success, and that of his three friends.

Julian, half-expecting that he would be successful, had come up with Owen early in the day, and received the news from the porter as he entered the college. Kennedy and Lillyston were not yet arrived, and Julian went to meet the coach from Roysley, hoping to see one of them at least for he was almost as anxious to break the disappointment gently to Kennedy, as he was to be the first to bear to his oldest school friend the surprising and delightful news of his success.

They were both in the coach, and Julian was quite puzzled how to meet them. His vexation and delight alternated so rapidly as he looked from one to the other, that he felt exceedingly awkward, and would very much have preferred seeing either of them alone. Lillyston was incredulous; he insisted that there must be some mistake, until he actually saw the list with his own eyes. It was quite by accident, and not with any view of being sworn in as a scholar the next morning, that he had returned to Saint Werner's on that day at all. Kennedy bore the bitter, but not unexpected disappointment with silent stoicism, and showed an unaffected joy at the happy result which had crowned the honest exertions of his best-loved friends.

He bore it in stoical silence, until he reached his own rooms; and then, do not blame him—my poor Kennedy—if he bowed his head upon his hands, and cried like a little child. There are times when the bravest man feels quite like a boy—feels as if he were unchanged since the day when he sorrowed for boyish trespasses, and was chidden for boyish faults. Kennedy was very young, and he was eating the fruits of folly and idleness in painful failure and hope deferred. In public he never showed the faintest signs of vexation, but in the loneliness of his closet do not blame him if he wept—for Violet's sake as well as for his own.

So once more he was separated from Julian and Lillyston in hall and chapel, for they now sat at the scholars' table and in the scholars' seats.

He was beginning to get over his feeling of sorrow when he received a letter, which did not need the coronet on the seal to show him that his correspondent was De Vayne. He opened it with eagerness and curiosity, and read—

"Eaglestower, April 30, 18—, Argyllshire.
"My Dear Kennedy—How long it is since we saw or heard of each other! I am getting well now, slowly but surely, and as I am amusing my leisure by reviving my old correspondence with

196

my friends, let me write to you whom I reckon and shall ever reckon among that honoured number.

"I am afraid that you consider me to have been slightly alienated from you by the sad scene which your rooms witnessed when last we met in health, and by the connection into which your name was dragged, by popular rumour, with that unhappy affair. If such a thought has ever troubled you, let me pray that you will banish it. I have long since been sure that you would have been ready to suffer any calamity rather than expose me to the foreseen possibility of such an outrage.

"No, believe me, dear Kennedy, I am as much now as I always have been since I knew you, your sincere and affectionate friend. Nor will I conceal how deep an interest another circumstance has given me in your welfare. You perhaps did not know that I too loved your affianced Violet; how long, how deeply I can never utter to any living soul. I did not know that you had won her affections, and the information that such was the case, came on me like the death-knell of all my cherished hopes. But I have schooled myself now to the calm contemplation of my failure, and I can rejoice without envy in the knowledge, that in you she has won a lover richly endowed with all the qualities on which future happiness can depend.

"I write to you partly to say good-bye. In a fortnight I am going abroad, and shall not return until I feel that I have conquered a hopeless passion, and regained a shattered health. Farewell to dear Old Camford! I little thought that my career there would terminate as it did, but I trust in the full persuasion that God worketh all things for good to them who love Him.

"Once more good-bye. When I return, I hope that I shall see leaning on your arm, a fair, a divine young bride.—Ever affectionately yours, De Vayne."

Kennedy had written home to announce that his name was not to be found in the list of Saint Werner's scholars. The information had disgusted his father exceedingly. Mr Kennedy, himself an old Wernerian, loved that royal foundation with an unchanging regard, and ever since that day Edward had been playing in his hall a pretty boy, he determined that he should be a Saint Werner's scholar at his first trial. He knew his son's abilities, and felt convinced that there must be some radical fault in his Camford life to produce such a disastrous series of failures and disgraces. Unable to gain any real information on the subject from Edward's letters, he determined to write up at once, and ask the classical and mathematical tutors the points in which his son was most deficient, and the reason of his continued want of success.

The classical tutor, Mr Dalton, wrote back that Kennedy's failure was due solely to idleness; that his abilities were acknowledged to be brilliant, but that at Camford as everywhere else, the notion of success without industry, was a chimera invented by boastfulness and conceit. "Le Génie c'est la Patience."

"You seem, however," continued Mr Dalton, "to be under the mistaken impression that your son read with me last term, and even 'read double.' This is not the case, as he has ceased to read with me since the end of the Christmas term: I was sorry that he did so; for if economy was an object, I would gladly, merely for the sake of the interest I take in him, have afforded gratuitous assistance to so clever and promising a pupil."

The letter of Mr Baer, the mathematical tutor, was precisely to the same effect. "I can only speak," he said, "from what I observed of your son previous to last Christmas; since then I have not had the pleasure of numbering him among my pupils."

When Mr Dalton's letter came, Mr Kennedy was exceedingly perplexed to understand what it meant, and assumed that there must be some unaccountable mistake. He simply could not believe that his son could have asked him for the money on false pretences. But when Mr Baer's letter confirmed the fact that Kennedy had not been reading with a tutor either in classics or mathematics during the previous quarter, it seemed impossible for any one any longer to shut his eyes to the truth.

When the real state of the case forced itself on Mr Kennedy's conviction, his affliction was so deep that no language can adequately describe what he suffered. In a few days his countenance became sensibly older-looking, and his hair more grey. His favourite and only surviving son had proved unworthy and base. Not only had he wasted time in frivolous company, but clearly he must have sunk very low to be guilty of a crime so heinous in itself, and so peculiarly wounding to a father's heart, as the one which it was plain that he had committed.

At first Mr Kennedy could not trust himself to write, lest the anger and indignation which usurped the place of sorrow should lead him into a violence which might produce irreparable harm. Meanwhile, he bore in silence the blows which had fallen. Not even to his daughter Eva did he reveal the overwhelming secret of her brother's shame, but brooded in loneliness over the fair promise of the past, blighted utterly in the disgrace of the present. Often when he had looked at his young son, and seen how glorious and how happy his life might be, he had determined to shelter him from all evil, and endow him with means and opportunities for every success. He had looked to him as a pride and stay in declining manhood, and a comfort in old age. Edward Kennedy had been "a child whom every eye that looked on loved," and now he was—; Mr Kennedy could not apply to him the only name which at once sprang up to his lips. He wrote—

"Dear Edward,—When I tell you that it costs me an effort, a strong effort to call you 'dear,' you may judge of the depth of my anger. I cannot trust myself, nor will I condescend to say much to you. Suffice it for you to know that your shameful transactions are detected, and that I am now aware of the means, the treacherous dishonest means you have adopted to procure money, which, since I give you an ample and liberal allowance, can only be wanted to pander to vice, idleness, and I know not what other forms of sin.

"I tell you that I do not know what to say; if you can act as you have acted, you must be quite deaf to expostulation, and dead to shame. You have done all you can to cover me and yourself with dishonour, and to bring down my grey hairs with sorrow to the grave.

"Oh Edward, Edward! if I could have foreseen this in the days when you were yet a young and innocent and happy boy, I would have chosen rather that you should die.

*"It must be a long time before you see my face again. I will not see you in the coming holidays, and I at once reduce your allowance to half of what it was. I cannot, and will not supply money to be wasted in extravagance and folly, nor shall I again be deceived into granting it to you on false pretences—Your indignant, deeply-sorrowing father, **T. Kennedy**."*

Kennedy read the letter, and re-read it, and laid it down on the table beside his untouched breakfast. There was but one expression in his face, and that was misery, and in his soul no other feeling than that of hopeless shame.

He did not, and could not write to his father. What was to be said? He must bear his burden—the burden of detection and of punishment—alone.

And the thought of Violet added keener poignancy to all his grief. For Kennedy could not but observe that her letters were not so fondly, passionately loving as they once had been, and he knew that the fault was his, because his own letters reflected, like a broken mirror, the troubled images of his wandering heart.

CHAPTER TWENTY EIGHT

KENNEDY'S DESPAIR

"When all the blandishments from life are gone,
The coward slinks to death;—the brave live on!"

Of all the sicknesses that can happen to the human soul, the deadliest and the most incurable is the feeling of despair—and this was the malady which now infected every vein of Kennedy's moral and intellectual life.

Could he but have conquered his pride so far as to take but one person into his confidence, all might have been well. But Violet—could he ever tell Violet of sins which her noble heart must render so inconceivable as almost to make it impossible for her to sympathise with one who committed them? And Eva; could he ever wound the tender affection of his sweet sister, by revealing to her the disgrace of the brother whom, from her childhood, she had idolised? He sometimes thought that he would confess to Julian or Lillyston; but his courage failed him when the time came, and he fed on his own heart in solitude, avoiding the society of men.

The sore burden of a self-reproaching spirit wore him down. He had fallen so often now, and swerved so often from the path of temperance, rectitude, and honour, that he began to regard himself as a hopeless reprobate—as one who had been weighed and found wanting—tested of God, and deliberately set aside.

And so step by step the devil thrust him into desperation, and strove thereby to clinch the hopelessness of his estate. With wild fierce passion, Kennedy flung himself into sins he had never known before; angrily he laid waste the beauty and glory of the vineyard whose hedge had been broken down; a little entrance to the sanctuary had been opened to evil thoughts, and they, when once admitted, soon flung back wider and wider the golden gates, till the revelling band of worse wickednesses rushed in and defiled the altar, and trampled on the virgin floors, and defaced the cedarn walls with images of idolatry and picturings of sin. Because he had sunk into the slough of despond, he would be heedless of the mud that gathered on his garments. Was he not ruined already? Could anything much worse befall him than had befallen him already? No; he would sin on now and take his fill.

It was a short period of his life; but in no other period did he suffer so much, or shake more fatally the foundations of all future happiness. It was emphatically a sin against his own soul, and as such it affected his very look. Those blue laughing eyes were clouded over, and the bloom died away from his cheeks, and the ingenuous beauty from his countenance, as the light of the Shechinah grew pale and dim in the inmost sanctuary. Kennedy was not mastered by impulse, but driven by despair.

Nor did he take any precaution to shield himself from punishment—the punishment of outward circumstance and natural consequence—as his moral abasement proceeded. His acquaintances shunned him, his friends dropped away from him, and the guiltiness of the present received a tinge of deeper horror from the gloom of the future.

All that could be done, Julian did. He warned, he expostulated, he reminded of purer and happier—of pure and happy days. But he did not know the bitter fountain of despondency whence flowed those naphthaline streams of passion. At last he said—

"Kennedy, I have not often spoken to you of my dear sister; it is time to speak of her now. Your conduct proves to me that you do not and cannot love her."

Kennedy listened in silence; his face bowed down upon his hands. "You could not go on as you are doing if you loved her, for love allows no meaner, no unhallowed fires to pollute her vestal flame. Your love must be a pretence—a thing of the past. It was only possible, Kennedy, when you were worthier than now you are."

He groaned deeply, but still said nothing.

"Kennedy," continued Julian, "I have loved you as a friend, as a brother; I love you still most earnestly, and you must not be too much pained at what I say; but I have come to a determination which I must tell you, and by which I must abide. Your engagement with Violet must cease."

"Does she say so?" he asked in a hollow voice.

"No, she does not know, Kennedy, what I know of you; but she will trust my deep affection, and know that I act solely for her good. The blow may almost kill her, but better that she should die than that her life should be ever connected—oh, that you should have driven me to say it—with one so stained as yours!"

"Aye!" said Kennedy bitterly, "stab hard, for the knife is in your hand. Fling dust on those who are down already—it is the world's way. I see through it all, Julian Home; you would gladly get rid of me, that Violet may wear a coronet. No comparison between a penniless and ruined undergraduate, and a handsome, rich young viscount."

"Unjust! ungenerous!" answered Julian, with indignation;

"you have poisoned your own true heart, Kennedy, or you would not utter the lie which you must disbelieve. Edward Kennedy, I will not attempt to rebut your unworthy suspicions; you know neither my character nor Violet's, or you would not have dared to utter them. No—it is clearer to me than ever that you are no fit suitor for my sister. Passion and weakness have dragged you very low. I trust and pray that you may recover yourself again."

A sudden rush of tears came to his eyes as he turned away to leave his earliest and best-loved college friend. But Kennedy stopped him, and said wildly—

"Stop, Julian Home, you shall hear me speak. I can hardly believe that you do this of your own responsibility—without Violet's—nay, nay, I must not call her so—without your sister's consent. And if this be so, hear me. Tell her that I scorn the heart which would thus fling away its plighted love: tell her that she has committed a great sin in thus rejecting me: tell her that she is now responsible for all my future,—that whatever errors I may fall into, whatever sins I may commit, whatever disgrace or ruin I may incur, she is the author of them. Tell her that if I ever live to do ungenerous acts, or ever yield to bursts of foolish passion, the acts are hers, not mine; she will have caused them; my life lies at her feet. Tell her this before it is too late. What? you still wish to hurry away? Go, then." He almost pushed Julian out, and banged the door after him.

Amazed at this paroxysm of wrath and madness, Julian went down-stairs with a slow step and a heavy, heavy heart; above all, he dreaded the necessity of breaking to Violet the heart-rending intelligence of his decision, and the circumstances which caused it. He trembled to do it, for he knew not how crushing the weight might prove. At last he determined to write to his mother, and to beg her to bear for him the pain of telling that which her womanly tact and maternal sympathy might make less overwhelming to be borne.

But Kennedy, after Julian's words, rushed out of his rooms, and it was night. He left the college, and wandered into the fields— he knew not whither, nor with what intent.

His brain was on fire. The last gleam that lent brightness to his life had been extinguished; the friend whom he loved best had cast him off; his name was sullied; his love rejected. It was not thought which kept him in a tumult, but only a physical consciousness of dreadful, irremediable calamity; and but for the wind which blew so coldly and savagely in his face, and the rain that soaked his clothes and cooled the fever of his forehead, he feared that he might go mad.

He did not return to the college till long past midnight; and the old porter, as he got out of bed to open the gate, could not help saying to him in a tone of reproach—

"Oh, Mr Kennedy, sir—excuse me, sir—but these are bad ways."

The words were lost upon him: he went up to his room, and threw himself, without taking off his clothes, upon his bed. No sleep came to him, and in the morning—damp, weary, and feverish as he had been—his look was inexpressibly pitiable and haggard.

The imperious demands of health forced him to take some notice of his condition; and he was about to put on clean clothes, and take some warm tea about ten in the morning, when the Master's servant came to tell him that the Seniority desired his presence.

He at once knew that it must be for his irregularity of the previous night, which, in the agitation of other thoughts, had not occurred to him before. He remembered, too, that the Senior Dean had only recently threatened him that, in consequence of his late misdoings, the next offence would be visited with summary and final punishment.

Kennedy received rather hard treatment at the hand of the Senior Dean, who was a very worthy and excellent man, but so firm and punctilious that he could neither conceive nor tolerate the existence of beings less precise in their nature than himself. Kind and well-intentioned, he was utterly unfit for the guidance of young men, because he was totally deficient in those invaluable qualities— sympathy and tact. He had early taken a dislike to Kennedy, in consequence of some very harmless frivolities of his freshman's year. Kennedy, in his frolicsome and happy moods, had, in ways, childish, perhaps, but completely harmless, offended the sensitive dignity of the college official, and these trivial eccentricities the Dean regarded as heinous faults—the symptoms of a reckless and irreverent character. There was one particular transaction which gave him more than usual offence, in which Kennedy, hearing a very absurd story at a don's party, while the Dean was present, parodied it with such exquisite humour and such complete command of countenance, that all the other men, in spite of the official presence, had indecorously broken into fits of laughter. It is a great pity when rulers and teachers take such terrible fright at little outbreaks of mere animal and boyish spirits.

The Dean was inclined therefore from the first to take the most serious view of Kennedy's proceedings, even when they were not as questionable as recently they had been. Instead of trying to enter into a young man's feelings and temptations with consideration and forbearance, the Dean regarded them from a moral watchtower of unapproachable altitude, and hence to him the errors which he was sometimes obliged to punish were not regarded as human failings, but as monstrous and inexplicable phenomena. He could not in the least understand Kennedy; he only looked at him as a wild, and objectionable, and irregular young man; while Kennedy reciprocated his pity by a hardly-concealed contempt.

So, as Kennedy took cap and gown, and walked across the court to the combination-room, he became pretty well aware that a very heavy sentence was hanging over his head. He cared little for it; nothing that Saint Werner's or its authorities could do, would wound him half so deeply as what he was already suffering, or cause the iron to rankle more painfully in his soul. He felt as a man who is in a dream.

He stood before them with a look of utter vacancy and listlessness, the result partly of physical weariness, partly of complete indifference. He was aware that the Dean, undisturbed this time, was haranguing him to his heart's content, but he had very little notion of what he was saying. At last his ear caught the question—

"Have you any explanation to offer of your conduct, Mr Kennedy?"

He betrayed how little he had been attending by the reply—

"What conduct, sir?"

The Dean ruffled his plumage, and said with asperity—

"Your conduct last night, sir."

"I was wandering in the fields, sir."

"Wandering in the fields!" In the Dean's formal and regular mind such a proceeding was wholly unintelligible; fancy a sensible member of a college wandering in the fields on a wet stormy night past twelve o'clock! "Really, Mr Kennedy, you must excuse us, but we can hardy accept so fantastic an explanation; we can hardly believe that you had no ulterior designs."

Kennedy was bothered and fretful; he was not thinking of Deans or Seniors just then; his thoughts were reverting to his father's implacable anger, and to Julian's forbidding him to hope for the love of Violet Home. Weary of the talking, and careless of explaining anything to them, and with a short return of his old contempt, he wished to cut short the discussion, and merely said—

"I can't help what you accept or what you believe."

The Seniors had a little discussion among themselves, in which the opinion of Mr Norton appeared to be over-borne by the majority of votes, and then the Senior Dean said shortly—

"Mr Kennedy, we have come to the decision that it is

204

undesirable for you to remain at Saint Werner's at present, until you have mended your ways, and taken a different view of the duties and responsibilities of college life. You are rusticated for a year. You must leave to-morrow."

Kennedy bowed and left the room. He, too, had been coming to a decision, and one that rendered all minor ones a matter of no consequence to him. During all the wet, and feverish, and sleepless night he had been determining what to do, and the event of this morning confirmed him still further. He was rusticated for a year; where could he go? Not to his father and his home, where every eye would look on him as a disgraced and characterless man; not to any of his relations or friends, who would regard him perhaps as a shame and burden;—no, there was but one home for him, and that was the long home, undisturbed beneath the covering of the grave.

The burden and mystery of life lay heavily on him—its lasting calamities and vanishing joys, its trials and disappointments. He would try whether, in a new state of life, the same distorted individuality was a necessary possession. Would it be necessary there also to live two lives in one, to have a soul, within whose precincts curse wrestled with blessing, good with evil, and life with death? As life went with him then, he would rather escape from it even into annihilation; he groaned under it, and in spite of all he had heard or read, he had no fear whatever of the after-death. If he had any feeling about that, it was a feeling of curiosity alone. He could not wholly condemn himself: he felt that however much evil might have mastered him good was the truest and most distinctive element of his being. He loved it even when he abandoned it, and yielded himself to sin. He could not believe that for these frailties, he would be driven into an existence of unmitigated pain.

He had no fear, no shadow of fear of the state of death, for he forgot that he would carry himself, his unchanged being— Conscience, Habit and Memory—into the other world. What he dreaded was the spasm of dying—the convulsion that was to snap the thousand silver strings in the harp of life. This he shuddered at, but he consoled himself that it would be over in a moment.

He took no food that day, but wrote to his father, to Eva, to Julian, Violet, and De Vayne. He told them his purpose, and prayed their forgiveness for all the wrongs he had done them. And then there seemed no more to do. With weak unsteady steps he paced his room, and looked at the old Swiss chamois-gun above the door. He took it down and handled it. It was a coarse clumsy weapon, and he could not trust it to effect his purpose. Shunning observation, he walked by back streets and passages until he came to a gunsmith's shop, where he bought a large pistol, under pretence of wanting it for the purposes of travel.

He carried it home himself, but instead of returning straight to his rooms, he was tempted to stroll for a last time about the grounds. The delightful softness of the darkening air on that spring evening, and the cheerful gleam of lamps leaping up here and there between the trees, and flickering on the quiet river, enticed him up the glorious old entwined avenue into the shadow of the great oaks beyond, until he found himself leaning between the weeping willows over the bridge of Merham Hall, looking on the still grey poetic towers, and the three motionless reposing swans, and the gloaming of the west. And so, still thinking, thinking, thinking, he slowly wandered home.

As he had determined to commit suicide that night, it mattered little to him at what hour it was done, and opening the first book on the table, he tried to kill time until it grew later and darker. The book happened to be a Bible, and conscious how much it jarred with his present frame of mind, and his guilty purpose, he threw it down again; but not until his eye had caught the words:—

"AND HE SAW THE ANGEL OF THE LORD STANDING IN THE WAY."

The verse haunted him against his will, till he half shuddered at the dim light which the moon made, as it struggled through the curtains only partially drawn, into the quaint old room. He would delay no longer, and loaded the pistol with a dreadful charge, which should not fail of carrying death.

Some fancy seized him to put out the lights, and then with a violent throbbing at the heart, and a wild prayer for God's mercy at that terrible hour, he took the pistol in his hand.

At that very instant,—when there was hardly the motion of a hair's breadth between him and fate,—what was it that startled his attention, and caused his hand to drop, and fixed him there with open mouth and wild gaze, and caused him to shiver like the leaves of the acacia in a summer wind?

Right before him,—half hidden by the window curtains, and half drawing them back,—clear and distinct he saw the spirit of his dead mother with uplifted finger and sad reproachful eyes fixed upon her son. The countenance so sorrowfully beautiful, the long bright gleaming of the white robe, the tresses floating down over the shoulders like a golden veil, for one instant he saw them, not dim and shadowy like the fading outlines of a dream, but with all the marked full character of living vision.

"Oh mother, mother!" he whispered, as he stretched out his hands, and sank trembling upon his knees, and bowed his head; but

206

as he raised his head again, there was nothing there; only the glimmer of lamps about the court, and the pale moonlight streaming through the curtains, partly drawn, into the quaint old room.

Unable to trust himself with the murderous weapon in his hand even for a moment, yet swept from his evil purpose by the violent reflux of new and better thoughts, he fired the pistol into the air. The barrel, enormously overloaded, burst in the discharge, and uttering a cry, he fell fainting, with his right hand shattered, to the ground.

His cry and the loud report of the explosion raised the alarm, and as the men rushed up and forced open the door of his room, they found him weltering in his blood upon the floor.

CHAPTER TWENTY NINE

EVA ENTERS THE CHAPEL

"I took it for a faëry vision
Of some bright creatures of the element,
That in the colours of the rainbow live
And play i' the plighted clouds; I was awe-struck,
And, as I passed, I worshipped."

Comus

The long, long illness that followed, and the weary time which it took to heal the mutilated hand, proved the greatest blessings that could have befallen the weak and erring heart of Edward Kennedy. They spared him the necessity of that heart-rending meeting with those whom he best loved, the dread of which had been the most powerful incitement to urge upon him the thought of suicide. They gave him time to look before and after—they relieved the painful tension of his overwrought mind—they calmed him with the necessity for quiet thought and deep rest after the anguish and turmoil of the bygone months.

When he awoke to consciousness, Eva was sitting by his bedside in the sick-room. Slowly the well-remembered objects and the beloved face broke upon his recollection, but at first he could remember nothing more, nor connect the strange present with the excited past. Still more slowly—as when one breaks the azure sleep of some unruffled mountain mere by the skimming of a stone, and for a long time the clear images of blue sky, and wreathing cloud, and green mountain-top, are shaken and confused on the tremulous and twinkling wave, but unite together into the old picture when the water has recovered its glassy smoothness—so still more slowly did Kennedy's troubled memory reflect the incidents, (alas! unbeautiful and threatening incidents), of the preceding days. They came back to him as he lay there quite still; and then he groaned.

"Hush! dearest Edward," said Eva, who had watched his face, and guessed from its expressive workings the progress of his thoughts; "hush, we are with you, and all is going on well. Your hand is healing."

He found that his right hand was tightly and firmly bandaged, and kept still by a splint.

"Was it much hurt? Shall I recover the use of it?"

"Yes, almost certainly, Dr Leesby says. I will tell papa that you are awake."

"Is he very, very angry?" asked poor Kennedy.

"He has forgiven all, dear," she said, kissing his forehead. "It was all very dreadful,"—and a cold shiver ran over her—"but none of us will ever allude to it again. Banish it from your thoughts, Eddy; we will leave Camford as soon as you can be moved."

She went to fetch her father, and as he came in and leant fondly over his son's sick-bed, and grasped warmly his unwounded hand, tears of afflicting memory coursed each other fast down the old man's cheeks. He had been hard, too hard upon Edward; perhaps his severity had driven him of late into such bad courses, and to the brink of such an awful and disgraceful end; perhaps if he had been kinder, gentler, more sympathising for this first offence, he might have been saved the anguish of driving his poor boy to lower and wilder depths of sin and sorrow. It was all over now; and amid the apparent wreck of all his hopes, even after the death-blows which recent events had dealt to his old pride in his noble child, he yet regarded him as he lay there—wounded and in such a way—with all the pity of a Christian's forgiveness, with all the fondness of a father's love.

"Oh, father, I have suffered unspeakably. If God ever raises me to health and strength again, I vow with all my heart to serve Him as I have never done before."

"Yes, Edward, I trust and believe it; think no more of the past;

let the dead bury their dead. The golden present is before you, and you will have two friends who never desert the brave man—your Maker and yourself."

A silence followed, and then Eva said, "I have just seen Dr Leesby, Eddy, and he says that if you are now quite yourself, and the light-headedness has ceased, you may be moved on Monday."

"And to-day is?—I have lost all count of time."

"To-day is Saturday. Won't it be charming, dear, to find ourselves once more at home; quietly at home, with no one but ourselves, and our own love to make us happy."

"And what am I to do, Eva?"

"Hush, Eddy; sufficient for the day—"

"Does she know, Eva? Do you ever hear from her now?"

"Yes, often—but do not think too much of those things just yet."

"And Julian?"

"He has often come to ask after you," she said blushing, "but he is afraid to see you, lest it should do you harm just now."

"Perhaps he is right. We are not all enemies, then?"

"Enemies with Julian and Violet? Oh no."

Though the engagement of Kennedy with Violet had been broken off by the common desire of Julian and Mr Kennedy, the two families still continued their affectionate intercourse, and bewailed the sad necessity which drove them to a step so painful, yet so unavoidably required by the welfare of all concerned. And from the first they hoped that all might yet be well, while some among them began to fancy that if Kennedy and Violet should ever be united, it would not be the only close bond between hearts already full of mutual affection.

So Julian still came daily during Kennedy's illness to see Eva and Mr Kennedy, and to inquire after the sufferer's health. And sometimes he took them for a walk in the grounds or the immediate neighbourhood of Camford, a place which they had never visited before, and which to them was full of interest.

Eva had often heard of the glories of Saint Werner's chapel, and on the Sunday she asked Julian if it would be possible for her to go with her father to the evening service there.

"Oh yes," said Julian; "certainly. I will get one of the Fellows to take you in. It is a remarkable sight, and I think you ought to go."

The Sunday evening came, and Julian escorted them to the ante-chapel, and showed them the various sculptures and memorials of mighty names. They then waited by the door till some Fellow whom Julian knew should pass into the chapel to escort them to a vacant place in the Fellows' seats.

Saint Werner's Chapel consists of a single aisle, along the floor of which are placed rows of benches for the undergraduates; raised above these to a height of three steps are the long seats appropriated to the scholars and the Bachelors of Arts; and again, two steps above these are the seats of the Fellows and Masters of Arts, together with room for such casual strangers as may chance to be admitted. In the centre of these long rows, on either side, are the places for the choristers, men and boys, and the lofty thrones whence the Deans "look down with sleepless eyes upon the world." By the door on either side are the red-curtained and velvet-cushioned seats of the Master and Vice-master, beyond whom sit the noblemen and fellow-commoners. By the lectern and reading-desk is a step of black and white marble, which extends to the altar, on which are two candlesticks of massive silver; and over them some beautiful carved oaken work covers a great painting, flanked on either side by old gilded pictures of the Saviour and the Madonna. Imagine this space all lighted from wall to wall by wax candles, and at the end by large lamps which shed a brighter and softer light, and imagine it filled, if you can, by five hundred men in snowy surplices, and you have a faint fancy of the scene which broke on the eyes of Mr Kennedy and Eva, as they passed between the statues of the ante-chapel, and under the pealing organ into the inner sanctuary of Saint Werner's chapel.

> "Could they behold—
> Who, less insensible than sodden clay
> In a sea river's bed at ebb of tide—
> Could have beheld with undelighted heart
> So many happy youths, so wide and fair
> A congregation in its budding-time
> Of health, and hope, and beauty, all at once
> So many divers samples from the growth
> Of life's sweet season—could have seen unmoved
> That miscellaneous garland of wild flowers,
> Decking the matron temples of a place,
> So famous through the world?"

It was Mr Norton whom Julian caught hold of as an escort for his friends into the chapel. I well remember, (who that saw it does not?) that entrance. It was rather late; the organ was playing a grand overture, the men were all in their seats, and the service just going to begin, when Eva entered leaning on Mr Norton's arm, and followed by her father and Julian. Many of the Saint Werner's men had seen her walking in the grounds the last day or two, and as Kennedy's sister a peculiar interest attached to her just then. But she needed no such accidental source of interest to attract the liveliest attention of such keen and warm enthusiasts for beauty as the Camford undergraduates. Ladies are comparatively rare apparitions in that semi-monastic body of scholars; and ladies both young and lovely are rare indeed. So as Eva entered, so young and so fair, the bright and graceful and beautiful Eva—with that exquisite rose-tinge which the air of Orton-on-the-Sea had given her, and the folded softness of the tresses which flowed down beside her perfect face, and the light of beaming eyes seen like jewels under her long eyelashes as she bent her glance upon the ground—as Eva entered, I say, leaning on Mr Norton's arm, and touched, with the floating of her pale silk dress, the surplices of the Saint Werner's men as they sat on either side down the narrow passage, it was no wonder that every single eye from that of the Senior Dean (Pace Decani dixerim!) to that of the little chorister boy was turned upon her for an instant, as she passed up to the only vacant seats, and Mr Norton caused room to be made for her beside the tutor's cushion by the chaplain's desk. She was happily unconscious of the admiration, and the perfect simplicity of her sweet girlish unconsciousness added a fresh charm to the whole grace of her manner and appearance. Only by the slightest possible blush did she show her sense of her unusual position as the cynosure for the admiring gaze of five hundred English youths; and that too though the dark and handsome countenance of Mr Norton glowed visibly with a brighter colour, (as though he were conscious of the thought respecting him, which darted across many an undergraduate's mind), and even the face of Julian, as he walked to the scholars' seats among the familiar ranks of his compeers, was flushed with the crimson of a sensitiveness which he would fain have hidden.

And I cannot help it, if even during the noble service—even amid the sound "Of solemn psalms and silver litanies," the eyes of many men wandered towards a sweet face, and gazed upon it as they might have gazed upon a flower, and if the thoughts of many men were absorbed unwontedly in other emotions than those of prayer; nor can I help it if Julian was one of those whose eyes and thoughts were so employed.

What an evening star she was! And how her very presence filled all hearts with a livelier sense of happiness and hope, and sweet pure yearnings for wedded calm and bridal love! But she—innocent young Eva—little knew of the sensation she had caused by the rare beauty of her blossoming womanhood. Her whole heart was in the act of worship, except when it wandered for a moment to her poor sick Eddy, whom they had left alone, or for another moment to one whom she could not but see before her in the scholars' seats. She did not know that men were looking at her, as she raised her clear warbling voice amid the silvery trebles of the choir, and uttered with all the expressiveness of genuine emotion those strains of poetry and passion which thrilled from the heart to the harp of the warrior-prophet and poet-king. And never did truer prayers come from a woman's lips than those which her heart offered as her head was bowed that night.

The service was over, and the congregation streamed out. That evening the ante-chapel was fuller than usual of men, who stayed nominally to hear the organ; but besides those musical souls, who always linger to hear the voluntary, or to talk in little groups, there were others who, on that pretence, waited to catch another glimpse—a last glimpse of eyes whose deep and lovely colour had flowed into their souls. They were disappointed though, for Eva dropped her veil. With a graceful bow to Mr Norton, which he returned with courteous dignity, she took Julian's proffered arm, and walked out into the court, her father following. A proud man was Julian that evening, and the subject of kindly envy to not a few.

But that little incident—the many eyes that had seen his treasure—determined Julian to take the step which he had long decided upon in his secret heart. He was half-jealous of the open, unconcealed admiration which Eva had excited, and it made him fear lest another should approach the object of his love, and occupy a place in the heart which he had not even demanded as his own. He was positively in a hurry. What if some undergraduate should get an introduction to Eva—some gay and handsome Adonis—and should suddenly carry away her heart?

So when Mr Kennedy went into the sick-room to read to Edward the lessons for the day, and Julian stayed with Eva in the sitting-room, he drew his chair beside hers, and they began to talk about Saint Werner's.

"Do you think you shall ever be a Fellow, Julian? I should so like you to be?"

"And if I am, I shall hope very soon to exchange it for a happier fellowship, Eva."

She wouldn't see what he meant, so he said, "Eva, shall I read to you?"

"Yes," she said, "I should like it so much; I used to enjoy so much the poetry we read at Grindelwald."

He took down Coleridge's poems from the shelf, and read—

212

"All thoughts, all passions, all delights,
Whatever stirs this mortal frame,
Are all but ministers of love,
And feed his sacred flame."

He went on, watching her colour change with the musical variations of his voice, until he came to the verse—

"I told her how he pined,—and ah
The deep, the low, the pleading tone
In which I sang another's love
Interpreted my own."

He saw her breast heaving with agitation, and throwing away the book, he bent down beside her, and looked up into her deep eyes, and said, "Oh, Eva, what need of concealment? You have read it long ago, have you not? I love you, Eva, love you so passionately—you cannot tell the depth of my love. Do you return it, Eva?" he said as he gained possession of her hand.

She had won him then—the dream of her latter life. This was the noble Julian kneeling at her side. She trembled for very joy, and whispered—"Oh, Julian, Julian, do you not see that I loved you from the first day we met?" She regretted the speech the next moment, as though it had been wanting in maidenly reserve, but it was the first warm natural utterance of her heart; and Julian sprang up in an ecstasy of joy, and as she rose he claimed as his due a lover's kiss.

She blushed crimson, but suffered him to sit down beside her; and they sat, hardly knowing anything but the great fact that they loved each other, till Mr Kennedy's voice had ceased in the adjoining room, and he came in.

"Oh, there you are," he said. "Edward is sinking to sleep. How good of you to be so quiet!"

They rose up, and Julian led her to him with her hand in his, and his arm supporting her. "Mr Kennedy," he said, "I am going to ask you for the most priceless jewel you possess."

"What? Is it indeed so? Ah, you wicked Julian, do not rob me of Eva yet. She is too young; and now that Edward seems likely to be ill so long—ah, me! I am bereaved of my children. Well, well, I suppose it must be so. Come here, darling, to the old father you are going to desert; I daresay Julian won't grudge me one kiss."

He kissed her tenderly, and she clung about his neck as she whispered, "But it will not be yet for a long long time, papa."

"What youth calls long, my Eva; but not long for those who are walking into the shadow down the hill."

213

O happy, happy lovers! how gloriously that night did the stars shine out for you in the deep, unfathomable galaxies of heaven, and the dew fall, and the moon dawn into a sky yet flushed with the long-unfading purple of the fading day! Yet there was sadness mixed with their happiness as they heard, until they parted, the plaintive murmurs of Kennedy's fitful sleep, and thought of all the sufferings of their brother, and how nearly, how very nearly, he had been hurried from the midst of them by self-inflicted death.

CHAPTER THIRTY

REPENTANCE

"This world will not believe a man repents,
And this wise world of ours is mainly right
For seldom does a man repent, and use
Both grace and will to pick the vicious quitch
Of blood and nature wholly out of him,
And make all clean, and plant himself afresh."

Tennyson's Idylls

Beautiful Orton-on-the-Sea! Who that has been there does not long to return there again and again, and gaze on the green and purple of its broad bay, and its one little islet, and the golden sands that stretch along its winding shore, and its glens clothed with fir trees and musical with the voice of many rills?

It was there that Kennedy had lived from childhood, and it was there that he now returned to spend at home the year of his rustication. They arrived at home on the Monday evening, and from that time forward Kennedy rapidly gained health and strength, and was able to move about again, though his hand healed but slowly, and it took months to enable him to use it without pain.

On that little islet of the bay was Kennedy's favourite haunt. It was a place where the top of a low cliff was sheltered by a clump of trees which formed a natural bower, from whence he would gaze untired for hours on the rising and falling of the tide. A little orphan cousin whom Mr Kennedy had adopted, used to row him over to this retirement, and while the boy stayed in their little boat, and fished, or hunted for seabirds' nests in the undisturbed creeks and inlets, Kennedy with some volume of the poets in his hand, would rest under the waving branches, and gaze upon the glancing waves.

And at times, when, like a great glowing globe, the sun sank, after the fiery heat of some burning summer day, into the crimsoned waters, and filled the earth, and the heavens, and the sea with silent splendours, a deep feeling of solemnity, such as he had never before experienced, would steal over Kennedy's mind. He could not but remember, that, but for God's special grace thwarting the nearly-accomplished purpose of his sin, the eyes which were filled with such indescribable visions of glory, would have been closed in death, and the brow on which the sea-wind was beating in such cool and refreshful perfume would have been crumbling under the clammy sod. Surely it must be for some great thing that his life had been saved: it was his own no longer; it must be devoted to mighty purposes of love and toil. Kennedy began to long for some work of danger and suffering as his portion upon earth: he longed ambitiously for the wanderings of the apostle and the crown of the martyr. The good deeds of a conventional piety, the quiet routine of a commonplace benevolence seemed no meet or adequate employment for his highly-wrought mind. No, he would sail to another world; there he would join a new colony in clearing away the primeval depths of some virgin forest, and tilling the glebes of a rich and untried soil; and, living among them, he would make that place a centre for wide evangelisation—the home of religious enthusiasms and equal laws; or he would go as a missionary to the savage and the cannibal, and, sailing from reef to reef, where the coral-islands of the Pacific mirror in the deep waters of their calm lagoon the reed-huts of the savage, and the feathery coronal of tropic trees, he would devote his life to reclaiming from ignorance and barbarism the waste places of a degraded humanity.

Such were the visions and purposes that floated through his mind—partly the fantastic fancies of dreamy hours, partly the unconscious desire to fly from a land which reminded him too painfully of vanished hopes, and from a scene which had been the witness of his error and disgrace. Perhaps, most of all, he was influenced by the desire to escape from a house which constantly recalled the image of a lost love—a lost love that he never hoped to regain; for Kennedy thought—though but little had been said about it—that Violet had deliberately and finally rejected him in scorn for the courses he had followed.

But he wished, before he quite made up his mind as to his future career, to see Violet once more, and bid her a last farewell.

Not daring to write and announce his intention lest she should refuse to meet him again, and unwilling to trust his secret to any of her family, he determined to see her by surprise, and enjoy for one last hour the unspeakable happiness of sitting by her side.

"Father," he said, "I am well now, or nearly well will you let me go on a little journey?"

"A journey?—where? We will all go together, Edward, if you want any change of air and scene."

He shook his head. "You can guess," he said, "where I wish to go for the last time."

"But do you think you can travel alone, Eddy, with your poor wounded hand?" asked Eva.

"Oh yes; the splints keep it safe, and I shall only be two days or so away."

They suffered him to fulfil his whim, although they felt that if he saw Violet, the meeting could hardly fail to be full of pain.

It was deep in autumn when he started, and arriving at Ildown, took up his abode in the little village inn. He kept himself as free from observation as he could, and begged the landlady, who recognised him, not to mention his arrival to any one. She had seen him on his former visit, and remembered favourably his genial good-humour and affable bearing. He told her frankly that he had come to say good-bye to Miss Home, whom he might not see again; but he did not wish to go to the house—could the landlady tell him anything about their movements?

"Why, yes; I do happen to know," she said, "and I suppose there can't be no harm in telling you, for I heard Master Cyril say as how they were all a-going a-gipseying to-morrow in the wood near the King's Oak."

"And when do you think they will start?"

"Oh, they'll start at ten, sir, in the morning, for I'm a-going to lend 'em my little trap to carry the perwisions in, and that."

This would suit Kennedy capitally, and musing on the meeting of the morrow, he sank into a doze in the armchair. A whispering awoke him, and he was far from reassured by overhearing the following colloquy:—

"Who be that in the parlour?" asked a rustic.

"Oh, that's the young gentleman as wer' Miss Violet's sweetheart," said the barmaid confidentially; "nobody don't know of it, but I heard the Missus a-saying so."

"Why bean't he at the house then?"

"Oh, ye know, he ain't her sweetheart no longer; there's been a muddle somehow, and they do say as how he shot hisself, but he don't seem to be shot much now, to look at 'im. He's as likely and proper a young gentleman as I've seen for a long time."

Taking his candle wearily, Kennedy listened to no more of the conversation, and went to bed. His bedroom window looked towards the pleasant house and garden of Mrs Home, and he did not lie down till he had seen the light extinguished in the embowered window of Violet's room. Next morning he got up betimes, and after dressing himself with the utmost pain and difficulty, for he did not like to ask for the assistance which he always had at home since his illness, he went down to breakfast. Hardly touching the dainties which the hospitable old landlady had provided, he strolled off to the wood, almost before Ildown was a-stir, and sat down in a place, not far from the King's Oak, in a green hollow, where he was sheltered from sight by the broad tree trunks, and the tall and graceful ferns.

He had not long to wait, and the time so spent would have been happy if agitation had not prevented him from enjoying the glories of the scene. Nowhere was "the gorgeous and melancholy beauty of the sunlit autumnal landscape more bounteously displayed." The grand old trees all round him were burning themselves away in many-coloured flames, and the green leaves that still lingered amid the rich hues of beautiful decay, suggested, in their contrasting harmony with their withered brethren, many a deep moral to the thoughtful mind: and everything that the thoughts could shape received a deeper emphasis from the unbroken silence of the wood.

The occupation of his mind made the time pass quickly, and it seemed but a few minutes when he saw the Homes approaching the King's Oak. The boys laid on the greensward the materials for the picnic, and then, while Violet and Mrs Home seated themselves on a fallen trunk and took out their work, Julian read to them, and Cyril and Frank walked through the wood in search of exercise and amusement.

As they passed near the spot where Kennedy was seated, they caught sight of a squirrel's nest, and Frank was instantly on the alert to reach the spoil. While he was scrambling with difficulty up the tall fir, Cyril stayed at the foot, and Kennedy determined to call him. Cyril had grown into a tall handsome boy of seventeen, and Kennedy knew that he could be trusted to help him, for he had won the boy's affection thoroughly when they were together in Switzerland.

"Cyril!"

The sound of a voice in that quiet place, out of earshot of his friends, startled Cyril, and he turned hastily round.

217

"Who's there?"

"Edward Kennedy. Come here, Cyril, and let me speak to you; Frank does not notice us."

"Edward—you here?" said Cyril. "Why don't you come and see mother?"—he was going to say Violet, but he checked himself.

"I want to see, not Mrs Home, but Violet," said Kennedy; "you know our engagement is broken off, Cyril; I have only come to say farewell, before I leave England, perhaps for ever. Call Violet here alone."

Cyril, who had heard of Kennedy's wild ways at college, and of the dreadful story that had raised against him the suspicion of intended suicide, hesitated a moment, as though he were half-afraid or unwilling to fulfil the commission. But Kennedy said to him sorrowfully—"You need not fear, Cyril, that you will be doing wrong. Tell Frank first, and then you can stay near, while I speak for a few minutes to your sister."

Cyril called down his brother from the tree, and told him that Kennedy was there. "Stay here, Frankie, while I fetch Violet; Edward wants to bid her good-bye."

He ran off, and said—"Come here, Vi; Frank and I have something to show you."

"Is it anything very particular?" said Violet, "for I shall disturb Julian's reading if I go away."

"Yes, something very particular."

"Won't you tell me what?"

"Why, a squirrel's nest for one thing, which Frank has found. Do come."

"You imperious boys, at home for your holidays!" she said, smiling; "Punch hasn't half cured you of your tyranny to us poor sisters." She rose to follow him, and when they had gone a few steps, he said—

"Vi, Edward Kennedy is in that little dell there, behind the trees; he has come, he says, to bid you good-bye."

The sudden announcement startled her, but she only leaned on Cyril's shoulder, and walked on, while he almost heard the beating of her heart.

"We will stay here, Violet; you see him there." Cyril pointed to a tree, against whose trunk Kennedy was leaning, with his eyes bent upon the ground, looking at the red splashes on the withered leaves, and the golden buds embroidered on "elf-needled mat of moss." Hearing the sound of footsteps he raised his head, and a moment after he was by Violet's side.

Taking her hand without a word, while her bosom shook with deep sobs as she saw his pale face and maimed hand, he led her to

218

the gnarled and serpentine roots of a great oak, and seated her there, while he sat lowly at her feet upon the red ground, "With beddings of the pining umbrage tinged."

How was it that she did not shrink from him? How was it that she seemed content to rest close beside him, and suffered her hand to rest upon his shoulder as he stooped? Did she love him still after all? Had Julian deceived him with the assertion of her acquiescence in the termination of their engagement? A strange rush of new hope filled his heart. He would test the true state of her affections.

"I have come," he said, in that tone of voice which was so dear to her remembrance—"I have come, Violet, to bid you farewell for ever. Since you have rejected me, I have neither heart nor hope, and I shall leave England as soon as I may go."

The tears were falling fast from her blue eyes. "Oh, Edward," she said, "why do you bid me farewell? Do you not think that I love you still?"

"Still, Violet? You love me, the ruined, dishonourable, disgraced—the—" She would not hear the dreadful word, but laid her finger on his lip.

"Oh, hush, Edward! Those words are not for you. You may have sinned; they tell me you have sinned. But have you not repented too, Edward? Have the lessons of sickness and anguish taught you nothing? I am sure they have. I could not wed one who was living an evil life, but now I see your true self once more."

"Then you love me still?" The words were uttered in astonishment, and the emotions of unexpected joy almost overpowered him.

"I never ceased to love you, Edward. Do you think that I am one to trifle with your heart, or to use it as a plaything for me to triumph by? Never, never. Had you died, or worse still, had you continued in sinful ways, I could not even then have ceased to love you, though we might have been separated until death. But now I read other things in your face, Edward, and I will be yours—your betrothed—again. Come, let us join the rest. There is not one of us but will welcome you with joy."

"Nay, nay, let us stay here for a moment," he cried, as she rose up; "let me realise the joyful sensation which your words have given me; let me sit here, Violet, a few moments at your feet, and feel the touch of your hand in mine, and look at your face, that I may recover strength again."

They sat there in silence, and the thoughts of both recurred to that other scene where they had sat on the great boulder under the shadow of the Alps, and watched the rose-film steal over their white summits on the golden summer eve. It was the same love that still filled their souls—the same love, but more sober, more quiet, more like the love of maturer years, less like the passionate love of boy and girl. It was more of an autumnal love than of old; and if the departing summer had flung new hues over the forest and the glen, they were the duller hues that recalled to mind the greater glory of the past. It was round a dying year that Autumn was "folding his jewelled arms." Yet they were happy—very happy, and they felt that, come what might, nothing on earth could part them now.

When Kennedy had grown more calm, Violet called for Cyril, and bade him break the fact of Edward's presence to her mother and Julian. The boy bounded off to do her bidding, and in a few moments Kennedy was seated among the Homes as one of them. They received him with no simulated affection; Frank and Cyril helped to take away all awkwardness from the meeting by their high spirits, and when they all sat down on the velvet mosses to their rural meal, every one of them had banished the painful hauntings of the past. Of course Kennedy accompanied them home; they drove back in the quiet evening, and Kennedy sat by Violet's side.

He stayed at Ildown till Julian returned to Saint Werner's, and, as was natural, he revolved in his mind continually his future course. At last he determined to talk it over with Violet, and told her of all his heroic longings for a life of toil and endeavour, if need were, even of banishment and death—all the high thoughts that had filled his heart as he sat alone in the island by Orton-on-the-Sea.

"Let us wait," she said, "Edward. God will decide all this for us in time, and if duty seems to call you to the hard life of missionary or colonist, I am ready to go with you."

"But don't you feel yourself, Violet, a kind of commonplaceness about English life; a silver-slippered religion, a pettiness that does not satisfy, a sense of comfort incompatible with the strong desire to do the work which others will not do in the neglected corners of the vineyard?"

"No," she answered, smiling, "I am content:—

"'The trivial round, the common task
Should furnish all we ought to ask;
Room to deny ourselves—a road
To bring us daily nearer God.'"

"True," he said; "well, I must try not to carry ambition into my religion."

"Of course you return to Saint Werner's next autumn?"

He mused long. "Ah, Violet, you cannot conceive how awful to my imagination that place has grown. And to return after

220

rustication, and live among men who will regard me with galling curiosity, and dons who will look at me sideways with suspicion— can I ever bear it?"

"Why not, Edward? They cannot affect you by their opinion. I heard you say the other day that your heart was becoming an island, and the waters round it broadening every day. If the island itself be beautiful and happy, it need not reck of the outer world."

"You are right, Violet. I will return if need be, and bear all meekly which I have deserved to bear. The one sorrow will be gone," he said, as he drew her nearer to his side, "that drove me into— Yes, you are right. I will go away home to-morrow, when Julian starts, and begin from the very first day to read with all my might. Hitherto I have had only the bitter lessons of Camford; let us see if I cannot gain some of her honours too."

CHAPTER THIRTY ONE

BRUCE IN TROUBLE

"Nuda nec arva placent, umbrasque negantia molles,
  Nec dudum vetiti me laris augit amor."

Milton

Bruce, when expelled from Saint Werner's, thought very little of his disgrace. It hardly ruffled the calm stream of his self-complacency, and, for some reasons, he was rather glad that it had happened. He did not like Camford; he had never taken to reading, and being thus debarred from all intellectual pleasures, he had grown thoroughly tired of late breakfasts, boating on the muddy Iscam, noisy wines, and interminable whist parties. Moreover, he had made far less sensation at Camford than he had expected. Somehow or other he had a dim consciousness that men saw through him; that his cleverness did not conceal his superficiality, nor his easy manners blind men's eyes to his ungenerous and selfish heart. Even his late phase of popular scepticism was less successful at Camford than it would have been at places of less steady diligence and less sound acquirements. In fact, Bruce imagined that he was by no mean appreciated. The sphere was too narrow for him; he was quite sure that in the arena of London society and political life he was qualified to play a far more conspicuous part.

Nor did he believe that Sir Rollo Bruce would care for his expulsion any more than he did himself; he fancied that his father was quite above the middle-class prejudices of respect and reverence for pedantry and pedagogues, and was too much a man of the world to be disturbed by a slight contretemps like this. He wrote home a careless note to mention the fact that his Saint Werner's career was ended, and attributed this result to a mere escapade at a wine-party, which had been distorted by rumour, and exaggerated by malice into a serious offence.

So when Vyvyan gaily entered his father's house, he felt rather light-hearted than otherwise. He expected that very likely some party would be going on, and quite looked forward to an agreeable dance. When he arrived, however, Vyvyan House was quite silent; a dim light came from a single window, but that was all.

"Sir Rollo and my mother not at home, I suppose," he said to the plushed and powdered footman.

"Yes, sir, they're in the library."

He entered; they were sitting on opposite sides of the fire, with a single lamp between them. They were not doing anything, and Lady Bruce appeared to have been crying; but neither of them took any notice of his entrance beyond turning their heads.

"How do you do?" he said, advancing gracefully; but not a little surprised at so silent and moody a greeting.

"How do you do?" was his father's cold reply.

"Dear me—I quite expected to find a party going on, but you seem quite gloomy. Is anything the matter?"

"Matter, sir!" exclaimed Sir Rollo, starting up vehemently from his chair, and angrily pacing the room. "Matter! Upon my word, Vyvyan, your impudence is sublime."

"You surprise me. What have I done?"

"Done!" retorted his father, with intense scorn. "You have been expelled from College; you have wasted your whole opportunities of education; you have thrown away the boundless sums which I have spent in your interest; you have lived the life of a puppy and a fool, and now you come back in the uttermost disgrace, with your name involved in I know not what infamy, and are as cool about it as if you returned to announce a triumph."

Not deigning a word more, Sir Rollo turned indignantly on his heel and left Bruce as much astounded by so unexpected a reception as if he had suddenly trodden on a snake. He relapsed into

222

uncommon sheepishness, and hardly knew how to address his mother, who sat sobbing in her armchair.

"My dear mother," he said at last, "what can be the matter that I am met by such tornados as my welcome on returning?"

"Don't ask me, Vyvyan. Your father is naturally angry at your expulsion, and you have grieved us both. But, dear Vyvyan, do not put on such an impertinent and indifferent manner; it annoys Sir Rollo exceedingly. Do submit yourself, my dear boy, and he will soon recover his usual suavity."

"But I never saw him like this before."

"No; these violent fits of temper have only come over him of late, and I am afraid that there must be some cause for them of which I am unaware."

Bruce sat silent and unhappy. Expelled from college, and insulted, (as he called it), at home, he felt truly alone and miserable. He went up to his own room, supped there, and coming down next morning to the awkward meeting with his parents, spoke a few words of regret about his position. Sir Rollo barely listened to them, breakfasted in silence, and immediately afterwards set out for his office. He did not return till late in the evening, and continued for some time to spend the days in this manner, seeing next to nothing of his wife and son, but sternly forbidding any festivities or balls.

One morning he called Vyvyan into his study before starting. Bruce laid aside his novel, yawned, and followed.

"Pray, sir, do you intend to spend all your time in reading novels?" said Sir Rollo.

"There's nothing else for me to do that I see."

"Very well. If you suppose that you are going to spend your days in idleness, you are mistaken. I give you a week to choose some occupation that will not involve me in further outlay."

Bruce took out his embroidered pocket-handkerchief, redolent with scent, and blew his nose affectedly. On doing so, an unopened envelope dropped on the floor, out of his pocket; picking it up, he glanced at it, tore it across, and flung it into the fire. Sir Rollo immediately picked up the pieces with the tongs and opened it.

"I see that this is a bill, and I shall proceed to look at it."

"Yes, if you like," said Bruce, in an indifferent tone—"it's from a dun."

It was a tailor's bill which had been sent after him, and it amounted to 150 pounds.

"And you suppose," said his father, "that I am going to pay these debts for you?"

"I suppose so, certainly—some day. Let the dogs wait."

Sir Rollo seemed on the point of a great burst of wrath; his lips positively quivered and his eye flashed with passion. He seemed, however, to control himself,—darted at his son a look of wrath and scorn, and left the room. A note that evening informed Lady Bruce that business detained him from home, and that he might not return for some days.

A week after Bruce received a letter with foreign post-marks, to the following effect:—

Dear Vyvyan—By the time you receive this, I shall be on the Continent, far beyond the reach of the law.

"I have been living for the last ten years on the money I embezzled from the company whose affairs I managed. The fraud cannot fail of being detected almost immediately.

"I feel acutely the position in which I am forced to leave your mother. I do not pity you in the least. I gave you the amplest opportunity to save yourself from this ruin, if you had not been a fool. You cared for nothing and for nobody but yourself. You never worked hard, though you knew it to be my wish; you assumed an air of spurious independence, and affected the fine gentleman. Your conceit and idleness will be their own punishment. You have made your own bed; now you will have to lie in it.

"**Rollo Bruce.**"

The truth was soon known to the world. Numberless executions were put into Vyvyan House. Every available fragment of property was seized by Sir Rollo's creditors; and as Lady Bruce's private fortune had long been spent, she and her son were left all but penniless. The gay and gilded friends of their summer hours were the first to desert them, and Sir Rollo's wickedness had created such a gust of indignation, that few came forward to lend his family the slightest assistance.

When Bruce found himself in this most distressing position—when he sat with his mother in shame and retirement in obscure lodgings, which had been taken for them by one of their former servants, and with no immediate means of livelihood—then first the folly of his past career revealed itself to his mind in its full proportions. Lady Bruce's health was dreadfully affected by the mental anguish through which she had passed, and it became a positive necessity that Bruce should work with his head or hands to earn their daily bread.

He found no difficulty in procuring a temporary post in a lawyer's office as a clerk. The drudgery was terrible. Daily, from nine in the morning to six in the evening, he found himself chained

224

to the desk, and obliged to go through the dullest and most mechanical routine, the only respite being half an hour in the middle of the day, which he spent in dining at an eating-house. Nursed on the lap of luxury, habituated to the choicest viands, and accustomed to find every whim fulfilled, this kind of life was intolerable to him. The steaming recesses of a squalid eating-house gave him a sensation of loathing and sickness, and the want of exercise made him look haggard and wan. In vain he appealed to men who had called themselves his father's friends; he found to his cost that the son of a detected swindler has no friends, and more especially if his own life have been tainted with suspicion or dishonour. Poor Bruce was driven to the very verge of despair.

He applied for a situation in a bank, but he was informed that it could not be granted him unless he could obtain a certificate of good character from his college, which, of course, was out of the question. He tried writing for the press, but his shallow intellectual resources soon ran dry. The pittance he could thus earn did not remunerate him for the toil and wasted health, and even this pittance was too often cruelly held back. He made applications in answer to all sorts of advertisements, but one after another the replies were unfavourable, until his whole heart died within him. No intelligence could be obtained of his father's hiding-place, and before a year had elapsed since Sir Rollo's bankruptcy and felony had been made known, Lady Bruce died at her son's lodgings, worn out with misery and shame.

This climax of the young man's misfortunes awoke at last the long dormant sympathy in his favour. An effort was made by his few remaining and unalienated friends to provide for him the means of emigration, which seemed the only course likely to give him once more a fair start in life. But to pay his passage, and provide him with the means of settling in New Zealand required a considerable sum, and Bruce had to suffer for weeks the agonies of hope deferred. And when he glanced over his past life, he found nothing to help him. He could not look back with any comfort; the past was haunted by the phantoms of regret. His violent and wilful infancy, his proud, passionate boyhood, his wandering and wicked youth, afforded him few green spots whereon the eye of retrospect could rest with calm. As the wayworn traveller who on some bright day sat down by the fringed bank of clear fountain or silver lake, and while he leant to look into its waters, was suddenly dazzled into madness by the flashing upwards upon him, from the unknown depths, of some startling image; so Bruce, as he rested by the dusty wayside of life, and gazed into the dark abysses of recollection, was startled and horrified, with a more fearful nympholepsy, by the crowding images and sullen glare of unforgotten and half-forgotten sins.

But in dwelling on his past life, Bruce bethought him that he might still find friends at school; and not long after his mother's funeral, he determined to call on his old masters, and get such pecuniary aid as he could from them and his schoolboy friends. To come to such a resolution was the very bitterness of humiliation; but Bruce was now all eagerness to escape from England, and recommence a new life in other lands.

He took a third class ticket to Harton, and when he arrived there, was so overcome with shame that he well-nigh determined to return by the next train, and leave the town unvisited, at whatever cost; but on inquiry he found that the next train would not start for some hours, and meanwhile he fully expected to be seen and recognised by those whom he had known before. And yet it was not easy, in that stooping figure, with the pale cheek and dimmed eye, to recognise the bright and audacious Vyvyan Bruce, who had been captain of Harton barely three years before. Poverty, ruin, disappointment, confinement, guilt, and sorrow had done their work with marvellous quickness.

Nerving himself to the effort, he turned his face towards Harton, and walked slowly up the hill. The reminiscences which the walk recalled were not happy—rather, far from happy. It was not because formerly when he was a flattered, and rich, and handsome, and popular Harton boy, all the prospects of his life had looked as bright as now they seemed full of gloom; it was not that then both his parents were living, and now one was dead, the other disgraced; it was not that then he was full of health and vigour, and now was feeble and wearied; it was not that then he seemed to have many friends, and now he hardly knew of one; no, it was none of these things that affected him most deeply as he caught sight of the well-known chapel, and strolled up the familiar hill; but it was the thought, the bitter thought, the cursed thought that there, as at Camford, the voice of his brother's blood was crying against htm from the ground.

By the time he reached the school buildings, it happened to be just one o'clock, and from the various school-rooms, the boys were pouring out in gay and noisy throngs. The faces were new to him for the most part, and at first he began to fancy that he should recognise no one. But at last he observed a boy looking hard at him, who at length came up and shook him warmly by the hand.

"How do you do, Bruce? Ah, I see you don't remember me; true, I was only in the Shell when you left, but you ought at least to remember your old fags."

The change of countenance between fifteen and eighteen is however very great, and it was not without an effort that Bruce recalled in the tall strong fellow who was talking to him his quondam fag, little Walter Thornley, now in his turn captain of the eleven, and Head of the school, whose admiration of Bruce we have already recorded in the first chapter of this eventful history.

"Where are you off to now?" said Thornley.

"To the Doctor's."

"Well, you'll come and see me afterwards?"

Bruce promised and then walked to see the Doctor, and his old tutor. To both he opened his piteous tale, and both of them gave him the most generous and liberal assistance; they promised also to procure him such other aid as might lie in their power. A little lighter in heart, he went to pay his visit to Thornley, whom he found occupying his old rooms. As Bruce recrossed the familiar threshold, the contrasts of past and present were almost too much for him, and he found it difficult to restrain his tears. He stayed but a short time, and then returned to London to his poor and lonely lodgings.

Walter Thornley heard his story from the tutor, and besides getting a large subscription for him among his own friends, wrote to ask if Julian could procure for the emigrant any assistance in Camford. Julian received the letter about the middle of the October term in his third year, and it ran thus:—

"**Dear Home**—Beyond knowing by rumour that I am head of the school, you will, I suppose, hardly remember a boy who was so low in the school as I was when you were monitor. But though you will perhaps have forgotten me, I have not forgotten you, or the many kinds acts I experienced from you and Lillyston when I was a little new fellow. Remembering these, I am emboldened to write, and ask if you or any of the old Hartonians are willing to assist poor Bruce to settle in New Zealand, now that he has no chance of succeeding well in England? I am sure that you personally will be glad of any opportunity to help an old school-fellow in his distress and difficulty, for report tells me that Julian Home is as kind-hearted and generous as he was when he won the Newry scholarship at Harton.—Believe me to be, my dear Home, yours very truly,—**Walter Thornley**."

Julian had almost forgotten the very existence of Thornley when this letter recalled him to his mind; but it was one of the pleasures of Julian's life constantly to receive letters of this kind from former school-fellows, thanking him for past kindnesses of which he was wholly unconscious from the simple and natural manner in which they had been done. It need hardly be said that he at once complied with the request which the letter contained, and that, (next to De Vayne's), his own was the largest contribution towards the handsome sum which the Hartonians and other Saint Werner's men cheerfully subscribed to assist their former comrade in his hour of need.

To avoid all unnecessary wounding of Bruce's feelings, the money thus collected was transmitted to the Doctor to be placed at Bruce's disposal. It completed the sum requisite for his outfit, and there was no longer any obstacle in the way of his immediate departure from England. He at once booked his passage by an emigrant ship, and sailed from England. The day after his departure, Julian received from him the following letter:—

"Dear Julian—Although you are one of those who would 'do good by stealth, and blush to find it fame,' I am not ignorant of the debt of gratitude which I owe to you for providing me with the means of recovering my fortunes, and beginning life afresh in another hemisphere.

"Our lots in life, since at Harton we ran a neck and neck race, have been widely different, and while the happy months have been rolling for you on silver wheels, and the happy hours speeding by you with white feet, to me Time has been:—

"'A maniac scattering dust,
And Life a Fury slinging flame.'

"How much I have gone through in the last year—the accumulated agony of remorse, bereavement, and ruin—no human soul can tell. No wonder my bark was wrecked after such mad and careless navigation; but, thank God, the blow of the tempest that staggered and shattered it, and drove it on the reefs, has not sunk it utterly, and now, like a waif or stray, it is being carried to be refitted across a thousand leagues of sea.

"I am not the Bruce you knew, but a wiser, sadder, and better man. I have not yet lost all hope. The old book of my life was so smutched and begrimed—torn, dogs-eared, and scrawled over— that it was scarcely worth while to turn over a new leaf. I have rather began a new volume altogether, and trust, by God's blessing, that when 'Finis' comes to be written in it, some few of the pages will bear re-perusal.

"'De Vayne!' how that name haunts me; how full it is of horror—De Vayne and Hazlet; and yet I hear that both have contributed to my help. It gives me new life to know that human hearts can be so full of forgiveness and of love.

"Starting almost for another world—without fortune, without friends, with nothing but head and heart, the wreck of what I was—I sometimes feel so sad that I could wish myself out of the world altogether. Forgive me, then, for once more bringing before you a name which you can only connect with the most unpleasant and sombre thoughts, and pray for me that my efforts, (this time they are genuine and sincere), to improve my life, my talents, and my fortune, may be crowned with success.

"We sail in an hour or sooner, for I hear them weighing anchor now. Good-bye. Accept my warmest thanks for all your kindnesses, and my wishes, (ah! that they were worthier!) for your happiness in life, and believe me, my dear Julian, your sincere and grateful friend—

"Vyvyan Bruce.

"P S—I am positively alone; not one soul is here even to bid me good-bye. Eheu! jam serus vitam ingemo relictam!"

Julian read the letter many times; he was touched by its delicate and eloquent sorrow—its fine and chastened thoughtfulness. He was no longer in a mood to work, but closed his books, and watched the faces in the fire. One thought filled him with joy and thankfulness; it was the thought that, though of his friends and acquaintances so many had gone wrong, yet God was leading them back again, by rough and thorny roads it might be, but still by sure roads to the right path once more. Hazlet, Bruce, Brogten—above all, his friend and brother Kennedy—were returning to the fold they had deserted, were learning that for him who has sinned and suffered, REPENTANCE IS THE WORK OF LIFE. And as these thoughts floated through Julian's mind, the words of an old prayer came back upon his lips—"That it may please Thee to strengthen such as do stand; and to comfort and help the weak-hearted, and to raise up them that fall; and finally, to beat down Satan under our feet."

CHAPTER THIRTY TWO

A QUIET PROSPECT

"Patet omnibus veritas; nondum est prorsus occupata."

Seneca, Epistolae 33

Julian's third year at Camford was by no means the happiest period of his life there, because the sad absence of Kennedy and De Vayne made a gap in his circle of friends which could not easily be filled up; but this was the annus mirabilis of his university career. He gained prize after prize; he was always first class in the college examinations; he won the chancellor's medals for Latin and English verse, and, indeed, almost divided with Owen the honours of the place. To crown all, he gained the Ireford University scholarship, which Owen had won the year before.

Of all the men of his year, he was the most honoured and respected; he wore the weight both of his honours and his learning "lightly like a flower," and there was a graceful humility, joined with his self-dependence, which won every heart, and prevented that jealousy which sometimes accompanies success.

The most important event in his intellectual progress was the attention which he began to turn at this time to biblical and theological studies. He was thankful in later years that he had deferred such inquiries to a time when he was capacitated for them by a calm and sound judgment, and a solid basis of linguistic and historical knowledge. He had always looked forward to holy orders, and regarding the life of a clergyman as his appointed work, he considered that an honest, a critical, and an impartial study of the Bible was his first duty. In setting about it, he came to it as a little child; all he sought for was the simple truth, uncrushed by human traditions, unmingled with human dogmas, untrammelled by human interpretations, unadulterated by human systems. He found that he had a vast amount to unlearn, and saw clearly that if he fearlessly pursued his inquiries they would lead him so far from the belief of popular ignorance, as very probably to bar all worldly success in the sacred profession which he had chosen. But he knew that the profession was sacred, and, fearless by nature, he determined to seek for truth and truth only, honestly following the prayerful conclusions of his clearest and most deliberate judgment. Even in these early days the freedom and honesty of his research drew on him slight sibilations of those whose religion was shallow and sectarian; in after years they were destined to bring on him open and positive persecution.

Not that Julian was ever in the least degree obtrusive in stating his beliefs when they widely and materially differed from the expressed opinions of the majority; except, indeed, in the cases when such opinions appeared to him dishonest or dangerous. He was scrupulously careful not to wound the conscience of those who would have been unable to understand the ground of his arguments, even when they could not resist their logical statement; and in whom long custom was so inveterate that the weed of system could not be torn out of their hearts without endangering the flower of belief. With men like Hazlet—I mean the reformed and now sincere Hazlet—he either confined himself wholly to subjects on which differences were impossible, or, if questioned, stated his views with caution and consideration. It was only with the noisy and violent upholders of long-grounded error—error which they were too feeble to maintain except by mean invective or ignorant declamation—that Julian used the keen edge of his sarcasm, or the weighty sword of his moral indignation. He was not the man to bow down before the fool's-cap of tyrannous and blatant ignorance. If he could have chosen one utterance from the holy Scriptures, which to him was more precious in its full meaning than another, it was that promise, rich with inexhaustible blessing, "And ye shall know the truth, and the truth shall make you free."

Perhaps there is no greater want in this age than a full, fair, fearless religio clerici; the men who could write it, dare not; and the men who dare write it, cannot. They say the age is not ripe for it; and if they mean that it would cause violent offence to the potent rulers of fashionable religious dogmatism, they are right. But I wander from my theme, and meddle with the subjects which this is not the place to touch upon.

The close of Julian's undergraduate life was as honourable as its promise had been. He obtained a brilliant first class, and was bracketed with Owen as the best classic of his year. Lillyston also distinguished himself, and all three determined to read for Fellowships, which, before a year was over, they had the honour to obtain.

Meanwhile a circumstance had happened which changed the course of Kennedy's intentions. After his conversation with Violet, he had often thought of his plans for the future, and written to her about them. Reconciled to the plan, of returning to Camford after the year of his rustication, he was now trying to settle his future profession. His way seemed by no means clear; he had never

231

thought of being a clergyman, and now, more than ever, deemed himself unfitted for such a life. The long tedious delay of the bar to a man without any special interest; the sickness of hope deferred during the prime years of life the weariness of a distasteful study, and the heavy trial of dusky chambers in a city to a man who loved the sea and the country with a passionate love, deterred him from choosing the law. He had no liking for the army, except in time of war; the life of the officers whom he knew was not altogether to his mind, and he was neither inclined to gaiety nor fond of an occupation which offered so many temptations to listlessness and indolence. There was no immediate necessity to decide finally, because in any case he meant to take his degree, and looked forward with some hope, after his year of unswerving diligence in the retirement of Orton, to honours in the Tripos and the pleasant aid of a Saint Werner's Fellowship as the crown of his career. But on the whole, he began to think that he might be both useful and successful as a physician. He had a deep reverence for this earthly tabernacle of the immortal soul, and a hallowed and reverend curiosity about that "harp of a thousand strings," which, if it be untuned by sickness, mars every other melody of life. Violet entered into all his views, and they determined to leave the matter thus until Kennedy should have donned his B A gown.

But about this period that public step was taken of throwing open to competition the Indian civil service appointments, which has been of such enormous advantage to the "middle-classes" of England by offering to them, as the reward of industry, the opportunity of a new and honourable profession, and which seems likely to be prolific of good results to the future of our Empire in the East. Directly Kennedy saw the announcement of the examination, he grasped with avidity the chance of a provision for life which it afforded, and easily obtained the assent both of his own and of Julian's family to offer himself as a candidate. Of course they contemplated with sorrow the prospect of so long a separation as the plan involved, but they saw that he himself was strongly desirous to win their approval of his proposition, and of course his wishes were Violet's too.

So Kennedy went in for the civil service examination, and acquitted himself so admirably that his name headed the list of successful competitors, and he was told that he must prepare himself to leave England in a year for the post to which they appointed him.

This happened about the time that Julian took his degree, and before the year was over Julian had been elected a Fellow, and the living of Elstan was offered to him. Being of small value—200 pounds a year—it had been rejected by all the Fellows of older standing, and had "come down" to Julian, who, to the surprise of his friends, left Camford and accepted it without hesitation.

"My dear fellow," said Mr Admer, "how in the world can you be so insane as to bury yourself alive, at the age of twenty-two, in so obscure a place as the vicarage of Elstan?"

"Oh, Elstan is a charming place," said Julian; "I visited it before accepting it, and found it to be one of those dear little English villages in the greenest fields of Wiltshire. The house is a very pretty one, and the parish is in perfect order. My predecessor was an excellent man: his population, of one thousand souls, were perhaps as well attended to as any in all England."

"Yes, yes," said Mr Admer, impatiently, "I know all that; but who will ever hear of you again if you go and become what Sydney Smith calls 'a kind of holy vegetable' in the cabbage-gardens of a Wiltshire hamlet?"

"Why, what would you have me do, Mr Admer?"

"Oh, I don't know; stay up here, edit a Greek play, or one of the epistles; bestir yourself for some rising university member in a contested election; set yourself to get a bishopric or a deanery; you could easily do it if you tried. I'll give you a receipt for it any day you like. Or go to some London church; with such sermons as you could preach you might have London at your heels in no time, and as you would superadd learning to effectiveness, your fortune would be made."

Julian was sorry to hear him talk like this; it was the language of a disappointed and half-believing man.

"I don't care for such aims," he said. "A mere popular preacher I would not be, and as for preferment it doesn't depend much on me, but for the most part on purely accidental causes. All I care for at present is to be useful and happy. Obscurity is no trial to me; neither success nor failure can make me different from what I am."

"Well then, at least, write a book or something to keep yourself in men's memory."

"I don't feel inclined. There are too many books in the world, and I have nothing particular to say. Besides, the annoyance and spite to which an author subjects himself are endless—to hear ignorant and often malicious criticisms, to see his views misrepresented, his motives calumniated, and his name aspersed. No, for the present, I prefer the peace and the dignity of silence."

"What on earth will you find to do, then, if you have no ambition?"

"Nay, I don't want you to think that I'm so virtuous or so

233

phlegmatic as to have no ambition. I have a passionate ambition, whether known or unknown, so to live as to lead on the coming golden age, and prepare the next generation to be truer and wiser than ours. If it be my destiny never to be called to a wider sphere of work than Elstan, I shall be content to do it there."

"And how will you occupy your time?" asked Mr Admer, who had long loved Julian too well even to smile at what were to himself mere unintelligible enthusiasms.

"Oh, no fear on that score. My profession will give me plenty of work; besides, what is the use of education, if it be not to render it impossible for a man to know the meaning of the word ennui? Put me alone in the waiting-room of some little wayside station to wait three hours for a train, and I should still be perfectly happy, even if there were no such thing as a book to be got for miles."

"Well, well, if you must vanish to Elstan, do. At any rate, remember your old Camford friends, and let us hear of you sometimes? I suppose you'll keep on your Fellowship at least for a year?"

"Insidious questioner!" said Julian; "no, I hope to be married very soon. You shall come down and see love in a cottage."

"Aha, I see it all now," said Mr Admer, with a sigh.

"Nay, you mustn't sigh. I expect to be congratulated, not pitied," said Julian, gaily. "A wife will sweeten all the cares and sorrows of life, and instead of withering away my prime in selfish isolation, and spending these still half-youthful years in loneliness, and without a real home, I shall feel myself complete in the materials of happiness. After all, ambition such as yours is a loveless bride."

So Julian accepted Elstan, and Lillyston went with him to London to help him in selecting furniture for the vicarage which was so soon to receive a bride.

"Are you really going to venture on matrimony with only 200 pounds a year?" asked Lillyston.

"I have some more of my own, you know, Hugh; Mr Carden's legacy, you remember; but even if I hadn't, I would still marry even on a hundred a year if I wished and the lady consented."

"And repent at leisure."

"Not a bit of it. If I were a man to whom lavender-coloured kid gloves and unlimited eau-de-cologne were necessaries of life, it might be folly to think of it. But if a man be brave, and manly, and fearless of convention, let him marry by all means, and not make his life bitter and his love cold by long delay."

"But how about his children?"

"Well, it may be fanaticism, but I believe that God never sends a soul into the world without providing ample means for its sustenance. Of course, such an assertion will set the tongues of our would-be philosophers waggling in scornful cachinnation; but, in spite of that, I do believe that if a man have faith, and a strong heart, and common sense, he may depend upon it his children will not starve. Some of the very happiest people I know are to be found among the large families of country clergymen. Besides, very often the children succeed in life, and improve their father's position. I haven't the shadow of a doubt that I am doing the right thing. I only wish, Hugh, that you would follow my example."

"Perhaps I shall, some day," said Lillyston.

"And meanwhile you will be my bridegroom's man, will you not?"

"Joyfully—if it be only to see Miss Kennedy's face again."

"And do you know that Kennedy is to be married to Violet the same day?"

"Is he? happy fellow! As for me, I am going to resign my fellowship, and to make myself useful at Lillyston Court. When is the wedding to be?"

"Both weddings, you mean, Hugh. On the tenth of next June at Orton-on-the-Sea—the loveliest spot in the world, I think."

So in due time Julian packed up all his books and prizes, and bade farewell to his friends, and turned his back on Camford. It is as impossible to leave one's college without emotion as it is to enter it, and the tears often started to Julian's eyes as the train whirled him off to Elstan. He had cause, if any man ever had, to look back to Camford with regret and love. His course had been singularly successful, singularly happy. He had entered Saint Werner's as a sizar, he left it as a Fellow, and not "With academic laurels unbestowed."

He had grown in calmness, in strength, in wisdom; he had learnt many practical lessons of life; he had gained new friends, without losing the old. He had learnt to honour all men, and to be fearless for the truth. His mind had become a well-managed instrument, which he could apply to all purposes of discovery, research, and thought; he was wiser, better, braver, nearer the light. In a word, he had learnt the great purpose of life—sympathy and love to further man's interest—faith and prayer to live ever for God's glory. And not a few of these lessons he owed to his college, to its directing influence, its ennobling associations, its studies—all bent towards that which is permanent and eternal, not to the transitory and superficial. To the latest day of his life, the name of Saint Werner's remained to Julian Home an incentive to all that is noble and manly in human effort. He felt the same duty with regard to it as the generous scion of an illustrious house feels towards the ancient name which he has inherited, and the noble lineage whence he has sprung.

The few months which were to elapse before his marriage, Julian spent in preparing the vicarage for his young betrothed, and he stored it with everything which could delight a simple yet refined and educated taste. There was an indefinable charm about it—the charm of home. You felt on entering it that its owner destined it as the place around which his fondest affections were to centre, and his work in life was to be done. Julian had not the restless mind which sighs for continual change; happy in himself and his own resources, and the honest endeavour to do good, the glory of the green fields, the changes of the varying year supplied him with a wealth of beauty which was sufficient for all his needs, and when—after some long day's work amid the cottages, reading to the sick at their lonely bedsides, listening to the prattle of the children in the infant schools, talking to the labourers as they rested at their work—he refreshed himself by a gallop across the free fresh downs, or a quiet stroll under the rosy apple-blossoms of his orchard or garden, Julian might have said with more truth than most men can, that he was a happy and a contented man.

CHAPTER THIRTY THREE

FAREWELL

"Hear the mellow wedding bells,
Golden bells!
What a world of happiness their harmony foretells!
Oh, from out the sounding cells,
What a gush of euphony voluminously swells!"

Edgar Poe

Merrily, merrily, rang out the sweet bells of Orton-on-the-Sea; more merrily than they ever rang before; so merrily that it seemed as if they would concentrate into every single clash and clang of their joyous peal a tumult of inexpressible happiness greater than they would ever be able to enjoy again. If you look up at the belfry, you will see them swing and dance in a very delirium of ecstasy, such as made everybody laugh while he listened, and chased away the possibility of sorrow, and thrilled the very atmosphere with an impression of hilarity and triumph.

All Orton is a-stir. Mr Kennedy is the squire of the parish, and the villagers may well love him as they do. The son and daughter of the squire are not often married on the same day; and besides the double wedding with its promise of an evening banquet, and dance on the hall lawn to all the people of Orton, Eva and Edward are known well to every cottager, and loved as well as known.

The hall is quite full, and the village inn is quite full, and all the neighbouring gentry who are invited, are hospitably entertaining such members of the two families as can find room nowhere else. Never had Orton seen such grand doings; the very stables and coach-houses are insufficient to receive the multitude of carriages.

Several Saint Wernerians are invited; and, (as both Julian and Kennedy prefer to be alone on that morning), Lillyston, who has visited the place before, is lionising them in the neighbourhood, and with Willie, Kennedy's orphan cousin, rows them over to the little islet in the bay. As they come back, the hour for the wedding approaches, and Lillyston says to Owen—"How I wish De Vayne were here!"

"But he is in Florence, is he not?" says Owen.

They have hardly spoken when a carriage with a coronet on the panels dashes up to the Lion Inn; a young man alights, hands out a lady, and enters the inn.

"Surely that must be De Vayne himself," says Suton running forward. Meanwhile the young man, after taking the lady into a private room, asks if he may see Mr. Home or Mr Kennedy, and is showed up to the parlour in which they are sitting.

"De Vayne!" they both exclaim in surprise.

"Yes, Julian!" he answered cheerily; "I only returned from Florence two days ago, heard of your marriage from the Ildown people, and determined to come with my mother a self-invited guest."

"Don't fear for my feelings," he continued, turning to Kennedy. "Nothing is so useless or dangerous as to nurse a hopeless love, like the flame burning in the hearts of the banqueters, at the feast of Eblis. No, Kennedy, I love Violet, but only as a sister now, and you must not be afraid if I claim one kiss after the marriage from the bride. You shall have the same privilege some day soon."

"Your coming is the completion of my happiness," said Kennedy, cordially shaking his hand. "I will run and tell Violet at once, lest she should be alarmed by seeing you."

"Yes, and to show her why we may continue to have communion as friends, tell her that there is a gentle Florentine girl, with dark eyes, and dark hair, and a sweet voice, who, as my mother will bear witness, has promised in a year's time to leave her Casa d'oro for Other Hall," he said smiling.

They took him down to see the others, who rejoiced to see him nearly as much as they did, and the time sped on for the wedding to be performed. The carriages had already started to convey the bridegrooms and their friends to church, when another carriage drove rapidly along the street, carrying another most unexpected guest.

It had been arranged that Cyril and Frank should come down to Orton on the morning of the ceremony, as there was a difficulty in finding room for them. It was very late, and they were beginning to be afraid that the boys had missed a train, and would not arrive till after the ceremony, when they made their triumphant entry into Orton in a carriage by the side of—Lady Vinsear!

Only imagine! Being left almost alone at Ildown while the others had gone to Orton to make arrangements for the marriage, Cyril had audaciously proposed to his brother that, as it was through them that Lady Vinsear's wrath had been kindled against Julian, they should go over and see whether the old lady would admit them into her presence or in any way suffer herself to be pacified. The proposal was quite a sudden one, and the thought had only come into Cyril's head because he had nothing else to do. But he had no sooner thought of it than he determined to carry it out. He felt certain that Lady Vinsear could not be so totally unlike his late father as to have become wholly ill-natured and implacable, and he was sure that no harm could result from his visit even if no good were done.

So the boys drove over in a pony-chaise to Lonstead Abbey, and knocking at the door, asked if Lady Vinsear was at home.

"Yes," said the old servant, opening his eyes in astonishment at the apparition of the two boys, whom he had only seen as children four years before.

"Then, ask if she will see Mr Cyril and Master Frank Home. Stop, though; is Miss Sprong at home?"

"Oh, no, Master Cyril; bless you, Miss Sprong, sir, has gone and married Farmer Jones this year gone."

"Has she indeed? Oh, then, take my message, please, James."

They had come at the right moment. In the large drawing-room of Lonstead Abbey, Lady Vinsear was sitting with no companion but the orphan girl of a villager, to whom she gave a home, and who was amusing herself with a picture-book on a low stool by the fire; for though it was summer, the fire was lighted to give cheerfulness to the room. When Miss Sprong married a neighbouring farmer, Lady Vinsear had given her a handsome dowry, and refused ever to see her again, being in fact heartily tired of her malice and sycophancy, and above all, resenting the new breach which she had caused between herself and her brother's family. Ever since her quarrel with Julian, Lady Vinsear had bitterly regretted the violence which had cut off from her that natural affection to which she had looked as the stay of her declining years. She had grown sadder as she grew older, and the loneliness of her life weighed heavily on her heart, yet in her obstinate pride she made an unutterable resolve never to take the initiative in restoring Julian to her favour.

And as she sat there by the fire, longing in her secret soul for the society and love of some young hearts of her own kith and kin, she glanced away from the uninteresting little girl whom she had taken as a protégée to the likeness of Julian's bright and thoughtful boyish features, (which still, in spite of Miss Sprong, had retained a place over the mantel-piece), and remembered the foolish little incident which had led to her rejection of him as her heir. The tears started to her eyes as she thought of it, and wished with all her heart that the two gay and merry boys whose frolic had caused the fracas were with her once more. How much she should now enjoy the pleasant sound of their young voices, and how gladly she would join in their unrestrained and innocent laughter.

So when the bewildered James asked in his never-varying voice, "whether Master Cyril and Frank Home might see her," Lady Vinsear fancied that she was seeing in a dream the fulfilment of her unexpressed wishes, and rubbed her eyes to see if she could really be wide awake.

"What's all this, James?—are you James, or am I in a dream?"

"James, your ladyship."

"And do you really mean to tell me that my nephews are outside?"

"Yes, please your ladyship."

"Well, then, don't keep them there a minute longer, James. Run along, Annie," she said to the little girl, "it is time for you to be in bed."

Annie had hardly retired, when—a little shyly—the boys entered, uncertain of their reception. But Lady Vinsear started from her seat, and embraced them with the utmost affection.

"My dear Cyril," she said, kissing him again; "how tall and handsome you have grown; and Frankie, too, you are the image of Julian when he was your age."

The boys were amazed at the heartiness with which she welcomed them, as though nothing had happened, and after she had given them a capital supper, she said to them, "Now, boys, I see you are rather puzzled at me. Never mind that; don't think of what has happened. We mean all to be friends now. And now tell me all about Julian."

They found, however, that Lady Vinsear knew a good deal about his college career from her neighbour Lord De Vayne, who had kept her acquainted with all his successes and honours up to the period when De Vayne left Other Hall. Since then she had not been able to gain much information about him, and had not heard the news either of his fellowship, his approaching marriage, or his acceptance of a college living.

She listened eagerly to the intelligence, and finally asked if he knew of their visit.

"No," said Cyril, laughing; "neither he nor any of them. Now, Aunt Vinsear, you really must do me a favour. You know Vi is to be married at Orton on the same day as Julian; won't you come with us to the wedding, and surprise them all? If you were to start by an early train, and take the carriage with you, we should drive up in time for the ceremony, and it would be such a happy joke for all concerned."

The old lady was delighted with the plan. Meeting on such an occasion, when the minds of all were so much occupied, would avert the necessity of anything approaching to a scene, which of all things she most dreaded. She felt a flood of new interests, occupations, and hopes; she made the boys stay with her until the appointed day, and looked forward to Cyril's triumph with a delight which made her happier than she had been for many a long year.

And thus it was that Cyril and Frank drove into the town in gallant style, accompanied by Lady Vinsear! They stopped at the door of the Lion, and hearing that Julian had started, got white favours placed at the horses' heads, and dashed on to the church. The brides had not arrived, but they were expected every moment; and Mr Vere, (who had most kindly come to perform the ceremony), was putting on his surplice in the vestry, while Julian and Kennedy, with Owen, Lillyston, and De Vayne, were strolling up and down a pretty, retired laurel walk behind the church. Hearing where they were, the boys, accompanied by their aunt, boldly invaded their privacy, and reached the end of the walk just as the gentlemen were approaching to enter the church.

240

"Good gracious! Lady Vinsear!" said De Vayne.

"Hush, hush!" she said. "Come here, Julian, and kiss your old aunt, and welcome her on your wedding-day, and don't think of bygones. I am proud to see you, my boy;" and he felt a tear on his cheek as the old lady drew down his head to kiss him.

"And now," she said, "don't tell any of the rest that I have come till after the marriage. I hear the sound of wheels. Put me in some pew near the altar, Julian, that I may have a good long look at your bride, and Violet's bridegroom."

They had just time to fulfil her wish when the carriages drove up, and the bridal procession formed, and, followed by their bride's-maids, Violet and Eva passed up the aisle, in all their loveliness, with wreaths of myrtle and orange-flower round their fair foreheads, and long, graceful veils, and simple ornaments of pearl.

Beautiful to see! A bride always looks beautiful, but these two were radiant and exquisite in their loveliness. Which was the fairest? I cannot tell. Most men would have given the golden apple to Eva, with the sweet, tender grace that played about her young features, almost infantile in their delicacy, and with those bright, beaming, laughter-loving eyes, of which the light could not be hid though she bent her face downwards to hide the bridal blush that tinged it; but yet they would have doubted about the decision when they turned from her to the full flower of Violet's beauty, and gazed on her perfect face, so enchanting in its meekness, and on that one tress of golden hair that played upon her neck.

De Vayne, as he looked on the perfect scene, took out a piece of paper, and wrote on it Spenser's lines:—

"Behold, while she before the altar stands,
Hearing the holy priest that to her speaks
And blesses her with his two happy hands,
How the red roses flush up in her cheeks
And the pure snow with golden vermeil stain,
Like crimson dyed in grain."

He handed the lines to Lillyston and Owen, and they saw from the happy smile upon his face that no touch of regret or envy marred his present meditations.

Has life any pleasure—any deep, unspoken happiness—comparable to that which fills a young's man whole soul when he stands beside the altar with such a bride as Violet or Eva was?—when he thinks that the fair, blushing girl, whose white hand trembles in his own, is to be the star of his home, the mother of his children, the sunbeam shining steadily on all his life? Verily he who hath experienced such a joy has found a jewel richer:

> "Than twenty seas though all their sands were pearl,
> Their waters crystal, and their rocks pure gold."

The service was over, and in those few moments, four young souls had passed over the marble threshold of married life. Violet felt that the presence of De Vayne removed the only alloy to that deep happiness that spoke in the eloquent lustre of her eye, and she told him so as he bent to kiss her hand, and as Lady De Vayne clasped her to her heart with an affectionate embrace. All the people of the village awaited them at the porch, and as they passed along the path, the village children, lining the way, and standing heedless on the green mounds that covered the crumbling relics of mortality, scattered under their happy feet a thousand flowers. One passing thought, perhaps, about the lesson which those green mounds told, flitted through the minds of the bridal party as they left the trodden blossoms to wither on the churchyard path, but if so, it was but as the shadow of a summer cloud, and it vanished, as with a sudden clash the bells rang out again, thrilling the tremulous air with their enthusiasm of happy auguries, and the sailor boys of Orton gave cheer on cheer while brides and bridegrooms entered their carriages, and drove from under the umbrage of the churchyard yews to the elms and oaks and lime-tree avenues of the hall.

Oh that happy day! The wedding breakfast had been laid in a large tent on the lawn, whence you could catch bright glimpses of the blue sea, and the islet, and the passing ships, while on all sides around it the garden glowed a paradise of blossom, and the fragrance of sweet flowers floated to them through the golden air. Rich fruits and gorgeous bouquets covered the table, and the whole tent was gay with wreaths and anadems. And then, what ringing laughter, what merry jests, what earnest happy talk! Let us not linger there too long, and from this scene I bid avaunt to the coarse cynical reader; who is too strong-minded to believe in love.

Only let the gentle reader fancy for himself how beautiful were the few words with which Mr Vere proposed the health of the brides, and how long they remembered his earnest wish, that though the truest love is often that which has been sanctified by sorrow, yet that they might be spared the sorrow, and enjoy the truest love. And he will fancy how admirably Julian and Kennedy replied—Julian in words of poetic feeling and thoughtful power, Kennedy with quick flashes of picturesque expression, both with the eloquence of sincere and deep emotion; and how gracefully De

Vayne proposed the health of the bridesmaids, for whom Cyril and Lillyston replied. Then, too quickly, came the hour of separation; the old shoe was flung after the carriages, the bridal couples departed for a tour among the lakes, and the villagers danced and feasted till twilight on the lawn.

Six weeks are over since the marriage day, and there, in Southampton harbour, lies the Valleyfield, which is to convey Kennedy and Violet to Calcutta. They have just spoken the last, long, lingering farewell to Eva and Julian, who are standing in deep tearful silence on the pier, and are watching the little boat which is conveying their only brother and only sister to the ship. The boat is but a few moments in reaching the Valleyfield, and, when they are on board, the vessel weighs anchor, and ruffles her white plumage, and flings her pennons to the breeze, and begins to dash the blue water into foam about her prow. Violet and her husband are standing at the stern, and as long as the vessel is in sight they wave their hands in token of farewell. It is but a short time, and then the Valleyfield grows into a mere dot on the horizon, and Eva and Julian, heedless of the crowds around them, do not check the tears as they flow, and speak to each other in voices broken by sorrow as they slowly turn away.

That evening Violet and Kennedy knelt side by side in their little cabin to join in common prayer, and Julian led his Eva over the threshold of their quiet and holy home.

And their path thenceforth was "as the shining light, shining more and more to the perfect day."

The End